HUNGRY GHOSTS

John D. Greenwood was born in [...] at the Universities of Edinburgh and Oxford. He is [...] professor at the City University of New York Graduate Center, where he specializes in the history of psychology. He is the author of eight books and numerous academic papers.

He was a lecturer in the department of philosophy at the National University of Singapore from 1983-1986, when he first fell in love with Singapore, her people and her history. He returned as senior visiting scholar in 1999-2000 and as visiting professor in 2008-2009. He considers NUS to be his second academic home. He also returns regularly to Singapore to visit old friends and old haunts, and considers a trip to Pulau Ubin followed by chilli or pepper crab in the evening at Changi Village to be a perfect day.

He lives in Richmond, Virginia, USA.

Praise for the Singapore Saga series

'Brimming with memorable characters, this colourful reimagining of the early history of Singapore ... brings the intrigues, personality clashes and violence of the era vividly to life.' Tim Hannigan, author of *Raffles and the British Invasion of Java*

'Singapore Saga reminds us just how much [Singapore's] development was owed to its early Scottish pioneers.' *The Scotsman*

'Greenwood seamlessly weaves invented characters and imagined events into a historically accurate narrative.' *South China Morning Post*, Hong Kong

'*Forbidden Hill* (Vol.1) is an imagined but historically faithful account of Singapore's transition from sleepy fishing village to major trading center.' *Asian Review of Books*

'100 years of early Singapore in new fiction series.' *Straits Times*

'*Forbidden Hill* (Vol.1) has pirates, concubines and lots of Scots.' *The Star*, Malaysia

HUNGRY GHOSTS

SINGAPORE SAGA, VOL. 3

JOHN D. GREENWOOD

monsoon

monsoonbooks

First published in 2020
by Monsoon Books Ltd
www.monsoonbooks.co.uk

No.1 The Lodge, Burrough Court,
Burrough on the Hill, Leicestershire LE14 2QS, UK

ISBN (paperback): 9781912049226
ISBN (ebook): 9781912049233

Cover design by Cover Kitchen.

A Cataloguing-in-Publication data record is available from the British
Library.

MIX
Paper from
responsible sources
FSC® C018072
FSC
www.fsc.org

Printed and bound in Great Britain by Clays Ltd, Elcograf S.p.A.
22 21 20   1 2 3 4

For Singapore and all her people.

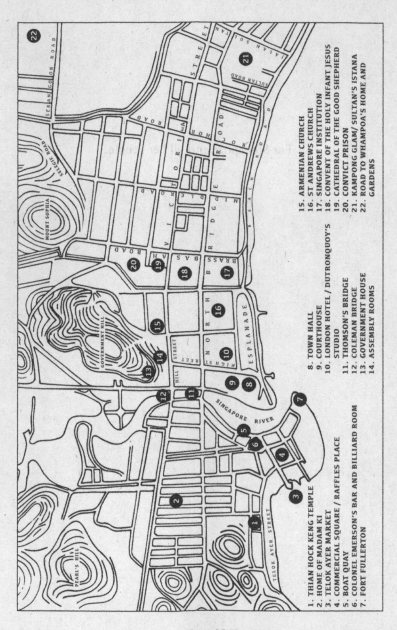

1. THIAN HOCK KENG TEMPLE
2. HOME OF MADAM KI
3. TELOK AYER MARKET
4. COMMERCIAL SQUARE / RAFFLES PLACE
5. BOAT QUAY
6. COLONEL EMERSON'S BAR AND BILLIARD ROOM
7. FORT FULLERTON
8. TOWN HALL
9. COURTHOUSE
10. LONDON HOTEL / DUTRONQUOY'S STUDIO
11. THOMSON'S BRIDGE
12. COLEMAN BRIDGE
13. GOVERNMENT HOUSE
14. ASSEMBLY ROOMS
15. ARMENIAN CHURCH
16. ST ANDREWS CHURCH
17. SINGAPORE INSTITUTION
18. CONVENT OF THE HOLY INFANT JESUS
19. CATHEDRAL OF THE GOOD SHEPHERD
20. CONVICT PRISON
21. KAMPONG GLAM / SULTAN'S ISTANA
22. ROAD TO WHAMPOA'S HOME AND GARDENS

Singapore, circa 1852-1869

Acknowledgements

Hungry Ghosts is the third volume of Singapore Saga, a series of historical fiction about the early development of Singapore. Once again, I am indebted to a number of people and institutions for their help and support in producing this work.

Thanks again to Donald McDermid for giving me the original idea for a historical novel about early Singapore; to my wife Shelagh for supporting my year-long sojourn to Singapore to complete the original manuscript; to Arne Adland and Stella Fogg for critiquing the original very long manuscript; to the late Beverly Swerling for persuading me to reduce that manuscript to three shorter novels, of which *Hungry Ghosts* is the third (with *Chasing the Dragon* the second and *Forbidden Hill* the first); to the National University of Singapore for providing me with the opportunity to spend 2008-2009 as visiting professor in Singapore, enabling me to complete most of my research for the book; and to the staff at the circulation desk of the NUS library for tracking down microfiche copies of the early Singapore newspapers, such as the *Singapore Chronicle*, the *Singapore Free Press* and *The Straits Times and Singapore Journal of Commerce*. Thanks also to Arnie Adland (again), my wife Shelagh, and Yingshihan Zhu for proofreading *Hungry Ghosts, and to my daughter Holly for creating the map of Singapore*, and to my daughter Holly for creating the map of Singapore.

Like the early newspapers, many of the books that I read while researching the novel provided the germ of plotlines that found their way into the three volumes of *Singapore Saga*. For *Hungry Ghosts*, a number of these deserve special mention. Charles Burton Buckley's *An*

Anecdotal History of Old Times in Singapore (Fraser and Neave, 1902) and Walter Makepeace, Gilbert E. Brooke and Roland St John Braddell's *One Hundred Years of Singapore* (John Murray, 1921) suggested some plotlines while also providing invaluable checks on my historical time line. The historical background to the stories of Hong Xiuquan, the Taiping Rebellion, the rise of Yehonala, the concubine Cixi, the Indian Mutiny and the Second Opium War is based upon Jonathan Spence's *God's Chinese Son: The Taiping Heavenly Kingdom of Hong Xiuquan* (Norton, 1996), Rayne Kruger's *All Under Heaven: A Complete History of China* (John Wiley, 2003), Keith Laidler's *The Last Empress: The She-Dragon of China (John Wiley, 2003)* and Saul David's *Victoria's Wars: The Rise of Empire* (Viking, 2006). Background material for the story of the Indian convict Shiv Nadir is drawn from John F. A McNair's *Prisoners Their Own Warders* (A. Constable and Co, 1899); for the story of the mui tsai Ah Keng from Maria Jaschok's *Concubines and Bondservants: The Social History of a Chinese Custom* (Oxford University Press, 1988), for the story the CSS *Alabama* and her layover in Singapore from Stephen Fox's *Wolf of the Deep: Raphael Semmes and the Notorious Confederate Raider CSS Alabama* (Vintage Books, 2007); for the story of the torture of the British negotiators during the Second Opium War from Henry Brougham Loch's *Personal Narrative of Occurrences During Lord Elgin's Second Embassy to China in 1860* (John Murray, 1900); and for the story of the ghost marriage from Marjory Topley's *Ghost Marriages Among the Singapore Chinese* (*Man*, Vol 55: Royal Anthropological Institute of Great Britain and Ireland).

I have, once again, done my best to maintain historical accuracy with respect to the real characters and episodes, to the best of my knowledge and ability. Some readers of *Forbidden Hill* and *Chasing the Dragon* told me they had difficulty distinguishing the real characters from the fictional, which I take as a compliment of sorts. I hope readers of *Hungry Ghosts* continue to find them both engaging.

Let me take this opportunity to thank Philip Tatham, the publisher of Monsoon Books, for his unstinting support and sharp editorial eye, and for enabling me to bring to fruition my personal homage to Singapore. Thanks also to Leslie Lim Boon Hup of Pansing for being such an energetic and enthusiastic promotor of my books in Singapore, and for indulging my passion for chilli and pepper crab.

John D. Greenwood

Prologue

1851

Shiv Nadir was not an evil man, at least not by nature. He came from a good Tamil family, had received some formal education at an English school in Madras,[i] and had worked in the office of the Glasgow firm of McIvor Fraser as an administrative assistant. His family had arranged his marriage, but he had loved his wife, a dark-haired and passionate beauty. She had not loved him, but had directed her passion to his younger brother, who was tall, muscular and handsome, while Shiv was short, thin and bookish. Yet Shiv Nadir had found his strength when he discovered them in his bed one day, having returned from work with a sick stomach. He had taken up the curry stone[ii] from the kitchen and dashed their brains out upon the saffron sheets, splashing their bright red blood across the whitewashed walls. When his pregnant wife died, his unborn child had died with her.

Shiv Nadir had been sentenced to life imprisonment for the murder. Yet his real punishment was expatriation. He was sent across the kala pani – the black water – in a jeta junaza – a living tomb – to a faraway land that he had heard about only in shipping schedules. He was dead to his former life, defiled and excommunicated from his caste. When he arrived in Singapore he

---

i Present-day Chennai, capital of the Indian state of Tamil Nadu.
ii Heavy stone used to grind herbs and spices.

was taken to the Bras Basah jail,[iii] a brick building that had been built in 1841 by the convicts themselves, under the supervision of Captain Henry Man, then superintendent of convicts. Shiv Nadir was registered, bathed and numbered, and inspected by the prison doctor. His own clothes were taken away and fumigated and he was issued with a set of prison overalls. His few possessions, including a small amount of money, were taken from him. He was issued a receipt and advised that they would be returned to him when he had earned his entitlement, which normally took two years, so long as he did not prove recalcitrant, in which case he would be reduced to a lower class.

* * *

She was sixteen years old when she arrived in Peking[iv] with her mother. They had travelled by barge to the capital from Wuhu, on the lower reaches of the Yangtze River. Her father, a captain in the Blue Bordered Banner regiment, had died the previous year, and they were going to live with her uncle Mu-fan, an official in the Imperial Board of Works. The sight of the capital city on the low plain took her breath away. Imposing battlements fringed the towering forty-foot walls that ran sixteen miles around the square enclosure of the outer city, with massive roofed towers at each corner, and elaborate fortified gates. As with other major cities in China, there was another inner walled city, the Tartar city, reserved exclusively for the Manchu conquerors. The Chinese city, which lay between the outer walls and the Tartar city, was laid out in a grid, and composed entirely of single-floor dwellings, so that nobody

---

iii So called because it was located on Bras Basah Road, built over the Bras Basah stream, 'bras basah' meaning 'wet rice', because early traders used to unload their cargoes of wet rice on its banks to dry.
iv Present-day Beijing.

could look down from an upper story if the Emperor happened to pass beneath. Within the Tartar city was the Imperial City, a fifteen-hundred-acre enclosure that housed the administrative offices of the Celestial Empire, and within the Imperial City, the purple walls and golden rooftops of the Forbidden City. At the centre of the Forbidden City, amid the elaborate palaces, temples, courtyards and gardens, lay the Dragon Throne, the centre of the Earth under Heaven, the throne to which the Qing Emperor Hsien Feng had ascended the previous year.

She was exquisitely beautiful. She was no more than five feet tall, with a perfectly proportioned body and dainty feet. Her face was round like the moon and her skin was soft and lustrous, without blemish, with dark brown eyes, soft red lips and jet-black hair – a classical beauty that made her the envy of her female relations and friends. She had a quick wit and wicked humour, and her voice was soft and sensual, like liquid velvet.

Her name was Yehonala. She was named after her clan, the Yeho-Nala, who were the last tribe to be subdued by the Manchu armies of the great warlord Nurhachi, before he declared war upon the Ming Empire in the early seventeenth century. When that long war had finally ended, Nurhachi's son Dorgun proclaimed the Mandate of Heaven for Shun-chih, the first Qing Emperor of China, in 1644. In that year of Manchu triumph, a marble tablet was discovered deep in the forests of Manchuria, the Manchu homeland. A prophecy was inscribed upon the tablet, which warned that if ever a Yeho-Nala female were to gain control of the fortunes of the Manchu, she would lead them to certain destruction.

PART ONE

'FLYING SEAGULLS AND WINDING DRAGONS'

1852 – 1855

1

1852

There were five classes of Indian convicts in the Bras Basah jail. The first class of prisoners comprised those who had demonstrated their trustworthiness and received conditional tickets of leave. They were allowed to work in their trades or professions outside of the jail, without supervision or interference, although they had to attend muster in the jail courtyard on the first of the month, and advise the superintendent of convicts of their work and home addresses. Some of the convicts lived by themselves or with their wives and families in huts they were allowed to erect outside the walls of the jail; others lived in the houses in which they worked as servants, or in the merchant godowns[v] where they worked as clerks or night guards. Their tickets of leave could be revoked if there were any complaints or trouble, but there were seldom any complaints or trouble.

The second class comprised those who had demonstrated sufficient trustworthiness to be allowed out to work in government offices or hospitals during the day, or serve as petty officers in the jail. The first superintendent of convicts, Lieutenant Chester of the 23rd Bengal Light Infantry, had quickly found that the well-behaved prisoners made far better warders than the police peons who had been assigned to him, two of whom he had been forced to prosecute for theft and the attempted rape of a female convict.

---

v Warehouse or other storage space, usually on a dockside.

Thus, the prisoners in effect became their own warders,[vi] although a British overseer always supervised them. As with convicts of the first class, the status of the second class was contingent on their continued good behaviour, but there was little trouble from them – they received three dollars[vii] a month in pay, which was more than many police peons and most labourers and stevedores received. Whether warders or public servants, they were allowed out of the jail after six in the evening, although they had to attend muster every morning at eight.

The third class comprised those who had successfully completed their probationary period and were allowed to work as labourers on the roads and public works. They were also instructed in various trades and professions: they were trained as carpenters, stone masons, bricklayers, brick-makers and tile-makers, cement and lime burners, quarrymen, blacksmiths, cattleman, slaters, painters, wheel-rights, coopers, plumbers, basket-makers, tailors, shoemakers, gardeners and boatmen, and some as medical orderlies, clerks and accountants. Volunteers from the community taught some of the convicts, but others were taught by convicts who had earlier served in these trades or professions, and who had worked out their probation in this fashion. Thus, the prisoners became their own teachers as well as their own warders. After work they were allowed out until six in the evening, and were assigned one rupee per month condiment[viii] money, to supplement their basic food ration of rice, vegetables and fish. Some of the convicts who worked on the roads or hill-stations were housed in temporary buildings outside of the town, in 'command' stations supervised by those who had attained the status of petty officers. Their rations were sent out to

---

vi After the book of the same title, *Prisoners Their Own Warders* (1899), authored by Major John McNair, the fifth superintendent of convicts in Singapore.
vii Spanish dollars, the primary currency in Singapore at the time.
viii Spices used to flavour their food.

them once a month, on which day they had to pass muster before a visiting British officer.

The fourth class of convicts comprised the newly arrived, those demoted from the upper classes because of bad behaviour, or promoted from the fifth class because of good behaviour. During their probationary period, they were kept in light double-leg irons. They were not allowed out of the jail, but were allowed to cook their own food.

The fifth class comprised those judged too dangerous to be given any degree of freedom, including those demoted from the higher classes for violent behaviour. They were kept in heavy leg and wrist irons, and only allowed out of their cells to work menial tasks, such as pounding and cleaning rice, or beating out coir[ix] from the rough husk of coconuts, to be used in the production of mats and sacking. They were not allowed to cook their own food, but had it delivered from the convict mess. If they served two years of exemplary behaviour they could be promoted to the higher classes, although few managed to rise above the fourth or third class. The most difficult and recalcitrant cases were given one to six dozen lashes of the cat o' nine tails whenever they engaged in violent or criminal acts. These were delivered on their bare buttocks in the presence of the medical officer and the other inmates.

There was also a sixth class of invalids and superannuated prisoners who were too weak or too old to do anything other than light work, and who were employed as sweepers, country night-watchmen or latrine attendants. The female convicts were kept in a separate wing under the supervision of a matron and were not allowed contact with the male prisoners, although by wile and guile contacts were often made. The youngest convicts were also kept apart from the rest, and were organized into special work gangs supervised by a petty officer.

---

ix Fiber from the outer husk of the coconut.

Shiv Nadir was placed in the fourth class when he arrived in Singapore. At first, he behaved like a somnambulant. He ate, drank and followed orders like any good prisoner, but did not seem to care about anything, not even whether he lived or died. Yet although he wore a heavy cloak of misery because of the bright future he had lost, he was an intelligent and strong-willed man, and as the days passed into weeks and the weeks passed into months, he began to observe those around him and see new possibilities in this mysterious new world. He was a stranger in a strange land, but this enabled him to have new dreams, and one day he threw off his cloak of misery and grasped his destiny in his own two hands.

2

Yehonala lived with her mother in her uncle's courtyard house within the Tartar City, comprising a series of pavilions that lay behind the high outer and windowless walls that faced the street, within which was a central courtyard planted with bamboo and willow. She became friends with her cousin Sakota, who was the same age as Yehonala, and fell in love with another cousin, the dark and handsome Jung Lu, who was a cadet at the Military Academy. Her future had seemed bright and cloudless and open horizoned, but now, one year since she had travelled from Wuhu to Peking, great iron gates closed before and behind her. She was summoned to the Forbidden City, having been informed by the Imperial couriers that she was one of the sixty virgins who had been selected as potential consorts for the Son of Heaven.

If she was surprised, she did not show it – she had been trained to always display a public face of passive humility and obedience. And it was not surprising that she had been chosen. There were many girls from the Yeho-Nala clan on the lists of eligible Manchu virgins that had been drawn up that year; since the time of the great warlord Nurhachi, the Imperial Manchu family had taken their first wives from the clan, in order to reinforce the relationship between the two most powerful northern dynasties. Yehonala's older cousin, the Empress Xiao De Xian, had been selected as the first wife of the Emperor Hsien Feng, but had died childless three years earlier. Now that the mandatory mourning period following the death of the old Emperor Tao Kwang had ended, an Imperial decree had gone out to Manchu officials throughout the kingdom to draw up lists of eligible Manchu maidens, based upon their ancestry, astrological projections, beauty and character.

***

On the appointed day, Yehonala was carried through the streets in an enclosed palanquin,[x] dressed in the best robes and jewellery her uncle could provide. The thick white powder that covered her face masked the mixed emotions she felt, and her lips were reddened into a public smile. She was proud to have been chosen as a potential consort of the Emperor, but heart-broken that she was forsaking her beloved Jung Lu. They made slow progress, but eventually arrived at the Tien An Men, the Gate of Heavenly Peace, where Imperial edits were lowered down to officials in the mouth of a golden phoenix from the great towers above the gate. They passed through the Tien An Men to the open plaza beyond the Meridian Gate, the formal entrance to the Forbidden City, where the Emperor announced the names of the successful candidates in the civil service examinations, and proclaimed the calendar prepared by the royal astrologers for each new year. Yehonala descended from the palanquin to the plaza, and sent the servants back to her uncle's house. There she waited patiently while the other girls arrived. Like Yehonala, they were arrayed in all their finery, with powdered faces and painted smiles. Before her lay the palaces, temples and courtyards of the Forbidden City.

Zhu Di, the fourth son of the first Ming Emperor Chu Yuan-chang, had built the Forbidden City in the early fifteenth century,

---

x Covered litter for one passenger, consisting of a large box carried on two horizontal poles by four or six bearers.

when he had decided to transfer his capital from Nanking[xi] to Peking. The main buildings were laid out in a north-south axis between 1410 and 1420, and over one hundred thousand craftsmen and over a million labourers were employed in their construction. The spectacularly carved palaces and temples were built entirely of wood, their walls bright vermillion[xii] and their roofs ablaze with yellow-glazed tiles. White marble bridges, staircases and balustrades sparkled in the sunshine and moonlight, emblazoned with royal dragons and phoenixes. The white marble was quarried in Fanshan, close by the city, and the roof tiles and paving bricks were produced locally, but the timber came from as far away as the southwestern provinces and northeastern forests, and sometimes took as long as four years to reach the capital. Over the centuries many of the original buildings had succumbed to fire and been rebuilt, and huge bronze and iron vats filled with water – heated in winter to prevent freezing – were distributed throughout the Forbidden City, to ensure a ready supply of water in case of future fires.

In the courtyard beyond the Meridian Gate, where Yehonala now stood, five marble bridges curved over the River of Golden Water, which was fed from the northeast corner of the city moat. Beyond these marble bridges lay the Gate of Supreme Harmony, guarded by giant bronze lions, which opened out onto the massive Supreme Harmony Square, laid with fifteen layers of bricks, to prevent intruders from tunnelling into the Forbidden City. At the northern end of the square, aligned along the north-south axis, were the three Harmony Halls, of Supreme, Complete and Preserving Harmony, which stood upon a three-tiered marble terrace. The three halls supported elaborately carved balustrades, and were emblazoned with over a thousand elaborately carved dragonheads, which also served as drains during heavy rains.

---

xi Present-day Nanjing.
xii Brilliant red or scarlet pigment.

3

As yet, Yehonala knew little of what lay beyond the Gate of Supreme Harmony, other than the stories she had heard from her cousin Sakota, who had heard them from her elder sister, Empress Xiao De Xian, the former first wife of the Emperor Hsien Feng. She stood with her cousin and the other Manchu virgins as the early morning sun shone down and sparkled upon the white marble staircases and bridges. Then a group of palace eunuchs, clothed in grey robes and blue coats, crossed over the bridges and led them westward to the Nei Wu Fu Pavilion, which housed the offices of the Imperial Household Department. The pavilion was hung with banners and lanterns, and furnished with sumptuous furniture and ornate statuary.

Presently the Emperor Hsien Feng entered and was enthroned, although he took no part in the proceedings. The Manchu girls were selected and ranked by Xiao Jing Chen, the Dowager Empress, the first wife of the former emperor Tao Kwang, on the advice of the Chief Eunuch, An Te-hai, who had followed the Emperor into the Pavilion. The girls were presented to the Dowager Empress in turn, after which tea was served, while the Dowager Empress carefully observed their ritual deportment. Yehonala was ecstatic when she was invited to join the Emperor's table for dinner, but her pretty smiles and witty repartee were wasted on him. Hsien Feng sat pale faced and listless all evening, stroking his thin moustache, seemingly oblivious to the chatter around the table. He hardly ate anything, and pointedly ignored the Dowager Empress at times. Was it sickness, boredom, wine or opium, Yehonala wondered to herself?

* * *

The Dowager Empress and An Te-hai were critical of this brood of Manchu virgins, and none of the twenty-eight selected from the sixty aspirants were assigned to the first class of concubine. Yehonala was glad to have been chosen, but deeply disappointed and humiliated by her relegation to the third class – only one rank above the lowest fourth class. Her cousin Sakota had been selected for the second class, and Yehonala knew that she was more beautiful and intelligent than her cousin. She supposed it was because her cousin was the sister of the Emperor's first wife, and she was grateful to have at least one friend in what was to all intents and purposes a gilded prison. The girls who had been chosen were now bound to live within the walls of the Forbidden City until they died, whether or not they were ever chosen for the Emperor's bed.

Yehonala knew that if she was to escape a life of lonely misery, she had to achieve three goals. She had to gain access to the Emperor's bed, she had to captivate him and be raised to the rank of first concubine, and she had to produce a son.

* * *

The method by which the Son of Heaven chose his first wife and consorts was simple and energetic. The eastern 'heated chamber' of the Hall of Mental Cultivation was the Emperor's lavish bedroom, ablaze with yellow silk sheets and red banners. Every evening the Emperor turned over one of the hundreds of jade plaques that lay on an ivory table at his bedside, which bore the names of the concubines of all four classes. The girl who was chosen for that evening was carried in a red silk sheet on the back of a eunuch and deposited naked on the stone flagstones at the foot of the Emperor's bed, at the optimal hour for intimacy determined by the court astrologers. Then she would crawl across the bed and submit herself to the divine will of the Celestial Prince, and his all too human perversions. As he worked his way up and down the female hierarchy, the Emperor would select those who were most pleasing to him and those who were judged most likely to produce sons – one of whom would emerge and display his dragon power as Hsien Feng's rightful successor and eventual possessor of All Under Heaven.

4

1853

Habib Noh bin Muhammad Al-Habshi was a majdhub.[xiii] Habib
Noh's ancestors were from Hadramaut[xiv] and he was a direct
descendant of the prophet Muhammad. According to legend, he
was born aboard a ship travelling from Palembang to Penang
during a storm, and his father named him 'Noh' in honour of the
prophet Noh[xv] when the sea calmed after his birth. Habib Noh
lived in Penang for some thirty years before travelling to the newly
established settlement of Singapore in 1819, at the invitation of
Habib Salim bin Abdullah Ba Samuyr, a Naqshbandi sufi.[xvi] A deeply
religious man, Habib Noh would spend whole nights in prayer and
contemplation, often on the hill overlooking Telok Ayer Bay known
as Mount Palmer. He was esteemed by the Muslim community as a
saint and a healer, and was known to have a great love of children.

***

Habib Noh was in the habit of walking by the shops that lined the
streets around the Sultan's compound at Kampong Glam,[xvii] usually

---

xiii One who undergoes the divine attraction.
xiv Present-day Yemen.
xv Noah.
xvi A major Sunni spiritual order of Sufism.
xvii Kampong (meaning village in Malay) named after the Glam tree,
whose resin was used for caulking ships, and whose leaves were used
for medicinal oil.

followed by a crowd of young children. He would tell them magical stories and relate religious parables, and they loved him as he loved them. Without warning, he would suddenly enter one of the shops and gather up all the money from the cash drawer, then throw it out to the children waiting in the street. The Arab shopkeepers did not protest, for they knew he was a holy man and mystic and that their businesses would prosper because of their service to the servant of God.

The Chinese and Indian shopkeepers who also plied their trade in Kampong Glam did not quite see it that way. In times past they had complained to Governor Bonham, who had had Habib Noh arrested and placed in jail. But Habib Noh was an awliya – a friend of God – and was not bound by the laws of man or nature. Within a few hours he would be seen again on the streets of Kampong Glam, and every time he was arrested and placed behind bars, he would reappear again on the streets a few hours later. Some Europeans who witnessed these miraculous escapes were so impressed that they converted to Islam. Habib Noh would receive them into his home, where they would recite the two declarations of the Islamic faith.

***

It was said of Habib Noh that he would often bid farewell to pilgrims in Singapore embarking on their Haj[xviii] to Mecca, who were amazed when they found him waiting to greet them on arrival in Jeddah, then were amazed again when he was there to welcome them home when they arrived back safely in Singapore.

---

xviii Pilgrimage to Mecca, which every adult Muslim is required to make at least once in their lifetime.

5

Yehonala quickly identified the two sources of power within the Forbidden City. The first was the Dowager Empress Xiao Jing Chen, who, although she was unlikely to help her gain access to the Emperor's bed, could easily make difficulties by relegating her to the role of servant or by raising objections to her elevation. She discovered that the Dowager Empress loved poetry and painting, in which Yehonala had some skill, and was prone to flattery. Yehonala was careful to compliment the Dowager Empress on her work while modestly disparaging her own considerable artistic achievements, which the Dowager Empress honestly admired.

The second was the palace eunuchs, especially the ruling elite, but they were a far tougher nut to crack. They had dominated the politics of the Forbidden City since the time of the Ming dynasty, whose rulers they had emasculated to the point that the Celestial Kingdom had become, in the words of one sage mandarin, an 'apple ready for plucking' by the Manchu. Shun Chih, the first Qing Emperor, had recognized the danger they posed to the new dynasty. Yet he and his successors were helpless in the face of the ingrained cultural mores that required the Emperor to remain aloof from his subjects, and mandated that the Celestial Prince maintain a large harem to satisfy his superhuman sexual needs. A Son of Heaven could not tolerate the presence of other males living in the Forbidden City – males who might pollute the Manchu maidens, and sire illegitimate sons and daughters that might be passed off as Imperial offspring. So the eunuchs had remained and retained their powers.

***

Becoming a eunuch was a painful and hazardous career choice for a young man. Before the operation the patient's stomach and thighs were tightly bandaged, and his genitalia washed in a solution of hot pepper to anaesthetize them. While attendants held his arms and legs, the physician sliced off both penis and scrotum with a razor-sharp curved blade, then washed and bandaged the wound. If the operation was a success, the wound would heal within a hundred days. If it was not, the man would die within a few days in excruciating pain. It was a risk, but for many young men it was a risk worth taking, given the potential rewards if they were accepted for service in the Forbidden City. In past centuries the mortality rate was extremely high – at least half would die in agony from the operation – but the professional castrators in the Imperial City had turned the surgery into a fine art, so that by the reign of Hsien Feng most operations were successful. The surgeons preserved the eunuch's organs – their 'precious' – in airtight jars, which were kept as proof of castration. When a eunuch died, his precious was buried with him to fool the gods that he was a whole man.

The eunuchs were chosen as palace servants not only because they posed no sexual threat, but also because it was believed that as a result of their operation they would be deprived of their masculine yang principle, and become as docile and submissive as wives were supposed to be because of their feminine yin principle. Yet this proved to be no truer for the eunuchs than it was for Yehonala, who had to compete hard to match their selfish determination. The eunuchs were despised by the nobility, the artisans and even by the peasantry, who mocked their glossy fat bodies, mincing gait and high falsetto voices, and called them 'crows' or 'foxes'. They were banned from major religious rituals and prohibited from ancestor worship, and received only a small allowance. Yet they were allowed to impose a tax – or 'squeeze' – on the precious metals, timber, livestock, household furnishings, rice and grain that were delivered in tribute to the Emperor each year, and to control the amount of tax they imposed, which was sometimes as high as thirty percent. Some of the eunuchs accumulated great wealth, for their opportunities for bribery and corruption were almost limitless, since they were also effectively their own police. They formed themselves into a self-supporting, self-protecting, self-serving hierarchical inner society that worked subtly to control and bend the Emperor to their will.

In this endeavour the eunuchs had all the advantages of their despised class. The Emperor was isolated by his exalted rank from even his nobles and chief ministers, but not from the eunuchs who attended to his every bodily need, who fed him, bathed him, dressed him and gently directed his sexual education. Of necessity they became his intimates, then his confidants, then his counsellors. By the time that Yehonala was selected as concubine third class, the Chief Eunuch An Te-hai directed the life of the Emperor Hsien Feng like a hidden puppet-master.

***

Yehonala despised them also, but took very great care not to show it, always treating them with courtesy, consideration and calculation. She appealed to their vanity and comforted them with soothing words when they were troubled. She knew that the high-ranking eunuchs controlled access to the Emperor's bedroom, the Jade Bedchamber, and she also knew that their co-operation did not come cheap. A very heavy bribe was required, but was no guarantee of access, since hundreds of girls vied for the same position, and many were richer than she. In any case they might take all of a girl's money and then regret their inability to influence the Emperor. Yehonala and her sisters all dreaded the fate of the neglected concubine, doomed never to share the Emperor's bed, doomed to remain forever a virgin and doomed to spend the rest of her days within the gilded prison of the Forbidden City. For these Manchu women were never allowed to leave the Forbidden City or to take other lovers or husbands. They all knew of the old maids who had lived there in miserable isolation for decades and were only waiting to die. Yehonala swore that it would never happen to her – she would find a way to the Emperor's bed. She made a special effort to ingratiate herself with the Chief Eunuch An Te-hai, whom she knew held the key to the Jade Bedchamber.

***

And then what! Then she had to so sexually satiate the Emperor that he would desire no other, that he would want to spend every night with her and would want to give her a healthy Dragon boy. The sexual sages of the Han dynasty had taught that there was no substitute for sexual practice to attain mastery in the art of love, and the palace eunuchs had applied this wisdom in the sexual education of the Emperor himself, through secret visits to the city brothels. Yet this route was not open to Yehonala – she had to be a virgin when she shared the Dragon Bed with the Emperor. Yet those ancient sages reckoned without the vivid imagination of a strong-willed girl intent on sexual domination. Each evening as she lay in her bedchamber, in one of the small blue-tiled pavilions in the Hall of Preserved Elegance, Yehonala enacted in her mind and body the positions and movements described in the *Secret Codes of the Jade Room*, the Taoist sex-manual that she had brought with her from Wuhu. She rehearsed them over and over again, so that her brain and vaginal muscles remembered the beauty and poetry of the myriad love dances of men and women. With the man on top, she imagined the Flying Seagulls and Winding Dragons. With the man behind, she dreamed of the Jumping White Tiger and the Dark Cicada Cleaving to a Tree. With the woman on top, her riotous fantasy explored the Cat and Mouse in One Hole and the Fluttering Butterflies. When her imagination was exhausted, she exercised her vaginal muscles with the help of a polished jade stone, until they obeyed her every whim, and practiced the sexual artistry of lips, tongue and teeth on an ivory replica of the male sexual organ. When the time came, she would be ready. Oh, she would be ready!

6

1854

'Bonjour, Madame Brown and Monsieur Thomas,' said Monsieur Dutronquoy, as he greeted his clients and let them into his photographic studio at the London Hotel. Gaston Dutronquoy had recently expanded his service by offering coloured daguerreotypes,[xix] which were far superior to regular daguerreotypes, especially for family photographs. 'But is Monsieur Brown not joining you?'

'I'm afraid he is too busy at work,' Margaret Brown replied, although that was not the reason. Her husband Richard was not interested in having a family photograph taken with his wife and son – he had already had his own photograph taken with Thomas at Dutronquoy's studio two weeks before. Margaret was furious when she had heard about this, and had wanted her own photograph taken with her son, and a photograph taken of her son without his father.

'Ah, the pressure of business, the pressure of business,' Dutronquoy replied, 'but we will make some fine prints of mother and son that you will treasure when you are apart – I know that Monsieur Thomas is returning to England to attend military school. Oh, but he will miss our fine weather in Singapore!'

***

---

xix Early method of photography that produced images on a silver-coated copper plate, developed by the French artist Louis Jacques Mandé Daguerre (1787-1851).

Margaret Brown was the only child of a prosperous lawyer and his social climbing wife, who were intent on making a good marriage for her daughter. Mr and Mrs Charles Claridge had lived in a fine townhouse in Leicester; they had gone to Bath and Bristol in the seasons, and to Bournemouth for six weeks in the summer. Margaret had had many suitors, for she was a very attractive young woman, with dark hair and eyes, full red lips, and a figure that was the envy of her female friends and jealous competitors. She had had little need of her mother's elaborate introductions and arranged meetings, and in any case, she had fallen deeply in love with Jonathan Barnes, the eldest son of Sir Gerald Barnes, a local landowner and country gentleman. Jonathan had sworn to her that he loved her like no other. They were meant for each other, he had said, like Odysseus and Penelope, and Aeneas and Lavinia.[xx] Jonathan was in line to inherit his father's estate on Sir Gerald's death, and had plans to serve in the government; his father was the local member of parliament for Rutland, and Jonathan planned to succeed him. They had already decided to get married, and had been waiting for an opportune moment to announce their planned engagement to their parents. Margaret had wanted to do so immediately, but Jonathan had asked her to wait until his father recovered from an attack of gout that was causing him great discomfort. She had not minded. Her life stretched out before her like a wonderful dream – she had never wanted in life, and she never would once she was married to Jonathan.

* * *

Then one day she came home after meeting a friend for lunch in town and was surprised to find her father's coat hanging on the stand in the hall. She had gone to the library to find him, because

xx Famous lovers in the Odyssey and Aeneid.

she assumed he had come home to consult the documents that he kept in his safe. Then she had smelt the burning powder in the still air, and knew he had shot himself. When she entered the library, Charles Claridge lay slumped over his desk, his brains blown out over his papers. That was what she remembered most vividly – the dark red stains on the white blotting paper.

After the coroner and undertaker had completed their business, her father's partner Mr Edward Henderson explained the reason for his suicide and the tragedy of their present situation. Charles Claridge had been an obsessive gambler. He bet on the racetrack and the dog-track; he bet at cards, on the verdict of court cases and the outcome of foreign wars; and he had lost heavily. He had left them nothing but debts, and the family was ruined – they would be forced by their creditors to sell their house and all its fine furnishings.

Margaret was heartbroken at the death of her father. She had loved him dearly, and had many fond childhood memories of him, but deep in her heart was a creeping anger at what he had done to her and her mother and younger sister. Yet she had managed to keep her anger at bay with the comforting thought that Jonathan would put everything right as soon as they were married, and ensure that her mother and younger sister were decently provided for.

But Jonathan Barnes, the heir to the estate of Sir Gerald Barnes, had not called on her when he received news of her father's death. He had not attended her father's funeral. He had not read her letters, which were returned to her unopened. When she had visited Maudsley Hall, the family's country seat, where she knew he was staying, she had been turned away by the doorman, who informed her with a supercilious sneer that the master wished him to inform her that she was not welcome at Maudsley Hall, on this day or any other day. She was not to bother him again.

When she returned home, her creeping anger towards her dead father had exploded into raging fury at Jonathan. He who had sworn he loved her like no other had rejected her because he did not want to be associated with the scandal of her father's suicide and ruinous debts. She was dead to him now, she knew, in reality as dead as her father was to her.

But what was she to do? She had no profession, trade or resources. She still had her beauty, but she no longer had the good reputation she had once enjoyed. She had been raised to become a wife to a man of noble birth and wealth, and all her mother's careful preparations for that day had come to naught. No man of noble birth and wealth would marry her now, and any man willing to take her as his wife would want nothing to do with her mother and younger sister. She felt helpless and betrayed, and her anger returned to her father's selfish foolishness.

Then, in the depth of her despair, Margaret had received a visit from Richard Brown, the son of a local merchant who was also a partner in a London firm. She had dismissed his attentions before, for he was trade, and she, like her father and mother and younger sister, had despised trade – she had known she could do far better than that. But now she knew she had to cut her cloth to fit her present condition, so she allowed him to visit, to take her out to the theatre and for supper afterwards, and to walk with her unchaperoned in the park. When he had proposed marriage to her she had accepted, even though she did not love him. She had thought she cared for him, for he had agreed to settle her mother and sister in a cottage on the outskirts of Leicester and provide them with a modest annual allowance. He was well-enough off to afford that, he said, since he had recently been appointed assistant manager of his company's offices in Singapore, for which city he was departing in four weeks' time.

It was this that made up her mind to marry him, she decided, when she thought about it later. Her mother and sister were provided for, and she could escape the whispering gossips and the memory of what might have been. And, if truth be told, Richard had painted a pretty picture when he described the sparkling white mansions and green lawns, the servants and gardeners, and the midnight balls at Government House – set amid the traveller's palms and the bright blanket of stars shining silver in the black velvet night. Although she was disappointed with the way things had turned out, she was excited by the prospect of life in the exotic East.

So, she had married Richard two weeks after he proposed to her, and they set out for Singapore two weeks later, after bidding a tearful farewell to her mother and sister. Yet she had found the reality of Singapore far less appealing than her dream. Margaret found the tropical heat oppressive, especially since she was expected to follow the men-folk in dressing as if she were attending an outdoor soiree on a cool autumn evening in England. She wore stockings and long dresses, starched blouses with long sleeves and tight collars, just as the men-folk dressed in dark suits, collars and ties, as if they were going to their offices in Leicester or London. The servants did everything – they dressed and undressed her, and did all the cooking – so there was little left for her to do but to attend the endless bridge and croquet parties with the other bored wives, to which she rode in an open gharry in the hot sun, as she gagged at the smell of the streets and the dust driven up by the pony's hooves. The governor only rarely gave a ball, and it was the same old people at the same old dreary parties, where the men got drunk while the women talked about their bridge and croquet – and their children.

That had been her saving grace. Richard had proved to be a poor lover. She had lost her virginity in a gruff fumbling moment, and their sexual relations had gone downhill ever since. She wondered if Richard enjoyed the physical act at all, as men were supposed to do, or whether he thought of it simply as a duty required for the purpose of procreation, as she knew some preachers taught – although she had not heard this view advocated at the Mission Church, that cramped and ugly wooden edifice where they were forced to take Sunday services, while waiting for the new English church to be built.

But he had given her a son, Thomas, a beautiful boy who was her life and joy. She had refused a wet-nurse, and had provided his nourishment in the first glorious months of his life, when he had gurgled in contentment at her breast, and she had rejoiced in the pure joy of motherhood – for a while she had managed to banish all her disappointments and sad memories. She had delighted in watching Thomas growing up – taking his first steps, saying his first words, and calling her 'mama' for the first time. She had grasped his tiny hand in hers as they had flown the brightly coloured kite that the Malay houseboy had fashioned, and he had squealed with delight as it soared into the bright blue sky. She had even indulged his love for his toy soldiers, which Richard had given him one Christmas morning, and helped him set up the tin armies of the Duke of Wellington and the Emperor Napoleon. But most of all she had delighted in reading stories to him before he went to bed – tales of pirates and buried treasure, of brave hunters who faced down fierce tigers, and of the fairy folk and their magical kingdoms – and kissing him good night before he fell into the deep and innocent sleep of childhood.

She had on occasion wondered about Richard's sexuality, and

whether he might prefer men or boys to his beautiful wife – for she took great care to preserve her beauty, taking her proper rest and using the latest creams that she bought from John Little and Co's department store in Commercial Square. But she concluded that this was not the case, for she soon learned that her husband and some of his business colleagues often took their pleasure in the European brothels on Malay Street, and sometimes in the Chinese ones on Smith Street. She was not sure whether it was because he needed the male camaraderie, the drink or the opium, the excitement of illicit sex or their more imaginative ways of pleasuring a man. She did not care – she had her son, and Richard provided well for them both. She had thought that of him at the time.

For a few years she had fallen into a comfortable routine, and had begun to reassert her independence. She went horse-riding in the cool hours of the early morning, she took an active role in the management of the house and hosted the occasional dinner party or musical soiree, which pleased her husband, and spent the rest of the time enjoying her infant son, and sharing his firsts with the other wives.

8

On February 6, a ball was held in the Assembly Rooms to celebrate the thirty-fifth anniversary of the founding of the settlement in 1819. After supper a toast was drunk to the health of the Queen, as was customary, and Governor Butterworth gave a speech celebrating the commercial success of the settlement. He noted that whereas the value of imports and exports in the first five years of the settlement had been two and a half million pounds sterling, their value according to the last returns was six and a half million pounds sterling. The governor attributed the prosperity of the settlement to the principle of free trade championed by the visionary founder of the settlement Sir Stamford Raffles, and called for another toast to prosperity and free trade, concluding by advising the company of his intention to name the new lighthouse about to be erected at Pulau Satumu,[xxi] the 'Raffles Lighthouse', in honour of the founder.

No mention was made of Colonel William Farquhar, the first resident and commandant of Singapore, who had done so much in the early years to secure the initial success of the settlement.

***

Duncan Simpson had recently returned from Hong Kong to report to his father on the successful establishment of an office of Simpson and Co in the Crown colony. His father, Ronnie Simpson, had landed on the island of Singapore with Sir Stamford Raffles and

xxi 'One tree island' in archaic Malay.

Colonel William Farquhar on January 29, 1819, when Temenggong Abdul Rahman had agreed to allow the East India Company to set up a factory[xxii] on the island. Ronnie was one of the many Scottish merchants whose canny business sense and ability to work with their Peranakan[xxiii] counterparts had contributed so much to the early commercial success of the settlement. The business that he had founded with his father John Simpson had thrived, and was now expanding into Johor[xxiv] and Hong Kong. It had not all been plain sailing. Ronnie and his wife Sarah had fought a running battle with the Illanun pirates who had murdered Sarah's sister and her family at sea, which only ended when Ronnie had set a trap that led to the destruction of the pirate leader.

Ronnie's son Duncan had joined the business as soon as he was old enough to play a role, but as part of his broader education, Ronnie had agreed to let him join James Brooke and Captain Henry Keppel in their expeditions against the Dayak pirates that plagued the rivers of Sarawak. Through a series of lucky accidents and judicious use of the guns and crew of *The Royalist*, James Brooke had managed to get himself declared ruler of Sarawak. Brooke had maintained good relations with the Sultan of Brunei, until the Sultan, on the counsel of Pangeran[xxv] Mahkota, the Serpent, had ordered the murder of Pangeran Muda Hassim, the former ruler of Sarawak, and Pangeran Badrudeen, whom Duncan had fought with side by side along the rivers of Sarawak. Hearing that Mahkota had joined a fleet of Saribus Dayak pirate prahus that were raiding the coastline and rivers of Sarawak, Brooke, now known as the White

xxii Early name for commercial settlement. The agents for companies who set up such settlements in Southeast Asia were known as factors.
xxiii Chinese merchants from Malacca and Penang who married into the local Malay community.
xxiv Southernmost state of the Malayan peninsula, sharing a sea border with Singapore.
xxv Prince or other male noble of high rank.

Rajah of Sarawak, had taken his revenge by organizing an ambush at Batang Marau, aided by the gunships of the Royal Navy. Duncan had joined James – now Sir James Brooke – on the expedition, since he had been a good friend of the murdered Badrudeen, but he had been shocked by the wholesale slaughter of the Dayaks in their wooden prahus, which had been no match for the ironclad paddle gunships of the navy. Duncan had been sickened by the carnage, in which hundreds had been killed or drowned, and had told James that he no longer wanted any part of it. Their parting had been cool, but Duncan still considered James to be his friend.

Matters had not ended there. When the navy claimed an extortionate bounty for all the Saribus Dayak pirates killed, questions had been raised in the British parliament about whether the Dayak fleet was really a fleet of pirates, and by what right Sir James Brooke, a private citizen, had called upon the services of Her Majesty's Navy to further his own personal ends. There had been calls for a public inquiry, partly stimulated by a damning indictment penned by Robert Carr Woods, the editor of the Singapore *Straits Times*, and supported by some of the Singapore merchants. Although Sir James and his friends back home had fought hard to prevent it, parliament had finally approved a commission of inquiry to be held in Singapore, to which Sir James had been summoned to appear. The commissioners, Charles Henry Prinsep, the Advocate General of India, and Humphrey Bohun Devereux, a government agent, had arrived in Singapore on August 7, and announced that the inquiry would begin on September 11.

Sir James was staying at the home of W.H. Read, one of the merchants who supported James' cause and who believed that the Dayaks were murdering pirates who got what they deserved. When Duncan arrived at Read's house to attend a dinner in honour of Sir James, Duncan could hardly recognize him. The once ramrod straight back was now stooped; the once boyish face was deeply lined and pock-marked, and the once bouncing brown curls had given way to a thin and receding hairline. Only the fierce blue eyes were recognizable, as they held his with undisguised hostility.

'And what role had your father in all this?' James Brooke demanded. 'I thought he had led an expedition against a bunch of Illanun pirates, and destroyed them and their leader. So, what sort of hypocrite is he to sign Wood's slanderous petition?'

Duncan did his best to keep his temper.

'He had no role at all, other than being one of the signatories of the petition, along with my grandfather,' Duncan replied. 'You're right, of course, he has no love of pirates, and would no doubt be happy to see them go down to the last man to a watery grave. I have assured him that the Saribus Dayaks were pirates, and he and my grandfather have accepted my word on that – I was there that day at Batang Marau, you may remember. I was sickened by the bloodshed, but I also know that these men had plenty of blood on their own hands. So, you won't have any trouble from him over the question of whether they were pirates.'

'Then why the hell did he – why did they – sign Wood's petition?' James demanded.

Duncan replied by pointing out what many of James' friends – including W.H. Read – had already pointed out to him. Many of those who had agreed to the call for an inquiry had done so because they honestly believed that the extent of the slaughter at Batang Marau – and the almost obscene amount of prize money awarded for that action – demanded some justification of the necessity of the action beyond the Rajah's mere say so. This was, he thought, a reasonable request, and if James would just let the inquiry take its natural course, it would soon become clear to most reasonable people that his actions were entirely justified.

But James Brooke refused to accept this.

'Never! Never I say! I will fight them every inch with every weapon I can lay my hands on. I will not let this scoundrel Woods get the better of me, or let my government treat me in the same disgraceful way that they treated the founder of this great port city!'[xxvi]

Duncan could not help but grin. For a moment James sounded like his old self. Yet the outburst seemed to drain his energy, and James remained sullen throughout the rest of the dinner, endlessly nitpicking over details of the inquiry, a man both obsessed and obsessive.

---

xxvi When Sir Stamford Raffles retired to England in 1832, he petitioned the Board of Directors of the East India Company for a pension and compensation for his administrative expenses incurred in the foundation of Singapore. The Board denied his request for a pension, for having willfully ignored their directions in the past, and presented him with a demand for twenty-two thousand pounds he owed the Company, having denied many of his administrative expenses, which they considered to be excessive.

9

Then Richard had dropped his bombshell. He informed her that he was sending their six-year-old son to the Royal Military Academy in London. She had always known that Richard intended a military career for Thomas – Richard himself had wanted a career in the army, but his father had refused him – and that one day Thomas would be sent back home for training, but she never imagined that he would be sent away to a boarding school at such a tender age. She feared for him. He was a sensitive child, and the Royal Military Academy was known for its strict discipline – Richard had boasted that they would make a man of him if anyone could, before his mother turned him into a proper pansy. But she also feared for herself. She did not think she could bear to be without him. That was the reason she had taken him to Monsieur Dutronquoy's studio, so she could at least have a picture to remember him by – and she could not forgive Richard's cruelty in not inviting her to the first photographic session.

***

Margaret was overcome with emotion when she kissed Thomas one last time, before he boarded the steamer with the servant who was to accompany him on his voyage to England. She made him promise to write to her regularly and tell her truly what was in his heart. As a parting gift she gave him a box made from camphor wood, which she said would always remind him of Singapore.

'Don't worry about me mama,' he said, although the tears formed in his eyes, 'I will be a good soldier and make you and father proud. And I promise I will write to you as often as I can.'

And then he was gone and she felt he was already dead to her. He would be lonely at first and miss his mother, she knew, but he would eventually make new friends and grow up into a young man, by which time he would scarcely remember her. Richard had refused to let the boy return to Singapore or to let Margaret travel to England to visit him until he had graduated as a cadet – he said it would only disturb the boy and interfere with his education. This she could not understand. Did he not love their son as much as she did? Or was he blinded by the hope that the boy would fulfil his own thwarted military ambition.

She worried that Thomas might not survive the harsh discipline, and then worried that he would be sent off to die in some dreadful foreign war, like the one that had recently broken out between England and France against the Russians in the Crimean peninsula. She hoped desperately that someday he would rebel against the discipline and the career that had been chosen for him, and be expelled from the academy, to return safely to her. Yet she knew in her heart that it would not come to pass, for she knew that the thing Thomas wanted most in all the world was to become a soldier – the tin soldiers that Richard had bought for him had done that trick.

10

Yehonala had been ready for a year now, but still had not received a summons from the Emperor Hsien Feng to the Jade Bedchamber. She had charmed the Dowager Empress, but had made little progress with An Te-hai or the other senior eunuchs, who found her amusing and charming, but treated her with the distance and disdain appropriate to a concubine of the third class. She had tried everything except bribery, because she knew she had insufficient funds, which the eunuchs might in any case take without keeping their part of the bargain, and seduction, since she knew it would be wasted on these 'half-men'. She had to find some flaw or failing that she could exploit. She was done with fawning obsequiousness.

And then the chance came to her. Bored with the daily palace routines, she had taken to wandering the Forbidden City at night, after the time had passed beyond which she was sure the Emperor would not summon her. She slipped out into the shadows, wearing only a long black hooded silk robe and black slippers, and wandered the edges of the palace buildings. She had no particular destination in mind – she just wanted to leave the constricting oppression of the concubine pavilions and breath free in the night air. Some evenings she would sit deep in the shadows of an outer court and watch the silver moonlight dance across the white marble bridges and the black surface of the River of Golden Waters. At other times she would visit the temples and gardens or play a game of following the eunuchs while they made their night rounds with their glowing lanterns.

She knew that such nocturnal wanderings were forbidden, and she knew the punishment if she was caught. She knew the danger, but she did it because she loved the danger – it was the only thing that kept her alive in the sumptuous, stifling prison. She moved like a fox spirit dancing around the half-men who patrolled the palace grounds in their stooped and mincing gait. They would never catch her!

***

Then one night as she had been about to return to her quarters, she had almost been discovered by two eunuchs, who suddenly emerged out of the shadows and disappeared down a corridor that led into an anteroom of the Palace of Eternal Spring. She caught her breath and pressed herself against the wall, but the two men passed without noticing her, so intent were they on whispering to each other as they slipped by. Her heart thumping in her breast, Yehonala followed them cautiously to the edge of the anteroom, where they moved about like shadow puppets in the darkness. They were whispering excitedly now, although she could not hear what they were saying. Then her eyes adjusted to the darkness, as the pale moonlight drifted down from the high ceiling, and she could see what they were doing. She could not believe her eyes. One of the eunuchs was An Te-hai, who had knelt down and prostrated his arms upon the floor. Was he offering a prayer? But why here? And why not in one of the temples? Then the other eunuch, a younger man whom she knew to be a favourite of An Te-hai, knelt down behind the chief eunuch and lifted his robe to reveal his pale buttocks. The younger man reached into his pocket and pulled out a small jar, whose contents he spread between the legs of the chief eunuch, who moaned gently in the ghostly moonlight. Then the younger man reached beneath his own robe and pulled out – and there was no mistaking it – his long hard penis! Yehonala watched in amazement as the younger man performed the Flying Seagull on the chief eunuch, who moaned and whimpered in pleasure with every stroke of passion. She found herself strangely aroused by the homosexual act, her arousal heightened by the danger of the moment. She waited patiently until the lovers' passion was finally spent. Then she stepped forward from her hiding place, her head bowed and her black silk hood pulled close around her face, and whispered loud enough for the two men to hear:

'I see you, An Te-hai, and I see your precious friend! You will hear from me this day!'

Then she turned back into the shadows and raced like a fox spirit down the corridor and out into the moon drenched courtyard before An Te-hai and his lover were able to raise themselves from the floor.

11

The Assembly Rooms at the foot of Government Hill[xxvii] having fallen
into grave disrepair, the trustees proposed that instead of rebuilding
the frail wooden structure, a more substantial building should be
erected in its stead, to be designated as the Town Hall. The trustees
of the Assembly Rooms petitioned Thomas Church, the resident
councillor, and the municipal committee to match the sum of money
raised by the community subscribers, which happily exceeded their
expectations. The resident councillor and the municipal committee
agreed to match the funding.

Around the same time the Grand Jury complained about the
present size and location of the Court House, being a mere house[xxviii]
with insufficient space for the court officers and public, and subject
to continual interruption by the cacophony of sounds emanating
from the nearby shipbuilding yard of Hallpike and Co.

***

The next day Yehonala requested a private audience with An Te-
hai, and to the surprise of the other senior eunuchs she was granted
it. He met with her in his private sitting room, where he offered her

xxvii Formerly known as Forbidden Hill (Bukit Larangan in Malay).
xxviii John Argyll Maxwell's house, which eventually became the first
Parliament House when Singapore attained full internal self-government
in 1959 under the newly victorious People's Action Party led by Lee
Kuan Yew. Later known as Old Parliament House, the building is
currently known as The Arts House.

a cup of plum wine, which she politely declined – she knew that the palace eunuchs had an intimate knowledge of poisons.

'What can I do for you, my child?' he said, in a simpering voice that reminded Yehonala of the hissing of a deadly snake. An Te-hai was short and stout, with a round face that would have done many women proud. He was smiling graciously, but Yehonala knew that his thoughts were anything but gracious. 'We both know why you are here,' he said, and his smile also reminded her of a deadly snake.

'I am here to ask a favour, An Te-hai,' Yehonala replied.

He looked at her carefully. Yes, she was as beautiful as he remembered. A perfect oval face, a cherry mouth with full lower lip, sparkling white teeth, dark brown eyes and jet-black hair, with a voice like liquid velvet. He had planned to use her, but she had been slow in offering him a bribe, although she had charmed him and his brothers with her wit and feline charm. She reminded him of one of those fox spirits who come to men in the form of beautiful young women, then suck their essence dry until they fade into death in their empty human shells. She was lascivious to her core, even a half-man like he could see that. She was also a danger, and by all rights he should have her killed without delay. Yet a danger to whom, he thought to himself? He might be able to harness her fox spirit to his own ends.

An Te-hai voiced his thoughts.

'Tell me of the favour you ask, concubine third class, but first tell me why I should not have you killed?'

'I do not think you would wish me dead, my dear An Te-hai,' she replied in her silken voice. 'Our secret will remain our secret so long as I remain alive and we remain friends, but it has been entrusted to one you will never suspect and it will be shared with the Emperor if anything ever happens to me.'

'You are bluffing, concubine third class. You dare not share this knowledge with anyone because I would be sure to find them out.'

'So sure?' Yehonala smiled, as she put her finger to her lower lip and raised her thin eyebrows. 'How many frustrated friends have I made? How many young eunuchs have I charmed? And how easy it was to get a message to the noble Jung Lu, my former betrothed, who would lay down his life in my service.'

'He cannot touch me. I am safe within the walls of the Forbidden City,' An Te-hai responded dismissively.

'Oh, I mean you no harm, my dear An Te-hai. I was only thinking of the harm that would befall your boyfriend if something should happen to me – I am sure it would be *very* painful.'

Yehonala giggled. She could not help herself. She was enjoying the tubby eunuch's discomfort.

'He means nothing to me. I could have him killed as easily as you. You make a dangerous enemy when you threaten me.'

'He seemed to mean a lot to you last night. ' She giggled again, but then turned serious. 'But I do not wish him death or to make an enemy of you, my dear An Te-hai. I only wish a summons from the Emperor to the Jade Bedchamber, which I know is in your power to bring about. He has ignored me this long year past, but only because he has never seen me in my true element and I have no champion in your court. Grant me this service and I will be eternally grateful to you and promise your star will rise with my own.'

'But how do I know you will not betray us if I do manage to arrange a summons from the Emperor?'

'Oh come,' Yehonala smiled sweetly, 'what would I gain by that, when I could instead gain a loyal and devoted servant who might one day serve the Empress Consort?'

He looked into her dark eyes and saw her passion and ruthless ambition. He knew she was more than his match. If he did not bend his will to her, he knew she would destroy him utterly. It was not a difficult decision.

'I would be honoured to try to facilitate an evening with his

Masterful Highness,' he replied in his singing, sugary voice. 'In the meantime you must be ready, and I must prepare you by sharing some of the secrets of the Jade Bedchamber.'

'Thank you, dear An Te-hai – from now on you and I must take good care of each other.'

Yehonala stepped forward and took hold of his chubby little hands, and kissed his bald forehead. Then they sat down together as Yehonala prepared to ask her questions and An Te-hai prepared to divulge the secrets of the Jade Bedchamber.

'But first, An Te-hai, you must tell me, although I mean your lover no harm, how is it possible for an intact man to serve as a palace eunuch? I thought there were regular inspections, before and after entry? Does a man's organ grow back, like the bud on a rose tree?'

Now it was An Te-hai's turn to giggle.

'No, no, my dear Yehonala, that is an old wives' tale – although some days I wish it were true. But one may buy the 'precious' of another man on the black market and pretend that it is one's own, just as a rich enough man may buy his way intact into our brotherhood. Remarkable as it may seem, the annual inspection only requires us to display our former accoutrements in their sealed jars – nobody thinks to check whether they belong to their rightful owner! Which shows how dangerous was your attempt to blackmail me – Lee Wang would only have had to display his "extra" set to demonstrate his innocence.'

'Not if ...' she began, but An Te-hai held up his hand and hushed her.

'Maybe there would still have been danger, and maybe I was not prepared to take the risk. But you should know that I have decided to co-operate with you out of selfish interest. It is plain to see that you are determined and ambitious, and willing to risk all for the greatest prize. With a friend like me, you could go far, very far indeed, and with a friend like you, dear Yehonala, I could rise much higher than my present station. You and I are kindred spirits, and I believe our fortunes are intertwined.'

'My thoughts exactly, my dear An Te-hai,' Yehonala purred. 'But you must call me Orchid and I will call you Little An. And you must tell me more about the Emperor Hsien Feng and the secrets of the Jade Bedchamber.'

12

1854

Hong Xiuquan came from a poor Hakka farming family in Guanlubu, a small village about thirty miles north of Canton. He had originally hoped for a career as a Confucian scholar, but his continued attempts to pass the state examinations had ended in failure. On one of these occasions, he had been presented with a Chinese tract, *Good Words for Exhorting the Age*, which had explained the basic tenets of the Christian faith. After another failed attempt at the state examinations, Hong had fallen dangerously ill and taken to his bed, where he had had a fantastic dream. He dreamed that he had met his father, God in Heaven, and his elder brother, Jesus Christ. God had told him to return to earth to spread the gospel of redemption, to drive out the demon-devils and their idols and false gods, and to bring about the time of Taiping, of Heavenly Peace on Earth. When he woke from his dream, he could not at first make any sense of it, but having reread *Good Words for Exhorting the Age* a year later, he had come to understand his Heavenly mission on earth.

With a few close friends, whom he baptized in the Christian fashion, he had left home to spread the gospel of redemption. Over time his converted God-followers had grown in number from hundreds to thousands to hundreds of thousands. Against all odds, the Taiping army had defeated the Qing armies sent to oppose them, as they battled their way across southern China until they captured Nanking, the southern capital, on March 19, 1853, which they had made their base of operations. When Hong Xiuquan conferred with his subordinate kings about their next course of action, they had all supported an advance on Shanghai, in the hope of forging an alliance with their foreign barbarian Christian brothers against the Manchu emperor, Hsien Feng. There they could purchase modern munitions and gunboats, which would enable them to control the approaches to the Grand Canal and the capital city of Peking.

But Hong Xiuquan had been adamant. The demon-devils were trapped like rats in their northern refuge, and they must immediately send an army to Peking to destroy them. Hong had divided the main Taiping army into three smaller armies. The first army of Wei Changhui, the North King, would remain and protect Nanking, while the second army of Shi Dakai, the Wing King, would secure the west. The third army of General Lin Fengxiang would drive north across the Yellow River and capture Peking. Yang Xiuqing, the East King[xxix] and the voice of God, was given charge of the overall military campaign and administration, while Hong Xiuquan devoted himself to the supervision of the printing of the holy books of the Taiping.

The northern expedition of General Lin Fengxiang, comprising seventy thousand veterans and new recruits, had set out on the two-thousand-mile march to Peking in May 1853. Without proper clothing, the Taiping were woefully unprepared for the northern winter, many freezing to death along the way. Constantly harried by Qing forces, some thirty thousand managed to fight their way to within thirty miles of the capital in late October – but there they were checked by numerically superior Qing infantry, reinforced by Mongol cavalry. While the beleaguered Taiping soldiers dug in for the winter, the Qing forces, commanded by the Mongol General Senggelinqin, built a ring of siege trenches that encircled the remnants of General Lin Fengxiang's army.

---

xxix There were originally four Taiping Kings. Xiao Chaogui, the West King and the voice of Jesus, had died in battle the previous year, as had Feng Yunshan, the South King.

***

After a seven-month siege, General Senggelinqin had ordered his soldiers to cut a ditch to divert the waters of the Grand Canal into the Taiping positions. When the work was completed in June, 1854, the Taiping camp was turned into a swamp and then into a lake. The Taiping suffered great losses as they fought their way out of the quagmire, but managed to fight a successful rearguard action as they fell back southward and set up a final defensive position in the Grand Canal city of Lianzhen. There they were quickly surrounded again by the forces of General Senggelinqin, who immediately began yet another siege of the doomed northern expedition.

The Taiping western campaign met with better success than the northern expedition, although not without its own setbacks. Shi Dakai, the Wing King, had driven south into Jiang and Hunan provinces. Over the next two years the fighting raged back and forth across the land, with cities taken and retaken by the Taiping and the Qing, the countryside ravaged to feed the marauding armies. Shi Dakai managed to establish control of most of Jiang province, which he set up as a Taiping base and valuable source of food supplies. He also captured the strategic capital city of Luzhou, at the confluence of the Yangtze and Tuo Rivers, but could not hold it in the face of determined Qing counterattacks. After some initial successes in Hunan, Shi Dakai failed to establish control of the province, where he faced the increasingly well-organized Hunan army of Zeng Guofan,[xxx] who managed to drive him back despite suffering some early crippling defeats. The two leaders were well matched. Both were young, well educated and commanded fierce loyalty from their men.

---

xxx The scholar-gentleman who founded the Hunan army from local militias, funded by the local nobles and gentry, to help the regular Qing forces defeat the Taiping.

3

In July the naturalist Alfred Russel Wallace and his assistant Charles Grant packed up their collections and thanked Father Maudit for his hospitality. They had stayed with him the past two months while collecting specimens of beetles and other insects in the forest of Bukit Timah[xxxi] Hill. Father Anatole Maudit was the priest of St Joseph's Church at Bukit Timah, and had allowed them to use his spare bedroom and washhouse while they did their work. In return, Alfred had contributed financially to Father Maudit's mission, with Charles, who was a crack shot, providing the occasional game for the evening table. Wallace was enormously impressed by Father Maudit's simple goodness and generosity of spirit – whatever he had he shared with his poor Chinese parishioners – and by his bravery during the recent secret society rampages on the island.

When Wallace and his assistant returned to Singapore town, they boarded a schooner for Malacca, where they spent the following two months collecting specimens in the jungle a few miles east of the town. There Wallace had a severe recurrence of the malarial fever he had contracted in South America. The government doctor prescribed massive quantities of quinine every day for a week, which seemed to cure him completely, so he made a point of stocking up on supplies of the drug for his planned travels into the remoter regions of the Malay Archipelago.

In October, they returned to Singapore, then travelled to Borneo, where they set up camp twenty miles southeast of Sarawak on the

---

xxxi Malay for Tin Hill.

outskirts of the Si Munjon coal works. Wallace continued to collect and record the many species of beetle he found there, but he also spent a good deal of time collecting specimens of orang utan; this was one of the reasons he had chosen Borneo as his next destination after Singapore and Malacca, because of their quantity and variety in the region. He was impressed by the fact that – at least according to his Dayak guides – there were three distinct species, which were quite numerous in the jungle around their camp, but were never to be found in the jungle closer to Sarawak. There appeared to be some invisible boundary line between them, which he was sure must be determined by a law of distribution, but he could not as yet determine its nature.

* * *

Little An and Orchid became the best of friends and the two self-serving schemers spent hours in each other's company. Little An told Orchid of the loneliness of his love for Lee Wang, and she comforted him, and Orchid told Little Ann of her thwarted love for Jung Lu, her former betrothed, and he comforted her. Orchid kept Little An's secret, and Little An kept his word. He told her to be patient and let him pick a propitious time for her first encounter with the Emperor – meanwhile he instructed her on the secrets of the Jade Bedchamber.

Although the Emperor shared his bed with one of his concubines every night, and did his best to bring them to orgasm, his own sexual satisfaction was severely constrained by tradition and ritual. He was only supposed to ejaculate seven times a year – three times in the spring, twice in the summer and autumn, but not at all in the winter. He restrained himself through yoga exercises and with the aid of a sheep's eyelid stretched over the end of his penis, so that his semen would return from his penis and travel up to his brain. In this way he would build up his Jing – his essence – and increase his longevity and fertility. And then, on the designated nights, on the stroke of midnight, the Emperor would explode in 'celestial fireworks'.

Yehonala grinned.

'Of course, it doesn't always work out like that,' An Te-hai concluded. 'You will have to use your imagination and your charm. But be sure of one thing – you must get him to explode his fireworks, for our path to success is through a male child.'

'I shall give him such a night of celestial fireworks that he will never forget me.'

'Oh, good girl! Good girl! Precious Orchid!'

14

It was early evening, and Dr James Legge[1] was in his study in the Mission House in Hong Kong, writing a letter to his brother in Scotland. There was a knock at the door, and he got up to open it. There were two men standing in the doorway, who greeted Dr Legge and introduced themselves. The first was a tall and blond-haired Swedish missionary, with piercing steel-blue eyes, the Reverend Olaf Andersson of the Basel Missionary Society, who had just returned from China. The other was a younger Chinese man, dressed in Western clothes but with his long hair hanging loose, who introduced himself in excellent English as Mr Hong Rengan. Reverend Andersson told Dr Legge that Hong Regan was the cousin of the Taiping King Hong Xiuquan, and had been trying to reach his cousin when he had heard of the Taiping victory at Nanking. Hong Rengan explained how he had travelled north with this purpose in mind, but that he and his companions had been attacked in their camp one evening by Qing forces, who had killed or captured most of his comrades. He had been one of the few to escape.

Reverend Andersson then explained that Hong Rengan had sought refuge with the missionaries. Since he had been on the point of returning to Hong Kong aboard a British steamer, he had agreed to smuggle Hong Rengan out, hoping that Dr Legge might be able to find some work for the young man, who seemed honest and industrious as well as a committed Christian.

'I'm sure we can work something out,' said Legge optimistically, inviting both men in and offering them tea.

* * *

Over the course of the next few months and years, the Scottish missionary and the Hakka cousin of the Heavenly King became the closest of friends. Dr Legge gave Hong Rengan a room in his home and had him conduct classes at the Mission school, where he was a great favourite with the students because of his fluency in Chinese and English and because of his cheerful disposition. He was patient with them when they had difficulty with their academic studies, and understanding when they were vexed by the Christian mysteries.

Hong Rengan also worked as a linguistic assistant to Dr Legge, who was preparing the groundwork for his ambitious project of translating the Chinese classics, with detailed learned commentaries. He often asked Hong for his advice on the translation of key Chinese terms, and the two men had long discussions about the proper Chinese words to characterize the Christian God, a subject that intrigued them both. Dr Legge was gratified to learn that Hong Rengan and Hong Xiuquan both used the term 'Shangdi' to represent the Heavenly Father, since he had been championing this translation for years. Hong Rengan joined Dr Legge in his Christian ministry among the Chinese, as they went together from house to house and from shop to shop spreading the message of love and redemption, and sometimes preaching the sermon together during the evening service at the Mission. But no matter how hard he tried, Hong Rengan could not persuade Dr Legge of the truth of Hong Xiuquan's vision. Legge had the greatest respect for many of Hong Xiuquan's moral prescriptions concerning the equality of men and women, his prohibition of opium and alcohol, and his condemnation of idolatry, but he simply could not accept that Hong Xiuquan was the younger brother of Jesus or that he had literally visited God in Heaven.

Dr Legge was so pleased with Hong Rengan's work that he allowed him to bring his family to the safety of the Mission House in Hong Kong. Sye-po, Hong Rengan's elder brother, quickly earned the trust of the Legge family and became their chief servant.

15

The Singapore inquiry dragged on for two stifling months while the friends and enemies of Sir James fought it out on the pages of the *Free Press* and the *Straits Times* and in the Singapore Chamber of Commerce. After a dilatory start, most of the witnesses called spoke to the issue of whether the Saribus Dayaks really were pirates. James' supporters had rounded up a rich collection of witnesses to testify that the Saribus Dayaks were in fact murderous pirates. These included Singapore merchants and Sarawak officials, and a host of ship's captains and sailors, European, Malay and Bugis, who happened to be in Singapore at the time.

But not all the testimony went James' way. Although some of Woods' witnesses were duds – some admitted that they had not read his petition before signing it, and some admitted they knew nothing about Borneo – others expressed genuine concern and raised legitimate doubts about James' apparent over-readiness to characterize all his opponents as pirates. James Guthrie, of Guthrie and Co, one of the more stalwart supporters of Woods' petition, stated that he was not prepared to take Sir James' word on the question of whether Saribus Dayaks were pirates – too often the Dayak people were forced into piracy by Malay or Illanun chieftains or by their own cruel masters – and questioned whether it had been necessary to let Sir James' own Dayaks and Malays loose on those who opposed him, taking their heads and burning their longhouses. But what irked him most, Guthrie said, was that Sir James had advised the home government that his report on the battle of Batang Marau had been approved by all the mercantile houses of Singapore, with the exception of three. This was a gross misrepresentation, since he and a good many other merchants had decidedly not approved it.

The work of the commission was completed in November. James was cleared of the charge of commercial exploitation of the natives of Borneo. He was also pleased to receive petitions of support (organized by his supporters) from the European merchants and from the 'Chinese merchants and residents of Singapore'. Yet for James it was a hollow victory. He felt that his government had betrayed him just as it had betrayed his hero Raffles before him. Duncan could see it in his eyes. Anyone could see it in his eyes. Rajah Brooke was a bitter man, and he would remain a bitter, suspicious and paranoid man to the end of his days.[2]

Although James was technically vindicated, there was implied condemnation in the final judgment of both commissioners, who concurred that in future Sir James should not be allowed to call upon the British Navy to further his interests in Sarawak and that he should not be entrusted by the British Crown 'to determine with any discretion which of these tribes are piratical'. This final insult demonstrated to James that his government had abandoned him – he was nothing more than a private citizen, whose authority was dependent on the indulgence of the Sultan of Brunei.

Duncan attended the farewell dinner given in Sir James' honour at W. H. Read's house in Tanglin, and rejoined him in the morning as James set sail for Sarawak on HMS *Rapid*. The two men shook hands, but Duncan thought there was no warmth to their parting, and that the man he had once so admired was already almost gone. He was never to see him again.

16

In February, Alfred Russel Wallace sat alone in his hut near the Si Munjon coal works. Charles Grant had gone back to Sarawak to pick up the mail and some supplies, and Wallace had finished mounting the specimens they had recently collected. The heavy rain precluded further exploration for the moment, so he sat down with pen and paper and wrote down some of his recent thoughts on the question of the transmutation of species. He was quite pleased with his work, and wrote up his notes into a scientific paper, which he entitled 'On the Law which has Regulated the Introduction of New Species'. The next time he was back in Sarawak he sent it off to the editor of The Annals and Magazine of Natural History, who agreed to publish it in the September issue. The paper included Wallace's statement of what came to be known as his 'Sarawak Law':

'Every species has come into existence coincident both in space and time with a pre-existing closely-allied species.'

But he still had no answer to the question of how this came to be.

***

In March, Hong Xiuquan, the Taiping Heavenly King, was dismayed to receive the news that after an eight-month siege, General Senggelinqin had broken through the defences at Lianzhen and annihilated the ragged remnants of the northern expedition.

General Lin Fengxiang had surrendered and been immediately beheaded – his body and severed head had been sent to Peking in a cage for public display. The Emperor Hsien Feng, the Celestial King, received the same news with great elation. His princely relations and senior mandarins assured him that his Bannermen would soon crush the remains of the rebellion and execute every last rebel 'God-follower'.

Hong Xiuquan received better news the following month, when he heard that after a series of carefully planned and executed advances Shi Dakai had scored a decisive naval victory at Jiujiang in Jiangxi, against the Hunan marines commanded by Zeng Guofan. So complete was his defeat that Zeng Guofan was driven to contemplate suicide, and in his report to the Emperor he called Shi Dakai 'the most cunning and strong of the Taiping'.

***

Temenggong Daing Ibrahim was the son of the late Temenggong Abdul Rahman, who along with Sultan Hussein had signed the treaty with Sir Stamford Raffles in 1819 that granted the East India Company the right to develop a trading settlement on Singapore island, in return for British protection and annual allowances. Like his father before him, Daing Ibrahim had profited from the agreement, which had been extended and formalized by John Crawfurd[xxxii] in 1824.

Daing Ibrahim had profited especially from his gutta-percha[xxxiii] monopoly, as well as from the sale and lease of his waterfront properties at Telok Blangah, which had become prime real estate

xxxii The second resident of Singapore.
xxxiii Malleable sap from the gutta-percha tree, a valuable export, which was used to make snuffboxes, walking sticks, dolls, chess pieces, bottle stoppers and temporary tooth fillings, and later to insulate telegraph and submarine cables and to produce a new 'gutta' golf ball.

with the development of the steamer wharfs and coaling stations at New Harbour.[xxxiv] When the slash and burn techniques of the Chinese gambier and pepper farmers exhausted the soil of the interior and north shore of the island, the Temenggong welcomed them to lease land from his estates in Johor, and the Singapore firm of Kerr, Paterson and Simons helped Ibrahim to expand the Johor trade. As Daing Ibrahim's fortunes rose, those of Tengku Ali, the son of the late Sultan Hussein who lived with his followers at the Istana[xxxv] at Kampong Glam, continued to fall. Although Tengku Ali still received the allowance that had been awarded to his father by Raffles and Crawfurd, the whole of it was now pledged to a Chettiar[xxxvi] to cover the interest on his debts, and he could not afford to support his dwindling band of supporters. Unlike Daing Ibrahim, Tengku Ali still refused to sully his noble hands with trade, although W.H. Read energetically employed the resources of Johnston & Co to try to gain some commercial advantage from the management of Tengku Ali's properties at Kampong Glam.

Governor Butterworth finally managed to negotiate a settlement between Tengku Ali and Daing Ibrahim, which they signed at an elaborate ceremony held at Government House on March 10. Both men got what they wanted, at least for the immediate present. Tengku Ali acknowledged Daing Ibrahim as the sole and absolute sovereign of Johor, while Daing Ibrahim agreed to pay Tengku Ali an allowance from the Johor revenues. Daing Ibrahim and Governor Butterworth formally recognized Tengku Ali as Sultan of Johor, but it was an empty honour, as W.H. Read complained when he learned of the terms of the settlement – Daing Ibrahim had clearly come out

---

xxxiv The naturally sheltered and deep-water harbor between the mainland of Singapore and the southern islands of Pulau Brani ('island of the brave') and Pulau Belakang Mati ('island of the back and beyond of death'), present-day Sentosa island.
xxxv Malay term for palace.
xxxvi South Indian trader and moneylender.

best in the arrangement. In the years that followed Temenggong Daing Ibrahim continued to invest his inheritance wisely, while Sultan Ali continued to squander his dwindling allowance.

On March 17, Governor Butterworth laid the foundation stone for the new Town Hall.

***

On March 19, shortly after Vespers on a beautiful evening, the Reverend Father Hypolito Huerta, of the Order of the Hermits of St Augustin, laid the foundation stone for the new school of the Christian Brothers of La Salle. Father Jean-Marie Beurel and the brothers were in attendance, as were the sisters of the Convent of the Holy Infant Jesus and their charges. Since March 19 fell on the Feast of Saint Joseph, the new school came to be known as St Joseph's Institution, although the building funds ran out soon after the dedication, and the school was not completed until years later.

Colonel Butterworth attended the ceremony, which was his last public act as governor of the Straits Settlements.[xxxvii] He relinquished the governorship the following day, and retired to England with his wife. Edmund Augustus Blundell, a civil servant who had served as resident councillor in Malacca and Penang, succeeded him the following day. Blundell had also served as acting governor of the Straits Settlements in 1843, and from 1851-1853 when Colonel Butterworth went on medical leave to Australia. Many of the residents of Singapore had thought that Blundell should have been appointed Governor in 1843, and he would have likely secured the position had it not been for Governor-General Lord Ellenborough's special affection for Colonel Butterworth. Yet at the end of his

xxxvii In 1826, Singapore, Penang and Malacca were formed into the Straits Settlements, an administrative unit of the East India Company, overseen by the Indian government.

twelve years it was generally agreed that Colonel Butterworth had served the settlements well, and he was given a rousing send off by the merchant community and by the military and civic leaders.

17

It was some months before An Te-hai could fulfil his promise to help Yehonala secure an evening engagement with the Emperor Hsien Feng. The Emperor and his court had moved to the Yuan Ming Yuan,[xxxviii] the Summer Palace, an elaborate complex of palaces and gardens five miles northwest of the Imperial City, which included the Hall of Jade Billows, the Hall of Joyful Longevity, the Enclosed and Beautiful Garden, the Golden and Brilliant Garden, and the Garden of Clear Rippling Water. The palaces and gardens were set in a landscaped park about five times the size of the Forbidden City, bounded by the expansive Kunming Lake, whose waters reached out to the distant haze of the blue-green hills beyond. There were dozens of halls, galleries, pavilions and temples, including some stone palaces in the European style that had been built by Jesuits, which contained a wealth of ancient Chinese art and antiquities, silks and furs, priceless gems and jade, and jewelled mechanical toys. Yet perhaps the greatest treasure of all was the harmony of nature and art that had been wrought by generations of artisans and gardeners, who had blended the yellow tiles and gold leaf of the palace and pavilion roofs with the brown flow of the branches and lustrous green of the leaves on the trees. They had formed magical paths, groves and grottos, with sparkling streams, cascading waterfalls and placid silver lakes, and had meticulously reproduced in miniature form many of the classical landscapes of China, which were breathtaking to behold. This was not art imitating nature, but

---

xxxviii Garden of Perfect Brightness.

art contriving to shape the very essence of nature.

And it was in these magical gardens that Yehonala and An Te-hai captured the ear and eye of the Emperor. She had worn her best silk robes and taken special care with her make-up and perfume. She sat in the pavilion known as 'The Deep Recesses Among Green Trees,' and sang a sad folk song her mother had taught her. When the Emperor passed by with An Te-hai, he was attracted by her sweet voice, and when he followed An Te-hai into the pavilion he was captivated by her almost perfect beauty: her slim ankles, her perfect skin and full lips, and her silken voice, which seemed to reach inside his heart. He stayed only a few moments, but when he returned to his chamber that evening he carefully selected Yehonala's jade plaque and placed it on the carved ivory table at his bedside.

* * *

There was a significant increase in piracy throughout the year, with Chinese pirates attacking junks on their way to and from Singapore, causing a significant disruption in trade. The government steamship the *Hooghly* was too slow to be of any use in suppressing the pirates, so Tan Beng Swee, W. H. Read, Tan Kim Ching, Jose d'Almeida and Dr Robert Little prepared and forwarded petitions to the Indian government, the houses of parliament and the admiral of the Far East Squadron, urging them to take vigorous measures to suppress the brazen acts of piracy taking place in the waters surrounding Singapore. Eventually a man-of-war was sent by the admiral of the Far East squadron, while local officials took the initiative by removing the rudders of suspected junks, which were often found to be without any cargo but fully armed and manned.

18

In July, Colonel Ronald Macpherson of the Madras Artillery, who had recently succeeded Captain Henry Man as superintendent of convicts in Singapore, received a visit from Dr Stanley Moon, the Inspector-General of Jails, who had travelled from Bengal. Captain Macpherson took Dr Moon on a tour of inspection of the Bras Basah jail, the living and sleeping quarters, and the training workshops. They also visited the field stations where the convicts laboured on roads, viaducts and government buildings, and met with some of the first class 'ticket of leave' prisoners who worked as clerks in the merchant houses and court offices.

'I have to admit I'm most impressed by your operation, colonel,' said Dr Moon as they dined in the colonel's quarters that evening. 'I don't think I've seen a more successful system for the industrial training of convicts anywhere, and certainly nowhere in the continent of India. Your prison is an example to us all. It just shows that if you give a man something to hope for – that he can once again become a respectable member of a community – then even the most recalcitrant criminals can be redeemed. And you say they rarely commit new crimes during their service? Quite remarkable!'

'Rare, but not unknown,' replied Colonel Macpherson, 'although mostly theft or other minor infringements, not much in the way of serious violence.'

'Are your prisoners mostly thieves, then? That might explain their docility.'

'On, no!' Colonel Macpherson laughed. 'No, no, Dr Moon,

they're mainly murderers! Many domestic affairs, of course, but we have plenty Thuggees – devotees of the goddess Kali who slaughter unwary travellers – and those regular armed robbers they call Dacoits.'

'Is that not a dangerous mix, colonel? Are you not troubled by the thought of prison rebellion or escape?'

'Not too much,' the colonel replied, 'although we keep the fifth class prisoners under double irons in isolation from the other prisoners, and we can call on the Sepoys[xxxix] for support if any serious trouble were to break out. But two factors tend to mitigate against these dangers, over and above the genuine commitment by most of our prisoners to work to improve their situation and gain an early ticket of leave.

'The first is that it takes all sorts to murder. We have men from all walks of life and every stratum of society, and a few women too – we have Benares Brahmins[xl], Sikh and Dogra Kshatriyas[xli], Nattukottai Chettiars, Bengali and Parsi financiers and peasants, as well as every variety of Untouchable. A more heterogeneous collection of scoundrels would be hard to find, so there's not much chance of communal rebellion, since there's not much sense of community among them – and as I said, most are intent on working their way toward their ticket of leave.

'And as to escape, where would they go? The local Indian community in Singapore is fairly small, so they could not easily blend into the general population, even if the local Indians were willing to aid and abet them, which they generally are not. Beyond here lies nothing but the jungle – full of dreaded tigers – and the open sea, where they are most likely to be returned for the bounty or sold into slavery by piratical Malays. No, there's not much for

---

xxxix Indian infantryman.
xl Highest ranking of four varnas or social classes in Hindu India.
xli Warrior class in Hindu India.

them to escape to, and most are intelligent enough to recognize that.

'Now the Chinese ... they're an altogether different kettle of fish. I've been pressed to take Chinese convicts from Hong Kong, but I wouldn't touch them with a ten-foot bargepole. They have every incentive to escape, and would simply disappear into Chinatown or the local plantations, where they would be protected by the secret societies. The Indian convicts are used to working with the British, and respect them in their way, but even the lowliest Chinese coolies think of us as barbarians. So, in a real sense we have our Indian prisoners to thank for our success!'

'I'll drink to that!' said Dr Moon.

19

Ronnie Simpson arrived for the meeting at Joaquim d'Almeida's house at seven o'clock in the evening.

'Good evening, Mr Simpson, and thank you for coming. I'm sorry your father could not make it. I think you know everyone here.'

'He's got a touch of fever, Joaquim, and sends his apologies,' Ronnie replied, greeting him and the two other men seated at d'Almeida's dining table. They were W.H. Read and Abraham Logan, the editor of the *Singapore Free Press*.

'Although he's as curious as I am as to what this meeting is about. Your note talked darkly about the threats to the future of our fair port city?'

His question was answered for him by the arrival of the next guest, Robin Carr Woods, the editor of the *Straits Times*. A few weeks before Woods had run an editorial urging the formation of a Reform League, aimed at persuading the British government to remove the administration of the Straits Settlements from the Governor-General of India, and to place them under the direct control of the Colonial Office in London. He wanted the government to make Singapore, along with Penang and Malacca, a crown colony. A meeting had been held a week ago in the Assembly Rooms, in which a motion proposing a transfer to the Colonial Office had been rejected, although Ronnie had spoken in its favour, as had Read, Logan, d'Almeida and Woods.

There had been an awkward silence when Woods first entered

the room. Woods and Logan had fired passionate editorials at each other condemning and defending Sir James Brooke during the Singapore commission of inquiry, while Read had tried his best to get the Chamber of Commerce to censure the editor of the *Straits Times.*

'Good evening, Mr Logan,' said Woods, trying to break the ice but putting his foot in it, 'I don't think we've spoken since ...'

He did not need to finish – they all knew to which circumstance he referred.

'I don't think we need to bother about that,' said W.H. Read, rising to his feet and offering his hand to Woods. 'Water under the bridge now, and we have bigger fish to fry.'

They all heartily agreed and with some relief got down to business.

'I suppose you all know by now why I invited you here,' said Joaquim d'Almeida. 'You all spoke for the motion to transfer the rule of our Straits Settlements from India to the Colonial Office. Although we lost the motion, I hope we – we small band of brothers – will take up Mr Wood's suggestion and create a Reform League devoted to the transfer. Nothing formal or official at the moment, but we should work together to try to persuade our colleagues, including the Chinese, Arabs, Parsis and the rest, that it would be in all our best interest. We will never get the financial and administrative support we need – and which, I might add, our competitor Hong Kong already receives – until we are brought under the direct control of the Crown.

'I'm all for that,' said Read, being the first to support d'Almeida's suggestion, 'but we also need to work with our friends in London to help persuade the home government. I know Mr Crawfurd, the former resident, will prove a strong ally – he and I talked about this directly the last time I was in London. But we have many other friends in the city, retired merchants and officials, who can talk to members of parliament and government ministers.'

'Hear, hear,' said Woods, and they all agreed to devote themselves to the task of persuading their business colleagues and communicating with their contacts in London. They also agreed to meet monthly at each other's houses to report on their progress and plan their future strategies.

'Well, we may end up goin' frae the frying pan in tae the fire,' Ronnie cautioned them, 'but from where I see it, the frying pan is pretty damn hot, and I want out! So I'm in with you gentlemen. Joaquim, let's drink on it! And none of your prissy Portuguese port – let's have the real stuff.'

Which they did, and with the real stuff, a highland malt that Ronnie had sold to Joaquim d'Almeida the previous month.

20

An Te-hai came early with the news, and to supervise the washing and shaving of her body. Then he carried Yehonala, his precious Orchid, in a red silk sheet to the Jade Bedchamber, which was hung with red banners. He deposited her naked at the foot of the Dragon Bed, spread out upon the yellow satin sheets. Before her at the head of the bed sat the Lord of Ten Thousand Years, the Emperor Hsien Feng, clad in a golden dragon robe. She lay there naked for a moment while his eyes gorged upon her – her slender feet and ankles, her tapering legs, the smooth curves of her stomach and buttocks, her tiny waist, her skin smooth and white as marble and crowned with two perfectly formed conical breasts, whose red nipples sparkled with hard desire in the flickering lantern light. Her ruby red lips pouted as she rolled gently on the bed before him, and her pink tongue flickered between them like a tiny snake. Her jet-black hair hung in lustrous strands over her shoulders and between her breasts, and Hsien Feng thought she looked like some goddess descended from Heaven. He was almost overcome with desire for her already, although she had made no move towards him. He opened his mouth to speak, to command her, but no words came out. She was not his to command.

Yehonala was in command now. She was in total command. Although it was forbidden, she held him with her dark eyes. She summoned within herself all the knowledge she had gleaned from the *Secret Codes of the Jade Room*, from the exercise of her body and imagination, and bound it to her single-minded will. She would make him remember this night forever, so that he would never want to leave her. Slowly, but very slowly, like a voluptuous cat she crawled across the bed towards him, whispering to him, begging him softly in her silken voice to share his celestial fireworks with her. But she was not to be rushed. She stripped him, kissed him, licked him, bit him and caressed him with her breasts, then took his swollen Celestial member in her mouth and drove him to the heights of the mountains and the Heavenly places. When she thought he could withstand the pleasure no more, she nipped off the sheep's eyelid from the top of his penis, and led him whimpering in anticipation into the warm moistness of her gently undulating vagina. She whispered to him the poetry of their lovemaking, as his Jade Stalk penetrated her Jade Gate and entered her Jade Garden, her Jade Juices flowed freely from her Jade Fountain, and the air was filled with the Jade Perfume of Love. He exploded his essence into her on the stroke of midnight, although not even An Te-hai was bothering to keep time.

***

The following night Hsien Feng turned over Yehonala's jade plaque once again, and every night thereafter. He was besotted with her and longed for her sweet voice and company as much as he longed for her body. He called her his Orchid, and he would have none other than his Orchid. On the seventh day of the seventh lunar month the lovers climbed up to the Porcelain Pagoda on Longevity Hill and searched the night sky until they saw the Cowherd star in the northeast and the Weaving Girl star in the northwest. And in the saturated silver moonlight she whispered to him of the bittersweet love between the Cowherd and the Weaving Girl:

Many years ago, there lived a young boy whose parents

had died, who worked for his elder brother and sister-in-law on the family farm. Because he tended the cows, the local farmers called him Cowherd. When he came of age, his brother and sister-in-law were afraid they would have to split the family farm, so they played a trick on Cowherd. They gave him the buffalo and a broken-down cart, which they claimed were the most valuable items from the family estate, and sent him off to seek his fortune in the world.

And so, the Cowherd set off and found himself some land to farm at the foot of a hill, sufficient for his needs. There he led a simple and contented life until one day, to his great surprise, the bullock began to talk to him. The animal told Cowherd that he was the Golden Bull Star, who had been banished to earth as a punishment. For the kindness the Cowherd had shown him, he was willing to help him find a wife. The following day the bullock instructed Cowherd to set off on a journey that would take him through a forest to the edge of a lake, where he would find seven sisters bathing. He was to search until he found the sisters' clothing in the bushes, and to take the red dress from among them. Then whoever came searching for the red dress would be his wife. The Cowherd journeyed through the forest and came to the edge of the lake, where he heard the sisters' laughter. Peering out from behind a tree he saw seven beautiful maidens bathing together, their clothes spread out over the bushes at the edge of the lake. He saw the red dress and removed it, but as he was returning to his hiding place behind the tree, one of the girls spotted him and cried out a warning. Six of the sisters rushed out of the lake and seized their clothes, then transformed themselves into doves and disappeared into the blue heavens. One girl remained, searching desperately for her dress.

Cowherd called out to her that he had her red dress, and told her not to be afraid, since he meant her no harm. He told her who he was and how he had been sent by the Golden Bull Star to find a wife. At first, she laughed at him, but then she became reflective. She told him that her name was Weaving Girl, because she wove the clouds in the sky. She was the granddaughter of the Heavenly Mother, who kept her working each and every day at the sky loom. She told him that her Heavenly Mother had been drinking heavily and had fallen asleep, so she and her sisters had taken the opportunity to enjoy themselves and explore the earth. She had found it a beautiful place – more beautiful, she said, than Heaven itself. Heaven was golden and dazzling, but it had no tinkling silver streams or soft breezes whispering through the green bamboo. Then Cowherd said that if she found the earth so beautiful, she should stay and become his wife, which, to his great joy and surprise, she agreed to do. And so, Cowherd and Weaving Girl were married, and were blessed with a boy and a girl. Cowherd tended the fields, while Weaving Girl spun cloth and looked after their children. They lived together in peace and contentment for seven years, until the Heavenly Mother noticed her granddaughter's absence, and in a fit of anger came down to earth in search of her.

When she found Weaving Girl, the Heavenly Mother was amazed that she could be so happy in such humble circumstances. But the Heavenly Mother had no pity for her, and carried her off into the sky. When his son ran into the fields to warn his father, Cowherd raced back to the farmhouse, only to see the Heavenly Mother and Weaving Girl floating upwards on a cloud. Then Golden Bull Star offered Cowherd his help and transformed himself into a cloud, and Cowherd and his children set off in pursuit of the Heavenly Mother. Cowherd's heart leapt as they began to gain on her, but fell when the angry Heavenly Mother turned and created a wide river in the sky, which even Golden Bull Star could not cross.

But then a great multitude of magpies rose up into the sky and formed a bridge across the raging river. Even the Heavenly Mother was moved by this act of kindness, although she would not allow Weaving Girl to return to earth. But she agreed to let Cowherd and Weaving Girl meet on the bridge of magpies on the seventh day of the seventh month of each year, and on that day each year young girls ask Cowherd and Weaving Girl to answer their prayers.

Emperor Hsien Feng smiled when she finished the tale and asked her: 'And what do you pray for, my sweet Orchid.'

'I pray that the child growing in my womb will be a Dragon boy,' she replied, smiling in return.

PART TWO

'NIGHT OF THE HUNGRY GHOSTS'

1856 – 1858

1

1856

Shiv Nadir had served his probationary period in the Bras Basah jail without incident, and moved quickly and easily up the classes. He had learned English and worked as an administrative assistant in Madras, two useful skills that first landed him a job teaching basic English and arithmetic to those fellow convicts who showed some intellectual promise, and then a part-time and later a full-time job as a clerk in the firm of John Purvis and Co. An earlier stint working in the granite quarries at Pulau Ubin[xlii] and on the extension of the Bukit Timah Road had put weight and muscle on his once spindly frame, so Purvis was happy to let him sleep in a small storeroom in his godown in return for his services as night watchman. It had taken five years, but he had managed to save enough money to purchase a small house of his own and secure a wife – albeit a former female convict, but an unbranded one – who was more than willing to share his bed and his rising good fortune. She had an older son by a previous marriage to a carpenter who had died of dengue fever, but Shiv Nadir was happy to take him on, for the boy was intelligent and hard-working, and she had given him a second son of his own. They would help him promote his business when they were grown up.

The money that Shiv Nadir had saved and which he continued to accumulate did not only come from his service with John Purvis and Co. It also came from a quite different business that he had

---

xlii Granite island.

89

originally run out of his prison cell, but which he now ran out of a room he had secretly rented above a tailor's shop in Chulia Kampong, the Tamil settlement north of Boat Quay on the edge of Chinatown. For Shiv Nadir had not only taught his fellow convicts new skills during his years as a lower-class prisoner, and it was not only the British authorities and merchants who profited from the variety of skills possessed by the convicts. Shiv Nadir had also learnt new skills from a master metalworker and silversmith, who – unbeknownst to the authorities, for he had been expatriated for the crime of embezzlement from his employer – was a master counterfeiter.

**

He had started small at first, working through two middlemen, Govinda Rudrappa and Ram Singh, both of whom were former assassins and enforcers who had served the goddess Kali.[xliii] But Shiv had carefully coached and trained them as master metalworkers – as well as master counterfeiters – until they had attained the first class and earned their tickets of leave, whereupon he had set them up in the room above the tailor's shop. Unlike most of the class five convicts, Govinda Rudrappa and Ram Singh had learned to accommodate themselves to their new situation, but they still retained the fierce demeanour of men who had been former enforcers. They dealt with the Ghee Hin secret society, whose members they employed as money runners, exchanging the counterfeit coins for genuine coins, in return for a percentage of the profits. The Ghee Hin also provided the solder, stolen from carriage makers and marine fitters, which they used in making the counterfeit coins – a solder base with a thin copper covering. Only Govinda Rudrappa and Ram Singh knew of Shiv Nadir's involvement in the enterprise, and they

---

xliii Hindu goddess of time, doomsday and death.

delivered his share of the profits at the end of every month. Shiv deposited some of his share in the Oriental Bank in Commercial Square, and loaned out the rest at good rates of interest to Indian businessmen and lightermen. Govinda Rudrappa and Ram Singh were happy with the arrangement, since they were also making good money, and they were careful not to squander it publicly in case they betrayed themselves. They also banked their share of the profits, for they both wished to purchase wives of their own. It was a good arrangement that served all parties well and none of them had any desire to disturb or threaten it.

2

In 1854 the Grand Jury had condemned the ruinous state of St Andrews Church as a disgrace to the community, and by the end of the year the old church had been torn down. The following year the Indian government agreed to bear the cost of building a new church dedicated to the worship of Almighty God according to the rites and discipline of the Church of England, under the name of St Andrew, on condition that the local authorities employed local convict labour in its construction. They also recommended that the church be built upon Government Hill, freeing up the original site for other government buildings, such as the proposed new Court House, but the recommendation was not taken up.

Colonel Ronald Macpherson drew up the plans for the new church. His design was loosely based upon Netley Abbey in Hampshire, and was an exemplar of the English Gothic architecture that was popular in England at the time. Macpherson maintained that he chose the Gothic form because of its simplicity and lack of ornamentation, which was best suited to the limited architectural skills of his convict workforce, although he prized their abilities as builders and carpenters. The Right Reverend Daniel Wilson, Lord Bishop of Calcutta, laid the foundation stone on March 4, before the civil and military authorities and representatives of the community.

* * *

On March 13, Colonel Macpherson announced the completion of

Johnston's Pier, named after Alexander Laurie Johnston, one of the early Scottish merchants, who established the firm of Johnston and Co in 1820. The pier, which was constructed of iron and wood and supported by piles and pillars, was forty feet wide and extended one hundred feet from the godowns of Johnston and Co at the mouth of the Singapore River into the sea. At the pier entrance were four ornamental lamp posts with fluted columns and turn-over leaves, surmounted by four copper lanterns glazed with plate glass. Because a red lamp was hung at the end of the pier to warn ships in the harbour, Johnston's Pier also came to be known as *lampu merah* in Malay and *ang teng* in Hokkien.[xliv]

***

On April 27, Yehonala's prayers were answered. She gave birth to a healthy dragon boy, who they named Zaichun. The Emperor Hsien Feng was ecstatic and named her Empress Hsiao Ch'in. Yehonala had attained her three goals. She had gained access to the Emperor's bed, she had captivated him and been raised to the rank of first concubine – now known as the Cixi concubine – and she had produced a son. Now it was time to consolidate her power and shield herself against her enemies.

The Emperor was now completely besotted with his Orchid and spent most of his time in her company, even when he was engaged in official state business. He read the state documents with her and valued her advice. She supported him when he resisted the constant pressure from British, French, American and Russian diplomats for the expansion of foreign trade. The red-haired barbarians wanted to open up all of China, both coastal and inland, to commerce, and they wanted an exemption from import taxes and legalization of the opium trade. But most odious of all, they were pressing their

---

xliv Both meaning 'red lamp'.

demands for foreign ambassadors to be established in Peking – a direct affront to the purity and sanctity of his Imperial Majesty.

Yehonala quickly became the Emperor's closest confidant and advisor. She urged him to send forth his reserves to quell the Taiping rebellion when news came of the destruction of the Taiping northern expedition at Lianzhen, and she made him steel his will when he was informed of the Taiping victories in the west. Yehonala encouraged him to promote Zeng Guofan to a position of greater military authority in Hunan, and to supply him with hard currency to help raise a larger Hunan army against the Taiping.

When she read Hsien Feng some of Zeng Guofan's eloquent dispatches from the battlefield, the Emperor felt invigorated, as if he himself had experienced the travails and triumphs of battle. The Emperor was confident that he could count upon the honest motives of this gentleman-soldier, and agreed to his elevation and the support of his Court.

Then in June there was more bad news. Hsien Feng learned that the Taiping East King Yang Xiuqing had attacked the Qing troops led by General Xiang Rong, which had massed close to the eastern wall of Nanking. The East King had driven them back in great disarray, in a brutal engagement that had cost the Qing ten thousand men.

3

On Monday, September 22, Thomas Church left the Straits Settlements for the last time, due to ill-health. He had originally served as a writer to Sir Stamford Raffles and then later served as deputy resident in Malacca from 1828 to 1830. He returned to England in 1831, after Lord Bentinck, then governor-general of India, had reduced the administration of the Straits Settlements. Church returned in 1834 as resident of Penang and served as acting governor of the Straits Settlements during the absence of Governor Murchison. Despite being unjustly demoted to assistant resident for Penang, he was appointed resident councillor in Singapore in 1837, a position he had held until his retirement in September.[3]

***

In November, H. C. Caldwell was dismissed as registrar for the court of judicature on charges of embezzlement. Caldwell was formerly senior clerk to the magistrates in Singapore and had commissioned the Irish architect George Drumgold Coleman to build him a house in 1840, which was completed in 1841. The house, which came to be known as Caldwell House, was purchased by Father Jean-Marie Beurel in 1852 to provide accommodation for the Sisters of the Holy Infant Jesus, who set up schools and an orphanage on the site bordering Bras Basah Road and Victoria Street.

For a number of weeks rumours had circulated that Caldwell had misappropriated significant sums of money entrusted to him for investment, misrepresenting the losses as money loaned out as mortgages. Originally little credence was given to these rumours, Caldwell having a long-established reputation for professional integrity, but further investigation revealed the extensive nature of his fraudulent activity, estimated in excess of one hundred thousand dollars. After failing to respond to repeated calls to provide an explanation of how he had disposed of this large sum, Caldwell was dismissed from his position and a criminal charge brought against him.

When the officers came to his house to arrest Caldwell, he was nowhere to be found, despite having been seen in town the previous day. An extensive search was conducted, but he was never found, leaving his creditors to speculate where he had gone with their money.

***

Captain Adil bin Mehmood made his weekly report to Inspector Thomas Dunman. There had not been much to report. A robbery at one of the merchant's godowns, with only minor losses; a missing wife who had turned up again; and a coolie caught passing counterfeit copper coins.

'But that's the third one in as many weeks,' said Dunman. 'Did you get any of them to talk?'

'Not a chance,' said Captain Mehmood. 'They pretend not to understand me, then swear to our Chinese interpreter that they thought the coins were genuine and got them from someone else.'

'Do you have any of these coins, Captain Mehmood?' asked Dunman. 'I'd like to see one.'

Adil produced one of the coins from his pocket and handed it over.

Dunman inspected it carefully. It was well made, and would

easily fool anyone who did not pay close attention.

'Professionally made, I believe,' said Dunman, 'I don't think your average coolie would be up to this.'

'I agree,' Captain Mehmood replied. 'I'm sure they must be runners for one of the societies, most probably the Ghee Hin. They must have some Chinese goldsmith or silversmith working for them. Hard to catch, since there are so many of them.'

'Well, have your men keep a close eye on them, and see if you can't trace some of these peddlers back to their source. No point arresting them, since it's impossible to make a charge stick unless we have some evidence of criminal intent. But let's try and nip this in the bud before it spreads too far, and before they start expanding their business. Whoever made this knew what they were doing.'

'I'll put some men on it right away,' Captain Mehmood replied.

4

While there was gloom at the Imperial court over the recent Taiping defeat of the Qing army besieging Nanking, neither was all well in the court of the Heavenly King. Yang Xiuqing, the East King and the voice of God, who had defeated Xiang Rong's army, criticized Hong Xiuquan for his lack of filial piety and other traditional virtues espoused by classical Chinese scholars such as Confucius and Mencius. Hong Xiuquan found this difficult to accept, since he had officially repudiated the teachings of Confucius and Mencius on the authority of his Heavenly Father and his elder brother Jesus.

Worse was soon to follow. After his great victory was proclaimed, Yang Xiuqing told Hong Xiuquan that he did not think it right and just that Hong Xiuquan, the Heavenly King, had the title of 'Lord of Ten Thousand Years', while he, Yang Xiuqing, the East King, the voice of God and the wind of the Holy Spirit,[xlv] had only the title 'Lord of Nine Thousand Years', and demanded to be elevated to the same status as Hong Xiuquan.

Hong Xiuquan recognized this threat to his authority but also his presently weak position. Yang Xiuqing had many supporters who shared his vocal commitment to traditional Confucian values, and he had dispatched Hong Xiuquan's most trusted generals, such as Shi Dakai, Wei Changhui and Qin Rigang, on distant campaigns. Hong Xiuquan graciously acknowledged the East King's achievements and agreed to his elevation. But he postponed the ceremony until September, on the day of Yang Xiuqing's birthday, which he claimed

---

xlv The Holy Ghost.

to be the most auspicious date for such an occasion. Meanwhile he sent out secret messengers to his trusted generals, warning them of the East King's treachery and ordering them to return to the Heavenly City immediately.

***

In the early hours of the morning, Yang Xiuqing woke with a start and heard the voice of God speaking through his mouth:

'Qin Rigang is helping the demons! Qin Rigang is helping the demons! They will set the city on fire! No one can save it.'

Yang Xiuqing called for his palace guard and sent out servants to summon his loyal troops to his palace. But he was too late. Wei Changhui, the North King, and General Qin Rigang had entered the city in secret at midnight with their battle-hardened veterans and were attacking his palace.

Yang Xiuqing tried to hide in a hollow wall, but he was quickly captured and beheaded, while his family and all his followers within the palace were slaughtered.

***

There were still some six thousand followers of Yang Xiuqing scattered throughout the city, who posed a continued threat. Hong Xiuquan pretended to have Wei Changhui and Qin Rigang arrested, then invited Yang Xiuqing's followers to witness their execution in the courtyard of his palace. On the day of the execution, Yang Xiuqing's followers assembled in the courtyard, leaving their arms at the gate, as was customary on such occasions. Then the gates were slammed shut and powder bags thrown in, which exploded amid the tightly packed crowd. When the explosions died down, the gates were thrown open again and the soldiers of Wei Changhui and Qin Rigang rushed in and massacred the defenceless survivors.

***

When Shi Dakai, the Wing King, finally returned to Nanking in October, he was appalled and disgusted to learn of the betrayal of the East King and the slaughter of his followers by Wei Changhui and Qin Rigang. He openly condemned them and claimed that their actions had weakened the Heavenly Kingdom. When he was warned that Wei Changhui and Qin Rigang were accusing him of treachery and planning his assassination, Shi Dakai slipped out of the city to join his army. When Wei Changhui and Qin Rigang found that Shi Dakai had fled his palace, they murdered his wife and children and all his servants.

***

Despite his youth, Shi Dakai was the most beloved of the Taiping Kings. While encamped to the west of Nanking, many new recruits were attracted to his banners, until his army had swollen in numbers to close to one hundred thousand men. With this enhanced force, he returned to the gates of Nanking, demanding that Hong Xiuquan deliver up the heads of Wei Changhui and Qin Rigang, the murderers of his wife and children.

When Wei Changhui and Qin Rigang got word of his demand, they planned to imprison Hong Xiuqan and set a trap for Shi Dakai, but Hong Xiuquan anticipated their treachery. He sent his elite bodyguard troops to execute Wei Changhui and Qin Rigang, then sent messengers to Shi Dakai to inform him that his request had been granted. In December, the Heavenly King welcomed Shi Dakai back to the Heavenly City, bestowing on him the title of 'Lightning of the Holy Spirit'.

5

The British were pressing the Emperor Hsien Feng to renegotiate the Treaty of Nanking, which had granted them most favoured nation status. Like the French and American traders, they had benefited greatly from the easing of restrictions and opening of the new treaty ports. Amoy, Foochow and Ningpo had been great commercial successes, and the roaring expansion of Shanghai had quickly transformed it into the great metropolis of China. By the mid 1850s there were about two hundred foreign companies operating in the treaty ports, mainly exchanging opium and guns for tea and silks, but also operating shipping, banking and insurance services from their factories in the foreign concessions. Giant firms such as the British Jardine, Matheson and Co and the American Dent and Co still dominated the China trade, but many smaller firms were also profiting hugely from the expanded opportunities, including the office of Simpson & Co in Hong Kong, which specialized in selling mechanical curios to the Chinese gentry. Yet they all knew that this was only the beginning, and they were clamouring for greater access to the Chinese markets.

The British now demanded that more Chinese ports and cities be opened to trade, that import duties be eliminated, and that the opium trade be finally legalized. They also insisted on the establishment of a permanent British ambassador in Peking. Yehonala urged the Emperor to reject all these demands, since if he gave in to them, it would be interpreted as a sign of weakness. They would continue to demand more and more until they and the other foreign powers would divide up the Middle Kingdom, like a traitor subjected to the slow dismemberment of lingchi – death by a thousand cuts. Hsien Feng saw the sense in what she said and instructed his ministers to enter into long and protracted negotiations with the foreign powers, principally Britain, France, the United States and Russia, but to reject all of their demands.

The British traders in Hong Kong, Canton and Shanghai bided their time and went on with their business, waiting for the opportunity to press their government into another war to advance their demands. On October 8, they got their opportunity, when a Qing river patrol boarded and impounded the *Arrow*, a Chinese owned and built lorcha,[xlvi] at the mouth of the Pearl River, and arrested twelve Chinese sailors who they charged with piracy and smuggling. Their action was entirely legal, since although the *Arrow* had originally been registered as a British vessel in Hong Kong, was flying the British ensign and skippered by Thomas Kennedy from Belfast, her registration had expired some twelve days previously, so she no longer enjoyed the privileges and protection afforded British vessels.

Harry Parkes, the British Consul at Canton, demanded the release of the crew, and when this demand was refused, he appealed to Ye Mingchen, the Governor of Guangdong and Guangxi provinces, who released most of the crew but insisted on keeping the vessel, which the crew had admitted was Chinese built and owned. This was not enough for Parkes or the local merchants, who felt that the British flag had been insulted, even though the *Arrow* had had no right to fly it. Parkes managed to persuade Sir John Bowring, the new governor of Hong Kong, to dispatch the gunboat *Coromandel* to capture the Chinese war junk that had seized the *Arrow*. He also asked Sir John to join him in demanding the release of the remaining crewmembers, and that Ye Mingchen issue a public

---

xlvi A type of sailing vessel with a European hull and Chinese junk rig.

apology to the British crown for the actions of the Qing navy.

In response, Bowring sent a naval squadron to blockade the Pearl River and bombard Canton, which levelled Ye Mingchen's palace on the outskirts of the city. Ye Mingchen responded by issuing a bounty for British heads and ordering the destruction of the British factories outside Canton. Browning sent an immediate request to Lord Canning, the Governor-General of India, to provide him with reinforcements to enforce his demands on the city, since otherwise their recent efforts to advance their commercial interests in China would be greatly impeded.

The French, fearing they might be disadvantaged by the British intention to press their interests over the *Arrow* incident, were eager to find an opportunity to advance their own. Some months prior to the *Arrow* incident, they had been presented with such an opportunity and were now eager to exploit it. Father Auguste Chapdelaine, a missionary of the Society of Foreign Missions of Paris, who had gathered many Catholic converts in Guangxi, had been arrested, then suspended naked in an iron cage until he died three weeks later from a combination of starvation, dehydration and exposure. When the French heard about this, they demanded an Imperial apology, reparations, the opening of more treaty ports, the granting of religious freedom to Chinese Christians and the free and protected passage of all Christian missionaries. After much delay and prevarication, all they got was the demotion of the local official who had ordered the arrest and punishment. The French Emperor Napoleon III determined to join the British in teaching the Chinese a lesson.

***

By the end of the year Yehonala had attained a position of great power and had become the Emperor's most trusted adviser. When she heard of the infighting among the Taiping leaders in Nanking, she urged the Emperor to order a new offensive against the God-followers.

'Now is the time to strike the wounded serpent,' she proclaimed, as she urged him on.

But Hsien Feng was in no position to follow her advice and take advantage of the situation. The Emperor was faced with a new Nien rebellion in the north, led by remnants of the White Lotus cult, which had broken out after the Yellow River had burst its banks and the Qing government had failed to provide effective relief to the starving farmers and peasants. This was because the government finances had been severely depleted by the indemnities paid to the European powers after the First Opium War and the heavy cost of the war against the Taiping rebels. The Emperor had been obliged to suspend many royal expenditures and ceremonies, and to melt down gold and bronze bells and statues to provide subsistence wages and supplies for the overstretched Qing troops. He was forced to send the Mongol General Senggelinqin, the victor of Lianzhen, against the fast-moving Nien cavalry, and could not spare sufficient forces or supplies for an all-out attack upon Nanking. Meanwhile there was trouble brewing elsewhere. A rebellion of Chinese Muslims led by Du Wenxiu broke out in the southwestern Yunnan province, after Qing soldiers had massacred Muslim miners protesting work conditions in the capital city of Kunming.

6

Siti had never ceased to be thankful for the good fortune in her life, even though much of it was of her own making. She had once been a slave in Sultan Hussein's palace, but she and her sisters had escaped one night to the home of Francis Bernard, then chief of police in the early years of the settlement. She had been taken into the service of the Malaccan merchant Tan Hong Chuan, first as a servant, then as his concubine and finally as his wife, after Hong Chuan's first wife Swan Neo had committed suicide to escape her heavy gambling debts – Swan Neo had secretly mortgaged Hong Chuan's properties to support her habit. They had almost been ruined, being forced to sell off some of their plantations and much of their land. Yet, they had gradually worked their way back to prosperity. Hong Chuan had taken over the chandlery business from his supervisor, and Siti had managed the pineapple plantations, doubling their profit in her first year. Twenty years later Tan Hong Chan was one of the most prosperous merchants in the Peranakan community, and although Siti still kept an eye on the pineapple plantations, she had eventually given up working and returned to managing her household and her children. They had moved from their shophouse in Chinatown to a more spatial home in Tanglin, where she also tended her extensive garden, her pride and joy after her husband and children. They had been blessed with two sons and a daughter, who was already married with a young daughter of her own.

So, she had good reason to be thankful. Yet today she was anxious, as well as bursting with eager anticipation of the return of their eldest son, Lee Cheng, who had been sent to study law at the University of Edinburgh three years before. He wrote regularly to them, describing his progress and the strange customs of the Scottish people, for whom he had the greatest respect and admiration. He had given her no special reason to be anxious.

However, still vivid in her memory was the story that her husband had once told her about the son of the Chinese merchant Whampoa,[xlvii] who had also been sent to Edinburgh to study at the university. When he returned to Singapore he had spoken with

xlvii Hoo Ah Kay, known in Singapore as Whampoa, after his birthplace in China.

a distinctive Scottish brogue, but much worse, he had cut off his queue and converted to the Presbyterian religion. Whampoa had immediately sent his son off to relatives in China, where he had been taught to learn proper respect for his ancestors and filial piety. She did not know if the story was true – she had met Whampoa's son recently with a fully formed queue and no trace of an accent – but still she was anxious. The accent she could handle, but not the abandonment of the ancestral gods or the cutting of his queue – both would make life very difficult for him in the local business community, not to mention the shameful reflection on his family.

She need not have worried. When Lee Cheng arrived home after her husband met him off the steamer, he was as tall and handsome as she remembered, his jet-black hair pulled into an elegantly formed queue that ran down the length of his back. He straightway went to make an offering to the family gods, and at the banquet in his honour that night he entertained them with stories about his time in Scotland in clear English prose as well as in the local Peranakan patois, which he had never forgotten in his absence.

'But my son,' Hong Chuan said during the banquet, 'how did you ever manage to improve your English living among the Scottish people, whose own English is often difficult to understand.'

'Oh, I managed to save some of the generous allowance you gave me, and took English lessons from the wife of the minister of the university church. She was a charming woman, who had me reciting English poetry and famous speeches.'

'Well, that will no doubt stand you in good stead with the merchants, although I think most of them would have preferred a true Scottish brogue. A useful talent though, especially in your line of work, where you will have to deal with judges and government officials.'

Then, her former fears returning, Siti said: 'I hope she did not try to turn you into a Protestant, Lee Cheng.'

'No mother, she did not,' he replied, 'nor was I ever tempted by the nailed god. However, there was a good deal of talk in the household and among my fellow students about the God-followers of Hong Xiuquan. They wanted to know if he was of the true faith – that is, the Protestant faith – or a blasphemer. They approved of his prohibition against opium, but had heard of his sacrilegious claim to be the brother of Jesus Christ.

'Although I was not tempted, a few of my fellow students from Canton were. Some openly condemned the Qing and were sympathetic to the God-followers, and some went so far as to cut off their queues, although whether it was from hatred of the Manchu or support for the Taiping I never could tell. I tried not to get too involved with them.

'And no, mother, I was not tempted by the Taiping, although I do have some sympathy for their cause. But, to use a word I learned from my Scottish friends, I am too canny to reveal my sympathy to others.'

'Well, we are glad to have you home, and glad you still want to work for Tan and Co,' said Hong Chuan. 'I am sure we can quickly put your education to good use. You can begin by looking at some of our standing contracts and those we are currently pursuing. Once you are rested and refreshed after your journey.'

'Oh, being home is sufficient rest and refreshment for me, especially having enjoyed this superb banquet you have laid on for my homecoming. I'm ready and rarin' to go, as my Scottish friends used to say.'

'I think perhaps it is best to leave behind those sayings of your Scottish friends,' Siti said, laughing. 'Getting back to legal work is all fine and good,' she continued, 'but our first order of business for our finely educated first born is to find him a suitable wife. I have been talking with my Nonya[xlviii] ladies and they have some excellent

---

xlviii Honorific term for a female Peranakan.

suggestions.'

'Oh mother,' Lee Cheng responded, 'not so soon, not so soon! Give me at least a few months of freedom!'

'For what, my son? There is no need, and you have had three years of freedom! No, we will arrange a meeting with the matchmaker as soon as we can, for you must marry before your younger brother, who, unlike you, cannot wait to be married! You are our first born, and you know you must marry first, as is the custom.'

'Very well,' Lee Cheng replied, without much enthusiasm, as both his parents noted. But he was a filial son, and they knew that he would honour them with a good marriage.

* * *

The next day Siti took Lee Cheng on a tour of her garden, her pride and joy. There were brilliant flowering plants and trees, ixora, magnolias and hibiscus, the air was sweet with the perfume of chrysanthemums, dahlias and frangipani, and in one corner, a beautiful small forest of dwarf bamboo. As they walked between the cool green stems and leaves the sunlight filtered through like ripples of water on a lake and he was moved by the natural beauty. As they emerged from the small forest, he complemented his mother on her garden.

'Oh, all I do is give the gardeners directions, and the beauty you see around you is mostly due to Wi Pek Chiat, who came to us a few years ago. She is the daughter of one of the sisters who fled with me from the Sultan's palace so many years ago. She also married a good man, although they were not blessed with any sons, only the one daughter Pek Chiat. Her mother and father were both taken by the cholera epidemic two years ago, and she had no relatives to look after her, so I persuaded your father to take her in. She has a room in the servant quarters – she insisted upon it herself, although she is no servant. She is free to come and go as she pleases, and sees to her own devices. Her work in the garden is entirely voluntary, but I don't think I could have found a better gardener no matter how much I paid.'

'I would like to meet this goddess of the gardens,' Lee Cheng joked, although Siti told him not to joke about goddesses – it was bad luck.

'You will meet her soon enough,' his mother continued. 'She is presently working for Whampoa, who begged us to let her come to his house at Serangoon and help his gardeners create a new display. But she is due to return next week.'

'I look forward to thanking her for making your garden so beautiful,' said Lee Cheng.

7

He met Pek Chiat by accident a week later, the morning after she returned to the house, having slipped into her bedroom in the servants' quarters late in the night. Lee Cheng had risen early and was enjoying the cooler air of the morning by taking a stroll in the garden. As he paused to admire again the dwarf bamboo, she stepped out of the small forest and stood before him. She seemed surprised to see him, more surprised than the mere act of meeting a stranger. For a long moment neither spoke, but their eyes locked in that long moment and he saw that her eyes were green, the green of the dwarf bamboo in the dappled morning light. She was not beautiful, he thought, at least not conventionally so, and was dressed in a dirty garden smock, but she had a presence. He found it hard to take his eyes from hers, but she turned her eyes downward, to arrange some cuttings in the basket she carried.

'You must be Lee Cheng, the young master,' she said softly, before looking up again.

'And you must be Pek Chiat,' he replied. 'May I complement you on your work in my mother's garden. She says you have a rare gift, and I am sure this garden is fit to rival Whampoa's own. Did you enjoy working for him?'

'I did, and he is a very kind man. He has beautiful gardens, as well as topiaries and an aviary, but I much prefer this garden, however small in comparison,' she replied, her voice as soft as the gentle breeze rustling the leaves in the bamboo forest.

'That is no doubt because it is a product of your own vision.

My mother tells me she has given you a free hand in the garden, because of your talent for coaching the beauty from the flowers.'

'Your mother exaggerates my talent, but I am very grateful to your parents for taking me in and allowing me to work in their garden,' she replied.

They stood in silence for the next few moments, until Pek Chiat bowed and said she was glad to have met him, and welcomed him home.

'But I have to return to my work or how else will the garden grow?' she said with a smile.

Lee Cheng replied that he had to leave too, but was glad to have met her and hoped they would get to know each other better, since he had a great interest in gardens.

Lee Cheng was generally a truthful young man, but this was a manifest untruth to anyone who knew him.

* * *

That night at dinner Lee Cheng told his parents he had met Pek Chiat in the garden in the early morning, and wondered why she did not join them for dinner.

'We asked her to, and told her that we look on her as one of the family, but she prefers to eat a simple meal after her work in the garden. She told me she is very grateful to us for taking her in – for saving her from who knows what dreadful fate – but does not wish to presume on our kindness. I have insisted that she does not, but she will not change her mind – she is a little proud I think, and certainly very independent.'

'Stubborn, I would call it,' said Hong Chuan, with a smile. 'But she is her own woman, a bit like our mother in fact."

'I will take that as a complement,' Siti replied. 'But let us not talk of Pek Chiat tonight. I have some good news. The matchmaker has arranged a meeting with the Lims next week, so we will get to meet their daughter Geok Chew. She is an excellent prospect, and we hope she lives up to all our expectations.'

'So soon!?' Lee Cheng exclaimed, but Siti gave him one of her looks that brooked no argument.

'We have already discussed this, Lee Cheng,' she replied, 'and will say no more on it until the marriage is arranged.'

'As you wish, mother,' Lee Cheng conceded with good grace.

* * *

That night he had a dream. He was walking through a giant forest of bamboo as dawn was breaking, the clear light filtering through the green leaves like the waters of a gently flowing stream, the moss beneath his feet like a carpet of green velvet. There was no sound in the forest, although he could feel a faint breeze on his skin, like a tangible whispering floating by him. Sometime after a while he heard a sound, very faint at first, but growing in intensity – someone was calling out his name. He recognized the voice – it was Wi Pek Chiat, who he had met in the garden that morning. He stopped in his tracks, when all a sudden she stood before him, no longer dressed in a garden smock, but in a long flowing gown of green silk – the colour of her eyes. He gazed into her green eyes, and she returned his gaze.

They stood together for what seemed to him an endless time, neither speaking. Then Pek Chiat and the bamboo forest faded into the deepest darkness, and he woke from his dream, amazed by its vividness.

8

Early next morning he went out walking in the garden again. He found Pek Chiat tending some climbing plants. He greeted her and she acknowledged him politely, although he thought he detected a hint of puzzlement in her face. He assumed it was only his imagination, born of his imaginings in the night.

That night he dreamt the same dream, and the night after that, and every night until his mother broke his reverie by informing him that the meeting with the Lims had gone exceptionally well. Geok Chew was an eminently suitable young lady, and the astrologer would compare their horoscopes to confirm their compatibility. He thanked his mother for helping to select his future bride, although he felt no excited anticipation. He did not confide this to his mother, nor mention the strange unease he felt at the prospect.

His unease increased when the night passed in dreamless sleep, and when he saw Pek Chiat in the garden the following morning, he was sure she had been crying. But she said nothing, only offering her normal polite bow and greeting.

***

Lee Cheng was confused, and he continued to be confused as he worked through the legal contacts, upon which he could not fully concentrate. The days passed and were followed by more dreamless nights. His father noticed his distraction and reminded him that he was a student no longer and had to concentrate harder on his work, on which the fortunes of the family depended. Lee Cheng noticed that Pek Chiat was distracted too when he met her in the mornings, and although he was never sure if she had been crying, he was sure she looked sadder than the day he had first met her.

Then one evening when he returned home from work with his father, Siti met them both in the entrance hall.

'I have bad news I'm afraid,' she told them. 'The astrologer was most insistent. Lee Cheng must not marry Geok Chew. Your horoscopes are badly crossed, and nothing but ill fortune would come from the marriage. I am very sorry, Lee Cheng, and I know how disappointed you must be. We will do our best to find you a partner as soon as we can – I am meeting with the matchmaker tomorrow to discuss some new prospects.'

'Thank you, mother – I know how much you and father wished for a successful union,' Lee Cheng replied, trying desperately to hide his complete lack of disappointment and huge relief. He did his level best to act out the part of disappointed suitor, and was so convincing that his father was led to remark:

'I'm sorry I was so hard on you at work today, my son. I know you must have been anxious to learn the astrologer's verdict.'

Which was of course true, although not for the reason his father supposed.

***

That night his dream returned and he met her once again in the giant bamboo forest. Yet this time she did not merely hold his gaze. She stepped closer and took his hands, and touched them to her lips. Although she did not open her mouth, he heard her voice saying, 'I love you, I have always loved you ...' Then she reached out and put her hands around his neck and kissed him full on the lips. As she did so, her green silken robe fell to her feet, revealing her full breasts and slender body, her jet-black hair tumbling down over her shoulders. He was overcome with passion, with his aching need for her as they lay down upon the mossy floor and made love in the silent green forest.

When he woke in the night, he found his semen on the bedclothes. Was it just a wet dream or was he bewitched by some spirit – a fox spirit come to draw away his *qi*, his life force? But he did not think so, for he had never felt more alive! He rose early, as dawn was breaking, and went down into the garden. He found her standing at the entrance to the forest of dwarf bamboo, this time with a hesitant smile on her face. He stepped up close to her and whispered in her ear:

'I dreamt of you last night, Pek Chiat, did you dream of me?'

'I did, my love. I dreamt of you long before I met you.'

'And in your dream,' he began, 'did we …?'

'Oh yes,' she said, 'oh yes, my love …'

She stepped backwards into the bamboo, and he followed her into the green stillness. Without a word they stripped off their clothes and made a bed among the fallen leaves, where they made love until he heard his father calling his mother in the house.

They rose and dressed quickly, then Lee Cheng said:

'I will come again tomorrow, at the same time.'

'No, my love,' Pek Chiat replied, 'it is too dangerous. Come to my bedroom in the night. It is separated from the others and opens onto the garden. I will leave the outer door unlocked.'

'Until then, Pek Chiat. I will come at the midnight hour. But my love will go with you all the long day.'

'And mine with you,' she replied, and kissed him one last time.

***

That day at work he was no longer distracted. He took to his legal papers like the newly minted lawyer that he was, and his father, delighted with his new enthusiasm for work, commented on it.

'I thought you had been having second thoughts about your vocation or were concerned about your future bride, but now I see you living the life that a young man should – engaged with your work and optimistic about your future. Do not concern yourself with this last mishap with the matchmaker – I am sure she will find the one to whom your fortunes are tied.'

'Oh, I am not concerned father,' Lee Cheng replied, although he did not mention the reason. He had found his one true love and knew that the matchmaker would always fail in her quest – at least until he announced that he would marry Pek Chiat.

9

1857

The introduction of the new Municipal and Police Acts, which were not well-understood by the non-Europeans, led to a general strike on January 2. The shops were closed, the markets were deserted and the boatmen and syces[xlix] refused to work. When an attempt was made by the police to force a shopkeeper to open for business, a riot broke out, mainly among the Chinese. The police, who suspected that the secret societies were at work instigating the riot, suffered minor injuries but no fatalities. The Sheriff called a public meeting, and a committee of merchants, which included Whampoa and Tan Kim Ching, was appointed to prevail upon Governor Blundell to issue a public statement, calling upon the populace to return to work and warning of severe punishment for any acts resulting in the injury of police or civilians.

Later that day the governor issued a proclamation in Chinese recognizing that the language of the new acts had been misunderstood and that new translations and explanations would be provided within the month, and that any objections raised would be carefully considered by the government. The governor urged everyone to go back to work, and was greatly relieved when most of the shops opened the following day.

Another riot followed the enforcement of the Municipal and Police Acts in February, this time by Indian Muslims holding a days-long festival at the Al-Abrar mosque on Telok Ayer Street.

xlix Grooms (for horses).

A license had been obtained, on condition that the celebrations terminate at ten in the evening. On the night of February 5, when Inspector Arthur Pennefather, his sergeant and some police peons were making their evening rounds, they found a large gathering of Indians blocking Telok Ayer Street, who had also created a barrier by driving stakes and plantain trees into the road. When the Indians refused the inspector's order to remove them, he sent for reinforcements, and soon after eight policemen arrived, some armed with muskets. When the Indians again refused to remove the obstructions in the road, Inspector Pennefather instructed the peons to remove them. As they attempted to do so, the Indians attacked them with sticks and stones, and two of the peons were knocked to the ground. The inspector and his men retreated to the police station on Telok Ayer Street, pursued by an angry mob who threw stones and bricks, and continued to do so when the police took cover inside the station. The police responded by firing into the crowd, killing one and seriously wounding about a dozen others, one of whom died the next day.

Order was eventually restored when further police reinforcements arrived, although great bitterness was felt within the Indian Muslim community. Inquests were held into the two fatalities and in both cases a verdict of justifiable homicide was rendered. However, the Commissioner of Police, Henry Mackenzie, then Resident Councillor, with the agreement of Governor Blundell, dismissed the inspector, his sergeant and one of the peons from their positions, on the grounds that their behaviour had been rash and unjustifiably provocative. At a public meeting of European residents on February 26, protests against the unfair treatment of the police were forwarded to the governor, who refused to reinstate the policemen who had been dismissed. Inspector Pennefather was committed to trial for manslaughter at the April criminal sessions, but after eight days he was acquitted of the charge.

When Gaston Dutronquoy had arrived in Singapore in 1839, he had established the London Hotel in Commercial Square. Two years later he had moved his hotel to premises on the corner of Coleman Street and the Esplanade,[1] where he set up the first photographic studio, specializing in portraits. When he relocated again two years later to premises on the corner of High Street and the Esplanade, he included space for the newly established Theatre Royal.

In the early 1850s Dutronquoy had set out to prospect for gold in the upper reaches of the Muar River in Pahang on the Malayan peninsula. He never returned, and it was rumoured that he had been murdered during an attack by a native tribe. His estate was dissolved in 1857, and Madame Esperanza took over the London Hotel, which she renamed the Hotel de l'Esperance. She closed down the photographic studio, having no expertise or interest in the business. The following year Edward A. Edgerton, a lawyer from Massachusetts turned photographer, set up his own photographic and stereoscopic studio on Hospital Road.

***

Tan Kim Seng had come to Singapore in the 1820s, where he established Kim Seng and Co. His training in English and Dutch at a private Chinese school in Malacca enabled him to quickly establish himself as one of the leading Peranakan merchants in Singapore, with offices in Malacca and Shanghai. With his successful business enterprises and extensive land holdings, Tan Kim Seng was one of the richest merchants in Singapore, but also a great philanthropist.

---

1 An open field in the centre of Singapore, reserved for public use, lying between Esplanade Road (later St Andrew's Road) and the seafront. Later known as the Padang, from the Malay word for 'field'.

He endowed Chui Eng, a free Chinese school, supported the Tan Tock Seng Hospital, and hosted many balls and dinners for his European friends. He was made a Justice of the Peace in 1850, and early in the year was appointed the first Chinese member of the municipal commissioners. In November he donated $13,000 to the Straits government to help bring a reliable source of good water to the town, having been advised that there was a plentiful supply at Bukit Timah, which could be relayed via pipelines to the principal areas of the town.

While they thanked him for his generosity, for years the Singapore authorities did nothing with the money except to buy some useless earthenware drain pipes.[4]

10

Inspector Dunman was frustrated. It had been almost six months. Despite Captain Mehmood's best efforts, he had not managed to get a trace on the counterfeiters. Mehmood's men had caught a runner every few weeks, but had never been able to trace any of them back to the source of the counterfeit copper coins. And now the problem had suddenly got far worse. A clerk at the German firm of Behn, Meyer & Co had received some counterfeit silver dollars from a Chinese shopkeeper, who swore he had received them from a customer. This was serious – if he did not get to the source of it soon, he would have the whole merchant community and the governor down upon his head. He looked at the counterfeit silver dollar that Captain Mehmood had given him. It was very well made, and would normally only be detected once the thin silver skin had worn away. The Chinese clerk at the office of Behn, Meyer and Co had identified it by its hollow ring, when he had struck it on the stone on his desk that he kept for this purpose. Dunman asked Captain Mehmood to redouble his efforts and to have some of his men watch the shophouses of the Chinese gold and silversmiths. Yet he knew this was a tall order, for there were a great many of them and his police force was already badly overstretched.

Once again, he wished he had been able to recruit some Chinese officers to the force, which would have helped greatly in this sort of investigation, but so far it had proved extraordinarily difficult to do. Some men, who had originally been willing, had been warned off by the societies, and others Dunman had rejected because he was sure they were society men themselves. So he had had to make do with his largely Indian and Malay force. They were good men, but like himself they had little inside knowledge of the societies and knew few Chinese willing to act as informers or witnesses. The Chinese were a tight knit and secretive bunch, and although Dunman generally got on well enough in dealing with their representatives, both the wealthy merchants and the heads of the societies (who were in many instances one and the same), he never really understood them.

11

In response to Sir John Bowring's request for reinforcements to enforce his demands on the Chinese, Lord Palmerston, the prime minister, appointed James Bruce, Lord Elgin, [5] as special Chinese plenipotentiary for Her Majesty the Queen, with an accompanying naval and military force commanded by Rear-Admiral Sir Michael Seymour and Major-General Thomas Ashburnham. Palmerston charged Lord Elgin to negotiate directly with the Imperial court, and to demand that the Manchu Emperor comply with all the provisions of the Treaty of Nanking. He was also to press the Emperor to open up more ports and cities to British trade, to pay reparations for the destruction of the foreign factories outside Canton, and to accept a permanent British Ambassador to Peking. Lord Elgin was only to use force as a last resort, if any of these demands were refused.

***

When the Emperor Hsien Feng and his court heard about the *Arrow* incident and Sir John Bowring's bombardment of Canton, they disagreed about how to react to the barbarian outrage. Prince Kung, the Emperor's brother, urged that they should adopt a conciliatory approach towards the British.

'Imperial majesty, we should talk to them, we should consider their demands, we should spin them out like a thin thread from a silkworm ... until we are ready to deal with them!'

But others would have no conciliation, and Yehonala begged

the Emperor to send the Qing armies to drive the invaders back into the seas from whence they came.

To no avail. Prince Kung, with the support of Su Shun, the Grand Secretary, and Tsai Yuen, the Prince of I, prevailed in the policy of appeasement. Hsien Feng reluctantly agreed that for the moment they would do nothing about the *Arrow* incident and the bombardment of Canton, which the Prince of I assured the Emperor had done little damage to the strong defences of the city.

12

The two lovers quickly fell into a blissful routine. Lee Cheng came to Pek Chiat's bedroom in the night, where they made love until just before dawn, when he returned to his room and prepared for the working day. Although lacking sleep, he worked with his mind as fresh and sharp as if he had slept all the long hours. She worked all day in the garden, where he would still visit her, sometimes with his mother, their interactions always polite and chaste.

And so it continued for three months, and as regular as the new moon his parents went to visit a new family and observe a young daughter, only to be surprised and dismayed to discover that their fortunes were badly crossed. Lee Cheng feigned disappointment and continued interest, but was not surprised, for he knew the reason for it. Only his and Pek Chiat's fortunes were bound together, in this and for all time.

***

Lee Cheng decided that the time had come to tell his parents that the only person he would marry was Pek Chiat. He did not like to deceive them, and had played along with the charade of the matchmaker in the hope that they might come to realize of their own accord that Pek Chiat was the only one he could marry. But now he had to tell them. He knew that when they consulted the astrologer they would find that their fortunes were bound as closely as any could be. Pek Chiat had been more hesitant. Although she loved him and would do anything for him, she was not sure his parents would agree to marriage and she did not like to go against the two people who had saved her from destitution.

Lee Cheng decided he would tell his parents that evening and came home early from work to forewarn Pek Chiat.

But when Lee Cheng went into the garden, he did not find her there. He went to her room, but there was no sign of her there either. He questioned one of the servants, who said he had not seen her since earlier in the day. He sought out his mother, and Siti told him that Pek Chiat had gone to work with Whampoa on a new garden project. He was disappointed, and doubly so, since they would not see each other for a while, and because he so wanted to tell his parents that evening that they wished to be married. He supposed he could tell them, but thought it better if Pek Chiat was with him when he did. He grudgingly accepted that he should wait the week or so while she was at Whampoa's, although his nights would be so very lonely without her.

Yet that night he dreamt of meeting her again in the giant bamboo forest – except that this time his dream had changed. He could see her approaching from a distance in her green silk gown, but as she drew closer, she seemed to slip back into the distance, her arms outstretched as she drifted further and further from his sight and finally disappeared into the darkness beyond. He was puzzled by the dream, but went about his business the next day without thinking too much of it. But that night he had another dream, again in the bamboo forest, but this time she was nowhere to be seen. He seemed to hear a whispering in the distance, but he could not make it out and eventually it faded to nothing, leaving him standing alone in the deep green silence.

The dream troubled him, and continued to trouble him the next day. He left work early, desperate to see her and to find out when she would be returning. But when he visited Whampoa's house and gardens on Serangoon Road, the head gardener informed him that she had not graced them with her presence of late – although he dearly wished she had, for she was like a magician in the garden, coaxing the most difficult plants and flowers to flourish. Lee Cheng thanked him, and agreed with his sentiment, then returned home to confront his parents.

'What has happened to Pek Chiat? he exclaimed, when he found them preparing to go into dinner. 'You told me she went to work with Whampoa, but I have just come from his home and the gardener informed me she never went there. What have you done with her?'

'I am sorry that I lied to you, Lee Cheng,' Siti replied, 'but we were afraid of what you might have done if we had told you at the time. We thought it best to send her away from this house, because we could not help but notice your romantic attachment to her. We tolerated it for a while, but things came to a head when one of the servants told us you had been visiting her in the night. We could not let her jeopardize your marriage prospects, so we sent her away.'

'But you had no right! I was going to tell you we were to be married the day you sent her away! Where have you sent her?

'We had every right,' Siti replied. 'We took her into our home and she betrayed us, so we sent her away so you can make a good match with one of the daughters of an established household, which will bring honour and prosperity to us all.'

'I will not marry anyone else,' Lee Cheng responded, in a voice that had quickly changed from angry exclamation to cold determination. 'Tell me where she has been taken so I may go to her.'

'We cannot tell you that,' Siti replied, 'because we know you would go to her. We have sent her far away, across the sea, to a place where she will be well cared for – we assure you of that – but somewhere you will never find her.'

'But I only want to marry Pek Chiat,' Lee Cheng lamented, tears beginning to roll down his cheeks. 'I love her as I love my own life.'

'You will never marry her,' Siti replied. 'You will marry someone fitting to your station. Let us hear no more talk of this, but let us go into dinner and forget about her.'

13

Lee Cheng did not go into dinner and did not forget about Pek Chiat. He took to his bed that evening and remained in his bed for the next five days, refusing all food and drink. They remonstrated and pleaded with him, but to no avail. He told them he did not want to live if he could not live with the one he loved and remained steadfast in his refusal to take any form of nourishment.

By the end of the five days they began to worry about him. They summoned their Chinese family physician, who told them that their son was fading fast and would soon die if he did not take at least something to drink. He told them they must persuade him to change his mind, that he would surely find happiness with a more suitable young woman. They also summoned Dr Little, the Scottish doctor, for a second opinion. Dr Little confirmed the Chinese doctor's prognosis and stated bluntly that he thought the young man was dying of a broken heart.

'What are you going to do about it?' he asked them.

The Tans had no reply for him, but that night Siti went to Hong Chuan and told him that what they had done was wrong.

'My husband, you married me when I was nothing, so how did we come to judge our son so harshly?'

'But you had proved your worth Siti, first as a servant and then as my concubine.'

'But Wi Pek Chiat has already proved her worth,' Siti replied. 'Look at what she has done in the garden. Remember we told her she was part our family when she came. If she has kept her distance from us, it is only because of her modesty and gratitude to us for taking her in. She came from a good family, and you and I might have considered her a suitable bride if her parents had lived.'

Hong Chuan thought long and hard about what his wife had said, then he replied: 'What you say is true, my wife, and I am ashamed of having treated her as if she were a wayward servant. She is the only person who can save our son. Let us send for her immediately and hope it is not too late.'

Fortunately, Siti had not in fact sent Pek Chiat far across the sea, but had placed her with some relatives in Johor. She gave orders to their most trusted male servant to take their fastest carriage to the river and hire the fastest boat that would take him to Johor, and bear their message that he was to return with Pek Chiat as soon as possible.

'Tell her that she is forgiven and that we have consented to the marriage. Tell her that Lee Cheng's life is in great danger and she must come immediately.'

Then Hong Chuan and Siti sat beside their son's bed and prayed that his life might be saved by Pek Chiat's return. For when they told him that they had consented to the marriage and that he must take something to drink, he did not respond.

14

The servant arrived with Wi Pek Chiat the following morning. She looked pale and wan, her eyes red with the tears she had shed when she heard that Lee Cheng's life was in danger. She ran straight to his bedside and wrapped her arms around his body, kissing his face and lips and begging him to take some food and water, so that he might live and they could be together again.

'Oh my love, come back to me – I love you with all my heart, and know that we are meant to be together.'

When Hong Chuan and Siti saw the depth of Pek Chiat's feeling for their son, they knew that they were meant to be together. They begged Pek Chiat to tell him that they had agreed to the marriage, that he must live for her and take some food and water. Pek Chiat took a cup of water from the bedside table and held it to his lips.

'Please drink, Lee Cheng,' she whispered to him, 'please drink and live for me.'

She raised his head and brought the cup to his lips, but he did not drink and the water ran down the sides of his mouth.

'Please drink, Lee Cheng,' she cried again, but to no effect. She gently laid his head back on the pillow, and her arm across his chest. As she did so, his eyes opened briefly, and she thought she saw a flash of recognition. But then the light went out of his eyes and she felt his breast go still as he died in her arms.

***

For a few moments Pek Chiat lay weeping over Lee Cheng's lifeless body, but then she raised herself up and dried her tears.

'Lee Cheng died because he loved me, and I will die for him because I love him.'

Then she went to leave the death-room, intending to lie down upon her own bed and deny herself food and drink until death took her also.

Siti saw at once what was on her mind and cried out to her: 'Pek Chiat, you cannot do this. You must live!'

'Why must I live?' Pek Chiat retorted angrily. 'I have nothing to live for!'

'You must live,' Siti replied quietly, 'you must live for the child in your womb.'

For Siti's sharp eyes had intuited what no one else had noticed, that Wi Pek Chiat was pregnant.

'Are you sure?' Hong Chuan said to his wife, as Wi Pek Chiat stood unbelieving in the middle of the room.

'Oh, I am as sure of this as I am of anything,' Siti replied. 'If Pek Chiat reflects on the passage of time she will know I speak true.'

Pek Chiat suddenly realized that her moon had passed and she had not bled. She had not noticed in her grief at having been taken from Lee Cheng, but now she had no doubt that what Siti said was true.

'But what am I to do?' she said, and burst into tears again. She was devastated and at a loss where to turn.

Siti went to Pek Chiat and wrapped her arms around her. 'You must stay with us, Pek Chiat, and we will help you raise the child.'

Pek Chiat looked at her doubtfully.

'We have wronged you deeply, Pek Chiat,' Siri said. 'Please forgive us and let us make it up to you by providing for you and your child.'

Pek Chiat was torn. She wanted to die as Lee Cheng had died, in the hope that she could be with him again, if only in the world of wandering souls. Yet she knew she could not let the child – the child that she and Lee Cheng had created together – die with her. So she agreed to stay with the Tans in their care, at least until the child was born. She did not know what she would do after that and did not want to think about it.

In the morning the undertaker came to prepare Lee Cheng's body for burial.

15

The following evening Siti had a dream in which Lee Cheng visited her from the spirit world. He apologized for the grief he had caused his parents and told her of his anguish at having left Pek Chiat alone in the world to care for their child.

'How I wish I could have lived and married her as I had planned!' he lamented.

He told his mother that he forgave her, that he knew she had only done what she thought was best for him and was glad that she and his father were reconciled with Pek Chiat. But he told her how lonely it was without her, so very lonely in the world of shadows. He had tried to reach Pek Chiat in her dreams, but without success and it broke his heart to have no contact with her.

When Siti awoke, her face was wet with tears and her heart ached for her son. Then she realized what she must do. She woke her husband and told him of her dream.

'It is very sad, my dear,' Hong Chuan replied, 'but there is nothing more we can do but pray for him.'

'There is something more we can do – we can arrange for Pek Chiat to marry our son.'

'But, but, you mean, you cannot mean, a … ghost marriage? I have heard this can be done, but have also heard it can bring ill luck to the family. Do we really want to risk such a thing …?'

'They only bring ill luck if the couple's fortunes are crossed, but we will consult with the astrologer to make sure it is not so,' she replied with confidence, since she knew in her heart that their fortunes would not be crossed, all tragedy aside.

Hong Chuan agreed to have the astrologer consult their horoscopes, but still seemed reluctant to give his consent to the ghost marriage.

'If you are concerned about ill luck husband, there is another thing you ought to consider. It is our custom that a younger son cannot marry before his elder brother, or else ill luck will fall upon the family. I do not think that Lee Cheng's ghost would try to take revenge, but there is no need for us to take that risk.'

At this Hong Chuan gave his consent to the marriage, and the astrologer was consulted to compare their horoscopes, which turned out to be perfectly matched.

'I have never seen a pair so well matched' the man exclaimed, 'they were clearly made for each other!'

Pek Chiat was also reluctant at first, but consented when she was told of their perfectly matched horoscopes. For then she knew that this was how it was meant to be.

***

Pek Chiat did not cry during Hong Chuan's funeral. She missed him desperately, but was comforted by the thought that, as his wife, she would one day join him in his grave. At her request, her poem to her deceased lover was inscribed on his headstone.

So far apart, our pledge remains
Bound by our love we will survive
Until like a pair of birds we fly in heaven

The ghost marriage was conducted in the Tan's home the day after Hong Chuan's funeral, by the same Taoist priest who had conducted the funeral, with a white cockerel substituted for

Hong Chuan during the ceremonies. As was the custom in a female marriage to a male ghost, Pek Chiat was obliged to take a vow of celibacy for the rest of her life, to which she consented without objection. When the ceremonies were completed, she felt a strange sense of relief and contentment as she was accepted into the Tan family as Hong Chuan's wife.

＊＊

On the night of the wedding, the ghost of Hong Chuan came to her in her dreams, in the same giant bamboo forest where they had first pledged themselves to each other. They made love on the forest floor and their hearts burst with happiness.

When Siti met Pek Chiat the next morning, tending to the dwarf bamboo in the garden, she could see the happiness on her face and knew that her son had come to his new wife in her dreams.

And on every night thereafter Hong Chuan visited his wife in her dreams. Six months later they both wept with joy when she told him of the birth of their son, Tan Chin Liew, and of his parents' delight in their grandson.

16

On May 10, at the garrison town of Meerut in Northern India, Sepoy units of the Bengal Army rebelled against the British authorities, murdering their British officers and their wives and children. The mutineers marched on Delhi, where they proclaimed the aged Bahadur Shah II, the King of Delhi and grandson of the last Mughal[li] emperor, as Emperor of all India. The 'devil's wind' had begun to howl – the Indian Mutiny, as the British knew it, or the Great Rebellion, as the Indians knew it, had begun.

The British were slow to respond, and by June many more Sepoys had joined the rebellion. On June 27, after three weeks of attacks on the garrison at Cawnpore, its commander General Sir Henry Wheeler surrendered to Nana Sahib, the dispossessed heir to the former Maratha Empire, in return for an offer of safe passage down the river Ganges to Allahabad. But as the soldiers and civilians boarded the transports at Satichaura Ghat, the rebels fired upon them and burned their transports, butchering them in the boats and the river, including women and children. The hundred odd survivors were imprisoned in a single-storey house at the edge of the city known as the Bibighar,[lii] where they were placed in the care of a prostitute called Hussaini Khanum.

---

li Mongol empire that controlled swathes of South Asia from the sixteenth to the nineteenth century.
lii 'The House of the Ladies'. A small six-room house that had been built for the Indian mistress of a now dead British officer.

***

When news of the mutiny reached Britain at the end of June, Lord Palmerston informed the Queen and parliament that Lord Canning, the Governor-General of India, had the situation under control, and that ten thousand British troops were scheduled to depart for India in July, along with four thousand more that had been requested by the East India Company. Yet by this time the mutineers already controlled large swathes of northern and central India, and many native princes in outlying states were waiting to see which way the wind would blow, before throwing in their lot with either the mutineers or the British. Unless Lord Canning and the beleaguered British forces in India could halt the spread of the mutiny – by persuading potentially rebellious units that it was in their best interests to remain loyal to the Crown, or disbanding or disarming them – then they could find themselves overwhelmed by the vastly superior Sepoy forces, which comprised over two hundred thousand men as opposed to the forty-five thousand regular British soldiers scattered in regimental units across the Indian continent.

17

James Bruce, the 8th Earl of Elgin and special Chinese plenipotentiary for Her Majesty the Queen, arrived in Singapore on the P & O[liii] steamer *Singapore* on Wednesday, June 3, en route to China, where his first intended action was to join with the French to press their demands for reparations over the destruction of the foreign factories in Canton. Lord Elgin planned to stop over in Singapore for a few days, while he awaited the arrival of his troop transports and HMS *Shannon*, which was to convey him to China.

Governor Blundell welcomed Lord Elgin at the dockside, where he received a military salute before the large crowd that had gathered to greet him. After the official ceremonies were over, Lord Elgin joined the governor in his carriage, which was to convey him to Government House.

'You have a very large Chinese population, sir,' Lord Elgin said to the governor, 'I did not realize it was quite so large. Do you expect any trouble on account of the coming China war?'

'None at all, your lordship,' Blundell replied. 'They're all here for the money, from the poorest coolie to the richest merchant, and in any case, they have no great love for the Manchu. But we have a much more serious problem, your lordship. The opium steamer *Fiery Cross* came in last night, with news that units of the Indian army have mutinied. They have destroyed the garrison at Meerut and captured Delhi, and the revolt is spreading across the country, among both Hindus and Muslims – the mutineers have declared a

---

liii Peninsular and Oriental Steam Navigation Company.

new Mughal Emperor. I have an urgent letter from Lord Canning that I was asked to deliver to you as soon as you arrived.'

Blundell took the letter from his inside pocket and handed it to Lord Elgin, whose face turned dark as he received it. James Bruce was a small man but stoutly built, with a bald head and thick side-whiskers. He wore a black frockcoat and hat, but had the bearing of a military man.

'We heard a rumour about the Meerut incident as we passed Point de Galle in Ceylon,' [liv] Lord Elgin said, 'but I was led to believe that it had been contained. Now it seems we're heading off to fight the dragon while the wolf is baying at our own back door.'

Lord Elgin tore open the letter from Canning, and read it on the way to Government House. George Canning was an old friend of James Bruce from his days in Oxford, where both men had taken Firsts in Classics at Christ Church. Canning explained briefly what had happened at Meerut and Delhi, and informed him that the rebellion was now spreading rapidly across northern and central India. Palmerston had promised to send reinforcements from Britain, but for some unimaginable reason they were being dispatched on sailing ships rather than steamers, and would not reach him until October – by which time the rebellion might well have spread to the whole subcontinent. Canning pleaded with his old friend to divert some of his troop ships for the China war back to Calcutta, so that he could nip the rebellion in the bud. Canning said that they would only be needed for a few months, and that he would send them back the moment their assistance was no longer necessary.

'Bad news?' Governor Blundell inquired gently after Lord Elgin had finished reading the letter, and had begun to fold it up again. 'Is it as bad as we've heard?'

'Probably worse,' Lord Elgin replied, 'and it leaves me with a

---

liv Present-day Sri Lanka.

hard choice, which I must quickly make. But I'm not going to think on it until I'm washed and fed, and listen to what advice you and your officers can give me on the matter.'

At that moment the carriage drew up at Government House, and Lord Elgin commented favourably upon its situation.

'That's why Raffles had it built up here,' replied the governor. 'It catches the sea breezes, and is far enough away from the noise of the town. It's also close to the tombs of the ancient kings of Singapore.'

'Is this the original building then?' said Lord Elgin, with some surprise. 'I would have thought you'd have had something grander by now, although I don't mind it for myself. I'm happy enough in a tent, so long I can get the breeze.'

'Well, it was renovated and expanded by George Coleman, the Irish architect responsible for most of the Palladian style buildings you will see around the town. But it was based upon Raffles' own plan, and still has the original verandah running round the house.'

'Now you've got Indian convicts here, I understand. Do you expect any trouble from them? Are they all safely under lock and key?'

'We have a rather unusual system here, your lordship, which has evolved over the years, and makes us the envy of many other penal settlements. Apart from a few incorrigibles – what we call class five convicts, who we do keep locked up in chains – the rest are pretty much on an honour system. Most of them live out on the plantations or in camps by the public building sites and road works, and come in for roll call once a month. The smarter ones have jobs as clerks with the merchant houses or as moneylenders. We have hardly any trouble with repeat offenders and absconders, although we did have to pick up a fellow named Kurruck Sing last week, who was trying to stir up the Sikhs. Not much chance of that, in my opinion, but we have confined him to one of the gunboats in the harbour as a precaution.'

'A most interesting system, Governor Blundell,' Lord Elgin replied. 'You must let me make a tour of inspection before I leave – I might learn something useful for future reference. But if one of your class five men gets out and cuts my throat in the night, I'll hold you personally responsible! And I'll expect to be buried with full military honours beside those ancient kings of Singapore!' he laughed.

* * *

That night Lord Elgin had dinner at Government House with Governor Blundell and his senior naval and army officers. Most of the talk was about the mutiny. Lord Elgin asked their opinion on the question of whether there was sufficient danger from the mutiny to warrant diverting at least some of his China troop transports back to Calcutta.

'I'm sure our boys there can handle a bunch of Hindus,' opined Colonel Barker, one of the commanders of the transports. 'I'd leave our lads back there to get the glory, so we can move on swiftly to sort out the Chinamen, before they get the idea we're reluctant to punish them for the *Arrow*.'

Perhaps,' replied Lord Elgin, who was himself concerned about the Chinese getting that idea, 'but we already underestimated them at Meerut and Delhi. There were two thousand British troops with artillery facing two thousand Sepoys without artillery, and they could not prevent them moving on Delhi. And I doubt very much if the revolt will be restricted to Hindus – we'll probably have the Muslim leader Ahmadullah Shah calling for a jihad against us.'

'But the Sunnis[lv] won't join in,' Lieutenant McNair, the new superintendent of convicts, interjected. 'They won't want to see a return to Shia[lvi] rule. And the Sikhs and the Pathans will remain loyal, as will the Gurkhas.'

'I'm sure you're right about the Sikhs, and the Pathans and Gurkhas,' Elgin replied, 'but we can't count on the Sunnis just because they won't join the Shia. They may very well start their own war.'

And so it went on late into the night. After all the guests had left, Lord Elgin sat alone on a wicker chair on the verandah, gazing out over the dark ocean. The stars shone sharply against a black velvet sky, and a soft sea breeze hushed through the traveller palms and long lalang grass. Lord Elgin downed the last of his brandy and walked to the end of one of the verandahs, and then to the other end, back and forth, back and forth, taking long and thoughtful steps. All night he paced, back and forth along the verandah, as he pondered his problem. If he turned the troop ships back now, and the mutiny was over before they reached the fighting, he would be a laughing stock, and his chances of becoming Governor-General of India after Lord Canning retired would be ruined. He might also jeopardize the China campaign by doing so. The Russians and Americans were holding back from providing military support for his expedition, and were content to preserve their stake in the outcome by sending advisors and observers rather than soldiers and sailors. The French might very well do the same, if they thought that they would end up doing the bulk of the fighting. In such a circumstance the Manchu might very well renege on the Treaty

---

lv Muslims who believe that following the death of the prophet Muhammad the leaders of their nation should be elected from among those capable of holding the position.

lvi Muslims who believe that following the death of the prophet Muhammad leaders of the Muslim nation should be selected from among the prophet's own family, or directly appointed by God.

of Nanking and drive the foreigners from the treaty ports. But if he sent the troop ships on to China, and the mutiny turned into a bloodbath for the British, the British public would never forgive him, and he would never forgive himself. He paced back and forth, back and forth along the verandah, alone with his thoughts and his destiny.

***

At seven o'clock, as the golden dawn was breaking over the lush greenness of Government Hill, Lord Elgin stopped pacing. He went inside, washed and shaved and changed. Then he summoned his adjutant, gave him his orders and went out again to the verandah, where the servants were setting tables for breakfast. Governor Blundell joined him ten minutes later and found him sipping a cup of coffee and munching on a slice of toast.

'You're up sharp, and looking bright-eyed and bushy-tailed, if I may say so, Your Lordship,' said Governor Blundell. 'Have you had any further thoughts about the Indian question?'

Lord Elgin laughed. 'Very nice of you not to mention the bags under my eyes, which I noticed while I was shaving this morning,' replied Lord Elgin. 'I was up all night, man, pacing this verandah. But I've made my decision. I've given orders for six regiments of the China expeditionary force to be sent back to Calcutta to relieve Delhi. So that's done! Now I think I'd like to hold a levee here at Government House while we're waiting for the *Shannon* to arrive.'

The levee was held on Saturday, June 6, and was attended by many European and Asian residents. Mr Peterson, deputy chairman of the Singapore Chamber of Commerce, presented an address to Lord Elgin, praising him for his leadership in the forthcoming China campaign. Lord Elgin replied that he was gratified to witness the remarkable progress of the mercantile community in Singapore, which was prospering under a system of just laws, in contrast to the desperate situation in Canton, where bad faith and mismanagement had devastated trade and spread ruin and desolation.

The following day, Lord Elgin began to wonder how his little speech had gone down with the Chinese members of his audience, and mentioned his concern to Major McDermid, Governor Blundell's secretary.

'Oh, you need not worry about the towkays,[lvii] my lord, they make more than their compatriots in China – and more than most of the Europeans here, who mainly work for European merchant houses. The Chinese keep their businesses in their own families, and many are millionaires, although it is hard to know how much some of them are worth. In any case,' he added with a grin, 'many of them would not have understood a word you said, for few of them speak English.'

But three days later, Lord Elgin was pleased to receive an address from a delegation of Chinese merchants, expressing their gratitude for the just treatment and benefits they had received from the British government. Tan Beng Swee, the eldest son of Tan Kim Seng, read the address in perfect English, which he had learned as a boy at the Anglo-Chinese College in Malacca. Lord Elgin thanked them in his own reply in English, and they nodded dutifully, although they were clearly taking their cue from Tang Beng Swee. When his reply was translated into Malay, they nodded again of their own accord and this time with understanding, Malay being the lingua franca of the merchant community.

The following day, June 10, Lord Elgin visited the sugar plantation of Jose d'Almeida & Sons, and that evening HMS *Shannon* arrived in port to take him on to China. The following evening the merchants held a supper and ball in his honour at the Masonic lodge. There Lord Elgin met Ronnie Simpson, who

lvii Chinese businessmen.

happened to mention that his son spoke fluent Chinese, which both men agreed was a great advantage in dealing with the Chinese.'

'I have great need of men like him,' said Lord Elgin, 'for we need to understand the Chinese if we are to make the best of our dealings with them. Where is your son, Mr Simpson?'

When Ronnie told him that Duncan was in Hong Kong, Lord Elgin said he would contact him when he got there the following week, and ask him if he might oblige Her Majesty by serving as an interpreter if needed.

'I'm sure he would be willing to serve his Queen,' Ronnie replied, though he found it intensely annoying that most of Her Majesty's servants, including Lord Elgin, the Earl of Kincardine and hereditary chief of the Scottish clan Bruce, insisted on calling her the Queen of England.

18

Lord Elgin arrived in Hong Kong on July 2 aboard HMS *Shannon*, the most powerful steam frigate of Her Majesty's Navy. She was one of the fastest vessels under sail, but she could also travel at full steam for five days against the wind with a single load of coal. She was heavily armed with sixty 68-pounder guns, plus some smaller cannon and swivel guns, and she carried a large contingent of Royal Marines. Lord Elgin looked out from the foredeck as the *Shannon* steamed through the smaller lorchas and junks in the harbour, and thought that she looked like a Triton among the minnows.

He was not the only one to have such thoughts. Dr James Legge and Hong Rengan were strolling together on Caine Road, each with an arm around the other's neck. As had been common of late, they had been discussing the question of whether the Taiping or the Manchu represented the best hope of securing China's future. As they watched the *Shannon* steam into the harbour and heard her sixty-gun salute rolling and thundering over the hillsides, Legge stopped and turned to face his friend. Then he swept his hand out toward the *Shannon* and declared with a sigh:

'I don't know about the future, my friend, but there is the knell of the past of China. It can do nothing against these leviathans.'

***

Lord Elgin conferred with the governor and local officials and traders about the situation in Canton. Sir John Bowring assured him there was no immediate danger from the Manchu, since they had enough on their hands dealing with the Taiping and Nien rebellions.

'They'll huff and puff and harm any man who goes near Canton, but otherwise they are contained for the moment,' he advised them.

Most of the traders pressed Lord Elgin for an immediate attack on Canton, but he informed them that his instructions were to negotiate first, and that he would not negotiate until his full naval and military force was reassembled, after the business in India was resolved. Lord Canning had assured him that he would have the troops returned by the end of the year, when he would be in a better position to press all of their demands, including his own.

Lord Elgin spent two weeks in Hong Kong, and one evening he invited Duncan Simpson for dinner on board the *Shannon*. They talked about the mutiny and the China situation, and Lord Elgin asked him if he would be willing to serve as an interpreter in Her Majesty's service should the need arise.

'We're desperately short of good men who can understand Chinese,' Lord Elgin told him, 'and you come highly recommended by the merchants of Singapore and Hong Kong.' Lord Elgin had made it his business to have his adjutant check up on Duncan's linguistic skills.

Duncan said he would be delighted to do so. If truth be told, he said to Lord Elgin, he was looking for new challenges, and his manager Ian Fraser was more than capable of running Simpson and Co in his absence. He did not say why, and Lord Elgin did not ask. He had no need, since Duncan's father had already informed him of the family tragedy.

Nearly six years had passed since his wife Marie and unborn child had died after being gored by a runaway buffalo, but for Duncan it was as if it had happened yesterday. He had been glad to get away from Singapore and from the memories of their house, which his father had sold for him. But he had found no escape or comfort in Hong Kong. Her ghost still sat with him at night as he looked out over the harbour, her hair still raven black against her white skin, her pale lips drawn into a thin sad smile. Probably the only thing that had saved him from despair was his friendship with James Legge, to whom he had been introduced by Joseph Jardine of Jardine Matheson and Co, and his fascinating friend, Hong Rengan, the cousin of the Taiping King, who claimed to be the younger brother of Jesus. Like Duncan, James Legge had lost his wife and youngest child, and although they did not talk about it, there was an uncommon bond between them founded on each man's knowledge of the other's private pain.

Lord Elgin asked Sir John Bowring to keep a sharp eye on the situation, but not to engage in any precipitous action, or be manoeuvred into doing so by the French or the Americans. Lord Elgin returned to Singapore on July 28 on the *Shannon*, with the steamships HMS *Pearl* and *Sanspareil* from Hong Kong. They departed for Calcutta two days later, where upon arrival the sailors and marines of the *Shannon*, *Pearl* and *Sanspareil* were formed into the Naval Brigade. Lord Elgin returned to Hong Kong on the P & O steamer *Ava* in late September, having received assurances from Lord Canning that he would get his troops back by December.

'You'd better keep your promise, Charlie,' Lord Elgin said to him as he departed, 'otherwise Palmerston will have my guts for garters!'

19

Brigadier-General Henry Havelock, having heard the news of the massacre at Satichaura Ghat, ordered the relief force hastily assembled at Allahabad to march on Cawnpore on July 7. They arrived on the morning of July 16, too late to save the prisoners in the Bibighar. Fearing that the survivors might bear testimony against him for the massacre, Nan Sahib had ordered their execution before he fled the city. Throughout the afternoon of July 15, five of the rebels, armed with swords and axes, cut and hacked and sliced their way through the crowd of screaming prisoners, until only three women and three children remained alive amid the charnel house of blood, brains, bonnets and children's shoes. Those surviving six were then thrown into an adjoining well with the rest of the mutilated corpses, where they suffocated to death. When Havelock's men arrived, they found the rooms of the Bibighar ankle-deep in blood.

A few days later, Havelock ordered his force to march on Lucknow, where three thousand British soldiers and civilians were besieged by a rebel force of over twenty thousand. He left Cawnpore under the charge of Colonel James Neill of 1st Madras European Fusiliers, forbidding the Colonel to issue any orders in his absence. But Colonel Neill was a no-nonsense Scot who was determined to teach the mutineers a lesson they would never forget. He ordered his men to hang any rebel they caught who could not immediately prove their innocence. Neill reserved his cruellest justice for the high-caste Brahmins whom he identified as the leaders of the mutineers. He ordered that these men be forced by the lash to clean up a portion of the blood of their victims – each man was forced to lick clean a patch of congealed black blood that his soldiers had watered down. After their sickly task was completed, they were made to eat pork and beef, before they were hung and then buried in shallow graves at the side of the road.

Colonel Neill knew that these Brahmin men would believe that by touching the blood of the sahib-logue[lviii] they would damn their souls to perdition.

'Let them think so,' he said.

The 'devil's wind' continued to howl.

***

Shi Dakai, the Wing King and Lightning of the Holy Spirit, remained in the Heavenly City for six months. He became increasing dissatisfied and frustrated, since Hong Xiuquan had delegated authority to his elder brothers, Hong Renfa and Hong Renda, who had been with him since the beginning of the rebellion, but who had no administrative talent or military expertise. Dismayed by the situation, Shi Dakai departed with his loyal troops in the summer, giving as his reason his need to return to the campaign in the West, and avowing his enduring loyalty to Hong Xiuquan.

He was never to see his Heavenly King again.

---

lviii Indian term for Europeans. 'Sahib' meaning superior; 'logue' meaning people.

20

Inspector Dunman now had the merchants and the government down upon his head. The counterfeit dollars seemed to be turning up everywhere – in the banks as well as the merchant offices and Chinese shophouses. He must get to the bottom of it, and fast, but he already had enough on his plate. The news of the Indian Mutiny was on everyone's lips, and the European population, who were still nervous after the Chinese riots of '51 and '54, were anxious that the rebellion might spread to the Indians in Singapore. Dunman did not think that likely, since most of the Indians in Singapore were southern Chuliahs from the Coromandel Coast, who would have little sympathy with the northern rebels; the convicts had too much to lose, and had little hope of support within the region. Unless of course the Indian government in their infinite wisdom decided to transport some of the captured mutineers – those that they had not summarily shot or hung – to Singapore. Then there would be trouble for sure. Although he got on well with his Indian officers and peons – he spoke their language and knew their families – he did not know how far he could count upon them if there was an uprising by the Indian community in support of transported mutineers, or as the mutineers called themselves, devotees of the Great Rebellion.

***

Brigadier-General Archdale Wilson took over command of the small British force encamped on the ridge overlooking Delhi in July, which at that time could do little more than observe and report on the comings and goings in the city. In August he was grateful to receive a modest body of reinforcements, including Brigadier-General John Nicholson and his 'movable column' of British and irregular troops, and ordered his expanded force to advance on Delhi in early September. Despite initial setbacks and some difficult street fighting, including a desperate attack on the Burn Bastion,[lix] which claimed heavy British casualties and the life of Brigadier-General Nicholson, the British forces finally captured Delhi on September 20, including the Red Fort and Palace. The Sikhs lit fires in the sacred Jama Masjid mosque, and the victorious army killed every adult male they came across.

The following day, Captain William Hodson and his small force of irregular cavalry set off in search of the Mughal Emperor Bahadur Shah. They captured him and his favourite wife Zeenet Mahal at the splendid marble tomb of his ancestor, the Emperor Humayun, on the outskirts of the city. Hodson had earned his reputation as an exceptional leader of irregular cavalry, when he had commanded a corps of guides in the Punjab in the early 1850s. He had raised his present force, later known as Hodson's Horse, at the outbreak of the mutiny.

The next day Captain Hodson heard that the Emperor's two sons, Mirza Mughal and Mirza Khizr Sultan, and his grandson Mirza Abu Bakr, had also sought refuge at Humayun's tomb. All three men had been commanders in the rebel army, and all three were implicated in the massacre of the European civilians that had taken place when the mutineers had captured the city. Hodson rode out again with his irregulars to capture them.

There were around five thousand armed rebels encamped at Humayun's tomb, but Hodson treated them with cold distain as he ordered the sons and grandson of Bahadur Shah to surrender to

---

lix Fortification close to the Kabul Gate.

him. The three men gave themselves up without a fight or protest, but as Hodson led them back to Delhi in a bullock cart, he found that his horsemen were increasingly harried by an angry mob that had quickly formed behind them.

Hodson halted the column and ringed it with troopers, their Enfield[lx] rifles trained upon the mob. He climbed aboard the bullock cart that held the three prisoners, and ordered them to climb down from the cart, strip themselves naked, and climb back in. Then Hodson borrowed a rifle from one of his troopers and without another word shot each man dead.

The Muslim and Sikh troopers of Hodson's company cheered. The Muslims applauded the act of retribution, and the Sikhs recalled the ancient prophecy that they would one day capture the city of Delhi and destroy the royal Mughal princes. The execution took place before one of the main gates to the city, which later came to be known as the Khooni Darwaza, the Gate of Blood. The mob, stunned by Hodson's action, dispersed in sullen silence.

For days the British troops plundered the city, while dozens of presumed mutineers were hung in the public squares. The victorious troops cheered and hurrahed as the mutineers danced on the gallows or were blown from the muzzles of British cannon – an old Mughal punishment that the British had appropriated to deny the mutineers any hope of salvation.

---

lx Rifled musket introduced to the British army in 1853.

21

Shiv Nadir decided to call it a day. His counterfeiting operation had been extremely successful, beyond even his wildest dreams, and he had already accumulated more money than most merchants managed to accumulate during their lifetimes, save for the Chinese millionaires like Tan Kim Seng and Whampoa. Yet he knew that since he had extended his operation to the coining of silver dollars, the police would be under great pressure to identify the persons involved and bring them to justice, and Shiv Nadir did not want to be brought to justice again – to be returned in leg irons to the fifth class after he had achieved so much. So he made up his mind to discontinue the operation, and planned to visit Govinda Rudrappa and Ram Singh in their little factory above the tailor's shop the following week.

***

On September 15, in the News Room in Commercial Square, Joaquim d'Almeida, W. H. Read, Robert Carr Woods, Ronnie Simpson and Abraham Logan put forward a motion in support of the European merchants of Calcutta, who had sent a petition to the British parliament demanding the abolition of the East India Company, which they claimed was the source of the present troubles, and requesting that India be brought under direct control of the crown. The motion was passed by a comfortable majority, and forwarded to the British parliament, along with an additional motion – also passed by a comfortable majority – requesting that the control of the Straits Settlements themselves be transferred from India to the crown. Only the Singapore merchants supported these motions; the Malacca and Penang merchants did not, since they believed it bordered on treachery to the Company by adding to its troubles during the time of its greatest danger.

22

Captain Mehmood had been lucky. He had received a tip that a respectable shopkeeper had tried to pass counterfeit silver dollars at the Oriental Bank, and the clerk had had the quick wit to send a boy to fetch him. The clerk had refused the coins, so the shopkeeper still had them on him when he and two peons followed the man back to his shop, which they kept under surveillance. They were rewarded for their efforts when a heavy-set Chinese man, who was obviously neither a merchant nor a shopkeeper, entered the shop and the two men started arguing over the coins. Mehmood knew enough of the language to know that the shopkeeper wanted to return the coins before he got into any more trouble, while the society man was insisting that he exchange them as soon as possible, since a new batch had already been prepared. Captain Mehmood and his peons entered the shop and arrested both men.

* * *

Captain Mehmood knew he could not hold them in jail for long, because they would deny knowledge of the origin of the counterfeit coins. The shopkeeper would claim they had been passed to him, and that he was as much a victim as any other who had received the forged silver dollars. The shopkeeper did claim this, but when Captain Mehmood went to interrogate the society man, he found him surprisingly friendly and accommodating, and willing to converse with him in Malay, the lingua franca of the settlement. He said that he would be willing to compensate Captain Mehmood for the trouble they had caused him, if he would only forget the whole matter of the counterfeit coins.

Captain Mehmood declined the offer, which was a blatant bribe, but one that he knew it was pointless to try to prosecute, since the society man would of course deny he had ever made such an offer. He wondered how many of his men had been offered similar bribes, and how many had succumbed. He turned away in disgust, but as he did so the society man called out after him.

'Be careful how you go, Captain Adil bin Mehmood, in case you meet with an accident. The streets are very dangerous places at night.'

Mehmood's blood rose at the clear threat, but instead of returning to rebuke the society man, he marched off to his office. He wanted to check something in the almanac, for he had had a sudden and desperate idea.

'Ha!' he said to himself when he confirmed what he thought he had remembered. Tomorrow was the night of the hungry ghosts.

23

'So you have decided to release me, Captain Mehmood,' the society man said with a knowing grin, as Adil unlocked his cell door.

'No, Cheng Hui Ming, if that is indeed your name, we are going on a little excursion,' Adil replied, 'at the end of which you will tell where to find the coiners who made the silver dollars that your runners pass off to honest traders.'

The society man, whose real name was Chew Choo Keng, snorted in laughter, but his laughter faded when two burly Indian peons grabbed him by the arms and forced him into a pair of hand irons, then pushed him out of the cell and along the corridor. They thrust him into a waiting gharry, and sat with him while Captain Mehmood drove it westward along River Valley Road. Eventually he drew up outside the Chinese graveyard, as the fading sun was sinking beneath the darkening blue sky. The two peons pulled Chew Choo Keng out of the gharry and brought him before Captain Mehmood.

'Take the gharry back to the station and send someone back to fetch us in the early morning,' Adil instructed his men, and then with his right hand pushed Chew forward in the direction of the graveyard. In his left hand he carried a coiled length of rope.

'What are you doing? Where are you taking me?' Chew demanded to know, but already there was fear in his voice as Adil kept pushing him further into the graveyard, as the twilight turned to deepening dusk and the darkness of night. As they passed between the graves, three large black dogs, with lean bodies and sharp pointed snouts, followed them at a distance, leaping from stone to stone like shadows in the night. Whenever Chew stopped and tried to protest, the dogs came on, closer each time, so he did not need much persuasion from Captain Mehmood to carry on. The moon rose high in the sky, bathing the dark stones in a ghostly silver light. Eventually they came to a tall Angsana tree, where Adil brought Chew to a stop, and turned him around. The black dogs came forward again and stopped close by them, watching from the silvered shadows.

'What – you plan to hang me!' Chew exclaimed, when he saw the length of rope in Adil's hand.

'No, no, that would be too easy, my friend. And I expect you to talk to me first,' Adil replied. He then tied the society man to the tree, so he faced back the way they had come through the graveyard, and saw the three black dogs baring their fangs in the shadows.

When he was sure that Chew was tied fast, Adil addressed the society man in a steely voice:

'I am a policeman,' he said, 'and I find it rewarding to bring criminals like yourself to justice. But I have a relation who is a bomoh, a shaman of sorts, and although I have never had the inclination to follow his path, I seem to have inherited some of his special gifts.'

'What kinds of gifts are those?' Chew replied in a trembling voice, his eyes flitting from the dogs to Adil and back again.

'Oh, I see the dead, and more vividly than most. Old men, young women, children and babies, Christians, Mohammedans, Buddhists and Taoists – all sorts really. I saw them as we walked through the graveyard. They are pale creatures and keep to the shadows, but no doubt they will reveal themselves in due course. And especially tonight, for as I am sure you know, tonight is the fifteenth night of the seventh lunar month, the night of the hungry ghosts, when the souls are released from hell to wander the earth. You do not see them now, but I assure you you will, and you can tell me all about it when I return.'

'You ... you ... you're not going to leave me here!' Chew exclaimed. 'No, I beg of you, don't leave me,' Chew pleaded, his face now white with fear.

'Oh yes I am,' Adil replied with a cold smile, 'and when I return you will tell me all I need to know.' Then he stepped backwards into the shadows and disappeared into the darkness.

24

Chew Choo Keng, a tiger general of the Ghee Hin, who had killed men, women and children on the orders of the society, stood trembling in the darkness, his eyes straining out of their sockets in terror of what he might see. The three black dogs stood like stone statues on the gravestones before him, so close now that he could see their bloodshot eyes fixed upon him, ready to rip him apart with their long fangs if he managed to escape; although there was little chance of that, for the policeman knew how to tie a man fast.

For a while he saw nothing but the dogs and the dark shadows of the gravestones stretching into the blackness of the night beyond. But then all a sudden he saw them, walking slowly through the graveyard, their ghostly shapes taking form in the silver moonlight. Some of them he recognized, men that he had killed, who to his great relief passed him by. Then he saw a young girl, a black-haired beauty with pale white skin and dark red lips twisted into a thin smile. He remembered her. He had poisoned her and her family. She came up to him and took him gently by the hand. Her hand felt cold and damp to the touch, and he was overcome with fear and revulsion. Then to his amazement the shackles and ropes fell from him, and she led him away through the graveyard. He did not want to go with her, but found he had no will of his own, and was carried along by the dead girl as if she were trailing a paper kite. He followed, mesmerized in fear and wonder, as she guided him between the silent ghosts, until the ground opened up and she led him down a long winding stone staircase into Hell. He knew it was

Hell because he recognized Yan Luo, the King of Hell, who records the names of the souls as they enter into Hell, from pictures he had seen in the Jade Record.

Then she led him into the first court of Hell, ruled by Lord Qin Guang, who presides in judgment over those who enter the netherworld. Those who had been good in their past lives or whose good deeds outweighed their evil deeds were sent across the golden and silver bridges to the western paradise. Those whose good deeds had equalled their evil deeds were sent directly to the tenth court of Hell, presided over by Lord Zhuan Lun, to await his judgment. Those whose evil deeds outweighed their good deeds were taken to the terrace of the mirror of retributions, where they viewed the evil deeds they had committed while among the living, and the torments of the ten chambers of Hell that awaited them, so that they came to understand the meaning of the proverb:

Ten thousand taels of yellow gold cannot be brought away:
But every crime will tell its tale upon the judgment day.

Chew looked into the great silver mirror and saw his own sins, the murders he had committed, including the poisoning of his ghostly female companion and her family, the robberies, the opium smuggling and kidnapping, the gambling and fornication with prostitutes. His spectral companion smiled a deathly smile and seemed to grip his hand tighter as she led him down into the second court of Hell, presided over by Lord Chu Jiang, with its sixteen dungeons, a place of dark clouds of dust, excrement and urine, of gnawing hunger, burning thirst and boiling cauldrons, where men like he who had abducted young children, owned slave girls and had stolen from their fellow men received their punishments.

Then she led him into the third court of Hell, presided over by Lord Song Di, with its sixteen dungeons, a place of insects and reptiles, of flaying and eye gouging, where ribs were pierced, faces scratched with copper and iron, and hearts and livers squeezed by pincers, where men like he who had defrauded their clansmen, incited others to crime and fabricated evidence received their punishments.

In the fourth court, the realm of Lord Wu Guan, Chew saw the sixteen dungeons where faces were swollen with steam, where shoulders were pricked with tridents and skin ripped off the body, eyes put out, holes bored into flesh, mouths pricked and bodies buried in stones, where men such as he, who had evaded taxes, used debased coinage and who had broken their promises, receive their punishments.

When they reached the fifth court, his spirit companion took him before Lord Yan Luo. There sinners were brought before the terrace for viewing the world, and saw their friends sneering over their coffin as it was lowered into the ground, their relatives fighting over their property, their wives and concubines prostituting themselves with worthless men and their children sold as slaves. When they had seen their memory debased on earth, those who like Chew had made a pretence of piety, who had used their strength against the weak and the sick, who had fought and gambled and raped women, were dragged off by Ox Head and Horse Face, the two soldiers of Hell, who appear with their tridents and chains to collect the dying from their deathbeds, to face the punishments of the sixteen dungeons of the fifth court. There the sinners were buried under wooden pillars, pierced with copper stakes, had their bodies ripped open and their hearts torn out, while their entrails were fed to dogs.

Chew Choo Keng had seen enough. His heart was filled with horror and he did not want to continue, but his spectral companion led him down into the sixth court of Hell, the court of Lord Bian Cheng, the black noisy Hell, where sinners who had suffered in the first five courts were punished in its sixteen awful dungeons, where they were placed up to their necks in filth, where their heads were struck until they were shelled like eggs, where they were sawn in two at the waist, and from head to toe, where their skin was stripped and coiled from their bodies, and where their screams echoed throughout all the courts of Hell.

Then down into the seventh court of Hell, the domain of Lord Tai Shan, who punished those who like Chew had drank excessively, spent lavishly, used drugs such as opium, and sold children. In his sixteen dungeons, sinners had their heads crushed by pillars, their skulls smashed open, their bodies disembowelled and where the devils boiled them in kettles of oil.

In the eighth court of Hell, the court of Lord Du Shi, those sinners who had not quickly repented of their sins, but had continued in their evil ways, were punished in his sixteen dungeons, in which their penises and vaginas were cut off, where they were buried in dung, and where they were hacked and gashed and pricked with steel prongs until they begged for oblivion from the merciless devils.

Then they entered the ninth court of Hell, where Lord Ping Deng commanded the devils to punish those who, like Chew, had broken the laws of the land, who had corrupted children and drowned baby girls, in the sixteen dungeons where their brains were crushed and tongues and teeth sucked out, squeezed in wooden presses until their heads and bodies burst, stung by swarms of bees, bitten by legions of scorpions and fed upon by thousands of ants, who sucked the juices from their bodies, and bitten by purple and scarlet venomous snakes.

Yet these punishments were not enough for those who, like Chew, had read the warnings of the Jade Record and had not heeded them. They were chained to a hollow copper pillar filed with fire, until their hands and feet and hearts and liver were burned off and then plunged into the great Avici Hell, where the devils thrust knives into their chests and lungs, where they were made to eat their own hearts after the devils had torn them from their breasts, and where they suffered unrelenting torment in the uttermost depths of hell.

Until they entered the tenth court of Hell, into which the poisoned daughter now led him. There His Infernal Majesty Lord Zhuan Lun turned the wheel of life in his dark kingdom and determined whether the tortured souls were to drink the Goddess Meng's wine of forgetfulness and be thrown into the red river of Hell, to be reborn as men, women, beasts, birds or crawling things, or be sent back across the bridge of sorrows to the courts of Hell for further punishment. Then his spectral guide let go of his hand and went forward and spoke to Lord Zhuan Lun. Chew did not hear what she said, but he quickly learned of Zhuan Lun's judgment upon him, as His Infernal Majesty pointed towards the dread bridge of sorrows, and the devils came forward with their tridents to drive him across it. Chew Choo Keng turned around in terror, and fled backwards into the black cloud of darkness that swirled around him like thick treacle, which slowed his movements until he came to a dead stop, and stifled all light, sound, smell, taste and feeling. It seemed to Chew as if he was floating in an empty black space, his body smashed to fragments and hurled into the void, his consciousness slipping away into nothing.

25

Captain Mehmood came forward out of the shadows. He had watched the society man writhing in unspoken terror for the past hour, opening and closing his mouth like a fish but without speaking or crying out, and he noticed with satisfaction the yellow and brown stains that ran down the man's dirty cotton pants. It was time he had a talk with this once brave tiger general, before he lost him forever.

***

Chew woke with a start, his arms straining against the ropes, his mouth dry as dust and his eyes staring wide at the black dogs with their bloodshot eyes, who still stood before him. Had it all been a dream, a frightening dream, a dream with a message, but nothing more than a dream? Then he saw the figure moving out of the shadows, and in his frenzy, he thought it was Horse Head come to take him down to Hell, but then he realized that it was only Captain Mehmood, and sighed with relief when he heard the Malay policeman's voice.

'Now, society man, you will tell me who the coiners are, and where they are to be found. And you will tell me who your accomplices are, and your real name so I can keep my records straight.'

'Please, captain, release me and take me from this dreadful place of shadows,' Chew pleaded, 'and I will tell you everything you wish to know.'

'I am not a patient man,' Adil replied. 'I have waited too long in this graveyard already, and I am weary of watching the dead go about their dreary search for food and drink and clothing and Hell money, to placate the devils who torment them. You will tell me now or I will quit this place and leave you to the ghosts and the dogs.'

So saying, he turned away and started walking back into the darkness. As he did so, Chew looked beyond where he had stood, and saw the pale skinned poisoned daughter walking towards him, with her arms outstretched and her cold eyes and lips beckoning to him.

He screamed and cried out to Captain Mehmood, 'Captain, captain! Save me, I will tell you everything, everything you want to know, here and now.'

Captain Mehmood returned to his side quick as a flash – as fast as one of the demons of Hell – and wrote down everything that Chew told him in his police notebook, including his real name. Then he untied the trembling society man and led him without protest back through the cemetery to the gate, where a police sergeant and peon had returned with the gharry. Before he climbed in beside his jabbering prisoner, Captain Mehmood turned around and clapped his hands loudly, and the black dogs that had followed them turned around and bounded back over the gravestones into the grey-silvered distance.

***

That night, while Captain Mehmood and Chew Choo Keng passed their time in the Chinese graveyard, the merchants hosted a dinner at the Hotel de l'Esperance to honour Commodore Keppel. John Harvey, who chaired the ceremonies, announced that Commodore Keppel had been promoted to Rear Admiral and was about to receive a knighthood from the Queen. After the dinner was over, the *Corps Dramatique* gave a moving performance of 'A Trick to Catch the Old One', after which a collection was raised for funds to build a new theatre. The following week the *Free Press* suggested that it would be wise to combine the subscriptions raised for the Town Hall and the new theatre, which could easily be accommodated within it, and both committees eventually approved this suggestion.

26

'I think we've got them, sir,' said Captain Mehmood, as he entered Inspector Dunman's office and informed him about the society man's early morning confession in the graveyard.

'An unusual tactic,' Dunman replied, grinning. 'I never knew your relation was a bomoh and that you could see the dead.'

'Thankfully, I have no such relation and cannot see the dead – it was just a ruse to fire his imagination,' Captain Mehmood explained.

'Well, it certainly did that! But my heart does not bleed for the villain – he would have cut your throat without a thought if he had the chance. But Indians, you say – by Jove that takes the biscuit! No wonder we could not track them down, we were on a wild goose chase after Chinese gold and silversmiths. Never thought of them working together.'

'No, neither did I,' Mehmood confessed, 'but you live and learn.'

'We surely do,' said Dunman, 'but where is your man now, and when do you plan your raid?'

'We'll raid the place tonight, just around dusk. I don't want the news to get out that we've broken the case, although I don't think our society man will be putting anything out any time soon. He's back in his cell still gibbering about the demons of Hell. I'll have my squads arrest the society men involved at the same time.'

'Let's hope his anticipation is just as bad as the real thing,' Dunman replied. 'But well done, Captain Mehmood. And good luck tonight – I trust you'll take your best men.'

'I will do, sir. You're welcome to come along if you like, although it might get a bit lively.'

'I might just take you up on that,' Dunman replied, 'if I can get my meeting with the governor over in time. Should be interesting.'

'Adil,' Dunman called out to the captain as he was leaving the office, 'but what about the black dogs and their bloodshot eyes?'

'Nothing to do with me,' Adil replied, 'they came on their own!'

***

Captain Mehmood had the tailor's shop in Chulia Kampong quietly surrounded, as the sun was setting over the river, sending shimmering slivers of gold over the dark regions of its upper reaches. The sun had already set and dusk was beginning to fall when Captain Mehmood led Inspector Dunman and his armed peons up the stairs to break down the door to the counterfeiters' hideout. But when they reached the door, they found it was already open, and when they rushed in they gagged at what they saw. The room was thick with flies, which were gorging on the mouths and eyes of the two dead Indian men, whose throats had been cut from ear to ear. The room had been ransacked, and although plenty evidence remained of their coining operation – special turning and stamping machines and bags of solder – everything of value had been taken.

'What do you think, captain,' said Dunman, scratching his head in puzzlement. 'A society reckoning?'

'I'm not sure,' Adil replied. 'But why would they cook their golden goose? Unless they thought our man had betrayed them, and that the Indians would bear witness against them. But it looks like these men were murdered before they and the society men were betrayed, so I don't think that's very likely. And they could have simply shifted their operation. So why now?'

But Dunman had no answer.

27

Lieutenant John Frederick Adolphus McNair, who had taken over as superintendent of convicts when Colonel Macpherson was transferred to Malacca as resident councillor, stepped out into the assembly yard as the jail bell rang at five in the morning, summoning the men of all classes to the monthly muster. As the lower classes were brought out of their cells for assembly, and the higher classes came in from the town and country, the duffadars[lxi] and petty officers dressed the ranks and took the roll call. After they had completed their duty, the senior duffadar reported that two men of the third class were in the prison hospital and too sick to attend, and that two men of the first class, Govinda Rudrappa and Ram Singh, were missing. Lieutenant McNair asked the senior duffadar if this was unusual, and the man reported that it was. He said that never in his time had these men failed to turn up for muster, except for one time when they had been given an official waiver. Lieutenant McNair ordered him to investigate the matter after the muster was completed.

It had been four months since news of the mutiny had reached Singapore. The townspeople had been on edge, to the point where some had panicked one afternoon and had fled to the ships in the harbour. But Lieutenant McNair had not had any trouble so far. He thought that he had already won the trust of many of the men of the three higher classes. McNair was fluent in Hindustani, and spent a considerable amount of time talking to his charges, learning about

---

lxi Non-commissioned officers.

their conditions and trying to help them manage their new lives as best he could.

Nonetheless, there had been some whispered reports about a possible riot, so he was anticipating trouble today as he walked down the lines inspecting the men, now and then stopping to exchange a few words with those he knew. As he approached the middle of a line, one of the convicts, Aakash Malik, rushed forward and dug out from a small area of loose earth the knife he had buried the night before. With a wild cry he leapt at Lieutenant McNair and stabbed him in the heart. As Lieutenant McNair staggered backwards, three other convicts came forward to retrieve the axes and knives they had buried, and attack the senior duffadar and his men.

But to Aakash Malik's amazement, Lieutenant McNair did not collapse from his mortal wound. Instead, McNair calmly drew his revolver and placed it against his assailant's head, and cocked the hammer. Aakash was amazed by the lack of blood on the lieutenant's breast, until he realized why. He had struck his enemy with only the handle of his knife – someone had removed the blade in the early morning. He turned to look to his comrades, and saw to his dismay that they too only carried the handles of their axes and knives, and had been quickly disarmed by a party of guards who had rushed forward and restrained them. Aakash felt his own arms being gripped from behind, before he was dragged away to join his fellow conspirators.

Lieutenant McNair conferred a disciplinary tribunal on the spot, found the men guilty of conspiracy to riot and passed sentence upon them. Each man was to receive two dozen lashes with the cat o' nine tails on their bare buttocks, and demotion to the fifth class. The medical orderly was summoned and declared the men fit for punishment. Then they were strapped to the wooden rails in the yard, and one of the guards, a huge Sikh with hairy arms like tree trunks, administered the bloody strokes before the hushed crowd. After the punishment was over, the convicts were dismissed and Lieutenant McNair returned to his office

***

Later that day, Lieutenant McNair summoned Shiv Nadir to his office, ostensibly to ask his advice on a matter pertaining to industrial training. While he waited for Shiv Nadir, his senior duffadar returned to report that the two missing men, Govinda Rudrappa and Ram Singh, had been murdered the previous day; very likely by Chinese secret society men, according to Superintendent Dunman, who had been at the scene of the crime.

When Shiv Nadir arrived at Lieutenant McNair's office, McNair waited until they were alone, then quietly thanked Shiv Nadir for warning him about Aakash Malik's plan to assassinate him and his officers. Shiv Nadir replied that he was glad to have been of service, as it was in everyone's interest to maintain peaceful relations. Why, he himself had almost regained respectability in the outside community.

'I agree,' McNair replied, 'and thank you once again. Although you know that strictly speaking a ticket of leave remains conditional on future good behaviour, as far as I am concerned – and I will pass this on to Superintendent Dunman and the governor – from this day on you are a free man, Shiv Nadir.'

'Thank you, Lieutenant McNair,' Shiv Nadir replied. 'You honour me, sir, and I hope I may remain your humble servant.'

He prepared to leave, but Lieutenant McNair stopped him with a question.

'These fellows who were missing – Govinda Rudrappa and Ram Singh. I just learned they were murdered the other day. Did you know them, Shiv? Do you have any idea who might have murdered them?'

Shiv replied that he had known the men briefly. They had been very bad men, he said, but he thought they had reformed. They had both worked their way up to the first class, and he himself had played some small part in rehabilitating them.

28

It had been very easy, and they had suspected nothing. When he visited Govinda Rudrappa and Ram Singh they had at first been surprised to see him, but welcomed him when he told them he had come to celebrate their successful five years working together, give or take a few months. He had brought with him a bottle of fine French brandy and some sweetmeats that his wife had prepared – although as he confessed to them, they were too sweet for his own sour palate. They had suspected nothing. These once ruthless brigands had even been touched by the generosity of the man to whom they owed their own advancement. They were effusive in their thanks when he left, but they were as dead as doornails when he returned an hour later; the poison had been quick acting. He cut their throats and ransacked the room to make it look like a murder and robbery, before taking their remaining share of the profits. Then he left them and returned to his wife and family, free at last – for they were the only two men who had known of his part in the counterfeiting operation. Now Shiv Nadir would be able to give up his job at John Purvis and Co and begin his new career as a businessman. For the moment he would continue as a moneylender, but he had other plans. He wanted to become a cattle importer, and for that he needed the services of an experienced cattleman. He knew just the right man.

***

Inspector Dunman was sure that Govinda Rudrappa and Ram Singh had been brutally murdered because of their role in the coining operation, and that their throats had been cut by whoever had surprised them and robbed their premises. For that reason he did not bother to ask the coroner to investigate for traces of poisoning, and Dr Curties recorded their deaths as 'death by throat cutting by person or persons unknown'. The case was never solved, although Inspector Dunman was gratified that thanks to Captain Mehmood's detective work, the source of the counterfeit coins had been identified and extinguished, and that no new counterfeit dollars entered circulation following the murder – at least until some years later, when the Ghee Hin set up their own operation. No case was brought against the society men because Chew Choo Keng could not bear witness against them. He had been committed to the Insane Hospital on Bras Basah Road, where he raved with the other lunatics, until he was brutally murdered by tiger soldiers from the Ghee Hin for having broken his oath of silence.

For his services Captain Mehmood was commended by the governor and promoted to the rank of Sergeant Major.

29

Arjun Nath had come down to Singapore with the Indian merchant and brickmaker Naraina Pillai in 1819. Naraina was very pleased with work that Arjun did for him, and had made him manager of his brick kilns. But Arjun did not want to remain a brickmaker all his life. He had had two dreams in life – one to raise dairy cattle on the island and the other to find himself a wife. Eventually he saved up enough money to buy some land and a small dairy herd, and met his wife – and a tiger – one evening by the well at Telok Ayer. Fortunately the tiger ran off, but some years later his cattlemen had been attacked by a tiger, during the time of the terrible cattle blight. He had helped Mr Carrol kill the tiger, and then worked for a while as the tiger-hunter's rifle bearer to tide him over until the blight that had decimated his herd had passed. He had managed to rebuild his herd and was now the prosperous cattle farmer he always wanted to be. He had a thriving business in the town and his wife had given him two sons and a daughter. He regularly made offerings at the Sri Veeramakaliamman Temple on Serangoon Road to thank the goddess Kali for his good fortune.

He was quite content with his present position and was not at all sure if he wanted to go into business with Shiv Nadir or if he wished his daughter to marry Shiv Nadir's son Jangveer. Shiv Nadir was a moneylender, with secure capital, and had made him a very good offer to join him in his new business importing cattle – and later he said, if business was good, sheep also – in return for his expert knowledge of the animals. Shiv had also suggested that his son Jangveer should marry Arjun's daughter Abhati, to demonstrate his commitment to their partnership, and to establish a personal as well as a professional bond between the two men. The offer was good, and Jangveer Nadir seemed an upright as well as a handsome young man. Yet Arjun hesitated. Shiv Nadir was a former convict and murderer, and Arjun did not think he wanted to go into business with a former convict and murderer.

Yet after he thought it over, Arjun realized it would be a hypocrisy on his part to make too much of this, since after all he himself had married a former convict and murderess, who had slain her husband for his crime as Shiv Nadir had slain his wife and brother for theirs. And Shiv Nadir has earned the respect of the merchant community, both European and Asian, while working his ticket of passage and there was no doubt at all that the man was an astute businessman. So he gave the matter serious thought, but still he was not sure.

Then he made his decision. He told Shiv Nadir that he would agree to become a partner in his cattle import business and would consent to the marriage between Jangveer and his youngest daughter Abhati if Jangveer would commit himself to the prosperity of their business enterprise and his marriage by carrying the kavadi[lxii] in the festival of Thaipusam, which fell in the month of Thai,[lxiii] in three months' time. Shiv Nadir agreed to this, and told his son to prepare for the holy pilgrimage.

* * *

Brigadier-General Henry Havelock and Major-General Sir James

---

lxii A physical burden carried during the festival of Thaipusam.
lxiii In the Tamil calendar. Mid-January to mid-February in the Gregorian calendar.

Outram fought their way through to Lucknow in September, but they suffered many casualties, including the death of Brigadier-General Neill, and could only reinforce but not relieve the garrison. They were finally relieved in November by Sir Colin Campbell, who had taken overall command of the British forces. Campbell moved on to split and disperse the rebel forces of Tatya Tope and Nana Sahib, removing the remaining threat to Cawnpore. Although there were still rebel forces roaming north and central India, everyone from Lord Canning down to the lowest private knew that the Indian Mutiny was now doomed.

Lord Canning felt he was now in position to keep his promise to Lord Elgin, and ordered the borrowed regiments back to the China War. On December 27 the troop transports arrived in Hong Kong, where Baron Gros, the French envoy, had joined Lord Elgin. Gros also had a French military and naval force at his disposal, which had recently been dispatched by the Emperor Napoleon III. Lord Elgin and Baron Gros presented their ultimatum to Ye Mingchen, the Governor of Guangdong and Guangxi provinces, whose palace Sir Henry Browning's bombardment had destroyed the previous year, and who had consequently offered a bounty for British heads.

Lord Elgin demanded compliance with the Treaty of Nanking, a permanent ambassador in Peking and reparations for property loss following the *Arrow* incident; Baron Gros demanded that Father Chapdelaine's murderers be brought to justice, freedom for Frenchmen to operate anywhere in Canton and reparations for the destruction of their factories. Governor Ye Mingchen tried to stall them, so Elgin and Gros ordered a joint attack on Canton, an action that had been strongly recommended to Lord Elgin by Harry Parkes, the British consul in Canton, and by Lord Clarendon, the British foreign secretary. After a heavy naval bombardment, British and French troops launched a successful assault on the city, which they then began to plunder – or, to use the Hindi word that the British regiments had learned during their sojourn in India – to 'loot' the homes and shops and godowns and palaces and temples of the long-suffering Cantonese. Lord Elgin deplored their behaviour, but personally authorized the removal of half a million pounds worth of gold and silver bullion in unofficial reparations. Governor Ye Mingchen was captured and deported to Calcutta, where he committed suicide by starving himself to death. Lord Elgin and Baron Gros then sent envoys directly to Emperor Hsien Feng in Peking, reiterating their demands for reparations, access to additional ports and inland cities by merchants and missionaries, compliance with the Treaty of Nanking and a permanent British ambassador in Peking.

30

1858

1858

Jangveer Nadir joined the other devotees in the late evening at the Sri Srinivasa Perumal Temple on Serangoon Road. He had maintained a strictly vegetarian diet, had fasted for forty-eight days and avoided all carnal relations with women and all thoughts of them. He had slept each night on a cotton cloth spread out on the floor of the temple and had not shaven, so that now his black hair hung over his shoulders and his black beard hung down over his chest. He had spent his days in meditation and prayer and had often entered into a trance state as he made his vow to Murugan to carry the kavadi on the festival of Thaipusam, and asked the God in return to favour his father's new business and his own marriage.

***

The festival of Thaipusam was held each year to celebrate the pilgrimage of the demon Idumban, who became a devotee of the god Murugan. Shiva, who was Murugan's father, had one day presented two hills in the Himalayas, named Sivagiri and Saktigiri, to a sage named Agastya, and entrusted him with the task of moving the hills to the southern region of India. Agastya had in turn assigned the task to the demon Idumban, who, accompanied by two sacred serpents, carried the two hills suspended on either end of a giant kavadi, a long wooden pole that he carried on his broad shoulders. When he approached the south he became weary and laid his burden down at a place called Palani, where he intended to rest for a day. But when he rose to resume his journey, he found that the hills had become fixed to the ground, and although he used every ounce of his great strength, he could not move them.

As he stood wondering how he could break the hills loose from the ground, he met a young boy carrying a wooden stick, who claimed to own the hills. Idumban replied that he had been entrusted to carry the hills to the south, and would defend them against anyone – man or boy – who tried to stop him. The boy fought with Idumban and eventually overcame him after a pitched battle. After the demon was subdued, the boy revealed that he was the great god Murugan in disguise. Idumban became a devotee of Murugan, and thereafter served as guardian at the gate of the temples devoted to Murugan.

During the festival of Thaipusam, devotees symbolically re-enact the journey of Idumban by carrying their own kavadi, or burden. This is a multi-layered wire frame, decorated with peacock feathers and attached to their naked flesh by hooks pierced into their chests and backs, to which are attached pots of purified milk. The devotees carry their burdens in a pilgrimage from the Sri Srinivasa Perumal Temple on Serangoon Road, dedicated to the god Vishnu, to the Sri Thendayuthapani Temple, dedicated to Murugan, on Tank Road. The temple was also known as the Chettiar's temple, because it had been built with donations from the Chettiar banking community.

***

Like the other devotees, Jangveer Nadir laid out his elaborate wire-caged kavadi at a place he had chosen in the temple grounds and began his preparations: he attached to its frame the many chains with their small hooks upon which he would support his load. The crowds began to increase at midnight and he knew they would grow larger and larger as the morning approached.

Earlier in the day, devotees had borne the processional image of Murugan out of the Sri Thendayuthapani Temple and placed it upon a ceremonial chariot, which was to be carried on a visit to his brother Ganesh, the elephant god, at the Sri Layan Sithi Vinayagar Temple on Keong Saik Road, about a mile and a half distant. When the deity was positioned, crowds of worshippers raised trays containing offerings of fruit, coconuts, incense, garlands and cloth, which were presented to the deity. The priests passed down sanctified water and viputi[lxiv] to the worshippers, who followed the procession down South Bridge Road until it stopped before the Sri Mariamman Temple – the oldest Indian temple in Singapore, built in 1827 by Naraina Pillai, who had once employed Arjun Nath, the cattleman, as a brickmaker. There the image of Murugan greeted the goddess Mariamman, an incarnation of Parvati, the mother of Murugan. A temple priest broke a coconut on the pavement in front of Murugan's chariot, and more trays of offerings were presented to him, the priests distributing sanctified water and viputi as before. The arati flames[lxv] were waved before Murugan on the chariot and Mariamman in the temple, before the procession carried on to its final destination, the Sri Layan Sithi Vinayager Temple on Keong Saik Road. There two coconuts were broken on the pavement, and after aratis were performed before Murugan on the chariot and Ganesh in the shrine, the processional image of Murugan was installed in the temple, where it remained for the rest of the day. At about seven in the evening, the image of Murugan was returned to the chariot, and the procession wound its way through Market Street, where many of the homes and businesses of the Chettiars were located, until it arrived back around nine at the Sri Thendayuthapani temple, where a great crowd of worshippers had gathered, and where more

---

lxiv Sacred cow dung ash.
lxv Holy flames.

offerings were raised up to Murugan. Then the image was carried in a clockwise circle around the temple, and affixed upon a swing before the main altar, where the worshippers continued to place their offerings. The first day of Thaipusam, or Murugan's journey, was then completed.

31

Early on the morning of the second day, the devotees of Murugan prepared to duplicate the mythic journey of the demon Idumban by carrying their own burdens for the two miles between the Sri Srinivasa Perumal Temple and the Sri Thendayuthapani Temple. Jangveer Nadir took a bath to purify his body, and marked his forehead and body with viputi. He set his kavadi upright on the temple ground, like a small altar, and made offerings of fruit, coconut and incense, spread out before the kavadi on a banana leaf. Then he dropped incense on a pile of heated coals, which created a dense white cloud of sweet-scented smoke. He fumigated his brass milk pots by placing their open necks over the smoke, then filled them with milk and sealed them with leaves stretched over their brims.

***

Jangveer's younger brother and one of his prospective brothers-in-law assisted him in his preparations. They sang gentle songs of praise and wafted incense in his face, as Jangveer tried to focus all his attention, every thread of his waking consciousness, on the image of Murugan he had formed in his mind, and after a few moments he entered into a directed trance, excluding everything from his mind but his present purpose. He bent forward and picked up one of the three long brass skewers, symbolizing Murugan's lance, and pierced it vertically through the skin of his forehead. He felt the cool brass slide through his pinched flesh, but he felt no pain and did not shed a drop of blood – a sure sign, his assistants knew, of the devotee's piety and the favour of the god. He then pierced the second skewer vertically through his tongue, and the third horizontally through his cheeks, again without pain or bleeding. His assistants rubbed viputi into the points of insertion and exit, and affixed limes to the ends of the skewers, to ward off evil spirits along the processional route.

When this was done, the elaborate process of fixing the kavadi to his chest and back was begun. The cage-like structure, supported by shoulder pads and adorned with peacock feathers, extended in four arches out from his body, and was affixed to his chest and back by chains that were fastened by hooks driven under his skin. The covered pots of milk were then attached to the kavadi and an image of Murugan in a shrine placed in its centre. Additional pots of milk and limes were then attached by hooks into his body, and viputi sprinkled over his pierced flesh.

* * *

Just after dawn the devotees were ready, and began their long procession from the Sri Srinivasa Perumal Temple to the Sri Thendayuthapani Temple, their families and well-wishers following beside them, forming a protective shield as they now walked, now danced along the road, their kavadis springing on their shoulders as they walked and danced, pulling the sharp hooks tight against their skin. Jangveer kept sharply focused on his purpose, his brain burning with the intensity of his devotion to Murugan, the people around him flashing by in a kaleidoscope of colours and sounds. Some of the other devotees stumbled under the weight of their burdens, and one man fainted, but Jangveer pressed on, his family and followers singing and chanting, 'Vel, Vel!'[lxvi] Along the route they stopped

---

lxvi Lance, Lance!

before the Sri Veeramakaliamman Temple on Serangoon Road and the Sri Sivan Temple on Orchard Road, where they danced before the doorways and broke coconuts in honour of the deities therein, before proceeding onwards.

As they drew close to the Sri Thendayuthapani Temple, where a great crowd awaited them, their pace quickened and their dancing reached a whirling, leaping crescendo as they entered the temple gate. There Jangveer and the other devotees danced clockwise round the interior of the temple, before they approached the altar and poured the contents of their milk pots over the deity. After receiving a sprinkling of viputi and a portion of the offerings of milk and food that had been made to the god, they returned to the temple grounds, where their attendants helped them remove and dismantle their kavadis. Jangveer did not flinch as the hooks were removed from his flesh and he pulled the skewers free from his forehead, tongue and cheeks, and there was scarcely a fleck of blood on his body.

That evening, after the festive meal that had been prepared for the two families by Shiv Nadir's wife, Arjun Nath declared that Jangveer Nadir had proven himself to be a pure devotee of Murugan and must surely have gained the favour of the god. He agreed to enter into a business partnership with Shiv Nadir, and was happy to give his daughter Abhati in marriage to Jangveer Nadir, who had proven himself true on the festival of Thaipusam.

32

In response to concerns about an attack by the Russian fleet during the Crimean War, and fears of a local uprising in the wake of the Indian Mutiny, Governor Blundell had written to Calcutta requesting the construction of defensive fortifications and a place of refuge for the population – by which he meant the European population – in the event of a native uprising. In January Captain Collyer of the Madras Engineers arrived from Calcutta, and began to draw up plans for the fortification of Singapore. Collyer examined the earlier plans that had been made by Captain Edward Lake of the Bengal Engineers in 1827 and by Captain Samuel Best of the Madras Engineers in 1843. These had included recommendations for a series of new fortifications and hill and shore batteries, neither of which had been implemented due to what had then been judged to be their prohibitive cost.

Captain Collyer originally agreed with Captains Lake and Best that Pearl's Hill was best suited 'as a place of refuge against any sudden attack of the enemy or an uprising among the Chinese', as Governor Blundell had put it in 1856, although since the mutiny the Indians had been added as an additional source of concern. While Collyer corresponded with Calcutta, the European Seaman's Hospital and the Tan Teck Seng Hospital were served government notices to quit their premises. The European Seaman's Hospital was to be rebuilt near the Sepoy Lines[lxvii] at the foot of Pearl's Hill, while the Tan Tock Seng Hospital was to be rebuilt on Serangoon Road,

lxvii Barracks of the Indian regiments.

on the site of Joseph Balestier's former sugar plantation, which was now known as Balestier Plain. Tan Kim Ching, the eldest son of the late Tan Tock Seng, consented to the move, but only after he was assured that the new hospital would not cost less money or be less well provided for than the first.

In February Philip Robinson, who had come from Melbourne the previous year to join Cursetjee and Co as an assistant, set up his own business in Commercial Place in partnership with James Spicer, formerly keeper of the Singapore jail, specializing in groceries and millinery. When the partnership was dissolved the following year, Robinson brought in a new partner, George Rappa, and founded Robinson and Co.[lxviii]

* * *

Alfred Russel Wallace had spent the past year travelling in the Mollucas,[lxix] in the Eastern Archipelago. He was living on the island of Gilola, where he had collected many specimens, when he was suddenly afflicted with a recurrence of malarial fever. Shivering tremors were followed by hot spasms, which laid him low for hours on end. One morning as he lay disabled on his cot, his thoughts drifted aimlessly from one subject to another. He recounted to himself the specimens he had collected the previous day; he remembered his foolish concern about saving his watch when his life was in danger as the *Helen* went down in the Atlantic[lxx]; he

---

lxviii For generations the premier department store in Singapore, it continued in business up to the present day.

lxix Islands located east of the Celebes, west of New Guinea and northeast of Timor. Formerly known as the Spice Islands, one of the earliest sources of nutmeg, cloves and mace.

lxx Years earlier when Wallace was returning from an expedition in the Amazon, the Helen, the ship on which he was travelling, caught fire and sunk, along with his collection of specimens. Wallace escaped in a longboat with other crew members and was eventually rescued by the Jordeson.

remembered his happy days at Hertford Grammar School, until his father was forced to withdraw him when he had lost all his money to a swindler, a fate that he had recently learned he shared with Sir Stamford Raffles; he thought of his friend Henry Bates, of how much he missed his company and how much they would have to discuss the next time they met.

And then, seemingly against his will, his thoughts began to travel down a peculiar and then a very exciting path. At first, he thought of his fever. How serious was it? Was it one from which he would quickly recover, as he had done so often in the past, or was it one that would linger on for weeks or months? Would he perhaps die from the fever? He wondered how many of the native peoples died from similar fevers.

Then he recalled Thomas Malthus' *Theory of Population*, which he had read a dozen years before. Malthus had explained how 'positive checks to increase' such as disease, accidents, war and famine had kept down the population of savage peoples more than civilized ones. Then he thought about animals. Surely something similar must keep the population of animals in check, since they breed more rapidly than humans, for otherwise the fastest breeding animals would overrun the whole world. Similar causes must account for the vast and continued destruction of animal populations – disease, conflict and famine must cull the vast herds and communities of animals.

Then he thought of the remarkable consequence, and struggled to sit up in his cot, for the thought burned like white-hot iron in his brain. Why did some live and some die? When faced with disease, in general the healthy survived. When faced with enemies, the strongest, the fastest or the cleverest survived. When famine raged, only the best hunters, or those with the best digestive systems, survived. Only those best suited to their circumstances would survive! Then the thought *suddenly flashed upon him that this entirely natural process* would *necessarily* improve the race, *because in every generation the inferior would inevitably be killed off and the superior would remain. This struggle for existence would naturally ensure that those best adapted would survive!*

Given the inevitable struggle for existence, the abundance or rarity of a species would be dependent upon its degree of adaptation to the conditions of existence. Useful variations would tend to increase; useless or hurtful variations tend to decrease. Thus, an antelope with shorter or weaker legs would necessarily suffer more from the attacks of the feline carnivores. The passenger pigeon with less powerful wings would sooner or later be affected in its powers of procuring a regular supply of food. If, on the other hand, any species should produce a variety having slightly increased powers of preserving existence, that variety must inevitably in time acquire a superiority in numbers. Suppose that some alteration of physical conditions occurred in a district – a long period of drought or a destruction of vegetation by locusts or the interruption of some new carnivorous animal seeking 'pastures new'. Then it was surely evident that, of all the individuals composing the species, those forming the least numerous and most feebly organized variety would suffer first, and, if the pressure were severe, they would soon become extinct.

Wallace fell back on his cot, exhausted by the effort this realization had taken. But he knew it solved the problem – it was the answer he had been seeking, the explanation of the transmutation of species! He thought of the problems of Lamarck's account of transmutation in terms of the inheritance of acquired characteristics, and realized that his account in terms of natural processes of selection could deal with them all. He did not need to appeal to any supposed innate drive of organisms to adapt themselves to their environment to explain their adaptation, for only those types that were best adapted were likely to survive. The giraffe did not acquire its long neck by constantly stretching its neck to reach the highest foliage and its offspring consequently inheriting longer necks, but because any varieties that occurred among its antitypes with a longer neck than usual at once secured a fresh range of pasture over the same ground as their shorter-necked companions, and on the first scarcity of food were thereby enabled to outlive them. *His theory also explained what had so impressed the theologians. Why it appeared – but yet only appeared – as if the transmutation of species was brought about by design. This was because through entirely natural processes the best adapted would be selected to survive and reproduce.*

The cold chills took hold of him once again and his teeth chattered in his skull, then as quickly as they departed his skin and face began to burn like fire. He was physically as weak as a kitten, but the excitement of his discovery gave him the strength of purpose to rise from his bed to make some notes on the subject, before he was overcome by the fever – or, God forbid, he died from it. He was determined to communicate his discovery to Darwin by the next post, which was only three days away. He knew Darwin would immediately recognize its significance.

Over the next two days he used his notes to carefully write out his theory in the form of a short paper on the transmutation of species, which he sent to Charles Darwin, asking him to send a copy to Sir Charles Lyell if he thought the theory of sufficient interest. The title of Wallace's paper was 'On the Tendency of Varieties to Depart Indefinitely from the Original Type'.

33

In March, the municipal commissioners of Singapore decided to honour some of the heroes of the mutiny by renaming some of the streets after them. Cantonment Road was renamed Outram Road, after Lieutenant-General Sir James Outram, who distinguished himself in the relief and defence of Lucknow; Salat Road was renamed Neil Road, after Brigadier-General James

Neill,[lxxi] who had brought his cruel brand of summary justice to the mutineers at Cawnpore and had been killed in the assault on Lucknow; and the road from the stone bridge over Dalhousie Canal to the police station on River Valley Road was renamed Havelock Road, after Major-General Sir Henry Havelock, who led the relief of Lucknow and died of dysentery during its defence, a few days after learning of his knighthood. The municipal commissioners did not consult with the Indian community in their decision to rename these roads.

The commissioners also decided to rename Flint Street as Prinsep Street, after the commissioner of the Singapore inquiry; Market Street as Crawfurd Street, after the second resident; Commercial Square as Raffles Place, after the founder of Singapore; and Tavern Street as Bonham Street, after the former governor of the Straits Settlements. None of the municipal commissioners in that year or future years thought of naming a street or square after Colonel Farquhar, who had been the first resident and who had done so

---

lxxi For some unknown reason the commissioners dropped the second 'l' in the brigadier-general's name.

much to secure the early success of the settlement.

**

The Emperor Hsien Feng, emboldened by Yehonala's fiery rhetoric, refused to accept the British and French demands. In response, Lord Elgin and Baron Gros sailed north in April with the allied fleet and blasted their way past the Taku forts at the mouth of the Peiho river, which controlled the approaches to Peking. When the Emperor still refused to negotiate, they sent their gunboats upriver to Tientsin, only thirty miles south of the Imperial capital.

Yehonala begged Hsien Feng not to give in to the barbarians, but the Emperor was in a state of high panic that even his Orchid could not assuage, and he appointed two high-ranking mandarins, Kweilang and Hwarhana, as Imperial commissioners to negotiate with the allies. Yet Hsien Feng had no intention of negotiating in good faith. He instructed the commissioners to do everything in their power to obstruct and delay, to give him time to recall some of the Qing battalions presently engaged with the Taiping and Nien for the defence of the capital. In early June, the Emperor thought that Kweilang and Hwarhana were conceding too much, so he sent the aged Chi-ying, the principal negotiator of the original Treaty of Nanking, to use his reputation as a man of honour and reason to spin out the negotiations, by playing the allies off against the other. The Americans and Russians had by this time joined in the negotiations, and Chi-ying promised them trade concessions if they interceded with the British to persuade them to withdraw their most objectionable demands – for a resident ambassador in Peking, and for the right to trade on the Yangtze River and the interior regions of the country.

As the negotiations grew more complex and Chi-ying's tactics grew subtler, Lord Elgin requested Duncan's help in dealing with the commissioners. He was still desperately short of men who understood the Chinese language and he did not trust the court interpreters. Duncan spent a day giving instructions to his manager in Hong Kong, before departing for Tientsin in Simpson and Co's own steamer, the *Highland Lassie*, named after his father's square-rigger. Yet before he arrived in Tientsin, Lord Elgin had grown impatient with Chi-ying and the Imperial commissioners. He was also angered by the interference of the Americans and Russians, with respect to matters that he considered none of their business. On June 26 he issued an ultimatum to the Imperial court – if they did not comply with all his demands, he would immediately advance upon Peking and install his ambassador at gunpoint.

Again Yehonala and her supporters tried to persuade the Emperor to stand firm and make the arrogant barbarians eat their words, but Hsien Feng was frightened for his life as well as his kingdom and instructed his commissioners to accede to all the British demands. Duncan arrived in time for the final negotiations over the Treaty of Tientsin, which was signed on July 3. The new treaty authorized the opening of eleven new treaty ports, including Tengchow, Danshui and Swatow; granted Britain the right to maintain a resident ambassador to Peking; the right to trade on the Yangtze river as far as Hankow; the right of British citizens to travel freely to the interior of China; and approved an indemnity of five million pounds of silver in reparations for British merchant losses and British military expenses. Lord Clarendon, the foreign secretary, had pressed Lord Elgin to include a clause legalizing the opium trade, but Elgin declined to do so because he thought it counterproductive – the Chinese were liable to refuse and jeopardize the whole treaty, and there was no need for it. Chinese officials all the way up to the Imperial court were happy to take their bribes, while British and American companies such as Jardine and Matheson and Dent and Co made their fortunes in the illegal trade out of Hong Kong.

The French concluded a similar treaty a few days later, with the added stipulation that French missionaries were to have access to all parts of China to spread the Christian gospel, and the Americans and Russians negotiated only slightly less favourable treaties a month later. Chi-ying was recalled to Peking, where he bowed to the wrath of the Dragon Emperor. He was put on trial for treason, for which he was found guilty. The punishment for treason was lingchi; the humiliating death by slicing the body into parts that denied the victim entry to the spiritual realm. At the last minute, Hsien Feng relented and demonstrated his Imperial magnanimity by allowing Chi-ying to commit suicide by hanging himself with a silken cord.

After the treaty was concluded, Lord Elgin invited Duncan aboard his flagship and thanked him for his help with the negotiations. Then he apologized, but only jokingly, that they had taken so little time.

'I'm sorry you didn't get a proper chance to get to know these inscrutable Manchu. For by God we need to get to know them if we are to divine their real purposes – I don't believe the half of what they report to me about what the Emperor is willing to accept and do.'

'Oh no, sir,' Duncan replied, 'I would not have missed it for the world. I learned a lot and found the negotiations absolutely fascinating. I just wish I had got the chance to visit Peking and the Forbidden City.'

'You might yet, Duncan, you might yet, for I don't trust the Manchu to stick to their end of the bargain and we may still have to enforce it. However, for the moment, I have another proposition that might interest you, if you really want to see more of the Celestial Kingdom. I plan to test the waters – if you'll excuse the pun – by sailing up the Yangtze as far as Wuchang, as provided by the treaty. You'd get to see some fine scenery and perhaps have a chance to meet Hong Xiuquan, the Taiping King, whose Heavenly Capital at Nanking we will pass on route.'

Duncan thought about it for a moment. He knew he ought not to neglect his duties to Simpson and Co, and he had said he would only be gone for a month or two at most. Yet he found himself so fascinated with the ways of the Chinese that he could not resist the offer, and the chance to meet the Taiping King clinched the matter. What stories he would have to tell to Dr Legge and Hong Rengan when he returned to Hong Kong! While he felt an obligation to his father and the company, he knew that he was not really needed. His manager Ian Fraser was more than capable of running the Hong Kong office in his absence, trade was booming and was only likely to increase with the new treaty. Indeed, he thought to himself, he was actually promoting the company's business by working with Lord Elgin to help open up the country to British commerce. But the real reason he kept to himself. His engagement with the devious Chinese officials had helped to blunt the lingering pain of his loss, which only returned to him when he woke alone in the grey hours before the dawn.

'I'm your man, sir,' he replied. 'I hope I will have time to send some letters off to my manager in Hong Kong and to my family in Singapore.'

'Of course, of course,' Lord Elgin replied, 'and you've plenty of time. You can go back to Hong Kong – or Singapore for that matter – before we depart, which won't be until October. I have to stop off in Shanghai first to negotiate the details of the new tariff agreements with the dear old Imperial commissioners. You can take part if you like, but it will be damn boring stuff, and Harry Parkes can take care of it.'

'In that case, I'll take you up on your offer, and return to meet you in Shanghai in October. Good luck with the tariff negotiations,' he said, shaking Lord Elgin's hand as he prepared to leave, 'and don't give them an inch.'

'Oh, I think I'll give them a tax on opium, with a wee bit to themselves, and then we'll all be happy. God speed, Duncan!'

34

When Charles Darwin received Alfred Russel Wallace's letter at his home at Down House in Kent, he was heartbroken. He had spent the years since he had served as gentleman-naturalist on HMS *Beagle* developing his own theory of the transmutation of species, in terms of the natural selection of traits conducive to the survival of organisms. Almost twenty years ago to the day, he too had been reflecting on Malthus' theory of population, when it had struck him that the competition for limited resources that Malthus described in his book would naturally ensure that favourable variations would tend to be preserved and unfavourable variations tend to be destroyed. He had immediately started a notebook on the subject, and had prepared a rough abstract of his theory, which he had planned to develop into a book, but only after he had organized the biogeographical evidence he intended to provide for its support. Yet twenty years later he had not much more to show than his abstract, and now here was Wallace, in a few short pages of text, stating very precisely the fundamental principles of the very same theory that he had spent so many years working on.

Darwin's first instinct was to cede priority to Wallace and arrange for the publication of his paper. But his friends Charles Lyell and Joseph Hooker argued against it, reminding him that he had presented a version of his theory to them as far back as 1844. After much anxiety and distraction, during which time he lost his two-year-old son to scarlet fever, Darwin agreed to a compromise suggested by Lyell and Hooker. They maintained that the fairest thing would be for them to arrange for Wallace's paper and Darwin's abstract to be read into the minutes of the Linnean Society,[lxxii] which was to meet on July 1. This was duly done, and they were recorded in the minutes with the following preface:

The accompanying papers, which we have the honour of communicating to the Linnean Society, and which all relate to the same subject, viz. the Laws which affect the Production of Varieties, Races, and Species, contain the results of the investigations of two indefatigable naturalists, Mr Charles Darwin and Mr Alfred Wallace.

These gentlemen having, independently and unknown to one another, conceived the same very ingenious theory to account for the appearance and perpetuation of varieties and of specific forms on our planet, may both fairly claim the merit of being original thinkers in this important line of inquiry; but neither of them having published his views, though Mr Darwin has for many years past been repeatedly urged by us to do so, and both authors having now unreservedly placed their papers in our hands, we think it would best promote the interests of science that a selection from them should be laid before the Linnean Society.

Hooker wrote to Wallace explaining what they had done and their reasons for doing so, and hoped that Wallace would not be offended by their action, which he claimed was the best course of action in the interest of science and the honour of both men.

* * *

In August, Captain Collyer was appointed chief engineer, and the convict body was placed at his disposal to aid in the construction

lxxii The Linnean Society of London, founded in 1788, is a learned society devoted to the study of natural history, evolution, and taxonomy.

of the new fortifications. However, Collyer was now convinced that the main fortification should be built on Government Hill, where its guns could command the town and most of the harbour. Governor Blundell continued to champion Pearl's Hill, but the Indian government accepted Collyer's new recommendations, including his suggestion that Fort Fullerton be rebuilt to three times its present size. The decision was received too late to reprieve the Seaman's Hospital and the Tan Tock Seng Hospital, whose staff and inmates had already been transferred to temporary huts at the foot of Pearl's Hill.

Although Captain Collyer and Governor Blundell disagreed on the best site for the main fortification, when considering the number of troops required for the defence of the port, they both adamantly condemned the idea of creating a volunteer corps comprised of Chinese, Malay and Indian citizens, on a par with the recently established European volunteer corps. Both thought that such a corps, even if it could be raised, would be of little defensive value.

Musa bin Osman, who owned a carriage business, used to take Habib Noh on trips around the island to visit pilgrims on the various plantations, who were working to pay for their Haj passage tickets. Many of these pilgrims – including those who worked on plantations in Johor – would visit him in the town, and receive his prayers for a safe journey to Mecca or their return journey to their homes in Java and the Celebes. But Habib Noh would often travel to them in Musa bin Osman's carriage, knowing many had not the time nor the money to visit him.

Late one evening, Musa was returning home alone with his carriage. There was no moon that night, and dark clouds blotted out the stars. He imagined that he saw robbers in every shadow of the road – not an idle fear, for armed robbers, both Chinese and Malay, waited to ambush unwary travellers outside the precincts of the town. He dearly wished that Habib Noh was with him in the carriage, and no sooner had he wished it, than he heard a soft voice behind him, saying:

'Slow down, Musa bin Osman, slow down. There is no danger and you have nothing to fear.'

Turning around in amazement, Musa saw Habib Noh sitting in the carriage behind him.

***

Syed Ahmad Alsagoff and his father Syed Abdul Rahman Alsagoff were Arab merchants who had come to Singapore in 1824. They had traded in spices and formed Alsagoff and Co in 1848. When his father died, Syed Ahmad had become the senior partner of the company and had expanded the family fortune considerably by marrying Raja Siti, the daughter of Hajjah Fatimah, whose business operations he took over after she died. He also had a lucrative business arranging Haj pilgrimages to Mecca for the Muslim faithful throughout the Eastern Archipelago.

One morning in June he was preparing to set sail for Penang, to meet with a business colleague. As he prepared to board the ship, an Arab boy came running up and called out to him:

'Syed Ahmad! Syed Ahmad! Habib Noh wants to remind you that you are expected for lunch at his home today. I have come to bring you there, so please do me the honour of accompanying me.'

Syed Ahmad was perplexed and ashamed, for he had no recollection of having arranged to have lunch with the holy man. In fact he was sure that he had not. But he did not want to offend the majdhub, so he informed the captain he would not be travelling with him that day, then followed the boy back to Syed Ahmad's home, where he shared a humble meal and the wisdom of the holy man. He made no mention of his failure to remember their arrangement, and Habib Noh made no mention of it either.

Some days later, he received the startling news that the ship on which he had planned to sail had sunk in a heavy storm just south of Penang, drowning all the passengers and crew. He knew then that Habib Noh had foreseen the event and saved his life, and thereafter he gave generously to support Habib Noh's ministry and relief of the poor.

36

Duncan joined Lord Elgin's flagship *Furious* in Shanghai in early October, and the naval squadron of five warships set off for Wuchang a few days later. When Duncan first met with him, Lord Elgin apologized that he no longer thought it politic to communicate with Hong Xiuquan or his subordinate kings as they passed through Taiping held territory, although he did promise to send word ahead before they reached Nanking to assure the Taiping leaders of their peaceful intent and neutrality.

'It would send the wrong sort of message to the Qing if we stopped to hold meetings with the Taiping, and I don't want to give them an excuse to renege on the treaty. The whole point of this little exercise is to demonstrate to them that we are quite capable of enforcing its terms without assistance from our allies or any rebels. Once we have established ourselves as the first representatives of Her Majesty's Government to sail up the Yangtze as far as Wuchang, our business will be done, and I see no reason why we can't go ashore at Nanking when we return, if we can negotiate a friendly meeting. I have to admit that I'd like to meet this Heavenly King myself. He sounds as mad as a hatter, but he must have something going for him to have achieved so much and come so far. And one can never be too careful, for I would not care to bet much money on the outcome of this civil war. The day may come when we might be grateful to have assured the Taiping rulers of our neutrality.'

'I believe that is all they honestly desire,' Duncan replied, 'so they can rid themselves of their foreign oppressors.'

'The Manchu,' he added, when Elgin's brow darkened, having so often heard the British described in these terms. 'The Taiping have no quarrel with us or with our desire to increase our trade. On the contrary, they would like to join with us as Christian brothers.'

'Whoa, Duncan!' Lord Elgin exclaimed. 'One step at a time! And since when were you a champion of Christian brotherhood? I didn't take you for a God-follower of any persuasion.'

'I'm not, sir,' Duncan replied, 'I was merely representing what I've heard from my friend Hong Rengan in Hong Kong, who works for Dr Legge. He's a cousin of Hong Xiuquan, so he should know.'

'Well, we shall see,' said Lord Elgin. 'In the meantime, you should enjoy the river scenery, so long as the weather holds. I'm told it's rather beautiful, in fact breathtakingly so.'

'I look forward to it, sir,' said Duncan, as he took his leave of Lord Elgin and went up on deck.

PART THREE

'DEATH BY A THOUSAND CUTS'

1858 – 1859

1

1858

Wang Zuoxin peered out from the hidden cave as his wife and daughter cowered behind him. All around was wanton destruction and devastation. First the Taiping hordes had come, then the Imperial army and now the Taiping again. What they had not eaten or stolen they had destroyed, and fires burned around them as far as their eyes could see. Wang Zuoxin had nothing left, save for a bag of rice he had managed to grab before he and his family had fled from their cottage and their farm. His rice paddies were destroyed, trampled under the horses' hooves, his livestock slaughtered and his cottage burned to the ground. They spent the long night in the cave, huddled together for comfort, fearing that they would be discovered at any moment. Yet they were not, and the Taiping soldiers moved on in the early hours of the morning.

When they surveyed the desolate landscape the following day, they felt hopeless. They had no livestock, no crops, no shelter and no seed, and they would starve if they stayed where they were. Wang Zuoxin decided to head east towards Amoy in the hope of finding some work so he could feed himself and his family. They joined the tens of thousands of other destitute peasants who made their way toward the coastal towns, the 'flowing people' who were displaced by the war between the Heavenly King and the Celestial Emperor.

They arrived in Amoy some weeks later. They had finished the rice long ago and they were starving. But there was no work for any of them in the port city that was already overcrowded with refugees from the civil war, and Wang's wife Chung Yee was desperately sick with a fever. She lay semi-conscious on a pile of rags under a stairway that led up to a merchant godown.

'We must get medicine for Mother,' pleaded Ah Keng, Wang's sixteen-year-old daughter, 'or she will die.'

Wang Zuoxin knew she was right, although he feared that his wife was already so sick that she was beyond helping. Her skin was hot to the touch, but she would not take the water they tried to make her drink. She had stopped vomiting, but only because she had nothing left to vomit. She retched and convulsed in pain, and her face was deathly grey. They decided to take a risk and leave her where she was, while they went in search of food – even if it meant stealing a handful of rice or searching through the rubbish for some rotten fruit. They passed through the narrow teeming streets until they came to a market square close by the harbour, where there were only a few stalls selling poultry and vegetables. Most of the space was taken up by traders who were hiring wives and children from poor men like himself, to be sent to work as servants in Manila, Saigon, Penang, Malacca and Singapore. Wang Zuoxin looked at Ah Keng, who met his eye, and he shook his head.

'I could never do that,' he said to her. 'Please do not be afraid, Ah Keng – I could not sell my own daughter.'

'But father,' Ah Keng replied, 'I am not afraid to work across the seas, and I could send money back to you. The money you could get today would buy us food and medicine for mother. Please, father, please hire me out to them or we will all starve and die.'

'No, my child,' Wang Zuoxin replied, in a stern voice. 'For it would be better for me to die than to sell you as a slave – for a slave is what you would be.' But as he said these words he knew he was probably condemning his wife and child to death as well as himself.

'Father,' she begged, but Wang Zuoxin grabbed her roughly by the arm and dragged her back to the place where Chung Yee lay dying. She was now unconscious and her breath was very faint. She looked almost at peace, which meant that death was surely near. Wang Zuoxin took his wife's hand in his and lay down beside her on the bed of rags. Overcome by exhaustion, hunger, hopelessness and shame, he fell into a fitful sleep beside her. Ah Keng sat beside them, the tears running down her dirty face.

Ah Keng rose quietly and made her way back through the narrow streets to the human market. She looked around until she found an older trader with a kindly face, with a thin white beard and a long grey queue. He was hardly taller than her own five feet, so she was not afraid of him.

'I have a proposition to put to you,' she said to the old man. 'You can hire me if you will let me take the money back to my parents, so my father can buy medicine for my sick mother. She is lying down by the merchant godowns.'

'Ah yes, little one,' the old man replied, 'but how can I trust you to return to me if I give you money?'

'You could come with me,' she replied, 'or send someone with me.'

The old man looked at the girl standing before him. She was ragged and filthy, but she had a sweet round face with large brown eyes and a small nose and chin. Beneath the streaks of dirt, she had smooth white cheeks and thick sensual lips. Her body was emaciated, but she was big boned, and would run to plumpness if better fed. She would command a good price in the brothels of Singapore.

'Of course,' he responded, 'but first we must feed you – you must be starving. Then we can settle on a price and visit your parents. Come with me.'

Ah Keng did not want to leave the market place, but she followed the old man down a side street. He went into a small shophouse, where a very ugly old woman presided over piles of wicker baskets, and she followed him into the back room, where a young girl sat by a table in the semi-darkness. The old man muttered a few words to her and the young girl rose and left.

'Please sit down,' he said to Ah Keng. 'She has gone to fetch you something to eat.'

Ah Keng was growing fearful and beginning to doubt the wisdom of her decision to approach the old man. But her spirits lifted when the girl returned with a bowl of rice porridge, which Ah Keng ate greedily. She could not believe how good it tasted after having gone so long without food, and thought of how happy her parents would be when they shared her good fortune. For a few moments she forgot about her fear and even experienced a secret thrill at the adventure she was about to embark upon, even though she knew she would miss her parents. So she did not notice the shopkeeper coming into the room, until he clamped his dirty hand across her mouth and seized her around her shoulders. Then the young woman came forward and held a foul and sharp-smelling rag to her nose, and her senses reeled. She kicked her legs and struggled to break free, but the man's grip was too strong, and she felt herself falling down, down, down ... into a deep dark pit.

When she woke she was still in the dark pit, but lying upon – a giant snake! She tried to scream, but her parched throat would not let her. As she came to her senses, she realized that she was not lying upon a giant snake, but upon a pile of oily ropes, and sighed with small relief. She looked around as her eyes adjusted to the dim light in the room, and saw other shadowy figures spread out upon the ropes and baskets littering the floor. Some whimpered and moaned, while others snored. She knew not where she was, but she knew she was at sea, for she could hear the waves slapping against the side of the junk as it moved out of the harbour. And she knew she would never see her mother and father again.

It was midnight when Wang Zuoxin woke. The full moon sent shivers of silver light into the darkness of the stairwell. Chung Yee's hand was cold to his touch – she had died some hours before. In the ghostly light he turned to his daughter and found to his horror that she was gone.

He searched for her all night and all the next day. He asked strangers in the street, the traders in the square, shopkeepers and hawkers, but nobody had seen her. One hawker took pity on him and offered him some rice, but he was too sick at heart to eat. He had failed his family. His wife was dead and he had no money to bury her, his daughter was lost, in all likelihood kidnapped or murdered. He wandered down to the harbour as evening fell, and a great darkness engulfed his heart and soul.

He looked down at the water and stepped forward, intending to drop down into the harbour and drown himself.

'Wait up!' a man's voice cried out from behind. 'Do you want to go to Hell, where the devils will stab you and saw you into pieces and rip out your guts, then feed them to their dogs! What kind of a man wants to do that?'

'A man who has lost everything,' replied Wang Zuoxin, turning to face the stranger who stood beside him. 'A man who has lost his whole family.'

The stranger was a young Chinese man dressed in a suit of European clothes, with a battered straw hat.

'Such a man has everything to gain,' the stranger responded, tipping his hat. 'I can give you a new life, far away from here and far away from your sad memories.'

'I will never forget them,' Wang Zuoxin said, but he stepped back from the water's edge. He was too tired to argue and too tired to decide whether to live or die. He accepted the stranger's rice and plum wine, and his offer of passage to Singapore as an indentured labourer for one year. During that time he could repay the cost of his fare and the food and clothing the agent would provide – and the cost of the opium. As the junk set out the following evening, Wang Zuoxin lay on the deck in an opium dream. He dreamed that he sat with Chung Yee and Ah Keng in the sunshine, watching the swallows swoop across the cloudless sky above their farmhouse.

2

The voyage was horrific. Ah Keng was kept in the dark hold of the junk night and day along with the others, most of whom were young girls like herself. They were fed some rice and water each day, but Ah Keng was seasick and could not keep it down. She felt so sick that she thought she was going to die, and wished that she could die, when she thought of the fate that awaited her, and of her poor mother and father, who she was certain never to see again. The other girls told her that she would be sold as a mui tsai[lxxiii] in Singapore, which was where the junk was bound; she would be sold as a servant or prostitute, or, if she was lucky, as a handmaiden to the woman of a great house, as a concubine to some rich towkay or as a nun to say prayers for the spirit of some unmarried woman when she died.

They arrived in Singapore about ten days later, although to Ah Keng it seemed like an eternity. When they were taken up on deck, her eyes were almost blinded by the fierce sunlight, as they were paraded before the men and women who had come on board to inspect the goods before purchasing them. When her vision recovered, Ah Keng recognized the ugly old woman from the shophouse in Amoy, haggling with the men and women who were offering bids for her girls.

Ah Keng and another girl about her age were sold to a woman whose name, she later discovered, was Madam Ki Chin Ho. They

lxxiii 'Little sister' (Cantonese). Young girls who worked as servants or prostitutes, often sold at an early age by their impoverished parents.

were then transferred to a smaller boat with other girls and their owners, and landed at the shore of a bay, which she later learned was called Telok Ayer Bay. Madam Ki led them through the narrow streets until they came to a small two-storey house. There they were fed, allowed to wash in the bathhouse at the back and given new clothes to wear. Although she was still grieving for the loss of her family, Ah Keng was pleasantly surprised at her treatment by the woman who had bought her, and who told her to call her Auntie Ki. There were four other girls in the house, two older and two younger than Ah Keng, although only by a few years. They were all very pretty, and although she had never thought of herself as attractive, they assured her that she was pretty too. Which was why Auntie Ki had bought her, they said, for she normally tried to place her girls as concubines with rich masters, which was why she kept them well-fed and cared for. As Ah Keng had quickly noted, they were not required to do any household work, which was done by the two servant girls and the old male cook, Hua Chew.

Although they were well treated in Auntie Ki's house, Ah Keng did not want to be sold off as a concubine to any man, however rich, as was plainly Auntie Ki's intention. For she gave Ah Keng books with graphic illustrations of how she would be expected to sexually please her new master, and gave her special coaching on how to stimulate the sensual appetites and raise the flaccid members of elderly men. The thought disgusted her, but more than that, she felt that Auntie Ki had no right to determine her young life. The other girls in the house had been sold to procurers by their parents, which was hard enough, but that was at least legal. Yet she had been kidnapped and her parents had never consented to her sale! Ah Keng decided that she would go along pretending with the other girls until she had grown strong and healthy, and then she would escape. She would make her way back to Amoy and try to find out what had happened to her parents – she was sure her mother would have died, but hoped her father had survived – and she would report the people who had kidnapped her to the authorities.

She was desperately afraid of what would happen to her if Auntie Ki caught her trying to escape. One of the older girls had described how Auntie Ki had punished another girl who had tried to do so. She had made her wear pants tied up at the ends, into which Auntie Ki had thrust a street cat, which she had promptly beat with a broom. In its frenzy to escape the blows, the cat had torn the girl's legs and vagina to bloody shreds – the girl had nearly died, and would never find a man willing to take her as a concubine. She was doomed to destitution and the lowest form of prostitution with drug addicts and paupers. But Ah Keng was still bitter at the way she had been treated and was willing to take the risk.

She knew there was no way she could escape by the main door, since it was secured by two heavy wooden beams each evening, and Hua Chew slept on a bench at the foot of the stairs. Nor could she escape through the window of the room she shared with another girl that was opposite to Auntie Ki's own, for the window was secured with iron bars. But there was a small staircase at the back of the house that led up to a skylight window in the roof, which served as an escape route in the event of a fire. Although it was also secured by a heavy wooden beam, Ah Keng thought she might be able to lift it quietly enough so as not to wake Auntie Ki, at least on those nights when she indulged herself by taking an opium pipe to her bed. Ah Keng had noticed that there was a drainpipe that ran from the edge of the roof to the alley behind the house, and she hoped – and prayed – that she would be able to lower herself down to safety. What she would do then she did not know, but she was too focused on her plan of escape to worry about that at the moment. She kept a small supply of dry food that she managed to secret away, and a roll of clothes tied up in a bundle ready for the day.

3

Lord Elgin had been right. The scenery along the Yangtze River was beautiful, especially after they had left Shanghai and it began to narrow about fifty miles inland. There the river was bordered by a series of lagoons fronting the flat alluvial plains, broken here and there by low woods that stretched to the river's edge, which was fringed with overhanging bushes and bamboo. Although it was late in the year, it was clear to Duncan that the land was richly cultivated, as he watched the farmers and tradesmen going busily about their work without apparent hardship.

One evening, as the sun was sinking low, they passed by a small creek shrouded on both sides by arching osier and weeping willows. Taking out his field glasses, Duncan peered through the golden gloom, and was rewarded by the sight of a small sun-shadowed lake bordered by fruit trees and flower gardens, in the midst of which stood a small courtyard house swathed with green creepers. He wondered who lived in that house, and he imagined a happy family sitting down to their evening meal. How he wished he could have lived in such a house, with his own dear wife and child, and the pain tore at his heart with such power that it seemed to him as if it were only yesterday that they had passed. The homely image vanished from view as the gunboat steamed upriver, but the pain lingered on like an open wound. He went down to his cabin and sat in the gathering darkness and wondered if he would ever know happiness again. He said to himself what he had said to himself so many times before – you must not think of them, for the pain is too hard to bear.

Don't look back! Don't look back! Then out of the corner of his eye he caught sight of her standing in the cabin doorway, her dark hair tumbling over her shoulders, as she looked down upon him. But when he turned to speak to her she was gone.

***

As they moved further upriver and entered the region controlled by the Taiping, the flatlands gave way to hills that rolled away into distant mountains. There they were amazed by the sight of villagers who waved to them in friendship as they passed. None had done so downriver, although they had been cursed on a few occasions as foreign devils and barbarians. On the evening of November 20, they came within sight of the great walls of Nanking, and they steamed towards it as the sun set in thin golden streamers over the mountains. Duncan watched in quiet wonder as the swallows and swifts swooped like flickering shadows over the darkening hills.

***

As the five steam-powered gunships of Lord Elgin's flotilla passed beneath the Taiping batteries on both sides of the river facing Nanking, the gunners at first watched in hushed awe, but then ran out their flags and sent a single round shot over the bow of the leading ship, the *Lee*. As ordered by Lord Elgin, the captain ran out her white flag of truce, to communicate their peaceful intentions, but in response the Taiping batteries opened up on the *Lee*, firing round shot in rapid succession into the side of the ship. The British ships responded with a furious barrage as they passed by the Taiping positions, until all the gunships were safely upriver and out of range. There was little damage to the ships, and few casualties, but Lord Elgin was outraged by the insult to the British flag of truce and, after consulting with his officers, decided to return the following day and teach the Taiping gunners a lesson they would never forget.

As dawn was breaking the following morning, the five ships slipped back downriver through the early morning mist and took up their positions, training their guns and rocket launchers on the Taiping gun emplacements on both sides of the river. Although it was a bitterly cold morning and he knew the danger, Duncan climbed up into the rigging to look down upon the Taiping gunners, whose bright red tunics made them easy to identify. For a few moments silence hung like the morning mist over the ships and the Taiping batteries, until the British ships fired their broadsides. The chill air was pierced with the screaming light of their rockets and exploding Moorsom shells,[lxxiv] and the thunder and whistling of their shot and grape. The barrage continued with ferocious intensity for an hour and a half, while those Taiping positions that had not been completely destroyed or abandoned during the initial barrage responded with a pitiful smattering of occasional shot and grape.

As Duncan looked down upon the carnage, he thought it was like the battle of Batang Marau all over again, only with different players. The ancient cannon of the Taiping were no match for the British heavy guns and rockets, and the battle was a foregone conclusion, despite the bravery of the Taiping gunners, who continued to fire intermittently as Lord Elgin turned his ships around and headed back upriver. He had to admire their courage, especially when he saw the Imperial Ming forces ranged upon the hills overlooking Nanking – it was surely only a matter of time before the city was captured and the rebellion crushed.

Lord Elgin was anxious to make headway, since he assumed the Taiping would be thirsting for revenge, and might attempt

---

lxxiv Percussion shell designed to explode in the air and scatter
　　　shrapnel, invented by Captain William Moorsom (1817-1860)
　　　of the British Navy.

an ambush while they were anchored at night. Yet his morning attack had precisely the opposite effect. When Hong Xiuquan, the Heavenly King, heard of the spectacular success of the steam gunships against his batteries, he remembered how his elder brother Jesus had told him that his greatest army commander would come from a foreign country. Hong Xiuquan began to compose a poem, written in vermilion on a yellow silk scroll, to Lord Elgin, younger brother from the Western sea, exhorting him to join the Taiping cause and help him annihilate the demon-devils. Yet as the Heavenly King was carefully composing his poem, Lord Elgin was steaming upriver at full speed, and by the time the special messenger was sent out to deliver the poem to younger brother from the Western sea, he had already passed beyond the territories controlled by the Taiping.

4

On November 19, at seven in the morning, Governor Blundell read out the Queen's proclamation of September 1. Before an assembled crowd of officials, from a special platform erected on the Esplanade and decked out with bunting, he declared that Her Majesty had taken upon herself the responsibility of government of the Indian dominions. The soldiers of the 43rd Madras Native Infantry, the Madras Artillery and the Singapore Volunteer Rifle Corps paraded before the governor, Resident Councillor Henry Somerset MacKenzie and Daing Ibrahim the Temenggong of Singapore and Johor. The band of the HMS *Amethyst* played 'God Save the Queen' and the Madras Artillery fired a royal salute.

Since the day was a public holiday, Ronnie Simpson joined W.H. Read and others in celebrating the event in the Hotel de l'Esperance. They looked forward to the day when a governor would proclaim the direct control of the Straits Settlements by the crown.

***

Hong Rengan felt a deep obligation to his dear friend Dr Legge, who had welcomed him in his hour of need and helped him bring his family to the safety of Hong Kong, and who had regularly implored him to have nothing more to do with the Taiping. James Legge believed that Hong Xiuquan's theological doctrines were blasphemous, and that the Manchu would crush the rebellion in the end. Dr Legge had implored him:

'Stay with me and do God's work.'

For years his work of translation and ministry had kept Hong Rengan fully occupied. Yet always at the back of his mind was the thought that if he could only get back to his cousin in Nanking, he could persuade him to represent his theological views in ways that were less likely to be condemned as blasphemy, especially by those Christian missionaries who were potentially sympathetic to his cause, and to adopt a more conciliatory attitude to the foreign merchants and their envoys.

During the summer two events had taken place that persuaded him it was time to return to his cousin. Hong's mother died, freeing him from one obligation, and Dr Legge returned to Scotland on medical leave, weakening the other. With a few Hakka men from Hong Kong whom he trusted, he boarded a lorcha for Canton, and travelled north by land and by river, disguised as a peddler, until he managed to slip through the Qing lines and reached the Heavenly Capital in late November.

* * *

Hong Rengan did not know what to expect when he was brought before Hong Xiuquan, now Heavenly King of the Taiping, whom he had not seen for ten years. So he was greatly relieved when Hong Xiuquan, dressed in a white silk robe embroidered with gold dragons, welcomed him like the long-lost cousin that he was. When Hong Rengan prostrated himself before his Heavenly master, the Heavenly King stepped down from his throne and raised him up, and embraced him with genuine warmth.

'I welcome you, dear cousin,' Hong Xiuquan said. 'Elder brother assured me of your return. You are destined to take part in the final battle against the demon-devils, which will destroy them forever and establish our Heavenly Kingdom over all.'

In his turn Hong Rengan promised that he would do everything in his power to work towards their final victory.

'I have learned much in Hong Kong,' he said, 'where I have lived with the great missionary Dr Legge among the foreigners. I have learned about their institutions and their science, and how we can use their knowledge for the betterment of our people. I have also studied their minds and hearts, and hope to help you persuade them to join us in a great brotherhood of Christians.'

'I know you will serve me well, Hong Rengan, my cousin and brother in Christ and the Heavenly Father,' Hong Xiuquan replied, holding his cousin's shoulders tight.

Hong Rengan looked at his old friend. He had aged a bit and was a little stouter. His short beard was a shade lighter, but his long black hair retained its velvet sheen. And one thing had not changed – his dark eyes shone with the piercing intensity of a God, or the son of a God. Hong Rengan knew he had done the right thing when he had forsaken his life in Hong Kong to serve his sovereign and Heavenly King, and he knew that his own destiny was at hand.

5

At first Hong Rengan was dismayed to learn that Hong Xiuquan had withdrawn from the everyday command and administration of the Taiping Kingdom, in order to devote himself to meditation and commentary on the books of the Bible – especially the Book of Revelation, which foretold the destruction of the demon-devils and idolaters. Yet he was relieved when he met Li Xiucheng, who commanded the Taiping armies defending Nanking and its satellite towns and villages. Li Xiucheng was clearly a capable commander, and Hong quickly realized that the defence of the city and the future Taiping campaigns were best left in his able hands.

Li Xiucheng was thirty-six years old, the son of a peasant farmer and charcoal burner, who had joined the Taiping forces as they marched by his village on their way to Yongan. He was a natural soldier who had risen through the ranks of the Taiping by his displays of military daring and cunning. His soldiers had come to adulate him and the Ming commanders to fear him. The Manchu were so concerned that Li Xiucheng would lead the Taiping forces to victory over them that they had tried to bribe him to come over to their side, but he had refused them. For his victories and faithfulness the Heavenly King had raised him to the rank of subordinate king, and had given him the title of Loyal King. Li was a wiry young man, tight-lipped and dark-eyed, fanatically devoted to Hong Xiuquan and his cause – which was just as well, thought Hong Rengan to himself, since he suspected Li was quite capable of usurping the role of Taiping King.

Hong Xiuquan also elevated Hong Rengan to the rank of subordinate king, and gave him the title of Shield King. The Heavenly King was greatly impressed by Hong Rengan's suggestions for adapting Western science and technology for the improvement of the Heavenly Kingdom. Hong Rengan sent him a long memorandum recommending the establishment of a postal service, plans for road widening and river dredging to facilitate the speed of travel, the establishment of banks and insurance companies, and new building techniques and methods of city planning. The Heavenly King welcomed these suggestions, but he did not act upon them – he advised Hong Rengan that they would have to wait until they achieved final victory over the demon-devils. The Heavenly King also refused to accept Hong Rengan's plea that they demonstrate their humanity and commitment to the divine commandment not to kill, by abolishing capital punishment in the Kingdom of Heavenly Peace. Hong Xiuquan insisted that all evildoers and demon-devils must be killed, a command that Loyal King Li executed with fearsome efficiency.

6

Lord Elgin's flotilla returned from Wachung in December, arriving within sight of the Taiping batteries guarding the approaches to Nanking on Christmas Day, where they anchored for the night. There Lord Elgin finally received Hong Xiuquan's apology for the Taiping aggression in November, which informed him that the 'ignorant scoundrels' who had fired upon his ships had been decapitated. When they reached Nanking two days later, Lord Elgin declined to go ashore and meet with the Taiping King – he meant to maintain his strict policy of neutrality. Yet he did counsel Duncan, Thomas Wade, his Chinese secretary, and Reverend Alexander Wylie to do so, to try to glean what information they could about conditions in the Taiping capital.

Thomas Wade arranged for their safe passage into the Heavenly capital, where they were ushered into the quarters of Li Xiucheng, the Loyal King. Li was seated at a golden table dressed in yellow satin, writing on a yellow scroll. As he removed his spectacles and rose to greet them, he welcomed them to the Heavenly City and begged them to take a seat on the sofas and armchairs that were spread out over the yellow carpet. Wade introduced Duncan and Reverend Wylie, and explained that Lord Elgin had determined that it was not an opportune time to visit, but had sent the present company in his stead. He then reported the message Lord Elgin had asked him to convey to the Heavenly King:

'Lord Elgin acknowledges his apology for the unfortunate incident in November, and regrets the casualties on both sides that resulted from it. He has also asked me to impress upon you the fact that as a result of our recent treaty with the Manchu Emperor Hsien Feng, many more British ships will be passing up and down the Yangtze, and we earnestly hope that you will guarantee them safe passage. We assure you that we intend to maintain our policy of strict neutrality, but also warn you that we will respond with devastating force if our ships are fired upon again.'

'Of course, of course,' General Li replied dismissively. 'Do not concern yourself on that score, Mr Wade. Are we not Christian brothers together, serving a common God.'

'I hope that is true, sir,' said Reverend Wylie, 'and we hope we can meet with Hong Xiuquan this day. We heard a rumour that he had died and been succeeded by his son.'

'The Heavenly King lives, but I am afraid he cannot see you today,' Li replied. 'He and his wife Lai Xiying are visiting the Heavenly Father and Elder Brother Jesus, but if you will stay the night I promise you an audience in the morning. I know he will be eager to meet with the representatives of our younger brother from the Western sea[lxxv].'

They were all quite astonished by Li's response, delivered with palpable sincerity and a straight face. Reverend Wylie stood with his mouth wide open in amazement.

Their embarrassed confusion was relieved by the arrival of Shield King Hong Regan, who had received word of their entry into the city. Duncan and his old friend were delighted to see each other again.

Reverend Wylie was eager to take up the matter of Hong Xiuquan's visit to Heaven, having recovered from his earlier discombobulation, but Li Xiucheng forestalled any discussion by inviting Reverend Wylie to stay overnight and meet with the Heavenly King the following day.

---

lxxv Lord Elgin.

'We would love to,' Wade replied, 'but we must be getting back to our ship to report to Lord Elgin.'

'At least stay for dinner – we can offer you English food if you wish.'

Again Wade declined, but then Hong Rengan interjected:

'I hope at least you can stay, Duncan, so you can report back to Lord Elgin and Dr Legge the true nature of our Taiping mission. We will see you safely returned to your countrymen in Shanghai. You can stay with me or with my English friend, Augustus Lindley. As General Li said, we can offer you English food ... and wine ... and Scotch whisky!'

'Well that settles it then!' laughed Duncan. He knew these men were making history, whichever way it turned out, and it would be interesting to get their perspective on the state of China. It might even be commercially useful, if the Taiping armies did vanquish the Qing and become the ruling dynasty. At least that was how he would justify it to his father if he questioned his action at a later date, for he would surely see the commercial possibilities if Duncan were to become a trusted friend of the new Taiping Emperor, or at least of his subordinate mandarins. The mind boggled at the prospect!

Duncan returned to the flotilla to seek Lord Elgin's permission to stay on in Nanking, which he readily granted, since their official business of enforcing the treaty by sailing up the Yangtze to Wuchang was officially completed and he no longer had any special need of Duncan's services. He also thought it might indeed prove useful in the future – 'you never know, you never know' he said – although he hoped that Duncan would rejoin him if he had need of him, if the Manchu tried to twist themselves out of the terms of the treaty.

Duncan promised that he would, and went ashore the following morning, as Lord Elgin, his mission completed, set off at full steam for Shanghai, on his way home to London.

7

The Loyal King and the Shield King may have been rivals in the power vacuum created by Hong Xiuquan's withdrawal from public affairs, but they agreed on a number of important things. They knew that in order to attain victory over the Manchu, they must first destroy the extensive Qing encampments ranged on the hills surrounding them. While they posed no immediate threat to the city, which was almost impregnable behind its massive walls, they were threatening its supply lines. The Loyal King and the Shield King also agreed that once the Qing battalions had been routed, General Li should lead a campaign downriver to capture Shanghai, to give them control of at least one seaport.

'But we should be very careful not to threaten the foreign traders in Shanghai, and assure them of our peaceful intentions and the security of their trade,' Hong Rengan cautioned. 'We do not want to frighten them into taking sides with the Manchu.'

'I do not fear them, and I can take Shanghai with or without their support,' Li assured him. 'However, I fully agree that we should do our utmost to reassure them, and not force them into an alliance with the Manchu. What we need most is a fleet of those great steam gunships that destroyed our river batteries with such terrible ease. If we can capture Shanghai and demonstrate our good will to our foreign brethren, we can purchase a fleet of such ships. Then we can control the Yangtze and send them up the Grand Canal to destroy the demon den.'

General Li's dark eyes flashed and his fists clenched tightly as he described the prospect.

'I concur, General Li,' said Hong Rengan. 'We have a million taels of silver in the common treasury, more than enough to purchase such a fleet. And I have every confidence that out foreign brethren will be just as willing to sell us these and other modern munitions as they are to sell us Manchester cottons and Scotch whisky. We need their new Enfield rifles and breech loading cannon to replace our old matchlocks and muzzle-loaders.'

'So we are agreed then,' Li said, rising from his throne. 'Let us advise Hong Xiuquan of our plans.'

Hong Xiuquan also agreed, and said that God would send his Heavenly battalions to help them crush the snake-tiger-dog devils.

***

It took a long time for Joseph Hooker's letter to reach Alfred Wallace, since he was travelling between the Moluccas islands at the time, and longer still for Wallace to get his off to the post, but on the last day of the year Hooker finally got his reply. Wallace thanked Hooker for the generous action he had taken by having his and Darwin's papers read into the minutes of the Linnean Society, and for his invitation to return to England to help promote the theory of evolution by natural selection. This latter invitation he regretted he would have to decline, because he could not abandon his present researches, which had reached 'their most interesting point'.

8

1859

Duncan stayed in Nanking for six months, despite the privation caused by irregular food supplies, and the danger posed by the Imperial troops massed on the hills around the city. He lodged with Augustus F. Lindley, an English adventurer who had joined the Taiping cause. Lindley had served as an honorary officer in General Li's guards, and now commanded the Loyal and Faithful Auxiliary Legion, which was composed of European and American mercenaries as well as regular Taiping soldiers. Duncan discovered that there were quite a few foreigners in Nanking, some of whom, like Lindley, had joined as volunteers, while others served as mercenaries or ran guns and food supplies from Shanghai to Nanking, slipping through the Qing blockades by night.

Lindley, or Foreign Brother Lin-le as the God-followers knew him, was a passionate supporter and advocate of the Taiping cause. He maintained that the Taiping were true revolutionaries, the first Christian movement in Asia, whose goal was to free the Chinese people from the oppression of the Manchu. They had created a truly egalitarian society in the regions they controlled, and abolished slavery, concubinage and degrading practices such as foot binding. Lindley assured Duncan – and with great passion – that save for a few unfortunate incidents, all the stories in the foreign press about the destruction wrought by the Taiping armies on ordinary Chinese villagers were lies and fabrications. When the Taiping took control of a village, town or city, they destroyed the idols in the temples and those Qing forces that resisted them, but the wanton destruction of property and food stocks was usually the work of the retreating Qing forces.

Duncan was not sure whether he believed that, for he doubted that Lindley was an unbiased observer. Yet he admired his sincere commitment to the Taiping cause, and granted that at least his judgment on the matter was obviously based upon observations made in the field, rather than the reports in the foreign press that too readily accepted the official Manchu representation of Taiping 'atrocities'. Duncan was also impressed by the simple piety of the Taiping men and women. Despite their defeats and privations, they retained a strong faith that the Heavenly King and the Heavenly Father would lead them to salvation, and that one day they would be united with their Western brethren in the Kingdom of Heavenly Peace on Earth.

He was particularly struck by their use of the term 'foreign brother', which seemed wholly genuine. Often, as he walked through the city, either with Lindley or by himself, one of the residents, either soldier or ordinary citizen, would come up to him and grasp him by the hand, welcoming him as foreign brother from across the seas. Each time they would express their joyful anticipation of the day when they would all be united in the Kingdom of Heavenly Peace, and they pressed him with questions about his own country across the seas. They asked him how people in his country prayed to 'Yesu', and whether they believed all the things that the Heavenly King had taught them.

Some would invite him to meet their family, and he would join them for their simple evening meal, before which they gave thanks to the Heavenly Father. Sometimes he went with Lindley to an early morning service, between six and seven, which was similar to a simple Protestant ceremony. The men and women stood on separate sides of the Heavenly Hall, while the preacher led the sermon and hymns; the only real difference was that the preacher concluded the ceremony by reading out a written prayer, which he afterwards burned and then consumed. A Buddhist relic, Lindley informed him, that he was sure would be abolished in due course – once the Heavenly King, with the help of Hong Rengan and others, had determined upon the proper form of the Christian service.

***

Duncan cautioned Lindley, Hong Rengan and the Loyal King to be ready to compromise in their dealings with the Western powers, especially concerning the matter of the opium trade. If the Western powers could be persuaded to support the Taiping, and they were victorious, then it would surely be possible to negotiate the abandonment of the trade on opium in return for other lucrative trading concessions.

There was no room for compromise as far as Hong Xiuquan was concerned, but fortunately for the Taiping cause, he played no active role in the day to day management of the campaigns against the Qing, and accepted news of victory or defeat with sublime insouciance. He assured the Loyal King and the Shield King that he had conferred with the East King and the West King in Heaven, and that together they had planned a strategy for the Heavenly armies. Hong Xiuquan no longer left the golden walls of his Heavenly Palace, but spent his days revising his commentaries on the Old and New Testaments, and issuing daily edicts on the nature of God and his sons and their commandments, written in his own hand in vermilion ink on yellow silk, and posted on the palace gate called the Holy Heavenly Gate of the True God.

Then much to Duncan's surprise, he was one day summoned to the presence of the Heavenly King. Hong Xiuquan had learned that Duncan was a friend of Lord Elgin, younger brother from the

Western sea, whom the Heavenly King believed was destined to join him in his mission to destroy the demon-devils. Hong Rengan warned him to be careful, for the Heavenly King could see into men's souls, and he would know that Duncan was not a true believer.

9

When Duncan was brought before Hong Xiuquan, the Heavenly King looked down upon him from his golden throne, dressed in a spectacular black and red dragon robe, his long black hair tumbling down over his broad shoulders, as if in contempt of the Manchu prohibition against unbraided hair. He looked like an ordinary man, except for his eyes – the dark eyes seemed to pierce the very depths of his soul. He knows I am not a Christian, Duncan thought to himself.

But the Heavenly King said nothing of this, but asked him directly if younger brother from the Western sea would soon join him in his fight against the hateful Manchu.

'We have seen the power of his ships and guns, and with such power we could drive the demon-devils down into Hell.'

There was a part of Duncan that would have liked to assure Hong Xiuquan of this, but he knew he could not.

'Heavenly King, I regret to advise you that no such alliance is possible, at least at this time. Lord Elgin's mission on the Yangze was to enforce the terms of the Treaty of Tientsin, which he has dutifully done. He did allow me to come ashore to find out more about the Taiping way of life, to which Hong Rengan and Foreign Brother Lin-le have kindly introduced me. Lord Elgin also expressed the hope that our nations could maintain a policy of neutrality towards each other.'

Hong Xiuquan was clearly disappointed by this piece of news, but did not immediately pursue the matter.

'And how did you find our Taiping way of life?' he instead questioned.

'I am greatly impressed, sir, by the simple piety and commitment to your cause.'

'But you are not a believer, are you?' Hong shot back.

'On that matter, sir, I also remain neutral,' Duncan responded, anxiously but honestly.

Hong did not respond to this heresy, but returned to his questions about Lord Elgin.

'But where is younger brother from the Western sea at this moment? Would he not agree to meet with me, so that we could discuss the wishes of our Heavenly Father?'

'His business is done here, Heavenly King, and he has already left China and returned to London.'

'When will he return?'

'He will not be returning, at least not unless ...'

'Unless what?' Hong quickly responded.

'Not unless the Manchu renege on the treaty.'

A broad smile spread across Hong's face, and his dark eyes flashed.

'Oh, they will renege on the treaty,' he said, 'of that you may be certain.'

But then the Heavenly King's smile turned to a look of puzzlement, and in a gentle voice he said to Duncan:

'But if you do not believe, then why has she come here with you? Surely you must believe in *her*? I can feel her great love and sorrow.'

As Duncan turned to his side he saw her standing by him, with her same sad smile.

He was amazed and at a loss for words.

He bowed before the Heavenly King and backed out of the throne room, tears streaming down his cheeks.

The Heavenly King closed his eyes and straightway began to dream of Elder Brother Jesus and younger brother from the Western sea.

***

Duncan's last day in Nanking was a Saturday, which was the day of the Taiping sabbath. As on every other day, the great gongs rang out from the Heavenly Palace, summoning the populace to prayer, rumbling out over the city to the villages beyond the great walls. As the golden rays of the early morning sun flung fantastic golden shadows all around, a great humming sound arose from the faithful at prayer, who against all odds still believed their Heavenly King and Heavenly Father would protect them, despite the sight of the fortifications and tents of the Imperial forces crowning the hilltops around them. Lindley and Duncan shared a simple meal with a Taiping family they had come to know well, whose father served in Lindley's Loyal and Faithful Auxiliary Legion, and who delivered the Taiping form of grace:

Heavenly Father, the Great God, bless us thy little ones. Give us day by day food to eat and clothes to wear. Deliver us from evil and calamity, and receive our souls into heaven.

As they left, Lindley remarked to Duncan:
'When I see these honest people, and the strength of their faith, I feel that God would surely never forsake those who so fervently believe his word.'

Duncan was not so sure about that, but he marvelled at how well the Taiping kept the sabbath.

Duncan had taken his leave of General Li and Hong Rengan the previous day, and said that he would do everything in his limited power to persuade the British authorities of their peaceful intentions. He would also champion their cause and commitment to opening up trade with their brethren from the Western sea. Hong Rengan had asked Duncan to send his fond regards to Dr Legge, with the fervent hope that he would understand his need to be with his cousin in his time of great trial and tribulation. Li Xiucheng had asked him to join them in their fight against the Manchu. Duncan had declined, but during this last quiet day of reflection and meditation among the Taiping men and women he had grown to admire, he thought about it once again. He knew it was a worthy cause and that a man ought to fight for what he believed in – but at the end of the day he knew he did not share their faith and felt that he would be a hypocrite pretending to do so. He also thought he could probably do better as an ambassador for their cause than as a soldier in their armies. Yet as he stood with Lindley on the city wall watching the sun going down and heard the murmuring sounds of the Taiping evening prayers rolling over the city like a gentle wave of hope, he wished them well, and hoped that they would prevail.

The following morning at dawn he bade farewell to Lindley, who brought him to the Irish gunrunner who would transport him back safely to Shanghai.

'Pray for us,' he said to Duncan, 'if only in your own way.'

'I will,' Duncan replied, 'and God be with you.'

The two men embraced, and then Duncan boarded the Irishman's lorka. A few minutes later they cast off and began the journey downriver to Shanghai.

10

Ah Keng was in a state of nervous excitement. She had been waiting for Auntie Ki to indulge her opium habit, but nearly two weeks had passed and she had shown no interest. Ah Keng wondered if she dared to try to escape anyway, but then one night, as she wavered over her decision, Auntie Ki gave her girls a smile and sent them to bed early, and then asked Hua Chew to prepare a pipe for her. Ah Keng listened for Hua Chew's footsteps on the stairs, his knock on Auntie's door and then his return to the bench by the front door.

She waited for almost an hour, forcing herself not to rush it – she would only have one chance, so she wanted to make sure both Auntie Ki and Hua Chew were fast asleep before she made her attempt. Then, when she was sure the other girls were asleep, she crept out into the darkness of the landing, and felt her way to the staircase at the back of the house. She lifted the heavy wooden beam with great care and patience, and was very pleased with herself when she managed to remove it and laid it down on the floor without making a sound. She pulled back the narrow wooden door and stepped onto the first set of stairs, pulling the door quietly behind her.

It was dark in the stairwell, but sufficient light filtered down from the skylight for her to see her way forward, as she tiptoed barefoot up the narrow flight of stairs. When she reached the skylight, she had a sudden fear. What if it was bolted too, or stuck fast with age and disuse? But it was not and although it took her every ounce of strength she managed to push it open with her two hands, and found herself looking out over the rooftops of Chinatown, their red tiles bleached dark silver in the moonlight.

She pulled herself through the skylight and crawled across the roof until she thought she was above the drainpipe, and then, inch by creeping inch, lowered herself down over the tiles until she felt her feet slip over the edge and into the empty space beyond. Now for the difficult part. She had to lower herself over the edge and gain a handhold on the drainpipe without slipping; otherwise she was likely to spill her brains on the packed laterite clay in the alley below. She held her breath and took her pack in her teeth, but suddenly the tile she grasped in her right hand came away from the roof! It clattered down by her head and fell into the alley below, while Ah Keng slipped down and toppled over the edge of the roof, her pack falling from her mouth as she gave a little gasp of despair.

In her desperation, she grasped for any surface she could get her hands on, and managed to grab the top of the drainpipe as she slithered off the roof, her body slamming into the brick wall with a force that almost caused her to lose her grip. She held on for grim life, as more loosened tiles tumbled over her head to crash to the ground below. To her ears, the sound of the tiles smashing into pieces in the alley sounded like great explosions, which she was sure would wake the household. She hung there petrified, waiting for the sounds of alarm, and Auntie Ki screaming curses at her – but there was no sound except for the human hum of the night markets and brothels, and the gentle whispering of the surf from the bay. She took a deep breath and began to descend the drainpipe, her heart in her mouth and her ears pricked for any suspicious sound.

Her heart leapt when she suddenly felt the solid earth beneath her feet, but immediately sank when someone gripped her arm with a force like an iron vice. She thought it must be some gangster or robber, but when she turned she saw it was Auntie Ki, her black eyes fixing her with a cold stare.

'So my pretty one,' she said to Ah Keng in a low whisper that was more frightening than if the woman had screamed at the top of her voice, 'you seek your freedom in the open streets of this town, away from the safe house that your Auntie Ki provides for you. Then let me show you the price of your freedom.'

Ah Keng shuddered with fear, her mind racing to the cat torture. But Auntie Ki did not lead her back into the house, but instead dragged her through the night streets. As they passed by the opium dens and brothels on Pagoda Street and Sago Street, they saw young men sitting on benches and leaning against the sides of shophouses, laughing and joking among themselves.

'These are society men. Mainly Ghee Hin and Ghee Hock, but the difference means nothing to you. They find a plum young girl like you alone on the streets, they will have your virginity, and then they will have you over and over, until you scream out for death to put an end to your pain. But they will not kill you, for you will be worth something to them still. They will sell you to the first brothel that will take you, where they will work you until you are too ugly or diseased to attract any more customers, and then you will be sold to service the coolies who work the gambier farms in the jungle, or the tin mines of Sumatra, until you die or end up like one of these!'

Auntie had stopped at the opening of an alley between a row of shophouses and the burnt out remains of a former merchant godown. The smell of urine and excrement was overpowering, mixed with the sickly smell of opium dross, the dregs of the drug that the poor women who lived there fought over – the yellow skinned and red scarred women who offered their bodies and mouths for the least comfort a man might bring them, however poor or diseased that man himself might be. As they stood before the dark entrance to that monstrous place, an old woman, the flesh hanging from her skinny frame like the shroud of a walking corpse, beckoned with lewd gestures of her bony fingers to the men who passed by. And then Ah Keng realized to her horror that she was assuming that the spectre before her was an old woman – for she really had no way of telling the creature's age.

'No more than twenty-five years,' Auntie Ki whispered, as if she had read her thought. 'And she was once a pretty and plump young thing like you.'

Ah Keng gasped as she looked into the woman's eyes, which were as lifeless as the eyes of the dead.

'Have you seen enough, my pretty one?' Auntie Ki asked her.

Ah Keng could not reply, for her throat was choked with horror, but she nodded her agreement, and Auntie Ki led her away and back to their house.

***

Auntie Ki did not subject Ah Keng to the horror of the cat torture. There was no need for it, and they both knew it. Ah Keng would never try to escape again. Or at least she would not until she was in a more powerful position than that of a fatherless, motherless, child alone on the unforgiving streets of Chinatown.

11

Hong Xuiquan had been right. The Manchu did renege on the treaty, objecting to the clause establishing a permanent British ambassador in Peking. The Imperial ambassadors claimed that they had only agreed to this condition under duress, but now realized that it would represent such a humiliation to the Emperor that it was likely to bring down the Manchu dynasty, and leave the Celestial Empire in the hands of the Taiping rebels.

But the British government would not reconsider the clause, and Frederick Bruce, Lord Elgin's younger brother, was sent out to China in the spring as the first British ambassador in Peking, to ratify the Treaty of Tientsin with the Emperor in the Imperial capital.

* * *

In May, Captain Collyer began work on the new fortification on Government Hill. Government House was demolished, and Governor Blundell went to live at the Pavilion[lxxvi] on Oxley Estate. Four hundred Chinese coolies worked to excavate a plateau on the top of Government Hill, while Indian convicts brought loads of cut stone from Pulau Ubin and bricks from the government kilns on Serangoon Road. To the great distress of the Chinese coolies, the

lxxvi The Pavilion was one of five houses built on the nutmeg estate of Dr Thomas Oxley (1805-1886), on a hill that came to known as Oxley's Hill, near Orchard Road.

summit of Government Hill was found to be infested with cobras, both the regular black cobras, or kala samp, and king cobras. A reward was offered for their capture, and to everyone's relief some of the Indian convicts proved to be experts at catching the deadly snakes. They showed no fear of them, but followed them to their burrows, and grasped them by the tail, running their other hand along the snake's body until they grasped it by the head, allowing the snake to wind itself around their arm. When they brought the snakes to the jail to collect their reward, they asked the snake's forgiveness for betraying them to their master before they were killed.

***

Frederick Bruce arrived in Shanghai in May, where he met with Monsieur de Bourbolon, the French minister and representative of the Emperor Napoleon III. They received a request from the Imperial court for the Treaty of Tientsin to be ratified in Shanghai rather than Peking, and by the Emperor's younger brother Prince Kung rather than the Emperor himself.

Lord Elgin's younger brother would have none of it. He insisted that as Her Majesty's ambassador to Peking, he would travel directly to the Imperial capital with a large military force, appropriate to his station, and ratify the treaty with the Emperor in person. In the middle of June, Frederick Bruce and Monsieur de Bourbolon arrived at the mouth of the Peiho river with sixteen warships.

Rear-Admiral James Hope, who was in charge of the allied naval squadron, reported to Bruce that the Chinese had laid three heavy iron booms across the mouth of the river, and had repaired and refortified the Taku Forts that had been destroyed the previous year. The British ambassador to Peking sent a message to the Imperial court demanding that the barriers be lifted, and their ships allowed to proceed up the Peiho river. Hsien Feng was prepared to acquiesce to their demands, but Yohonala and the Prince of I worked together to persuade him to refuse their insolence. The Emperor replied that he would not remove the barriers, but would be happy to arrange for carts to take the civilian members of Mr Bruce's party to Peking.

When Her Majesty's ambassador to Peking received the Emperor's response, he ordered Rear-Admiral James Hope to destroy the barriers and raze the forts.

* * *

On the morning of June 25, Rear-Admiral Hope led the assault on the Taku forts with eleven steam gunships, bearing forty-eight guns and over five hundred sailors and marines. In their failed attempt to remove the booms across the river, one of the gunboats was sunk and six disabled, with heavy casualties, as they faced intense and unremitting fire from the Qing batteries in the forts. Later in the day the marines and sailors launched a land assault on the South Fort, but were cut down by relentless Qing shot, canister and musketry, and retreated back to the ships after suffering five hundred casualties. A despondent Frederick Bruce ordered the wounded Rear-Admiral Hope to turn the fleet around and return to Shanghai.

12

When news reached the Imperial court of the defeat of the foreign barbarians at the Taku forts, there was great jubilation and celebration. Although the Qing army of Zeng Guofan had been recently defeated by the Taiping at the Battle of Sanhe,[lxxvii] the victory against the British showed that the Dragon Emperor could still breathe fire upon his enemies, and send the British Lion scurrying away with its tail between its legs. Hsien Feng felt empowered by the great victory, and needed little persuasion from Yehonala and the other hawks at court to repudiate the terms of the Treaty of Tientsin. He also felt invigorated, and on the night after the news of the great victory was received, his Jade Stalk grew long and hard, and he exploded his royal essence into the Jade Garden of his beloved Orchid, first concubine Cixi, the Empress Hsiao Ch'in.

***

Duncan arrived back in Shanghai at the end of June, and travelled on to Hong Kong before returning to Singapore. He consulted with Ian Fraser, the manager of Simpson and Co, on how their business was doing in Hong Kong. Fraser assured him that it was doing just grand. Duncan also went to visit Dr Legge, who had returned from his medical leave, and conveyed Hong Rengan's messages to him.

'I understand his position, Duncan,' Legge replied, 'and why he felt he had to join his cousin. It is his war, and no doubt his destiny, whatever the outcome. I get the occasional message smuggled

---

lxxvii Three Rivers.

through. He even sent me a large sum of money to support our Christian mission, which I'm afraid I could not accept – at least not until this civil war is settled. But how I miss my dear old friend! I don't believe I've ever enjoyed another man's friendship over his. But you must tell me all about your time in Nanking, and what you learned about the Taiping ways. But wait, let me get a pen and paper, so I can take notes.'

Duncan spent the next few hours recounting his experiences, while Dr Legge peppered him with questions about the mysterious God-followers and their beliefs and practices. When Duncan finally left, Dr Legge thanked him profusely for his time and trouble, and wished him safe passage to Singapore.

'But I suspect we will see you again sooner rather than later, Duncan,' he said, 'for I doubt that matters are settled in China yet.'

* * *

Duncan arrived back in Singapore in July. His family were overjoyed to see him and anxious to hear about his adventures in China. He told his father, grandfather and brother-in-law Charles Singer that, despite the recent setbacks and civil war, their trade with China was bound to continue to expand, and he recommended the development of their offices in Hong Kong and Shanghai – and perhaps in Peking or Nanking one of these days.

By the time they went to their beds, only one thing was decided, which was that Duncan would have to go back to Hong Kong to develop their office there. Duncan warned them that if he did so he might be called into government service again, since the British government was bound to respond vigorously to the shameful defeat at the Taku Forts. Yet they all agreed that even if this proved to be the case, it would very likely be in their commercial interest in the long run.

13

It was the time of the mid-Autumn festival, when country people in China prayed to the moon and celebrated the harvest bounties. It was celebrated in Singapore on the fifteenth day of the eighth lunar month, when the night markets in Chinatown displayed choice delicacies and cakes, and the normally shadowy streets were emblazoned with the lights of hundreds of lanterns hung from the windows and the five-foot ways.[lxxviii] Of all the delicacies and cakes displayed, the most popular were the mooncakes, which celebrated renewal and completeness in the family.

Siti had taken her grandchild, Kai Kam, to the celebrations. Kai Kam was the daughter of Tan Eng Guan, the son of Song Nao, who had been Tan Hong Chuan's first wife, and who had committed suicide to avoid the shame of her gambling debts. Tan Eng Guan had married six years ago, and Siti was secretly delighted when their first child had been a girl (everyone else had been hoping, as usual, for a boy). Siti had given Tan Hong Chuan two other sons (and although Lee Cheng had died tragically, he and Pek Chiat had produced another son), but she had always wanted a girl, and had decided that, if she could not have her own daughter to love and spoil, she would love and spoil Kai Kam.

Earlier in the evening she had taken the child, who was dressed in the pretty red silk dress that Siti had bought for her, to her first

---

lxxviii The Singapore town plan of 1823 specified that each house should have a covered passageway with a depth of five feet, which became known as 'five-foot ways'.

Chinese opera, performed by a travelling company who had set up their stage on stilts on the western bank of the Singapore river. As they travelled in their palanquin from the opera to Chinatown, where Siti intended to purchase a box of mooncakes from the best confectioner there, Kai Kam begged her grandmother to tell her the story of the origin of mooncakes.

'But I have told you that story many times before, Kai Kam,' Siti laughed in response. 'Surely you are tired of it by now. And it is not really a proper story for little girls – although I dare say that is why you like it,' she laughed again.

'Well,' Siti began, leaning forward and whispering conspiratorially to her granddaughter, as if they were sharing some great secret, which Siti knew she loved:

During the time of the Yuan Dynasty, China was ruled by the Mongols, whose first Emperor was Kublai Khan, a grandson of Genghis Khan. The people were oppressed by the foreigners, who occupied all the positions of power in the government, from the highest mandarin to the lowliest local magistrate. The Mongols knew they were hated by the people, and were in constant fear of rebellion, so they decided to station a Mongol warrior in each household, to prevent the local people meeting together in someone's house to organize an uprising. However, some of the men managed to congregate while working in the fields to collect the harvest, and they decided to plan an uprising on the night of the mid-Autumn festival. That evening the conspirators went from house to house, delivering to each a cake in the shape of the full moon, which they told the master of the house to cut open that night to reveal the filling. When they did so, they found a message written on a strip of rice paper, instructing them to kill the Mongol soldier in their house on the stroke of midnight, which would signal the beginning of a general rebellion.

And so, on the stroke of midnight, the people fell upon the hated Mongols as they slept in their beds, sending them to Hell with swords, axes, knives, and heavy stones. In the morning the people joined together and took up arms against the remaining foreigners. Zhu Yuanzhang, a poor farmer himself, led his people to their freedom, and consequently founded the Ming dynasty. So, on the night of the mid-Autumn festival, we eat mooncakes to celebrate our freedom, and the renewal and completeness of our family, as Zhu Yuanzhang restored the completeness of our country.

Siti did not mention that the Manchu, another set of foreigners, had overthrown the Ming Dynasty two hundred years ago, or that foreign barbarians, including the British, who ruled Singapore, were threatening to divide up the country among themselves. Let her enjoy her mooncakes, Siti thought, in innocent ignorance of the great struggles that were taking place in China.

Siti looked out through the curtains of the palanquin and saw that they were only a street away from the market that had the best mooncakes, so she told the bearers to let them out at the next corner, and wait for their return. Then, taking Kai Kam by the hand, she made her way through the crowd to her favourite confectioner, and spent some time carefully comparing the mooncakes on offer; when she and Kai Kam had sampled one of those she had chosen, and agreed that they were delightfully sweet, she agreed to buy a box of them to take home.

As she reached into her purse to take out her coins with her right hand, she kept a firm hold on Kai Kam with her left, although it was a difficult manoeuvre. But as she handed over the coins, Kai Kam cried out 'Grannie, grannie, look at these,' and her little hand slipped from Siti's grasp as she pulled away to inspect the brightly coloured mooncakes she had spotted. When Siti turned to retrieve Kai Kam's hand she realized that the girl was gone. She summoned the servants and they searched the market and the streets beyond, but there was no sign of Kai Kam. The child had vanished like a fox-spirit in the night. Siti's heart, which had been so full of joy a moment before, was now filled with dread. She had lost her eldest son – she could not bear to lose her only granddaughter.

14

Mother Mathilde stifled her yawn. It had been a long day, but she did not wish to betray to the other sisters how tired she was. She knew they all worked as hard as she did, and she did not want them to fuss over her during their simple evening meal, which they always took together in

the semi-circular room on the first floor of Caldwell House.

The nuns of the Convent of the Holy Infant Jesus had been in Singapore for five years now, and it was a wonder they had survived. Their convent school had attracted few fee-paying students, but had attracted increasing numbers of orphans, often abandoned on their doorstep, as well as the sick and dying of all nationalities and faiths. The nuns could barely feed and clothe themselves, but they would not turn anyone away, and did their very best to provide comfort and hope to those whom God had entrusted to their care. To her great disappointment, Mother Mathilde had received little support from the Christian community in Singapore, either Catholic or Protestant. The Convent of the Holy Infant Jesus would probably not have survived without Father Beurel's support from his own pocket, and the benefaction of some of the wealthy Chinese merchants, who did not share their faith but appreciated the shelter and nourishment they provided for abandoned Chinese babies and orphans. One of these, Cheang Hong Lim, a licensed opium and spirit merchant, had recently donated money for new buildings to house the boarders and orphans, to replace the plank and attap[lxxix]

---

lxxix Thatch made from the leaves of the attap palm.

huts that had been hastily erected during their first year.

While she waited for the others to join her for dinner, she heard a knock on the door downstairs. A few minutes later, Sister St Margarite came in and told her there was a man downstairs with a Chinese child, practically naked, whom he had brought to them.

'Well, then, Sister Margarite, we must make the child welcome in the House of our Lord.'

'Yes, Reverend Mother,' Sister Margarite replied, 'but I am not sure we should.'

'Dear Lord, why ever not?' Mother Mathilde replied. 'You know that we do not turn children away, whatever their race or creed.'

'I understand, Reverend Mother,' said Sister St Margarite, 'but the man says he wants money for the child. He has heard that priests and nuns will pay money to convert heathen children to our faith. Surely that is not true, Reverend Mother?'

'It most certainly is not!' replied Mother Mathilde, her jaw dropping. 'Yet we must see to the child's care. I will come down and meet with this man. But I want you to leave by the back door this instant and summon the police, because I suspect this man is not the child's relation.'

She had heard this rumour before, although she had only heard it in reference to Catholic priests working on the Chinese mainland. She supposed this man must have come from there or heard it from some recent arrival. She knew the rumour was false, but she knew how dangerous it was, for it encouraged evil men to trade in children.

She went down the stairs to the hall, where the man stood waiting with the child. He was dressed in black pants and a dirty singlet, the child in her undergarments.

Mother Mathilde did not address the man, but asked Sister St Connolly, who had a gift for languages and had quickly learned the

Chinese dialects, to ask the girl if the man she was with was her father, or any sort of relation. The child did not reply and the man was angered by the question, demanding to know whether they would pay for the child or not – it was no business of theirs whether he was related to her or not.

When his reply was translated, Mother Mathilde instructed Sister St Connolly to tell the man that of course it was their business, since they would only take a child from a caring parent or relative, and would never buy a child in order to raise it in the faith. While Sister St Connolly was conveying this reply, the little girl nodded her head from side to side in silent response to Sister St Connolly's original question and then broke away from the man's grasp and ran towards Mother Mathilde, who grasped her to her black habit.

The man gave them a dark look, and then, before anything else could be said, turned and bolted back through the front door, leaving the tearful girl in their care. A few minutes later Sister St Margarite arrived with two police peons. More men were summoned to search the streets, but they could find no trace of the kidnapper.

Without waiting for the evening meal, Sister Mathilde had the police peons take her to the office of Superintendent Dunman. That night Tom Dunman and Mother Mathilde travelled in a police carriage to the homes of the leaders of the Chinese community, where they met with Whampoa, Seah Eu Chin, Tan Kim Ching and Cheang Hong Lim. They asked of them two favours: first, their help in locating the parents of the child, who, although she was too afraid to talk to them, Mother Mathilde was sure had been kidnapped; and second, to put the word out to their communities that the rumour that priests and nuns would pay money to convert Chinese children to the Catholic faith was a false and evil rumour. Inspector Dunman added that they should also convey to their communities the fact that any person caught trafficking in children would be severely punished.

A few days later Tan Hong Chuan and Siti were alarmed when a woman dressed completely in black came to visit them. At first, they thought she was an evil spirit come to warn them of some new calamity, but were overjoyed when Mother Mathilde brought forward their granddaughter Kai Kam from a waiting carriage and explained what had happened to her. Then and there Hong Chuan promised to make a donation to the Convent of the Holy Infant Jesus, and Mother Mathilde thanked him for his generosity, which she said would enable them to serve God's children for a little longer. After Mother Mathilde had left and they had stopped smothering their granddaughter with hugs and kisses, they asked Kai Kam if she was hungry and what did she want to eat.

And her answer was mooncakes.

15

Work continued apace on Captain Collyer's new fortification on Government Hill, whose summit had been raised to form a level surface for the seven acres of defensive ramparts, and already seven 68-pound gun emplacements had been set up overlooking the sea. Fort Fullerton was also being rebuilt to three times its original size, extending from the river to Johnston's Pier, and armed with 56- and 68-pound guns. As if to emphasize the new militarization of the town, Lord Canning had appointed Colonel William Orfeur Cavenagh as the new governor of the Straits Settlements in August, Governor Blundell having resigned in July. Colonel Cavenagh was a career soldier who had distinguished himself in the Punjab wars, when he had lost a leg, and during the mutiny, when he had taken early precautions to prevent Fort William in Calcutta being overrun by the mutineers. He was a short, stout man with a bald head, rimless spectacles on a pug nose and wispy grey sideburns. He always wore his uniform and decorations, and retained his military bearing, despite his wooden leg, which was considerably offset by the charger that he rode around town when on official business.

***

On December 24, John Murray and Company published Charles Darwin's book-length treatment of his theory of the transmutation of species through natural selection, entitled *On the Origin of Species by Natural Selection, or the Preservation of Favoured Races in the Struggle for Life.* In the introduction to the work, Darwin acknowledged that Wallace had independently developed the same theory of natural selection:

'Mr Wallace, who is now studying the natural history of the Malay archipelago, has arrived at almost exactly the same general conclusions that I have on the origin of species.'

The book was an instant success – the first print run of 1250 copies sold out on the first day of publication – and immediately generated a storm of scientific and religious controversy.

The following day Alfred Wallace, who was collecting beetles on Ceram, one the Moluccas Islands, wrote to his old friend H.W. Bates, congratulating him on the publication of his recent book on the fauna of the Amazon valley. Wallace told Bates that he was developing a theory of the distribution of species in the Malay Archipelago and was contemplating writing a book on the subject.

***

The years of dissolute behaviour were taking a heavy toll on the health of the Emperor Hsien Feng, but he remained buoyed by the victory over the barbarians at the Taku forts. Yehonala assured him that the cowardly big-nosed curs would not dare to enforce their treaties now, and that they would soon attain final victory over the Taiping rebels. The Imperial Jiangnan army group had two hundred thousand infantrymen and cavalry ringing the hills surrounding Nanking, and would soon crush the long-haired dogs.

Back in Britain, Lord Palmerston, the prime minister, informed his cabinet that they must make the Chinese pay for their latest outrage. He suggested that they send a combined military and naval force to occupy Peking, and force the Emperor to accept their demands. Lord Elgin, who was now a member of the cabinet, supported the proposed expeditionary force, but cautioned them about the dangers of occupying Peking. He suggested instead that a thirty-day ultimatum be delivered to the Emperor, demanding an apology for the hostilities at the Taku forts, the payment of new reparations to compensate for the loss of life and property and his promise to ratify the terms of the Treaty of Tientsin. Although Palmerston and most of his cabinet were intent on war, they deferred to the old China hand and reluctantly agreed to Lord Elgin's suggestion.

16

In early March, Frederick Bruce, Her Majesty's ambassador to Peking, dispatched Lord Palmerston's thirty-day ultimatum to the Emperor Hsien Feng. Bruce had received instructions to deliver the ultimatum the previous year, but had delayed doing so, because he did not think that Palmerston's threat to cut off rice supplies to the city by blockading the Peiho river would have any force until rice shipments from the provinces were due to be delivered in the spring.

The Emperor and Yehonala convinced themselves that the long-delayed ultimatum was a sign of fear and weakness on the part of the British government, who had not dared to send their armies and gunboats against them again after their humiliating defeat. They treated the ultimatum with the scorn they thought it deserved and quickly rejected all its terms. The Emperor would never apologize to the barbarians – it was they who must apologize to him and withdraw their insulting treaty demands.

***

Hong Xiuquan's son Tiangui Fu, the Young Monarch, was now eleven years old. Hong repeated to his son the message that his Holy Father – Tiangui's Holy Grandfather – had given him many years before. Tiangui should have no fear, for God and Jesus would always be by his side. In April, Tiangui had a dream. Two giant serpents had encircled the Heavenly City, but he had gone out through the great gates and slain them with his demon-destroying sword. The following day the Heavenly King issued an edict with an interpretation of Tiangui's dream, which prophesied the relief of the city and victory over the Qing armies arrayed against its walls.

***

In April, Lord Elgin was once again appointed Her Majesty's Special Plenipotentiary to China, with extraordinary powers to determine when and where to negotiate with the Chinese, what terms to impose, and – in consultation with the military and naval commanders who headed the British expeditionary force – whether to advance on, attack and occupy the Imperial capital. He set out for Shanghai at the end of the month, where he planned to join up again with Baron Gros, who would have authority over the French expedition. When Lord Elgin arrived in Shanghai in late June, he was pleased to hear that Duncan Simpson was also there exploring the prospects for setting up an office of Simpson and Co. He immediately sent a request for Duncan to join him on the new expedition, as an aide in what were bound to prove difficult negotiations with the Manchu, and to join him for dinner to recount his adventures in the Taiping capital.

The British and French forces had already set up their forward bases south of the mouth of the Peiho river. The British troops, thirteen thousand strong, commanded by Lieutenant-General Sir Hope Grant, a veteran of the first China War and the mutiny, were established at Tahlien Bay; the French force of six and a half thousand men, commanded by General Charles Montauban, were at Chefu to the west. The British forces were well equipped, and their supply train contained a corps of over two thousand coolies recruited from Hong Kong.

Although the Sepoy regiments were still issued with percussion muskets, the British regiments were equipped with new Enfield rifles. Some of the artillery brigades were equipped with the new breech-loading and rifled Armstrong guns, which were far more accurate and had a greater range than the old smoothbore and muzzle-loaded cannon, and which could fire fused shells that could burst into shrapnel in the air, as well as regular shot, canister and shell.

17

In May, Li Xiucheng and Hong Rengan set their earthly campaign against the Qing in motion. Li Xiucheng, the Loyal King, broke out with a few thousand battle-hardened Taiping veterans, dashed across the Yangtze delta and threatened the city of Hangzhou. When the Qing sent heavy reinforcements to relieve the city, General Li force-marched his troops back to the weakened Qing emplacements, where he was joined by the army of Shi Dakai, who had fought a continuous campaign through fifteen provinces in the west since he had left Nanking three years before. During a snowstorm they fell upon the Qing battalions, while Hong Rengan rode out of Nanking and took them in the rear as they fled down from the hills towards the city. In the slaughter that followed, the Imperial Jiangnan army group lost over sixty thousand men, including many of its senior commanders, and fled in disarray into the north. After their great victory, Shi Dakai returned to his campaign in the west, while General Li led his victorious forces east and captured the city of Suzhou, some thirty miles from Shanghai, where his troops massed for their final assault.

When the Emperor heard of the humiliating defeat of his armies before Nanking, he was furious at the incompetence of his commanders, whose suicides he demanded. Although it proved very difficult in the face of his fit of blind anger, Yehonala managed to persuade Hsien Feng to appoint Zeng Guofan as commander of the southern armies. Zeng Guofan, with his able lieutenants

Zuo[lxxx] Zongtang and Li Hongzhang, had driven the rebels out of Hunan and Guangxi provinces, and were advancing north towards Nanking.

* * *

'Mr Duncan Simpson to see you, sir,' said the adjutant, opening the door to Lord Elgin's rooms at the British Consulate in Shanghai. Duncan stepped inside.

Lord Elgin was sitting at a desk in blue uniform trousers and shirtsleeves, rolled up to the elbows. He laid aside the book he had been reading and rose to greet Duncan.

'Grand to see you again, Duncan, and I'm so glad to find you here. I need you more than ever. There will be some difficult dealings with the Emperor's people, I'm sure, and I want to leave nothing to chance. There's no telling which way this thing is going to go, with the Taiping having raised the siege at Nanking and taken Suzhou. My God, man, they are almost at the gates!'

'I'm most happy to be of service to Her Majesty's government again, sir, and hope that some good will come of it,' Duncan replied. 'I heard about the Taiping successes, but please be assured that we have nothing to fear from them. They only want a peaceful agreement with us, whom they call their Christian brethren. But let me tell you what I learned about them during my stay at Nanking – I perhaps did not express myself as well as I might in my letters to you.'

Lord Elgin poured them both a glass of sherry, then put his booted feet up on his desk, while he listened to Duncan try and persuade him of the Taiping's commitment to a Christian brotherhood of man. Duncan told him how the Taiping had

---

lxxx Known in the West as General Tso, after whom the spicy and sweet fried chicken dish is named.

abolished slavery, concubinage, the hated queue and foot binding, and how they treated men and women as equal citizens, having abolished private property, with all goods and services held for the common good and distributed equally among the citizenry. He also described their humble faith in their loving Heavenly Father and his Son who had redeemed them, even though Duncan himself did not share their faith – or optimism – about their future.

After Duncan had finished, Lord Elgin removed his feet from his desk and sat looking thoughtfully at him. Eventually he spoke.

'Fascinating, quite fascinating. You may be right, Duncan – we may be looking at a genuine social revolution in China. But don't you realize how dangerous these ideas are, young man? The Western powers wouldn't take kindly to the abolition of personal property, I can tell you!'

'Oh, but that's only for the Chinese,' Duncan replied. 'The Taiping are perfectly willing to let Western merchants trade throughout the land, and Western missionaries to travel wherever they please.'

'But not to trade in opium, I'm sure,' Elgin reminded him.

'That is true enough, sir, but why should they? Why should they allow their people to become addicted to that poisonous drug?'

'Because, I'm afraid – and now I'm speaking about the Manchu – the revenue from the opium trade is too lucrative for them,' Lord Elgin replied. 'Which is why, in a nutshell, I am back here negotiating with them.'

He saw Duncan's face flush red and held up his hand to block what he expected would be a spirited defence of the Taiping ban on opium.

'But hold up. I am not here to bless or blame, but only to carry out the directives of Her Majesty's government. It may be that we will be forced to take Peking and break the power of the Manchu Emperor, in which case the Taiping will likely prevail. And they may prevail in any case – they seem to have some very capable military commanders. My only hope is that they do not provoke an incident in Shanghai. Are you sure they will communicate their peaceful intentions to my brother?'

'I am certain of it, 'Duncan assured him. 'I was promised this by General Li himself.'

'Good, good,' Lord Elgin replied, 'then we should have nothing to fear.'

As Lord Elgin rose from his chair, Duncan noticed the book that he had been reading – Charles Darwin's *On the Origin of Species*.

'Do you think the principle of natural selection – the survival of the fittest – applies to men and societies, Lord Elgin?'

'Good question, Duncan,' Elgin replied. 'Darwin says nothing about man in his book, although the bishops and the popular press are complaining that he says we are all descended from apes. Still, I'm sure it does, with the qualification that societies are unfortunately not always left to develop naturally. I dare say if we left the Taiping and Qing to fight it out between themselves, the best adapted would survive, but we're not going to do that. We're going to intervene in their affairs again in a major way – as we did in India – and I don't think anyone can foresee the consequences, for ourselves or for China.'

'Well, if I were the prime minister,' Duncan responded, 'I would offer up Shanghai to the Taiping, and supply them with modern munitions and gunboats so they could triumph over the Manchu, and regain their own country. But don't worry, sir, I will maintain my neutrality while negotiating with the Manchu, as I hope we will maintain our neutrality in our dealings with the Taiping.'

'I hope so too,' said Lord Elgin, pulling on his jacket and buttoning it up. 'But now let's go and meet my brother and have some dinner.'

***

On July 8, Lord Canning, the Governor-General of India, declared the Indian Mutiny at an end, and declared that a 'State of Peace' reigned throughout the subcontinent. A special day of thanksgiving and prayer was held three weeks later.

***

The new Tan Tock Seng Hospital, which had been relocated at the junction of Serangoon Road and Balestier Road, was completed in the middle of the year, although the patients were not moved from Pearl's Hill until the following year. John Turnbull Thomson, the government architect who had designed the original hospital building, also designed the new classically proportioned building. Tan Kim Ching, Tan Tock Seng's eldest son, supervised the move and contributed more than half of the cost, with the government contributing the remainder. His mother, Lee Seo Neo, Tan Tock Seng's widow, contributed funds for a female ward, and a leper ward was also added. Conditions did not improve much at the new hospital, where overcrowding remained a problem, and its situation at the edge of a swamp was not conducive to the health of the patients, who were nonetheless glad to have been moved from the makeshift huts on Pearl's Hill. Among the Malays, the new hospital gained the nickname 'rumah miskin', or 'pauper house'.

18

A year had passed since Ah Keng had tried to make her escape. The two older girls had been sold, one as part of a rich bride's wedding dowry, the other to what Auntie Ki had called a good family, by which Ah Keng now understood meant she went to a higher-class brothel, where the girls had to serve only half a dozen men a night, and sometimes only one, when a rich client could pay for the whole night.

Ah Keng had begun to wonder what would happen to her, when Auntie Ki seemed to read her thoughts once again.

'Do not worry, my pretty one,' she said, 'I have great plans for you. I am going to find you a man that will make both our fortunes.'

Over the next few weeks a number of men came to visit her, mostly young or middle-aged men. They asked her questions and had her parade up and down before them, then made her show them her breasts and behind. Then she would be dismissed and she would hear Auntie Ki haggling with them over the price. But although she found some of the men quite attractive, and thought that there were far worse fates than being a concubine or servant to such men, they never returned, for Auntie Ki never completed the sale.

Then one day Auntie Ki rose early and spent all morning preparing Ah Keng's make-up and hair, then brought out a beautiful red silk dress and embroidered slippers. The old woman fussed and muttered to herself, and pinched Ah Keng with her fingers when she would not sit still or co-operate with her instructions. When Auntie Ki finally seemed satisfied with her work, she smiled broadly, then sent Hua Chew out for a carriage and instructed the driver to take them to a house in Tanglin. Ah Keng had heard of Tanglin from the other girls. She knew that was where the rich Chinese had their houses.

The house they arrived at was grander than any house she had seen before, in Singapore or Amoy. It was built of grey stone and had an imposing wrought iron gate, beside which stood two giant white marble lions, the male with his paw resting on a ball and the female with her paw resting upon a cub. She had seen such pairs before, outside the doors of temples. She knew the master of the house must be a rich man to afford such an expensive extravagance.

They were taken into the main entrance hall of the house, which was furnished with heavy dark teak tables and chairs and cabinets, ornately carved. It was decorated with jade and ivory statues and elaborate painted screens, and hung with rich tapestries from its high walls. In the centre of the hall the mistress of the house sat upon a high chair in silken robes, her tiny bound feet tucked neatly beneath her. She had a long thin face with high cheekbones, which might have been beautiful were it not for her thin red lips, which even when she smiled betrayed her cruel nature. When she spoke, her voice tinkled in a high sing song, but it was not musical – it reminded Ah Keng of breaking glass.

Auntie Ki gently nudged her forward, and the young woman began asking her questions. Was she a virgin? How old was she? Was she healthy? Was she honest? Then she ordered Ah Keng to turn around before her and, seemingly satisfied by what she saw, clapped her hands and then signalled to one of the young girls who served her, who left the room on her command.

For a moment nothing happened, while the young woman sat in silence and Ah Keng stood in silence. Then the old man entered the room, wearing only a black silk robe and a pair of ragged slippers. He was a very old man, bent almost double as he shuffled his way across the marble floor, with almost translucent skin and deep, sad brown eyes. If he had been a friend's grandfather, Ah Keng might have looked kindly on him, but she knew his intent was not that of a grandfather. As he drew close to her she could see that he was missing most of his teeth, as his gums parted in a lurid grin. He inspected her breasts, he smelt her armpits and then stepped round behind her, where, to her shame and embarrassment, Auntie Ki held up her dress to reveal her buttocks and exclaimed with laugher:

'See, Mr Ho, even her bottom makes music!'

The old man also found this funny and emitted a low chuckle, although the mistress of the house retained her thin cold smile.

Then he walked round to face her again and, on his command, Auntie Ki came forward and pulled aside her dress to reveal her vagina. The old man summoned one of the servants to come forward with tray of fruit, and taking a fresh date in his hand, handed it to Auntie Ki, who, to her shock and dismay, gently inserted the fruit into her vulva, then slowly withdrew it again and handed it back to the old man.

The old man smelt the date with infinite care, then popped it into his mouth, clearly savouring the taste. Then he called for Auntie Ki to come forward, and the negotiations began between Auntie Ki and the old man and the mistress of the house, while Ah Keng was taken to wait in another room. When Auntie Ki returned to join her, she was beaming from ear to ear. In the carriage on the journey home, she told Ah Keng that they had driven a hard bargain, but she had finally got them to accept a price one and a half times what she had been prepared to accept! She had shown them the high offers from the younger suitors, and that had made all the difference, she said, and in the end the old man, whose name was Ho Bee Swee, had grown impatient with his daughter-in-law's quibbling and had agreed upon the price for the virgin concubine.

19

Lord Elgin joined the British forces at Tahlien Bay on July 11, accompanied by Duncan and the Honourable William de Norman, cousin of the Marquis of Northampton. De Norman had come out to China as an aide to Frederick Bruce, but had asked to join Lord Elgin's staff so he could accompany him to Peking, when he learned that Frederick Bruce would be remaining in Shanghai. Lieutenant-General Sir Hope Grant advised Lord Elgin that he was prepared to move against the Taku forts, but was waiting for General Montauban to procure mules for his field guns. They had already decided not to make the mistake of the previous year by attacking the forts from the mouth of the river, but were instead planning to land their men further north and take them from the rear.

The allied fleet – over two hundred men-of-war, gunships and transports, containing nearly twenty thousand men, horses, munitions and supplies – set out on July 26. On July 31, they anchored at the mouth of the Pehtang river, about nine miles north of the Taku forts. The following day, the army disembarked unopposed. They had expected strong resistance, but found that the forts commanding the river and town were deserted. As they advanced south, large bodies of Tartar cavalry, commanded by General Senggelinqin, who had destroyed the Taiping northern expedition, challenged them, but these were quickly dispersed by allied artillery and cavalry counter-attacks.

***

When the British ambassador Frederick Bruce heard that the Taiping army was massing at Suzhou, he was outraged and quickly conferred with his French counterpart, M. de Bourbolon, who agreed that they should organize a military and civilian force in defence of Shanghai in the event of an attack. On August 16 Ambassador Bruce issued a public declaration, a copy of which he ordered sent to General Li Xiucheng aboard a gunboat, warning that if armed bodies of men approached the city they would be considered as commencing hostilities against the British and French forces stationed there and would be dealt with accordingly. Unfortunately, the gunboat steamed past the Taiping line of advance, so the message was never delivered. General Li never learned that Ambassador Bruce had decided to renege upon the policy of neutrality toward the Taiping, which had been affirmed by Governor Bonham and Lord Elgin.

***

While General Li Xiucheng was camped with his victorious army outside Suzhou, he met with a party of French merchants and other European nationals, who invited him to come to Shanghai to establish friendly relations and discuss future trading agreements. General Li was greatly encouraged by the meeting. He was confident that the Chinese defenders of Shanghai would yield up the city with only token resistance, as they had done at Suzhou, to avoid significant bloodshed. And now he was optimistic that his Western brethren would welcome them with open arms. But heedful of the advice of Hong Rengan and Commander Lin-Le, he sent a letter to all the foreign ambassadors, assuring them of his peaceful intentions toward them and advising them of the precautions they should take when his troops entered Shanghai.

General Li also issued a harsh admonition to his troops not to fire upon or attack any of their foreign brethren and issued an edict that all their property must be protected. And in order not to alarm his foreign brethren, General Li did not advance on Shanghai with his full army on August 18, but with only a force of three thousand men drawn from his own personal bodyguard. This small force quickly dislodged the Qing troops from the outlying forts and then marched in peace upon the western gate of Shanghai.

20

Having displaced the Qing from the forward outposts, the Taiping soldiers advanced toward the city walls, eager to unite with their foreign brethren. They were not met with hospitality and friendship, but with shot, shell, canister and musketry from the British, French and American forces arrayed along the city walls. As the hail of iron and lead tore through their ranks, the Taiping soldiers stood astonished before the city walls, like men of stone – unbelieving – obedient to their general's order not to attack their foreign brethren. As they waited in the deadly storm, they prayed that their Christian brothers would recognize their error, and waved to them to signal their desire for peaceful communication, but they waited and prayed and waved in vain.

* * *

Among the Westerners firing down upon the Taiping forces that day were the remains of the Foreign Arms Corps, a force of well-armed foreign mercenaries raised by Frederick Townsend Ward,[6] which had been financed by the rich Shanghai and Ningpo merchants Xuan Yang and Yang Fang.

Ward had arrived in Shanghai earlier in the year and had originally contemplated offering his services to the Taiping. Instead he served as executive officer aboard the American gunship the *Confucius*, financed by the 'Shanghai Pirate Suppression Bureau'. Impressed by Ward's initiative in taking the fight to the pirates, the

Shanghai officials invited him to raise a mercenary force of foreign nationals to help defend Shanghai against the encroaching Taiping forces. Backed by his merchant financiers, by late June Ward had assembled an assorted force of drunks, deserters, discharged sailors and adventurers, whom he had lured with promises of generous pay, adventure and pillage. They were some hundred strong, armed with the best rifles and revolvers money could buy in Shanghai, and were supplemented in July by eighty Filipino Manilamen. The British authorities had originally tried to discourage Ward's mercenary activities, because of their professed neutrality towards the Taiping, but they lost what influence they had over him after he married the daughter of Yang Fang and consequently became a Chinese subject.

Ward was a small wiry man, with wavy black hair, moustache and goatee beard, whose amiable and cheerful disposition belied the fierce intensity of his fighting spirit, which only the piercing blackness of his eyes betrayed. While his detractors dismissed him and his mercenaries as paid gangsters, Ward had proven his worth by capturing the Taiping held town of Sunkiang, albeit with heavy casualties, including himself – he received a minor wound as he led his men into battle armed with nothing more than his walking stick.

Buoyed by their victory, Ward had led his men into action again in early August against the Taiping forces occupying the town of Chingpu. As his men stormed the town walls, Ward rejoiced in what appeared to be an easy victory, but his rejoicing turned to self-reproach when he led his men into a deadly Taiping ambush. Half his force was destroyed and Ward received an incapacitating wound to his left jaw, which forced him to return to Shanghai for medical treatment. He left the remains of his Foreign Arms Corps in charge of his second in command, Henry Andres Burgevine, the son of a French officer in Napoleon's army. Burgevine had settled in North Carolina, but had served in the Crimea and also for a time as a foreign mercenary with the Taiping.

Burgevine was in command of the men of the Foreign Arms Corps arrayed on the western wall of Shanghai, who cheered mightily as they shot down the men of the Taiping advance guard, who stood like targets on a rifle range.

***

When the Taiping soldiers stood off the following day on General Li's command, the French soldiers came out of the city and set fire to the outer suburbs, to deny the Taiping rebels any cover. They burned the factories of the Chinese wholesale merchants and the ancient temple to the Queen of Heaven, and murdered, raped and pillaged the local population, whom they assumed to be Taiping sympathizers. British gunboats moved upriver and lobbed their ordinance into the standing Taiping divisions, while Burgevine and his Foreign Arms Corps joined the French pillage of the Shanghai suburbs.

***

On the morning of the third day, the remnants of General Li's specially selected force ventured forth one last time to plea for peace and communication, and once more were decimated by allied fire from the city walls and the gunships in the river. The Loyal King, who had led the Taiping armies to spectacular victories against the Qing, was stunned and shocked by the allied response, but finally recognized that the situation was hopeless and ordered his men to withdraw.

Augustus Lindley, who had watched the slaughter with mounting horror, felt deep shame at the actions of his countrymen. He could not understand why Christians would join with the cruel and pagan Manchu in slaughtering fellow brothers in Christ – it was beyond his comprehension. He was ashamed, but also afraid, for he knew that the violation of neutrality by the Western powers sounded the death-knell of the Taiping rebellion.

Nonetheless, Lindley fully expected General Li to order his great army at Suzhou to advance and capture Shanghai, whatever the consequences of waging war on the Europeans and Americans, and he ordered the men of his Loyal and Faithful Auxiliary Legion to prepare for battle. Yet to his great surprise and disappointment, General Li did no such thing. Greatly distressed by the allied response, the Loyal King still retained an almost childlike faith that his foreign Christian brethren would listen to reason, so instead of ordering an overwhelming military response, he sent a conciliatory letter to the foreign ambassadors, pleading with them to reconsider their position. But the foreign ambassadors did not favour him with a reply, and after waiting a full week, the Loyal King pulled his army back to deal with a Qing army that was threatening his northern flank.

21

She hated Auntie Ki for having bought her, for having sold her and for having sold her as a concubine to an ugly old man. Yet when the time came for her to leave and join Ho Bee Swee, Ah Keng knew that a part of her heart would miss the old lady, who had been her only protector since she had been kidnapped and taken to Singapore to be sold as a mui tsai.

Before she left for the house of Ho Bee Swee, the old lady bombarded her with advice about how to treat the old man, both sexually and socially, and how to turn her relationship to him to her best advantage. She also warned her to watch out for Mui Chi, the daughter-in-law who ruled the household, who would jealously guard her own position of power as first wife of Ho Bee Swee's eldest son. And when Auntie Ki said goodbye to her, and said that she would visit her once she was settled, Ah Keng found herself hoping desperately that she would. Then she did her best to hide her tears as the carriage bore her from the only home she had known for the past two years, into the arms of an old man who was a complete stranger to her.

***

Ho Bee Swee was a successful businessman who had sold up his commercial holdings in Canton at the very beginning of the Taiping Rebellion, after the Qing forces had been defeated at the battle of Jintian. He had seen that the rebellion would bring great turmoil to the Middle Kingdom and pose a serious threat to his commercial enterprises. Following the advice of his nephew in Singapore, he had transferred his capital and his family there, where he had purchased land and shophouses, which he had let out to local businessmen and tradesmen. When he had left Canton, he had been in vigorous health for his fifty-five years, having fathered four sons and a daughter by his first and second wives and concubine. Yet almost from the moment he had stepped off the junk in Singapore his health had begun to deteriorate.

He had set up his leasing agency to run smoothly under the day to day control of his manager, Mr Sng Chon Yee, which was just as well, since all four of his sons had turned out to be a great disappointment to him. Despite their expensive education, they had no head for numbers and no business sense and seemed content to live off their father's largesse, spending their generous allowances on fine clothes and entertainment, and gambling much of it away on lotteries and games of chance. At first Ho Bee Swee had chastised them and reduced their allowances, but his paternal fire and authority had diminished when his first wife, then his second wife and finally his beloved concubine had all died in the space of a few years. The spirit seemed to have gone out of him and he had suddenly begun to look like the old man he was. He had lost interest in his businesses and his life, scarcely caring to feed and clothe himself, and he became a virtual invalid, whose only purpose seemed to be his preparation for death. He had ordered a magnificent black lacquered coffin, which he had placed at the foot of his bed, in preparation for his journey to Yan Luo, the King of Hell.

* * *

As first wife of the first son, Mui Chi managed the household and most of the finances, since her father-in-law rarely quibbled about her expenses these days, not even the heavy debts she incurred at the mahjong[lxxxi] table. The sons and daughter and daughter-in-laws all waited in anticipation of the old man's death – in eager anticipation when they thought of the division of his estate – although they were careful to hide it from him. In the meantime it was Mui Chi's responsibility to care for her invalid father-in-law, to ensure that his physical needs and desires were satisfied, and to listen with patient but firm disapproval of his desire to take another concubine to bring him the pleasure he had been denied for so long. Yet she had grown so disgusted by the old man's habits and so resented the time she wasted away from the mahjong table, when she had to put up with his lascivious dreams of renewing his essence, if only for one last time, that in the end she had decided to kill two birds with one stone. She had decided to indulge the old man's sexual fantasies by purchasing a mui tsai, who could also serve as his nurse. She had heard that Madam Ki kept the best girls and prepared them well for their sexual duties. She was more expensive than most, it was true, but vastly cheaper than bringing some beauty from the home country. The young girl Ah Keng was pretty enough for Ho Bee Swee, whose eyesight was dim even if his taste and smell remained sharp, and she would keep him occupied and out of her hair.

---

lxxxi Chinese tile-based board game.

22

The British and French advance parties arrived behind the two northern Taku forts on the evening of August 20. They launched an attack on the fort closest to the river early the following morning, after an artillery barrage that began at dawn and lasted for two and a half hours. The Chinese guns returned a vigorous fire, even after a British mortar shell exploded their magazine, and the Chinese defenders put up a fierce fight. But by eight thirty the fort fell to the British and French, at the cost of thirty-four allied and fifteen hundred Chinese dead. The allies brought up fresh infantry for an assault on the remaining three forts, but there was no need, for the Chinese soon raised white flags of surrender. Meanwhile, General Senggelinqin pulled his cavalry back north to defend the approaches to Peking.

Later in the day Harry Parkes, the British consul at Canton, met with Hang-Fu, the provincial governor. They agreed that the allied armies would advance thirty miles upriver to Tientsin, where they would meet negotiators appointed by the Imperial court. Lord Elgin sent four gunboats up the Peiho River to Tientsin with Parkes, Duncan and two of Lord Elgin's secretaries, Lord Loch and Thomas Wade, to prepare for the meeting with the commissioners.

***

Lord Elgin and Baron Gros arrived in Tientsin on August 24, with the bulk of the allied armies. They met with governor Hang-Fu and with Kweilang and Hwarhana, the two commissioners who had negotiated the original Treaty of Tientsin. The allied demands were harsh – unconditional ratification of the original Treaty of Tientsin, with special insistence on the establishment of a permanent British ambassador in Peking; an apology from the Emperor for the attack on the British forces at the Taku forts the previous year; the opening of Tientsin to British trade; and an indemnity of three million pounds sterling, with Canton and the Taku forts remaining under allied occupation until the indemnity was paid.

As they had done in the past, the commissioners did their best to obfuscate and delay, and pleaded over the difficulty of paying the indemnity, but they finally agreed to the terms on September 4, as the last of the allied troops reached Tientsin.

***

When news of the capture of the Taku forts reached the Emperor, he was sick with worry and fear. He wanted to abandon the Imperial city and flee across the Great Wall to his secure palace at Jehol in Manchuria, the ancestral homeland of the Manchu. First the defeat of his besieging armies outside Nanking by the Taiping rebels, and now the capture of the Taku forts, which he had been assured were impregnable. Yet Yehonala, with the support of other hawks at court, managed to convince Hsien Feng that the barbarians would never reach the Imperial city, since General Senggelinqin had massed thousands of Mongol cavalry to block their passage north. They assured him that the only reason the foreign devils had managed to capture the Taku forts was because they had sneaked up behind them, like cowards in the night. Aroused by their patriotic arguments by day and Orchid's fierce sexual imagination by night, on September 4 the Emperor issued a defiant Imperial edict to his subjects:

My anger is about to strike and exterminate them without mercy. I command all my subjects, Chinese and Manchu, to hunt them down like savage beasts. Let the villages be abandoned as these wretches draw near. Let all provisions be destroyed that they might secure. In this manner, their accursed race will perish of hunger, like fish in a dried-up pond.

The Emperor offered a bounty of one hundred taels for the head of a white barbarian, and fifty taels for the head of a black barbarian.[lxxxii]

While Yehonala managed to persuade the Emperor that the Imperial capital was not under threat, the local population was not so sure. As garbled reports and rumours reached the city about the defeat at the hands of the allies, some of the richer merchants began to flee for their homes in the country.

***

As Lord Elgin and Baron Gros prepared for a military review to celebrate the new agreement on August 8, the Imperial commissioners suddenly informed them that they did not have the authority to sign the agreement. Lord Elgin was furious, and the following day ordered the army north towards Peking. He informed the Imperial commissioners that he would resume negotiations at Tang-chao, four miles east of the city. Two days later he received a letter advising him that the Emperor had appointed two new commissioners, Tsai Yuen, the Prince of I, and Mu Yin, the President of the Board of War. The letter also requested that the allies not advance on Tang-chao until their representatives had met there with the new commissioners, for fear of alarming the local people.

Lord Elgin would not halt the advance, but he sent Parkes, Wade

lxxxii An Indian Sepoy.

and Duncan ahead, where they met with the new commissioners on September 14. Duncan found both men subtle and intelligent in their demeanour, although he thought that the Prince of I, who was tall and dignified, concealed a wicked look behind his soft indulgent eyes, and that Mu Yin was clever like a fox. Yet after eight hours of intense discussions, to their great surprise the commissioners agreed to sign a letter on behalf of the Emperor agreeing to all the allied demands.

They returned to report this news to Lord Elgin the following day. They also advised him that they had provisionally agreed with the commissioners that the allied armies would be allowed to advance without interference to within ten miles of Tang-chao, where they would remain while Lord Elgin and Baron Gros proceeded under escort to ratify the revised Treaty of Tientsin. Lord Elgin agreed to this, in part because Lieutenant-General Hope Grant was having difficulty supplying his troops on the march, and the French were slow in bringing up theirs. Parkes also suggested that, after a day's rest, he should return to Tang-chao under a flag of truce, to make final arrangements for the meeting with the Emperor in Peking.

'But are you sure we can trust them?' Lord Elgin asked him.

'I'm sure we can, sir,' Parkes replied. 'They've never violated a flag of truce in the past, and they have no reason to do so now.'

'Better take a small escort, just in case,' Lord Elgin insisted.

23

On the following day, which was a Sunday, Christian services were held in an abandoned Chinese Temple in Ho-se-woo, after which the negotiating party prepared for their meeting with the Imperial commissioners in Tang-chao. Lord Elgin decided that Harry Parkes would be accompanied by Lord Loch, Lord Elgin's secretary; Duncan Simpson, as interpreter attached to Lord Elgin's staff; William de Norman, who had come up with Lord Elgin from Shanghai, and Thomas Bowlby, a correspondent with *The Times* of London. Their escort would comprise six King's Dragoon Guards and twenty Sikh troopers from Fane's Horse, commanded by Lieutenant Robert Anderson.

***

They set out early on Monday morning. It was a glorious day, with clear blue skies and a cool morning breeze. They saw little evidence of Qing troops as they rode along the road, save for a few pickets and squadrons of cavalry, who retired a respectful distance as they passed. They arrived at ten thirty in the morning and found that a temple had been prepared for their reception.

The commissioners arrived a little after one, and after they had taken tea and exchanged the usual compliments, Duncan translated a letter from Lord Elgin, accepting the provisions of the agreement previously negotiated by Parkes and Wade, and urged the commissioners to make speedy arrangements for Lord

Elgin to travel to Peking, so that he might personally deliver the letter to the Emperor that he carried from the Queen of England. The commissioners immediately began raising objections to the agreement, and the discussion dragged on in an increasingly acrimonious fashion throughout the afternoon.

And then, to their amazement, at around six in the evening the commissioners did a complete about-face and dropped their objections. They speedily arranged for the encampment of the British and French armies before Tang-chao, and Duncan helped Parkes draw up a proclamation to inform the populace that the Celestial Emperor had agreed to peace with the allies. Greatly relieved, they went to bed early, eager to convey the news to Lord Elgin in the morning.

24

Over breakfast the next day, Parkes assigned their respective duties. He would leave early with Loch, accompanied by the Dragoon Guards and three Sikhs from Fane's Horse, to inform Lord Elgin of their successful progress and the arrangements for the disposition of the armies. Duncan would stay in Tang-chao with William De Norman and Thomas Bowlby, under the protection of Lieutenant Anderson and the remaining Sikhs. When he returned, they would meet with the commissioners once again to finalize the details of the revised treaty and try to arrange suitable accommodation for the embassy officials.

***

Parkes' party retraced the route they had travelled the previous day. As they rode across the flat and open country, they became alarmed by the contrast with their outward journey. On their way to Tang-chao they had encountered only small pockets of Qing soldiers, but as they rode back toward the allied armies, they passed by regiments of Qing infantry heading in the same direction. When they reached the fortified town of Chang-kia-wan, they found it was full of Qing infantry and cavalry. They were allowed to proceed, but became increasingly anxious at the apparent treachery of the Chinese – they were convinced that such massing of troops could only mean that the Emperor Hsien Feng had decided on war rather than peace.

Parkes conferred a quick council of war in the middle of the road. They decided that Parkes would go back with Private Phipps of the King's Dragoon Guards and one Sikh trooper, bearing a flag of truce. He would warn the others left behind in Tang-chao, and seek an audience with the Prince of I, to try to defuse the dangerous situation. Loch would take the remaining Sikh troopers and Dragoon Guards and try to pass through the Qing cavalry ahead of them to warn the allied commanders – he would ask them to hold off from engagement with the enemy until Parkes had time to warn the others and meet with the Prince of I.-

When Parkes reached the temple at Tang–chao, he warned Lieutenant Anderson and the others of the danger, then rode off in search of the Prince of I.

***

Loch and his company rode through the head of the Tartar cavalry without incident, and after they had ridden another half mile they came upon Captain Brabazon, leading the advance guard of the allied armies. Captain Brazabon led Loch back to Lieutenant-General Sir Hope Grant, who was at the head of the column about a half-mile behind the advance guard. Loch warned the general about the Qing manoeuvres, of which he was already aware. Hope Grant had given orders for the army to halt, having received intelligence about large bodies of Tartar cavalry massing on his left flank.

Loch described the Qing positions in as much detail as he could, and begged Hope Grant to delay engagement with the enemy for as long as possible, in the hope that Parkes and the others could return to the safely of the allied camp.

'I will do my best, Mr Loch,' Hope Grant replied. 'I will in any case need some time to bring up the baggage and form the regiments in line. But you must understand that we will engage the enemy immediately if he fires upon us.'

At that moment General Montauban joined them. When he heard of the Qing treachery, he demanded that the allies attack immediately, but Hope Grant managed to persuade him to wait as long as they could.

Loch thanked them for their forbearance, and then asked permission to return to Tang-chao, to urge the others to leave and to help them find some safe means of escape. Hope Grant agreed to this, but not before warning Loch that he might be going to his own death, which Loch acknowledged. Hope Grant assigned two Sikh troopers from Probyn's Horse to accompany him, and granted Captain Brabazon's request to join the party. Loch took out his white handkerchief and tied it to the end of one of the trooper's lances. Then, with their flag of truce in place, they rode back towards Tang-chao. They reached the Qing lines without incident, but knew they had passed the point of no return when a squadron of Qing cavalry swept behind them to block their rear. As they rode back down the road towards Tang-Cheo, Loch was struck by the great change that had taken place in even the short time since they had passed on their way to the allied lines. There was Qing infantry and cavalry in broad view rushing towards the front, and gun emplacements being prepared east and west of them.

25

Loch, Captain Brabazon and the two Sikh troopers rode back as fast as they could, although they were slowed by Qing regiments still making their way to the front. When they reached Tang-chao, Lieutenant Anderson told them that Mr Parkes had gone off to meet with the Prince of I, but had not yet returned. Loch warned them of the Qing treachery, and instructed them to have their horses saddled for immediate departure when Parkes returned. When Parkes arrived back half an hour later, he warned them that the Prince of I had said that until the demand concerning the delivery of the letter from the Queen of England was withdrawn, there would be no peace but must be war. They all knew that Lord Elgin would not withdraw the demand. So there must be war. They were betrayed, and were at the mercy of their enemies.

Parkes still hoped they would respect the flag of truce, and allow them to return to the allied lines, if they could reach them before the fighting commenced. They set off at a brisk pace, Loch estimating that they had about ten miles to travel and less than an hour to spare – assuming that Hope Grant managed to hold off his attack for the two hours that Loch had requested.

They reached the town of Chang-kia-wan without incident, although by then it was clear that some of their horses were tiring. They made their way through the town with good speed, despite the press of soldiers, and as they emerged onto the plain beyond, Loch encouraged them onwards. Duncan said a silent prayer and crossed his fingers.

Duncan heard the Qing artillery barrage open up ahead of them, which was answered by an Armstrong shell[lxxxiii] from the allied lines, which burst with a brilliant white light in the clear blue sky. The battle had begun, and they were trapped behind the enemy lines. Duncan uncrossed his fingers and cursed the Manchu to the deepest layers of their Chinese Hell.

Parkes, who was leading the party, halted them on the road, and they discussed their next course of action. Unless they wished to surrender, Parkes said, their best chance of escape was to ride east through the enemy lines, and then try to ride clear of their right flank – as the Qing would be focused on the battle before them, they might hope to get away with it.

But Parkes was mistaken. As they turned off the road, they found their way blocked by a squad of Tartar cavalry, who quickly surrounded them. The officer in charge told them he would respect the flag of truce and arrange for their safe passage. However, he was first obliged to take their leaders to General Senggelinqin, whose camp was close by – for only the general could issue the necessary passes to enable them to pass through the Qing lines. They had no option but to obey, so it was quickly decided that Parkes and Loch should go, accompanied by the trooper bearing their flag of truce.

As Parkes assured them they would return as soon as they could, Loch tried to make light of their danger, and joked with Mr Bowlby:

'Now I think you'll get your wish and see how the Chinese really fight, Mr Bowlby!'

---

lxxxiii An explosive cast iron shell that burst into shrapnel in the air, created by the British inventor William George Armstrong, 1st Baron Armstrong (1810 –1900), who also invented an early breech-loading field gun designed to fire such shells.

But Bowlby did not appear assured, nor anxious to see how the Chinese fought while inside their lines.

Half an hour passed, and then an hour. Lieutenant Anderson asked the Qing officer to take him to their comrades, but was refused. Duncan noticed that the squad of cavalry surrounding them had grown larger as the time had passed, and the sound of the battle had grown louder in the distance. Then they were ordered to dismount and lead their horses back through Chang-kia-wan and north to Tang-chao. Duncan knew then that they would be not be reuniting with Parkes and Loch and receiving safe passage through the Qing lines. He loosened his holster flap and resolved to take as many with him as he could.

26

When Duncan and his party led their horses into Tang-chao, they were ordered to give up their arms. Duncan looked toward Lieutenant Anderson – if they were to fight and lay down their lives, now was the time to do it. He laid his hand upon the butt of his pistol, and wished he had Badrudeen's kris[lxxxiv] with him now, so that he could drive it into the black heart of one of his captors. Anderson caught his eye and read his intent, but asked him to hold off.

'I understand your feelings, Duncan,' he said earnestly, 'but I have to think of the civilians. If they had meant to kill us, I'm sure they'd have done it by now. We pose no real threat to them, and the arrogant bastards would not be much hampered by our small arms. There may still be a chance that we will get through this, but none if you draw your pistol.'

Duncan saw the look of fear in Bowlby's eyes and reluctantly complied with Anderson's request. He slowly withdrew his pistol from its holster and flung it on the ground, along with his short saber. Bowlby and de Norman surrendered their weapons, as did Private Phipps and the Sikh troopers, although with great reluctance. They were immediately searched, and all their valuables were taken from them, down to their rings and cufflinks. Duncan cursed them in English and then in Chinese, after they discovered and removed the dirk he had hidden in his boot. In response, his captors struck him on the head with their musket butts, and he fought to retain

---

lxxxiv Dagger with distinctive wavy blade favoured by Malays.

consciousness as he fell to the ground. Then they were allowed to remount, and led through Tang-chao and north towards Peking.

***

They were halted at a joss house on the road to Peking, where they rested for the night, and were given a simple meal of rice and tea. The Sikhs refused to eat the rice, but Lieutenant Anderson persuaded some of them to do so – otherwise they were giving in to their enemies, he told them. In the early morning Captain Brabazon was taken away, along with a French priest, the Abbé de Luc, who had been brought in during the night, along with two French officers. As they mounted their horses in the morning and set out for Peking with their guard, Lieutenant Anderson told the party that the two men had been sent back to communicate with the allied army and negotiate their release.

When they were a short distance down the road Duncan rode up close behind him, and whispered conspiratorially to the lieutenant.

'Is that true, Anderson? Are they really being sent back to negotiate our release?'

'I have no idea,' Anderson replied, 'I only said it to calm Mr Bowlby's nerves – the poor fellow is close to wetting himself with fear. I just hope to God someone is trying to negotiate our release.'

***

Unbeknownst to them, someone was trying to negotiate their release. The battle of the previous day, which had taken place near the village of Chang-kia-wan, had not gone well for General Senggelinqin and his army. When the fight was joined, the Qing had the numerical advantage. They fielded close to thirty thousand men against the ten thousand brought forward by the British and

French, with ten thousand Mongol cavalry under the personal command of General Senggelinqin. They also had the advantage of surprise, since their battalions were already drawn up and their artillery deployed when Generals Hope Grant and Montauban gave their orders to engage. Hope Grant had managed to hold off the attack for an hour and a half to give Loch time to return, but had been forced to join battle when the vanguard of the Anglo-French force was fired upon by Qing artillery.

Fifty or even ten years before, the battle would very likely have been a foregone conclusion in favour of the Qing, given their numerical advantage and the bravery and discipline displayed by their infantry and cavalry. Yet the Chinese cannon were mainly ancient muzzle loading devices that fired stone shot, whereas the allied forces were equipped with new breech-loading Armstrong guns, which had greater range and accuracy, and fired exploding cast iron shells that burst into shrapnel in the air. Most of the Chinese infantry carried ancient matchlocks, whose range and accuracy was comparable to the smooth-bore 'Brown Bess' muskets borne by British troops for the past fifty years, but vastly inferior to the new high velocity and rapid-loading Enfield and Minié[lxxxv] rifles carried by the allied expeditionary force.

The Chinese attackers were astounded by the ferocity of the allied artillery barrage and infantry fusillade, and by the end of the day were driven back to Tang-chao with heavy loss of men and guns. The vanguard of the allied army pursued the Chinese beyond Tang-chao and down the road towards Peking, but then pulled back and entrenched before Tang-chao to bring up supplies and reinforcements.

---

lxxxv Rifled musket introduced to the French army in 1849, adopted to accommodate the Minié ball, a conical-cylindrical soft lead bullet that provided spin for greater accuracy, invented by Claude-Etienne Minié (1804 –1879).

That evening, Thomas Wade, from Lord Elgin's staff, approached one of the gates of Tang-chao under a flag of truce. He tried to communicate with the Chinese authorities concerning the fate of the negotiating party, in the hope of securing their release and arranging a new peace conference. But the Chinese in Tang-chao claimed that they had no knowledge of them, and no authority to make any new arrangements, and they repeated the same story when Wade approached them again the following day.

27

The following morning, Duncan and his party arrived in Peking. When they rode through the Chi Hua gate,[lxxxvi] great crowds from the city came out to meet them, to stare in curiosity and wonder at the defeated barbarians. As they passed by the massive walls of the Forbidden City, they were ordered to dismount and sit upon the ground, where they were fed another meal of rice and tea. While they ate, their cavalry escort created a passage through the crowd and eight yellow liveried servants carried an ornate golden sedan chair to within a few feet of them. As Duncan looked up, he saw a woman of exquisite beauty gazing down upon them. The expression on her powdered face and painted lips was impossible to fathom – whether it was of pity or contempt or hatred, Duncan could not tell. Then the curtain was quickly drawn and the golden chair was carried away.

Yehonala turned to An Te-hai, and said with a smile that was half a sneer.

'Ugh! Those foreign barbarians look like pigs!'

'And they smell like pigs too, Orchid,' An Te-hai replied, and they both giggled together as they were carried away to the Summer Palace, where the Emperor Hsien Feng had relocated his court.

***

After they had finished their meal, they were ordered to remount, and were led two miles outside of the city, where they were ordered to dismount before what Duncan and Lieutenant Anderson took to be army barracks.

'What do you think they are going to do to us,' Bowlby asked, trying to hide the fear in his voice.

'Don't worry,' Anderson replied, 'I'm sure they're going to use us as bargaining chips. Otherwise we'd be dead by now.'

A mandarin approached them from the barracks, followed by a party of soldiers. The mandarin gave the order, and they were knocked to the ground by the soldiers, who tied their wrists and legs tightly behind their backs with leather cords. Within the hour they were all trussed up on the ground – they were kicked and beaten whenever they tried to rest upon their sides, and quickly pulled back upon their stomachs.

There they lay the rest of the day, parched in the hot sun, then shivering as night fell over them like an icy blanket. Duncan slept fitfully, dreaming he was being rescued by Hong Rengan leading the Taiping army against Peking, but woke to find the Chinese guards pouring water on the cords that fastened their hands and feet. He knew why. When the cords dried, they would contract, binding their wrists and ankles tighter together and further reducing their circulation. He also knew the inevitable outcome. Without relief, his hands and feet would swell until they turned black, and finally burst under the pressure, leaving gaping wounds that would be magnets for vermin and maggots. He shivered at the thought and wondered how long they could last.

They remained tied up on the ground for the following two days and nights. Their bonds were watered during the nights, and they were fed a little rice and water in the mornings. On the third day a party of soldiers came down from the barracks and loaded them with chains, and then bundled them into mule drawn carts. The soldiers drove the carts as fast as they could along the deeply rutted road, while their prisoners groaned in agony, tossed back and forth, their bindings and chains preventing them from gaining any sort of secure hold on the side of the carts. In the early dawn they arrived at a small fort, where they were dragged from the carts and carried to a basement prison, the only light coming from a narrow air-slit that ran along the roof, at the edge of the main slab-stone square. As they were carried to their prison, Duncan noticed the wooden posts in the middle of the square. He knew their purpose was for some form of punishment or execution, and tried not to imagine what it might be. He just hoped it would be quick.

The prison was stifling hot by day and freezing cold at night. The following day, which passed without them receiving any food or water, Lieutenant Anderson became delirious. Duncan and de Norman and the dragoon named Phipps tried to comfort him, but it was no use. The jailors had laid the heaviest chains upon him, with all the weight borne by his wrists, so he was the first to succumb to the biting cords. His hands had already swollen to about three times their normal size, and were black as pitch. He called out to Major Fane, urging him to charge the enemy, and to a girl called Jenny, whom he promised never to leave again. He lapsed in and out of consciousness, but he never recovered his wits.

28

On September 21, the day before Duncan and his party arrived in prison, the allied armies advanced beyond Tang-chao towards Peking. The Qing forces met them at Ba Li Gao,[lxxxvii] the marble bridge that spanned the Yang-Liang canal, the waterway connecting the Peiho River and Peking. General Senggelinqin's army was well prepared, with his artillery positioned in the woods and on the high ground. Yet he gambled his success on his veteran Tartar cavalry that he flung at the centre of the allied line. His Bannermen thundered forward in superbly coordinated waves, adjusting their formation by means of signalling flags. Yet all to no avail. The Armstrong shells and new Hale rockets[lxxxviii] cut deep swathes in their ranks, prompting Hope Grant to exclaim:

'Aye, and to think it was the Chinese who invented rockets. Once we have broken their cavalry, you may advance against the bridge, General Montauban.'

'As you wish,' the general acknowledged.

Still the Tartar cavalry came on, their ranks now shredded by grape and canister, until they were stopped dead in their tracks by the massed fire of the 52nd Highland Regiment. As the cavalry fell back, the French forces advanced on the bridge, and the British attacked the right flank of the Qing army. Although they had suffered heavy

---

lxxxvii Eight Mile Bridge.
lxxxviii Rotary rocket created by the British inventor William Hale (1797–1870).

losses, the Qing put up a spirited defence of the bridge, especially the elite Imperial guard, commanded by General Senggelinqin, who repulsed attack after attack by the French. General Senggelinqin was wounded twice, the second time by a fragment from an Armstrong shell that blew away most of his jaw. The general screamed in agony, and swore that he would have his revenge. He ordered his men to bring forward the two allied prisoners that were held behind their lines, Captain Brabazon and the Abbé de Luc, and behead them in full view of the allied forces. This was quickly done, but the intended affront to the allied armies had no effect, for the smoke of battle hid the brutal act from them. The Imperial guard held on for seven desperate hours, but were eventually driven back and fled with the remains of the army towards Peking, although many left the road for the safety of the open countryside.

The French lost almost a thousand men taking the Ba Li Gao, but the Qing casualties numbered over twenty thousand by the day's end. The allied forces halted on the enemy side of the bridge, oblivious to the severed heads and bodies of their unfortunate countrymen that lay beneath the Qing corpses piled high on the riverbank.

***

Bowlby woke Duncan from his doze.

'I fear we are all going to die,' he said, in a voice that Duncan thought was strangely calm. 'They don't give a toss about poor Lieutenant Anderson, and we'll all go his way in the next few days. '

Duncan was about to speak, but Bowlby shook his head vigorously and raised his bound hands, indicating that he wanted to finish what he was trying to say.

'I'm not a brave man,' he continued, 'and I'm not afraid to admit that I've come close to embarrassing myself these past few days. But now I think I'm resigned to it, you know – I'm not afraid to die, although I'm sorry to think I won't see my dear wife and children again. But I made arrangements for them when I left with Lord Elgin last year, in case anything happened to me. My brother died in a shipwreck off Wales about six weeks before we left, which made me think on my own mortality, and consult a lawyer to draw up a will. I have a pension and insurance policy with the *Times*, thanks to the efforts of Mr Russell, who served them so well in the Crimea.'

Duncan turned to look more closely at Bowlby, and saw that the drawn anxious face of yesterday was now set in calm determination. He was a small man, in a grey check suit, with receding brown hair on a massive brow, and a thick mane of hair spreading out from behind his ears. He sported magnificent mutton chop whiskers with a dapper moustache and goatee beard. His dark eyes had a fierce intensity that Duncan had not noticed before.

'Was your brother lost at sea or did you manage to retrieve his body?' Duncan asked him. A morbid subject he knew, but he was glad to engage Bowlby in conversation on any matter, and the man seemed intent on discussing mortal questions.

'The strangest thing,' Bowlby replied. 'I searched the shore where the *Royal Charter* went down, but the bodies that washed up all looked the same. Their faces had been washed off by that time, you see, so it was impossible to recognize him that way. But my brother had a deformity on his right foot, which was twisted. We both shared it, and that's how I recognized him.'

'So what do you think the outcome of this war will be?' Bowlby continued, suddenly changing the subject. 'I just hope our treatment, horrific and dishonourable as it may be, does not drive Lord Elgin to all-out war, with the powers that call themselves Great dividing up this ancient civilization into their special spheres of influence – British, French, German and no doubt soon enough

Austrian, Russian and American – and forcing their Christianity upon the poor wretches. Not that I have any more affection for the present Manchu rulers than the Han Chinese who suffer under them, but they'll be a lot worse off if the Western powers get to divvy up their country, that's for sure.'

Duncan saw de Norman raising an eyebrow, and trooper Phipps looked downright offended. The Sikhs said nothing. They had fought and lost a fierce war against the British over control of the Punjab, and then helped save the British during the mutiny, so he supposed they saw both sides of the story – or were just trying to stay alive.

'Surprised to hear me say that?' Bowlby said. 'Yet I share these views with a distinguished colleague, our good Lord Elgin, no less. We have no business determining the destiny of this great nation, with its rich culture and noble history.'

'Which is not to say that I recommend we accede to the Manchu demands,' he quickly added, 'nor, I'm sure, will Lord Elgin accede to them – we must make them abide by the terms of our treaty with them.'

'Well I'm glad to hear you say that, at least,' said de Norman, and trooper Phipps nodded in agreement.

'What do you think of the Taiping, Thomas?' Duncan asked him. 'Don't you think it would be better for us to throw our weight behind them rather than the Manchu, since we all agree the Manchu are corrupt as hell and do nothing for the Chinese people.'

'Well, I'm not sure, Duncan,' Bowlby replied. 'There is much to admire in them, their courage and military skill, for example, their elimination of concubinage and foot binding, their proscription of opium and hard liquor, equality of men and women before the law, and so forth. But this story about him being the son of God and younger brother of Jesus is stuff and nonsense, and won't wash with the Western powers. Can you imagine our pious politicians back home agreeing to an alliance with such a blasphemer? What would the bishops have to say about that? Or Her Majesty, for that matter? No, Duncan, I don't see us throwing our lot in with the Taiping, and you must know that most of the Chinese elite see him as a threat to their Confucian order. Now, if he had only stuck with good old Church of England Christianity and kept his original line that Confucianism is compatible with Christianity, that might have been a winning combination! But I think their time has already passed, and the Manchu – no doubt with some help from us – will eventually destroy them.'

'I suspect you're right, ' Duncan replied, and then told Bowlby that he had met General Li and Hong Rengan in Nanking – and Hong Xiuquan himself – when returning with Lord Elgin's expedition from Wuchang.

'Oh, how interesting!' Bowlby replied. 'Please do tell us all about that,' and the others concurred. So Duncan told them about his meetings with the Loyal King, the Shield King and the Heavenly King, and of his stay with Augustus Lindley, while Lieutenant Anderson moaned softly in his delirium.

29

When news of the defeat at Ba Li Gao reached Peking, there was widespread panic in the city, and uproar in the Summer Palace when the Emperor learned of the capture and imprisonment of Parkes and the other barbarians. He had not intended his edict offering a bounty for the heads of invading barbarians to include officials negotiating under a flag of truce. The Emperor wanted to leave at once for his northern palace at Jehol on the other side of the Great Wall. The palace was close to the ancient Manchurian capital of Mukden, where successive generations of insecure Manchu rulers had laid up stocks of arms and treasure. He also wanted Parkes and the others released immediately and returned to the foreign barbarians – he was terrified that they would use this treachery as grounds for all-out war against his Heavenly Kingdom.

But Yehonala, with the help of the Prince of I, managed to persuade him against both courses of action. The captured foreign emissaries had insulted his Illustrious Majesty, the Son of Heaven, many times over and deserved to be imprisoned. To release them now would be a sign of weakness that the barbarians would surely exploit to their advantage; it would be better to hold them in prison to strengthen their hand in any future negotiations with their enemies. And to leave the capital now would be to abandon his army and subjects: it would demoralize the fighting men and create a panic in the city. The soldiers would desert their positions and the population would leave their homes – they would follow him north, leaving the capital open to the plundering enemy hordes.

'How can the Celestial Emperor abandon his loyal subjects to the barbarians?' Yehonala reproached him. 'You are the Emperor of All under Heaven, and they must fail, if you strike them down with your Bannermen and exterminate them without mercy.'

'But our troops have already lost two battles against them, Empress of the Western Palace, and they are closing in on us,' Hsien Feng responded.

'That is true, Complete Abundance,' Yehonala granted, 'but they are a puny force, and your armies still outnumber them many times over! They will crush them like beetles if they dare to approach our sacred capital.'

'She is correct, Son of Heaven,' the Prince of I assured him. 'Their forces are stretched thin, winter is about to close in, and our cavalry can easily sweep behind them and cut their supply lines.'

This was exactly what Lord Elgin feared as he lay in his tent at Tang-chao. He tried to distract himself by reflecting on the 'grandeur' of Mr Darwin's view of life, according to which 'from so simple a beginning, endless forms most beautiful and most wonderful have been, and are being, evolved.' But his mind kept coming back to supply trains, winter storms and vengeful Tartar cavalry.

* * *

Bowlby died that night, and the following morning they saw why. Sometime during the past few days, either during the time they were tied and beaten or when they were transported in the carts, he had sustained a wound to his neck. As he lay on his side upon the earthen floor, his eyes staring wide and empty, they saw the dark moving mass of maggots swarming over his neck, and the pool of shimmering blood around his head. De Norman vomited, and Duncan found it hard to keep his own bile from rising; he looked at his own bound hands, which were swollen and aching with pain.

Lieutenant Anderson continued to rant and rave, and cried out to them to help him loosen his cords:

'Bite on them, I beg you!' he cried, 'bite on them and free me, for I fear I shall lose my hands, and what use is a soldier without hands?'

Mohamed Bux, a Sikh duffadar, crawled across to try to help him, but the Chinese guards kicked him away. As punishment, the guards denied them food and water for the day, and left the dead Bowlby where he lay, the dark mass slowly engulfing his head. When they finally retrieved his body, they carried it out on a wooden beam.

'God, do you hear what they're saying, Duncan!' whispered de Norman, 'My God, My God!'

'I do,' Duncan whispered in reply, but he did not translate for the others. They were joking about how the pigs and dogs would have a fine feed on Bowlby's large head.

***

'C'mon, sirs, cheer up!' cried Phipps, the trooper of the King's Dragoons. His hands were black and swollen as bad as Lieutenant Anderson's, but he still had his wits about him, and he did his best to distract them from the horror.

'Where are your family from, Mr Simpson?' he asked.

'From Ardersier, near Fort George, just east of Inverness,' Duncan replied.

'Well, how do you tell if an Ardersier girl is a virgin?'

'I don't know,' Duncan responded.

'Ha! A trick question, Mr Simpson! There are no virgins in Ardersier!'

In another time and place, Duncan might have taken offense, but he laughed at the joke, and it seemed to release the tension in his body, at least for the moment. Phipps continued to regale them with a series of jokes, mostly bawdy, some downright filthy, mostly at the expense of the Scots, but some at the expense of the Frogs, on account of the French officers in their company, and even a few for the Sikh troopers.

'And have ye heard the one about the trooper holed up in a Chinese jail with a Scotchmen, two Frogs and a bunch o' hairy Hindus!' he roared, and they all roared back in laughter with him, while the Chinese jailors looked on in amazement.

30

The allied armies had advanced only a few miles beyond Tang-chao, where they waited for supplies and reinforcements to be brought up, including their siege guns, which would be needed if the Qing withdrew their forces into Peking. Mindful of the threat from the Tartar cavalry to his extended baggage and communication lines, Lord Elgin wanted to accumulate a sufficiently large store of supplies and arms to ensure his freedom of action as winter came on. He sent word to the Imperial commissioners threatening serious consequences if any harm came to the prisoners, while Mr Wade continued to try to negotiate their release. In response, the Imperial commissioners urged him to drop his demand that he present a letter from Queen Victoria to the Emperor and warned him that if the allied armies advanced any further the prisoners would be executed. Lord Elgin immediately responded that he would not discuss any matter with them until the prisoners were released, and if they were not released he would march on Peking and destroy it, including the Forbidden City. Lord Elgin was not only acting as a cool-headed commander who put his mission over the lives of the prisoners, but also thought his tough line of response was his best hope of saving them. Anything less would surely be perceived as weakness on his part. And if he waited while negotiations dragged on, winter would set in and he might find his army encircled and threatened by reinforcements of Tartar cavalry, and his weakness rewarded by the execution of the prisoners. For he had little doubt that they would be executed if the Emperor thought that he had defeated the barbarians.

***

A few days later, General Senggelinqin mounted a counter-attack against the vanguard of the allied army that was probing the outskirts of Peking, close to the Chi Hua gate. The Qing forces were driven back with great losses, many of the infantry being trampled to death by the retreating cavalry. On the following day, they were routed a second time, again close by the Chi Hua gate. When the news reached the Emperor at the Summer Palace, northwest of the city, his nerve broke and, ignoring Yehonala's exhortations, decreed that he would leave at once for his northern palace at Jehol, leaving his brother Prince Kung to negotiate with the barbarians.

Pandemonium broke out as the Son of Heaven and his concubines, the royal princes and the mandarins, the eunuchs and the officers of his household, piled themselves and their treasures into every available conveyance. The Emperor and his entourage departed in a cowardly haste that for many was a shameful reminder of the manner in which the last Ming Emperor Zhu Youjian had fled the city, when he was driven from it by Hsien Feng's own ancestors, the Manchu Bannermen who had established the Qing dynasty.

Yehonala, usually so self-confident and controlled, was in a state of anxious turmoil. Her consistent council of defiance to the barbarians had now been officially and publicly repudiated, and she knew that as a consequence her influence over the Emperor was weakened – a disadvantage she knew her enemies would be quick to exploit, even to the point of assassination en route to Jehol. Worse, in the chaos of their flight from the Summer Palace, she had been separated from her son, Zaichun, the heir to the Dragon throne, and her own trump card in her dealings with the Emperor. If Zaichun were to meet with some mishap, she would find herself in the greatest danger.

Yet fortune continued to favour the Concubine Cixi. After a frantic search, her devoted eunuchs found her son in the care of his aunt, Yehonala's cousin Sakota, the Empress of the Eastern Palace. Then she learned that by some lucky chance, their Bannerman escort to Jehol was led by Captain Jung Lu, her former betrothed, and was comprised mainly of soldiers from her own Yeho-Nala clan, whose loyalty could be counted upon. She no longer feared assassination and began to plan her strategy for dealing with her enemies when they reached Jehol.

31

Conditions were growing increasingly desperate for Duncan's party, despite Phipps' continual banter. Mohamed Bux, the Sikh duffadar, cursed the Chinese jailors for bringing him pig to eat, and treated them with regal disdain and disgust, but both his hands had been eaten away by maggots. Lieutenant Anderson continued to call out to Captain Fane and Jenny, and sometimes they humoured him by responding. Yet it could not be long now, for his blackened fingers and nails had burst open, the bones of his wrists were exposed and the maggots crawled all over his body. Duncan looked at his own hands. They were swollen and black, but not as far advanced as Anderson's or, as he now noticed, de Norman's. He was torn between moving them to aid his circulation and keeping them still to avoid breaking his skin, but he knew that whatever he did, he would suffer the same fate as the others if he did not do something about it soon. But what? Thoughts of escape were futile. He could think of no way to loosen the cords that bound him, far less get past the armed guards that watched over them day and night.

He decided to betray his knowledge of the language and to try to communicate with one of the jailors, an ugly fellow with a cruel mouth and a long scar down his left cheek, but who never indulged in the wanton cruelties of his fellows. At first the man refused to talk or respond – he was amazed and afraid when Duncan first spoke to him in his own language. But the next day Duncan managed to get him to disclose that there had been a major battle between the barbarians and the Imperial forces, and that the barbarians were advancing on Peking.

'But the Imperial forces will drive the barbarians back and show them no mercy, you can be sure of that. Then you had all better watch out,' the man said, shaking his fist in the air, 'for then your lives will be worth nothing.'

'But what if they do not?' Duncan insisted. 'I know the Imperial armies have been beaten many times by the Taiping, and the allied forces have modern cannons and rifles. Then your lives will be forfeit, if not worse. My friends here will tell you what the British did to the Indians when they mutinied in 1857 and killed their prisoners. They were made to lick the blood of their victims from the floors and walls of their prisons, and then their bodies were blown to pieces from the mouths of their cannon.'

Duncan could see the man was terrified by that prospect, despite his bluster, since it meant that there would be no place in Heaven or Hell for his dismembered body.

'Bah, I don't believe you,' the man replied, recovering his former authority. 'The armies of the Son of Heaven will surround the barbarians and starve them to death, like fish in a dried-up pond. Those who have dishonoured the Emperor will be shown no mercy!'

'But are you willing to take that chance' Duncan retorted, 'when even a small act of mercy may save you from wandering through the world as a ghost for all eternity?'

The man said nothing in reply and returned to his station at the door to their prison.

***

The following morning Mohamed Bux passed away, having bled to death from his maggot-eaten stumps. One of the French officers, who had received a minor wound to his head, lapsed into unconsciousness, as the maggots swarmed into his nose, ears and mouth, and still Lieutenant Anderson rambled. But as the jailor who Duncan had talked with the previous day brought the prisoners their daily ration of rice and water, he bent down and loosened the cords that bound Duncan's hands and feet. They tingled with stinging pain as the blood flowed back into his fingers, and he very slowly began to flex them to encourage the circulation – he only hoped he was not too late to save his hands and his life. The jailor proceeded to loosen the cords binding the others, save for those who were clearly too far gone, like Lieutenant Anderson and the French officer, and Jawalla Sing, the Sikh trooper whose hands had already burst open. Duncan managed to crawl across to de Norman, and began to gently massage his hands and feet; after he had tired, de Norman did the same for him. Trooper Phipps followed their example with the Sikh trooper sitting next to him, and their hopes began to rise, if ever so faintly – they wondered if perhaps they might survive their ordeal after all.

Yet that evening as Duncan was drifting off to sleep, there was a great commotion outside the door and a mandarin entered with three attendants, who arrested the jailor who had helped them and dragged him away in chains. They expected that at any moment the other jailors would return and tighten the cords that bound them, but they seemed too agitated by their colleague's treachery to pay much attention to their prisoners. The next morning passed uneventfully, but at noon those who were still conscious were dragged out of the prison into the courtyard, where they saw their former jailor stripped to the waist and tied to a wooden post.

Duncan heard the official read out the charge, 'In violation of Qing Code Article 267, Plotting Rebellion and Sedition by Rescuing Prisoners', and the sentence, 'Lingchi – To Be Put to Death by Cuts'. To the right of the condemned man a party of soldiers had set up a small altar, in front of which was a small brick stove that supported a cauldron of boiling water. Another soldier arrived shortly after carrying a basket containing five long swords, which he then placed carefully into the cauldron – the Great Lord, and the Second, Third, Fourth and Fifth Lords. To the left of the condemned man was a canvas booth in which sat three mandarins, representatives of the Board of Punishments.

'Gawd's truth,' hissed Phipps to the others. 'He's going to get the death by a thousand cuts. They're going to slice him up alive afore our bleedin' eyes, the poor bugger. And he was only trying to do a bit of good for us.'

As Phipps spoke, the executioner arrived, clad in red and green silk and wearing a yellow leather apron caked in blood.

'No they're not,' gasped De Norman, who was having trouble breathing. 'The dreadful thing about lingchi for a Chinaman is not the cutting – he'll be put to death on the second stroke of the sword through his heart – but the dismemberment of his body, which means his lost soul must forever wander the earth.'

Duncan had no words. He knew that this poor man who had helped them was about to receive the self-same form of punishment that Duncan had threatened him with the previous day. He forced himself to look into the man's eyes to try to convey his pity and regret, but they were filled with horror, as the executioner withdrew the Great Lord and with its heated blade sliced off the man's left breast. With his second stroke he drove the sword through the prisoner's heart, and he died before their eyes. Then the executioner proceeded to slice the flesh from the man's body with the different swords, first his other breast, then his thighs, buttocks, back and legs, until all the skin was stripped from his body down to the bone. He then dismembered the body, cutting off the ears, nose, lips, head, hands, feet, knees, hips, arms and legs, until the prisoner lay in a scattered bloody heap at the foot of the wooden stake.

Then the executioner announced 'Sha ren li!'[lxxxix]

The mandarins got up and left. Two undertakers robed in white arrived and loaded the poor man's remains into a wooden barrow, which they carried away to bury in an unmarked grave. They all wondered anxiously if they were going to receive the same punishment, but they were dragged back to the prison after the undertakers had left, with nothing more than a flew slaps and kicks for their trouble, which they accepted in resigned silence.

Except for Phipps, who cursed as they pushed him back down on the earthen floor of the prison.

'Fuck! Fuck! Fuck!' he cried as he stared at his hands, which had split open like the others. 'Fuck them to hell! If I ever get out of here, I'm going to slice up these bastards myself, with my carving knife and razor!'

By the morning his hands were dark with maggots, and De Norman had lapsed into a coma. Duncan began to despair, but Phipps continued his usual banter, and led the surviving Sikhs through a series of bawdy ballads and defamatory regimental songs.

lxxxix 'The prisoner has been killed!'

32

After a night in which his delirium drove those still conscious to distraction, Lieutenant Anderson finally died – the great wonder was that he had lasted so long. The French officer also died later in the day, and the jailors carried the bodies out – to where they did not like to think. Although de Norman had no wounds on his body, and his hands were not so badly swollen as before, he looked deathly pale and had great difficulty breathing. Duncan ceased trying to engage him in conversation, to avoid exhausting the man's dwindling resources, but did not think de Norman had long to go, for he had now lapsed into unconsciousness. Phipps continued his banter, although his hands were now alive with maggots, and they all knew he had the death sentence upon him. Duncan felt duty bound to try to keep up with his lively jesting, but also felt exhaustion setting in, as waves of nausea swept over him. He hoped desperately that it was not cholera.

***

Duncan prepared for death. Phipps had died that morning, abruptly; he had continued to buoy their spirits with his banter and songs, but had breathed his last in mid-sentence. As the jailors carried out his body, Duncan looked around him. Now it was only he and three Sikhs who remained conscious, and he could see that they were preparing to meet their end in whispered prayers. Although the sunlight streamed in through vents in the roof of their prison, a dark film hung over his eyes like a thick cobweb, and as he looked at their faces, he thought he could see their skulls beneath their skin. He turned away and began to say his own prayers, but then as he raised his head he saw her sitting there, cross-legged on the floor before him, her raven black hair spread out over her shoulders and her full red lips smiling at him. His heart leapt up with sudden joy, even though some part of him knew she was a hallucination of his fevered brain. She raised herself to kneel before him and massaged his hands and ankles. Her hands felt cool against his fevered skin, and he could smell her sweet soft breath as she leant before him. Then she took him by his hands and raised him up and led him away into the velvet blackness that soon engulfed them and extinguished his every anxiety and fear.

33

Lord Elgin ordered the army to advance. To the south and east of Peking the suburbs extended for miles beyond the walls, making a frontal assault difficult, so the allied armies skirted the northeast edge of the city, heading towards the An-ting gate, where the ground was open save for a few temples and villages. The French were in the vanguard of the advance, followed by the British cavalry, but both had become detached from the rest of the British army during the course of the day. In the late afternoon, as the French pickets approached the high outer walls of the Summer Palace, the Yuan Ming Yuan, Prince Kung fled with the Dowager Empress and their entourage from the rear of the Palace, returning to the city by the An-ting gate.

When the French entered the Yuan Ming Yuan, The Gardens of Perfect Brightness, they found Chinese peasants looting the grounds, the palace guards having fled with Prince Kung back into the city. The French quickly drove out the Chinese peasants, then proceeded to loot the palaces, pavilions and temples themselves, carrying away clocks, watches, china, silks, paintings, tapestries, gold, silver and jade, and every form of treasure and curio.

When Lieutenant-General Hope Grant reached the Yuan Ming Yuan in the afternoon and saw the French at their work, he immediately rescinded the British standing order forbidding looting, and the officers on his staff immediately joined in the general plunder. When Lord Elgin and Hope Grant entered the main palace later in the day, they were appalled by the gratuitous destruction and devastation. But Lord Elgin would not be distracted by it, even though the looting went on throughout the following day. He ordered the siege guns brought up and preparations made for an assault on the An-ting gate, since he did not expect Prince Kung to surrender the prisoners or accede to his demands.

Yet he did not relish the prospect. The walls of Peking were forty feet high and sixty feet thick, and Lieutenant General Wolseley had informed him that they had insufficient rounds to make an effective breach.

***

News of the allied looting of the Yuan Ming Yuan reached the Emperor at Jehol the day after the French began it. His rage over the pillage of his beloved palaces and pavilions consumed him, and he screamed that he would have his revenge, whatever the consequences. Without any persuasion from Yehonala or the Prince of I, he ordered a death warrant drawn up for the allied prisoners, which he signed in vermilion ink and impressed with his royal chop.[xc] A courier was immediately dispatched to carry the warrant south to Prince Kung.

***

In the night the jailors came for them. They carried Duncan's lifeless body outside and loaded it onto a waiting cart, then carried out the Sikh who had died in the night and laid the heavily bearded man beside him. The Sikh's face glistened olive green in the moonlight, but Duncan's shone as white as marble on a funeral statue. The remaining Sikhs were made to sit on either side of the cart, the driver cracked his whip, and they lumbered out of the fort gates and

---

xc Seal employed to sign documents.

into the night. No escort accompanied them, and the Sikhs knew not where they were going. Their Chinese driver did not understand Hindustani, and merely shrugged his shoulders when they asked him.

***

The courier from the Imperial court in Jehol managed to slip through the British lines and gain entry through the Dongzhi gate[xci] northeast of the city, although he had been forced to send his vermillion scroll up in a basket before they would allow him entry. Once inside the city, he rode straight to the Forbidden City, where he delivered the death warrants to Prince Kung. But he was too late. The barbarians were already dead or gone.

---

xci East Straight gate.

34

When the following morning passed with no sign of the surrender of the An-ting gate, Lord Elgin had Thomas Wade deliver an ultimatum to Prince Kung. Unless the An-ting gate was surrendered by noon on October 13, four days hence, and the prisoners released, the allies would attack the city; if they accepted his demands, he would keep the troops out of the city and respect the lives and property of the civilian population. Two days later Wade received word that some of the prisoners would be returned the following afternoon, but no mention was made of the surrender of the An-ting gate.

***

Later that same afternoon, Lord Elgin was delighted to learn that Prince Kung had stayed the execution of Parkes and Loch, and that they had been escorted to the British lines. As they were led by a staff officer to the temple where Lord Elgin and Hope Grant had made their headquarters, soldiers of all ranks ran forward to greet and cheer them. As Lord Elgin's orderlies plied them with food and drink, they described how they had been trussed and beaten, then taken to the Board of Punishment, where they had been kept in chains and interrogated. They had been told they were going to be executed, and had prepared for death, but then suddenly they had been released in carts with some French soldiers through the An-ting gate.

***

On the afternoon of Friday, October 12, four carts were brought into the allied camp, bearing a party of French soldiers, three emaciated Sikhs and two bodies, one Sikh and one European, which was immediately identified as the body of Duncan Simpson, who had been an interpreter on Lord Elgin's staff. When Lord Elgin and Hope Grant questioned the Sikh troopers, whose wrists demonstrated the torture they had endured, they were horrified and enraged. Although neither man said anything, both were of a mind to launch an immediate assault on the city, and hang the consequences for trade or the Taiping. They questioned the Sikhs as to the fate of the other prisoners, and they related how Lieutenant Anderson, Mr de Norman, Mr Bowlby, Private Phipps, the French officer who had been with them, and their fellow Sikhs had all died, although they did not know what had happened to their bodies.

As they were concluding their account, two medical orderlies unloaded the bodies from the cart in which they had ridden.

'Gawd's truth! This un ain't dead!' one of them cried. 'Close to it, but he's not gorn yet – there's a breath of a pulse.'

'My God, you're alive Duncan! God bless you!' Lord Elgin exclaimed. He immediately summoned his aide-de-camp and ordered that his own personal physician, Sir Henry Potter, be immediately brought to attend to him. When Sir Henry arrived a few moments later, he examined Duncan on the stretcher that the orderlies had laid on the ground.

'He's alive, your lordship, but only barely,' Sir Henry advised Lord Elgin. 'I don't think I can save him.'

'Do your best man, do your best!' Elgin urged him.

Word of the treatment of the prisoners spread rapidly through the ranks of the allied army and by nightfall every man was thirsting for revenge. Some of the Sikhs from Fane's Horse were so incensed that they seized some Chinese villagers and bound them in the same way as the prisoners who had been tortured, and their lives were only spared by the intervention of one of the officers.

There was still no word from Prince Kung about the surrender of the An-ting gate, so Lord Elgin ordered Lieutenant-Colonel Wolseley to prepare the batteries for an artillery barrage the following day and instructed Sir Hope Grant to prepare for a general assault on the An-ting gate.

***

Lieutenant-Colonel Garnett Wolseley stood beside the main breaching battery, his pocket-watch in hand, as the hours and minutes ticked by on the morning of Saturday, October 13, the day that Lord Elgin's ultimatum expired at noon. He had mixed feelings as eleven thirty passed and there was still no sign of surrender. Wolseley did not think they had enough heavy shot to make an effective breach in the walls or the gate, but if they did, he dreaded the consequences. If the British had to fight their way into the city, there would be no holding them back, for they were thirsting for revenge. Many innocent Chinese – men, women and children, who had played no part in the treacherous actions of their Manchu masters – would be slaughtered.

Eleven thirty passed. Then eleven forty. At eleven fifty, Wolseley ordered the embrasures unmasked, and the guns sponged, loaded and run out. Then just as he was about to give the order to fire, an officer from Lord Elgin's staff rode up to inform him that the Chinese had opened the An-ting gate.

With only minutes to spare, Lord Elgin led five hundred men of the 97th Regiment of Foot and the 8th Punjabs through the An-ting gate. The British flag was raised over the wall, and Lord Elgin brought up Desborough's battery, who deployed their guns to cover the streets, as huge crowds came out to stare in wonder at the dreaded barbarians who had gained entry to their capital city, which was the centre of the Earthly Kingdom under Heaven.

35

Late in the evening the remaining bodies were brought in on carts, in wooden coffins filled with quicklime – Lieutenant Anderson, William de Norman, Thomas Bowlby, Trooper Phipps, Mohamed Bux and two Sikhs from Fane's Horse. The bodies were hard to recognize, partly because night had fallen, and they had to be inspected by torchlight, but also because they were so badly decomposed. They identified Lieutenant Anderson and de Norman by items of their clothing, and Trooper Phipps by his high cavalry boots. Bowlby was completely unrecognizable, his naked body a bloody pulp after being savaged by the pigs and dogs; at the last minute the jailors had decided to preserve his body, and had pulled it away before the animals could consume it whole. Ironically, like his brother before him, Bowlby was only identified by the deformity of his right foot – he had told the same story to Hope Grant that he had told to Duncan. The surviving Sikhs identified duffadar Mohamed Bux and the other troopers.

Lord Elgin walked from one cart to another, peering into the coffins. His face was ashen grey and his lips were drawn tight in suppressed anger. When he reached the last cart he snapped out an order for the coffins to be closed, and stood aside in the gloom, in raging silence, clenching and unclenching his fists, his muscles weaving like bare wires under his skin. Then without a word he turned on his heel, and marched back to his quarters in the temple on the outskirts of the Yuan Ming Yuan.

***

Lord Elgin spent a sleepless night. There was no grandeur in his view of life as he raged at the inhumanity of the Manchu. Shortly after dawn he sent a messenger to Prince Kung, informing him that he would have no further communication with him until he had decided upon a suitable punishment, which would demonstrate his detestation of the torture and murder of the allied officials and soldiers who had been protected by a flag of truce. He was so angry that he seriously contemplated sacking the Imperial city and destroying the remaining Qing forces in the north, leaving the Celestial Empire to the mercy of the Taiping. But he also knew the danger. Winter would soon be upon them, and the bulk of the Qing army would probably escape from the city. He had not enough troops to surround it, or cover all of the city gates, and he could find himself cut off from his supply lines and surrounded by reinforced Qing armies. Still he was up to it, God damn it!

But he knew it would never do – it would not wash back home. The British government did not want another expensive foreign war, and they certainly did not want another foreign colony, with India having proved more than enough to handle. He knew that if he attempted anything beyond the ratification of the revised Treaty of Tientsin he would be speedily withdrawn. He put the idea from his mind.

But what to do? It was worthless trying to punish those responsible for the treatment of the prisoners. If he demanded it, the Chinese would no doubt trot out some mandarins for execution, who would simply be replaced by others. The big fish responsible were long gone and safe at Jehol – the Emperor Hsien Feng, the concubine Cixi and the Prince of I. He could not imprison or execute Prince Kung, for it was Prince Kung who had released the prisoners and opened the An-ting gate, and only he had the

Emperor's authority to ratify the Treaty of Tientsin.

***

Two days later, Lord Elgin attended the funerals of the British dead in the Russian cemetery a mile northeast of the city. All that night he paced the elevated courtyard outside his quarters, which looked out over the Yuan Ming Yuan, trying to decide what to do; as he had paced all night on the verandah of Government House in Singapore three years before, when he had wondered whether to divert the troop ships of his first Chinese expedition back to India to help quell the mutiny. As dawn broke golden over Kunming Lake and the mountains beyond, Lord Elgin made his decision. He did not like it, and he knew he would never hear the end of it, but he knew it was the best thing to do under the circumstances. He went back into his quarters and washed and shaved, and called his orderly to bring him his breakfast. He dictated a letter informing Prince Kung of his decision, which was that the Yuan Ming Yuan would be burnt on the 18th, 'as a punishment inflicted on the Emperor for the violation of his word, and the act of treachery to a flag of truce.'

Baron Gros protested to Lord Elgin that such an appalling act of revenge and vandalism served no useful purpose, and indeed was liable to drive Prince Kung to flee the city and seek refuge with the Emperor at Jehol, in which case there would be no one left with the authority to ratify the treaty. Gros refused to allow French troops to take part in such a wanton act of destruction of the treasures of Chinese civilization. Yet that was precisely why Lord Elgin had decided to burn the Yuan Ming Yuan. It would demonstrate to the Chinese that their Emperor was not the divine being they believed him to be, but a fugitive who was unable to prevent the destruction of his beloved Gardens of Perfect Brightness, a place almost as sacred to the Emperor as the Forbidden City itself.

Lord Elgin ignored Baron Gros' hypocrisy, given the earlier French looting of the Yuan Ming Yuan, but took to heart his warning that he would be remembered as a despoiler of art, as his father, the Seventh Earl of Elgin, was remembered as the despoiler of the statues from the Parthenon in Athens, now known the world over as the 'Elgin Marbles'. He was not, however, moved by it. Lord Elgin gave the order, and on the morning of October 18, Sir John Mitchell moved his division to the Yuan Ming Yuan and began firing the buildings.

Baron Gros was wrong about Prince Kung. As the thick black smoke rose from the wooden buildings of the Yuan Ming Yuan, and burning embers and ash rained down upon the Imperial city, Prince Kung sent word to Lord Elgin that he accepted all of his demands, including his most recent demand for compensation for the families of all those who died in the Chinese prisons. Six days later, on October 24, Lord Elgin was borne into the Forbidden City in a scarlet palanquin, along a route lined with allied soldiers. The two men exchanged formally polite but icy looks as they sat down together in the Hall of Ceremonies, where Prince Kung ratified the revised Treaty of Tientsin, which included all of Lord Elgin's demands – including the opening of Tientsin as a new treaty port, the ceding of Kowloon peninsula facing Hong Kong island to the British government, and the payment of a war indemnity of three million pounds sterling. A day later, Prince Kung ratified a new Franco-Chinese treaty with Baron Gros.

The second China War, or the second Opium War, was finally over.

PART FOUR

'THE GHOST SHIP'

1860 – 1869

1

1860

Things had not worked out as Mui Chi had expected for any of them. Ah Keng was at first revolted by what she was expected to do, and especially by what she had been instructed by Auntie Ki to do to ensure that the old man could achieve and maintain an erection, if only for a few moments. And she had been heartbroken when she had first managed to stimulate him, and then had immediately lost her treasured virginity to the old man. Yet it had not been as disgusting as she had anticipated, and although she had felt a sharp pain when he had pierced her hymen, it was all over very quickly, and with only a little blood on the sheets – although the little blood had pleased the old man immensely. And she had not anticipated just how much she could please the old man. He told her afterwards before falling asleep – a blissful sleep, he had assured her the following morning – that she had returned his happiness to him, and that he felt like a young man again.

In the months that followed he demonstrated that this was no idle talk, for he behaved liked a man rejuvenated by some magic elixir. Once again, he took an active interest in his business affairs, he ate and drank with his old vigour, and took pleasure with his new concubine most nights when she was not menstruating. He felt that his essence was being renewed, and that his journey to King Yan Luo was postponed for many years, so he gave orders that his coffin be removed from the bedroom he often shared with Ah Keng.

Ah Keng found herself surprisingly content with the

arrangement. She quickly became accustomed to Bee Swee's nightly fumblings and discharges, which she came to treat as little more than a distasteful chore, which, when all was said and done, was preferable to many of the servant's chores, such as feeding the pigs or collecting the night soil. She knew that she could just as easily have been bought as an ordinary servant, and she knew how badly things could turn out for them. One of Mui Chi's personal servants, a mui tsai who had been part of her dowry, had been spitefully sold to one of the lowest brothels on Cross Street, after Mui Chi's eldest son had raped the girl while she was attending to him in his bath.

Ah Keng was also amazed by how much pleasure she could give Bee Swee for such a small outlay, and was touched by his overwhelming gratitude for her sexual favours. And he was not stingy in the expression of his gratitude, but provided her with lavish presents of clothing, jewellery, all sorts of dainty sweets and exotic fruits, lap dogs and kittens (of which she quickly tired, and then wondered where they disappeared to). On special occasions such as feast days or his birthday, he would give her generous gifts of money to dispose of as she pleased, which she kept carefully hidden from Mui Chi.

However, Ah Keng was under no illusions about her position. She had no recognized social status in the family, including Bee Swee, for whom she was in reality nothing more than a sexual slave, however grateful he might be for the pleasure she brought him. Yet she did not feel like a slave. She was more or less free to go as she pleased, into town or the countryside, albeit always accompanied by a servant, and she was allowed to receive her own visitors, albeit only female ones. She also found herself delighted – despite her lingering hostility – to receive monthly visits from Auntie Ki, who acted to all intents and purposes as if she were her foster mother, and from some of the mui tsai she had known who were still living with the old lady. And she in turn would visit Auntie Ki and the girls when she travelled to Chinatown to shop.

Yet although Bee Swee, Ah Keng and Auntie Ki were happy in their different ways, Mui Chi and the rest of her family were not. They all knew that Boo Swee's generosity to his new concubine posed a threat to their prosperity, both for the present and after his death. So pleased did he appear to be with his new concubine that there was a real danger that he might leave a significant amount of his estate to her in his will – something they agreed that they must prevent at all costs.

Thus in every little way, they made it known to her how much they despised her, a low-born girl with unbound feet who had been sold as a high-class prostitute, but as a prostitute nonetheless. Mui Chi always handed over the money to Ah Keng that Bee Swee instructed her to, but she always made a fuss over it, making out to her in subtle and not so subtle ways that she thought that Ah Keng was as good as stealing from her poor ailing father-in-law – although as both well knew, he was neither poor nor ailing at that moment in time. They snubbed her at every social opportunity, finding complicated ways of refusing to serve her at the family dinner in the evening, or managing to knock over her plate or spill sauces over her dress whenever they found they could, profusely apologizing in their offensively false public ways.

Yet her life had hardened Ah Keng to such pettiness. She patiently waited until Mui Chi handed over the money, which seemed to infuriate the first daughter-in-law even further, for it gave Mui Chi no reason to make complaint against her. She grew a little weary of the childish behaviour over dinner, so she persuaded Bee Swee that they should in future take dinner in their bedroom, so as not to waste any opportunity for lovemaking. To this he readily consented, ordering that the best dishes be first sent to them, while the rest of the family simmered in their anger at the dinner table. They were angry at the offense caused to them, but even angrier that their best opportunity for poisoning the hated concubine had been denied.

2

Hong Xiuquan woke at dawn, his dream still vivid. He had seen the three dead kings [xcii] riding out with him and his heavenly soldiers to destroy the demon-devils in the Golden Dragon Palace, and he had heard his followers shouting out, 'ten thousand years, ten thousand years of Heavenly Peace on Earth!' Then he knew that his victory over the demon-devils was assured, and he rejoiced within his heart, and thanked his Heavenly Father and Elder Brother Jesus.

Hong Rengan, the Shield King, was close to tears with frustration. Despite his initial enthusiasm, Hong Xiuquan had not initiated any of Hong Rengan's recommendations concerning the modernization and reform of Taiping society, economy and industry, and had not yet confirmed him as joint commander of the Taiping armies with General Li, the Loyal King. Hong Rengan had been entrusted with the care of Hong Xiuquan's son, Tiangui Fu, the Young Monarch. When Hong Rengan had betrayed his disappointment at the humiliating role assigned to him, Hong Xiuquan had assured him that on the contrary, it was the most important role in the Heavenly Kingdom. This was because Hong Xiuquan now devoted all his energy to spiritual matters, leaving his son Tiangui Fu to deal with the everyday running of the Heavenly Kingdom. And since the Young Monarch was only eleven years old, he needed a trusted advisor.

---

xcii Xiao Chaogui, the West King, Feng Yunshan, the South King, and Wei Changhui, the North King.

***

On November 26, Colonel Cavenagh, the governor of the Straits Settlements, reviewed the Singapore Volunteer Corps, commanded by Captain W.H. Read, on the Esplanade. There was nothing Colonel Cavenagh loved more than a military parade, as he sat oblivious to the sweltering heat in his full-dress uniform and medals, seated upon his magnificent white charger. Captain Read led the corps through a series of martial manoeuvres, marching by in fast and slow time, forming square, and firing two well-timed volleys before reforming facing the colonel and presenting arms.

The governor then addressed the company and celebrated the utility of volunteers at home and abroad. He cited his own experience with the company of volunteers he had commanded in Calcutta during the mutiny, which had successfully maintained order in the city, enabling the regular soldiers to take the field against the mutineers. He then informed them that since their own corps was the first to be officially acknowledged in India, they were entitled to bear the inscription 'Primus in Indis'[xciii] upon their company colours. At this news the volunteers gave three hearty cheers for the governor, before marching off to their headquarters in the Masonic Hall, on the corner of Coleman Street and the Esplanade, accompanied by the band of Her Majesty's 40th Regiment of Madras Native Infantry.

In March, the government had purchased seventy acres of land in Tanglin, formerly the nutmeg plantations of William W. Willans and Whampoa, and at the end of the year Captain Collyer began construction of the new infantry barracks, a set of airy attap-roofed plank buildings raised on stilts, with open verandahs running round the walls of the buildings, each housing fifty men. The area was considered a very healthy site, with a freshwater stream running through. This was in marked contrast to the cramped conditions of

---

xciii 'First in India.'

the abandoned buildings of the European Seaman's Hospital and the original Tan Tock Seng Hospital in which the troops were presently quartered, both Sepoys and European artillery, where the drinking wells were fouled by the water used by the local population for washing and bathing.

***

Suddenly he saw her face emerge from the depths of the darkness. It was the face of an angel, smiling down upon him. He knew she was an angel because he could see the bright red ring of celestial fire surrounding her face, and because he heard the soft whisper of her voice assuring him that everything would be all right. And then the darkness engulfed him once again.

***

After the revised Treaty of Tientsin was ratified, the allied troops were withdrawn from Peking, leaving a large force in occupation in Tientsin, now declared a free port, and at the Taku forts, until the war indemnity was paid. Lord Elgin and Sir Hope Grant returned to England, and Baron Gros and General Montauban – now awarded the title of Comte de Palikao by the Emperor Napoleon III, after the strategic bridge his men had captured – returned to France. Brigadier General Charles Staveley was put in charge of the remaining British troops when they were garrisoned in Shanghai the following year.

***

In early December, the Agri-Horticultural Society was established, on an acreage of land in Tanglin that the government had donated to the society. This had formerly been part of Whampoa's nutmeg plantation, which he had exchanged for land on Boat Quay, where he and Gilbert Angus had established their ill-fated icehouse in 1854.[7] The Botanical and Experimental Gardens, which had originally been planted on Government Hill, and which had fallen into disrepair and suffered great damage during the work on the new military fortification, were relocated to the society's new Tanglin premises.[xciv]

---

xciv The site of the present-day Botanical Gardens.

3

Hong Kong
December 12, 1860

Dear Mr and Mrs Simpson

I write this note in haste in the hope that I can make the mail-streamer and reach you in time for Christmas, to give you the news that your son Duncan is safe and well, and no longer in any danger. I am not sure how much Lord Elgin communicated to you about Duncan's time in the Chinese prison, and regret that I was only able to inform you of his delirious and dangerous state of health when he arrived at the Mission Hospital here last month. He suffered mightily from the tortures inflicted upon him by his Chinese jailors, who bound his wrists and ankles until they turned black, and were in great danger of putrefaction, but I think he suffered most by seeing his comrades die one by one of their frightful wounds while he survived. He still feels guilty about that, and has a passionate hatred of the Manchu rulers – if that dynasty has in fact survived, and there is currently some doubt about it – and a burning ambition to rejoin the Taiping in their war against them. I have counselled strongly against this, and common sense has prevailed, at least with the help of Nurse Angela Findlay – or nurse Angie as we call her – who has helped me persuade him that he must return to Singapore to recuperate and be reunited with his family, who had thought they might never see him again. I have to tell you that Nurse Angie has been a perfect angel to him, staying by his bedside night and day during the worst of his danger and delirium. Your dear son thought she was a real angel come to take him up to heaven when he first regained his senses, and saw her shining, smiling face, with its ring of burning red hair!

But enough for the moment or I shall miss the mail. I will have Duncan write to you himself as soon as he is able and will send him back to you as soon as he can travel.

With fond memories of our meeting many years ago in Singapore,

Yours most sincerely
Dr James Legge

***

Christmas day had come and gone – a day like any other day, Margaret Brown reflected. Like the other merchants, Richard had spent the day at work. She had made some effort to decorate a Chinese juniper tree with Christmas decorations, and had invited Mr Singer and his wife to dinner. The evening had gone well, but Richard had left her soon after their guests departed. She did not mind, and preferred to be alone, as she sat out on the verandah looking up at the night stars, shining brightly against the blue-black sky.

She thought of her son Thomas, and wondered if he sometimes looked up at the same stars and thought of her. It had been six years since she had last seen him, and in that time there had been three major wars: the Crimean War, the Indian Mutiny and the

Chinese War. It would be another six years before he became a commissioned officer and they could return home to see him again. And then what? He might be sent off to another war ... and she might never see him again.

She did not know if she could bear to wait another six years. Thomas still wrote to her, but more and more dutifully as she sensed his memory of her was fading – his letters talked of field manoeuvres and current affairs rather than his memories of Singapore. He had sent her a picture of himself in his cadet's uniform for Christmas. She still recognized his face, but his smile now seemed so adult and distant and she felt that she had already lost her child.

He was all she had to live for, as she went through her dreary days and her pretence of being a devoted wife, but she feared in her heart that one day he might be taken from her forever, on some foreign battlefield. She thought she would kill herself if that ever happened and could scarcely bear the thought of it. She thought of what her life might have been and of what it had become. She felt that all the beauty and promise had gone from her world, and all the colours, even when she stood among the flowers in her garden in the bright sunlight. It was as if she waited in the shadows, waiting for the dark night to finally engulf her.

4

Ah Keng's life settled into a kind of normality, and for the most part she enjoyed life, despite the restrictions of her position. She particularly enjoyed being allowed out to visit the town in a palanquin, even though she was always under the guard of a servant, when she would purchase some small gift for Bee Swee or Auntie Ki. She found that these small actions gave her intense pleasure, that she, who had never owned anything in the world, could now give something of her own to others, even though she was now owned by one and had been owned by the other in the past. She missed her parents, and hoped that they still lived, but doubted she would ever see them again. Even if she could somehow gain her freedom and return to Amoy, she would not know where to look for them, for she did not know what had happened to them. And in her heart, she doubted if they still lived – she knew her mother had been close to death when she had left them, and she knew that the civil war still raged as fiercely as it had done when they had been forced to flee their home – there would be nothing but bare fields and burnt ruins to return to.

She tried to put these thoughts to the back of her mind and focus on her good fortune, at least in relation to those other mui tsai in Singapore, who were not well-fed and clothed, who did not sleep in soft beds, and did not have any money of their own to buy small presents for their benefactors, notwithstanding the self-interest of their benefaction.

Her reverie was interrupted when the palanquin was brought to a sudden halt. She drew aside the curtain to ask her escort what was happening. He replied that there was a sick man lying across the road, who was blocking their passage. He assured Ah Keng that the man would be quickly moved, but he was not, for nobody was rushing to help the filthy old man, least of all her escort or her bearers. In frustration she climbed down from the palanquin, which had been laid on the ground, to see what was going on and in the hope that she could hasten the process. As she approached the front of the palanquin, two coolies were pulling the old man to the side of the road. She was about to turn back and retake her seat when suddenly she saw his face. It could not be! She must surely be dreaming! He was filthy and ragged and old, much older than she remembered. But still she remembered him as vividly as if it had only been yesterday, when she had left him on the dockside in Amoy. He was her father, and he was alive, even though his eyes stared out into space from the dark sockets of his skull.

But what should she do? Her mind raced. She could not take him home, for she knew Bee Swee would not have him in his house or let her care for him there. She could not take him to the Tan Tock Seng Hospital, for the old hospital had closed down and the new one was not yet built. There was only one thing she could do. She gave each of the coolies a copper coin and told them to put her father into the palanquin and then told the bearers to carry him to Auntie Ki's house – they knew the way, since they had taken her there often enough before. The servant who was her escort protested and said he would inform Bee Swee of what she had done.

'You will tell him nothing, Ah See,' Ah Keng hissed, bearing her teeth like a serpent bearing its fangs. 'You will promise this to me now or I will swear to my master in the name of the Queen of Heaven that you tried to force yourself upon me.'

'I have known the master far longer than you have,' Ah See

replied haughtily, 'I was his servant when we were in Canton.'

'I know you have, Ah See. But does he love you as he loves me? Do you give him as much pleasure as I do? And do you really want to take that chance?'

Ah See said nothing in reply, but stood considering the question in silence.

'And why should you? Why does Bee See need to know?' Ah Keng continued, adopting a more conciliatory tone. 'It would only upset him and where is the harm in it? This man is my father, even though he has fallen on hard times. I am only doing my filial duty.'

'Mistress, you did not tell me he was your father. My master would not hold this action against you, but still I think it is best that he does not know; you are right to take him to Madam Ki. Let us go quickly, for he is in desperate need of medical care.'

Auntie Ki was shocked when they turned up at the door with the dirty and ragged old man, but agreed to take him in when Ah Keng told her he was her father, and offered to pay for his board. They sent out for a doctor, while they cleaned him up as best they could. Wang Zuoxin was barely conscious and feverish, mumbling incoherently while his teeth chattered, despite the heat of the day. Long before the doctor arrived, Auntie Ki recognized what was wrong with him.

'He has been chasing the dragon too long, Ah Keng. He is an addict, and in his condition, he probably smokes the poorest chandu.[xcv] I will give him some of my own, which is of top quality.'

While he could not converse with them coherently, or stand on his own two feet, Wang Zuoxin knew well enough what was being offered him when the pipe was put in his hand, for he straightway put it to his mouth and deeply inhaled the sweet-smelling smoke. His expression gradually turned from deep anguish to calm serenity, and the haunted look passed from his face as he turned towards

---

xcv Opium dross, the residue left after opium has been smoked.

them and seemed to see them for the first time.

'Father, it is me, Ah Keng! Oh father, you are alive! You are very sick, but we will look after you and bring you back to health!'

Wang Zuoxin stared at her for a long time, and then the recognition seemed to dawn on him.

'Is it really you, Ah Keng, my only daughter?'

'It is really me, father. Tell me what happened to you ... and to mother.'

'Your mother died. I could not save her ... I ...'

But then he drifted away in an opium dream as the doctor arrived.

5

The doctor told them that Wang Zuoxin was badly undernourished, but whether it was a result of his opium addiction or some other cause he could not say – only time would tell. He gave them an elixir to restore his blood and a balm to put on his open wounds. He advised them on a suitable diet and promised to return in a week's time to check up on the patient. The doctor said it would be unwise to deny him opium, since he would suffer very badly from withdrawal symptoms and his weakened body and mind might not be able to bear it. But they should give him only good quality opium and gradually reduce the dosage.

Ah Keng paid for the doctor and for the servant whom Auntie Ki hired to look after her father. The servant looked to his physical needs, while Auntie Ki looked to his spiritual ones. It was she who prepared and offered him his pipe, and she who sat with him while she took her own. Ah Keng visited as often as she could without arousing suspicion and gradually Wang Zuoxin regained some of his strength and mental composure, although he remained desperately thin. He told Ah Keng that her mother had died shortly after she had left, and cried in shame when he explained that he had abandoned her body while he had searched desperately for his daughter. He told her that he had been about to drown himself, but had been persuaded against it by a man on the dockside who had offered him a new life in Singapore. He had not cared much about that, he said, but he had been eager to take the pipe that brought him peaceful oblivion.

In any case, the man had lied. When they arrived in Singapore, he and the other sinkeh[xcvi] were transferred to another vessel, a native prahu, which had taken them to the tin mines of northern Sumatra. He had not been able to save any money, he confessed, because what little had been left over after his food and board he had spent on opium, to which he had become hopelessly addicted – it had brought him the only relief from his misery and exhaustion. A few years passed and he still had not paid his passage debt, but his body was so wasted that he was of no further use to his employers so they had thrown him out of the mining camp. After a nightmare journey through the jungle, during which he had staggered and crawled along the ground without food, water or opium, and during which he felt sure he was going to die, he finally reached a Malay kampong at the mouth of a small river, where a family had taken pity on him and nursed him back to some semblance of health. They had helped him secure passage on a pilgrim ship travelling to Singapore, where he thought he might have some chance of finding his long-lost daughter – the other men on the ship had told him that most of the girls were taken to Singapore and sold as mui tsai. But in his weakened state he had been unable to find work, and his opium cravings had driven him into madness. He had begged, borrowed and stolen to maintain his habit, but had only managed to procure the poorest chandu – not the sweet black balls that Auntie Ki had provided. He had known that in his condition he had not long to live, and had been waiting for Ox Head and Horse Face to bear him off to Hell. Then suddenly he had been snatched back into the land of the living, into the arms of his beloved daughter, whom he had shamed.

Ah Keng assured her father that it had not been his fault – it was she who had run away, and she who had been stupid enough to get herself kidnapped. When she said this, Wang Zuoxin smiled

xcvi Chinese immigrants.

a thin, wan smile, and his eyes filled with tears.

'Enough of this,' said Auntie Ki, 'you must get back, Ah Keng, before you arouse suspicion at home.'

***

Ah Keng did arouse suspicion at home. Bee Swee asked her why she went to town so often, and she told him that she was visiting Auntie Ki, who was sick. Bee Swee was satisfied when Ah See confirmed that Ah Keng had been visiting her sick aunt. Ah See had formed a grudging respect for Ah Keng's filial piety, when previously he had thought of her as her nothing more than a money-grabbing concubine, and in any case he had been well-paid for his story. But Mui Chi was not so easily persuaded, and suspected that Ah Keng and Ah See were both lying. She determined that she would discover their secret and use it against the hated concubine.

6

In February, Rear-Admiral Sir James Hope, the commander of the British naval force that had been repulsed at the Taku forts in 1859, took an armoured squadron up the Yangtze River to Nanking, where he met with General Li and Hong Rengan. After lengthy negotiations, the Taiping leaders agreed not to advance to within thirty miles of Shanghai for one year. In return, Rear-Admiral Hope agreed to maintain British neutrality and to open a consulate in Nanking and two other Taiping held cities. The following month the Taiping reopened the Yangtze for trade, having closed it the previous year after their setback at Shanghai.

With the Emperor Hsien Feng isolated and ailing in Jehol, the Imperial Dragon was headless and the British were taking no chances. If the Manchu dynasty collapsed, they would have to deal with the Taiping one way or another. And despite Hong Xiuquan's dreams of Heavenly armies triumphing over the demon-devils, General Li and Hong Rengan were taking no chances either. They knew one day soon they would have to deal with the British, hopefully as Christian brothers – but if not, their earthly armies were preparing to return to Shanghai in force.

***

Frederick Townsend Ward sat alone in a waterfront bar in Shanghai. He had been in Hong Kong for treatment of his wounds, and had only recently returned. The bar was normally frequented by

American sailors, but today it was almost empty, and he knew the reason why. The southern states of America had seceded from the union, and civil war between the Federal north and Confederate south had broken out after the Confederates had fired upon the Federal arsenal at Fort Sumter in Charleston, South Carolina on April 12, when President Lincoln had ordered the Union navy to reinforce it. Most of the Americans had returned to their ships or tried to find some other way home, to join either the northern or the southern side.

After General Li had been repelled from Shanghai, he had turned part of his army around and driven back the Foreign Army Corps with heavy losses. The force that had once been Ward's pride and joy no longer functioned as an organized fighting unit – the best of the Americans had left for the civil war, except for Burgevine, who remained in nominal change of the Corps. Ward contemplated returning to his native Massachusetts and offering his services to the Union armies. Yet he knew it would come hard to take orders from others after he had been commander of his own army, and he was likely to be subordinated to some newly minted West Point officer who had never seen a shot fired in anger. But the chances of reviving the Foreign Army Corps seemed grim, given their recent losses and failures, and he thought it unlikely that the Shanghai merchants, including his father-in-law, Yang Fang, would be willing to finance such a project.

Yet in this he was proven wrong, for that night he received a visit from Li Hongzhang, the mandarin in charge of the Imperial forces in Shanghai. Li Hongzhang requested that he raise and command another army, this time composed of Chinese soldiers, who would be trained by Ward and his American and European officers. The Chinese merchants of Shanghai would pay for the recruitment and equipment of these men, who were to be trained in Western military tactics and systems of command, and the use of small arms, Enfield rifles and mobile artillery. Ward immediately agreed to do so, and set about recruiting and training his new army, which he equipped with Western type uniforms, including turbans modelled on those of the Indian Sepoys.

***

In May, as the fortification on Government Hill was nearing completion, it was found that its highest point of elevation was lower than Pearl's Hill, which had been the original site favoured by Captains Lake and Best and Governor Blundell. Accordingly, Captain Collyer gave orders that the summit of Pearl's Hill be reduced to a level below that of the new fortification. The European artillery regiment was transferred to the new fortification, which the government decided to name Fort Canning, after the Governor-General of India. Government Hill, which had once been called Forbidden Hill, now came to be known as Fort Canning Hill. The new Fort Fullerton was also completed, and the new sea wall, extending from Fort Fullerton to Telok Ayer Market, was named Collyer Quay, after the chief engineer. The new army barracks at Tanglin were also completed, and prepared to receive the European regiment that had been promised to reinforce the defences of Singapore. But with the Crimean and China wars concluded and their threats removed, the dispatch of these reinforcements was delayed and finally cancelled, and the barracks quickly fell into disrepair.

The new Fort Canning was the hot topic of discussion at the ball for the European merchants hosted by Tan Kim Seng at the Masonic Lodge during Race Week. While most agreed on the need for a strong military and naval presence in Singapore, most complained that they would likely be expected to bear the cost until the Straits Settlements were transferred to the crown, which did not seem likely to be anytime soon. As to Fort Canning itself, many thought its guns were set too far back and consequently not powerful enough to protect against a naval force threatening the ships in the harbour from out at sea – they could only reach the merchant ships already in the harbour, which was not much use to anyone. Some speculated, although not to Tan Kim Seng, that the guns were not intended to fire upon an enemy at sea, but upon Chinatown in the event of another serious riot. As for its potential use as a refuge for Europeans in the event of such a riot, by Chinese, Indians or perhaps even Malays, most thought they would be better off taking their chances with the merchant ships or naval vessels in the harbour, since all the wells in Fort Canning were dry, making it unable to withstand any extended siege, and the gun embrasures were open to easy attack by enemy snipers.

7

They met him off the P & O steamer from Hong Kong as it docked at Johnston's Pier.

Duncan had scarcely stepped off the gangplank when his father and mother rushed forward to embrace him, their tears of joy running freely down their cheeks.

'Grand tae have ye hame again, son,' Ronnie told him, 'we were sae worried aboot you.'

As he embraced his mother, Duncan could not help smiling when he heard his father's words. In all his years away from Scotland, his Highland accent had not changed one bit – even when he demonstrated his fluency in Malay, Chinese and Hindustani.

'But wait up, I have someone I would like you all to meet,' he said, turning his back to them and then bringing forward the young lady who had followed him down the gangplank.

'Father, mother, grandpa John, Charlie and Annie, I would like you to meet Miss Angela Findlay – Angie, as we call her – who saved my life and is my fiancée.'

They all welcomed her as if she was some long-lost relative, which in a manner of speaking grandpa John thought that she was.

***

Yehonala and her son had survived the trip to Jehol, but she now found herself in great danger. The dying Emperor blamed her for

357

the disasters of the war against the barbarians, while her enemies spread vicious lies about her. When Hsien Feng finally died on August 21, his infant son Zaichun ascended the Dragon Throne, and took the royal name Tung Chih. The Prince of I and his fellow noble conspirators declared themselves regents, and planned to assassinate the concubine Cixi on the return journey back to Peking. But Yehonala outfoxed them all. She rode ahead to Peking with Tung Chih and her sister Sakota, under the protection of her former lover Jung Lu and his loyal Yeho-Nala Bannermen. She bore with her the seal of authority that authorized all Imperial proclamations, which (through the machinations of An Te-hai) the eunuch masseur who attended to Hsien Feng in his final days had smuggled out of the Emperor's bedchamber. Armed with Imperial proclamations bearing the late Emperor's seal, Yehonala had the regents arrested, tried and sentenced to death. She was now firmly back in control. [8]

***

On October 1, St Andrew's Church was finally opened for service, having been completed in December the previous year. The church, which was designed in the Gothic style by Colonel Macpherson, the executive engineer and former superintendent of convicts, was completed under the direction of Major John F. A. McNair, who had taken over from Macpherson in 1857. Like the previous church, the new building was constructed using convict labour, and the inner and outer walls were coated in chunam plaster.[xcvii] The steeple of the church, with its lancet windows, turret-like pinnacles and decorated spire, was said by some to resemble the

---

xcvii A plaster made of shell lime beaten with egg whites and course sugar into a thick paste, then blended with water in which the husks of coconuts had been soaked. When the plaster dried, it was polished with round stones to a smooth and shiny finish.

steeple of Salisbury Cathedral, although, like the rest of the church, it was adapted to the demands of the tropical climate, having a large porte-cochere[xcviii] under the steeple, to shade the congregation arriving by coach. Tall windows lined the sides and the nave of the church, to maximize light and ventilation. An elaborate system of punkah fans hung from iron rods embedded in the roof, which were operated by Indian boys who pulled on the ropes that were drawn out through the side windows. This provided a light breeze that cooled the brows of the worshippers, although some found that the motion of thirty-two punkahs moving in different directions caused them to experience nauseous feelings akin to seasickness. A trio of lancet windows in stained glass commemorated the memory of Sir Stamford Raffles, John Crawfurd and Colonel William J. Butterworth.

The first wedding to be held in the new church was between Duncan Simpson, the son of Ronnie and Sarah Simpson, two of the earliest European inhabitants of Singapore, and Angela Findlay, the daughter of the Reverend and Mrs James Findlay of Aberdeen. Her parents having both passed away some years previous, the bride was given away by Captain William Scott, a highly respected and much-loved member of the European community.

'They mak a bonnie couple,' William Scott said to his old friend John Simpson after the ceremony, as they shared a glass of Champagne at the reception held in the Hotel de l'Europe[xcix] on Beach Road.

'That they dae,' John Simpson replied. 'I just hope they hae better luck wi their bairns.'

Duncan honeymooned with his new wife in Siam,[c] where they

---

xcviii Covered porch.
xcix The hotel was opened by the Frenchman J. Casteleyns and his wife in 1860, who had transferred their establishment from the smaller premises that they had opened on Hill Street in 1857.
c Present-day Thailand.

stayed at the home that Tan Kim Ching had built for himself when he visited his businesses there.

***

Zeng Guofan, now Imperial commissioner with overall command of the Qing armies, aimed to bring the war against the Taiping to a speedy end. While General Zuo Zongtang re-established control of the southern provinces of Guangdong and Fujian, where the Taiping rebellion had begun, Zeng Guofan and his brother Zeng Guoquan laid siege to the crucial Anqing river base, which controlled the Taiping lines of supply and communication to the north and west. When their Xiang army group starved the city into submission, they massacred the sixteen thousand Taiping rebels who garrisoned it.

When news of the fall of Anqing reached General Li Xiucheng and Hong Rengan, they knew they had no choice. They had to capture Shanghai, with or without the co-operation of their foreign brethren, otherwise Nanking would soon be starved into submission, and the Taiping Heavenly Kingdom on Earth would be destroyed by the demon-devils.

Yehonala and Zeng Guofan also anticipated that the Taiping would try to capture Shanghai. They ordered Li Hongzhang, in command of the Qing forces there, to defend the city at all costs, and to urge the foreign barbarians that it was in their best interests to join them in their fight against the Taiping, who would destroy the very trade that they had so recently fought a war to protect.

***

'You seem more than usually cheerful tonight, John,' said Captain Scott to his old chess companion, as he poured them both a generous portion of malt whisky. 'Are you under the illusion that you are going to beat me tonight, after all your recent defeats.'

'Nae illusion, Willie,' John Simpson responded. 'Ye ken I've been distracted with the weddin' and a', and now with the excitement of a new bairn in the offin'. I'm sae glad for my grandson – he deserves a bit o' happiness at last, after all he's been through.'

Duncan had recently announced to his family that Angie was pregnant with their first child.

'I quite agree, and I'm very glad for him,' Captain Scott replied. 'Which is not to say I intend to let you beat me tonight. Now how long ago was it when you last beat me? Was it this year or last?'

'Away with ye man, and pay attention to yer game – or it will a' be over too soon, and I'll hae to beat ye a' over again.'

That night John Simpson played one of the finest games he had ever played, and an hour later had his old friend in what he thought was a sure checkmate. He moved his queen into position.

'Let's see ye get oot of that, then, Willie!' he grinned as he rose from the table. 'I hae to step outside, since nature is calling, but ye could fill my glass while y'r thinking on it.'

When he returned, Captain Scott remained seated at the table, staring at the chessboard. But he had not filled their glasses, and he was not staring at the chess pieces. His soft blue eyes were staring empty into space, for he had passed away while John Simpson had been in the garden.

John Simpson sat down and looked with sadness at his old friend for a few moments. Then he leaned forward and gently closed his eyes, but not before he had tipped over his queen in silent surrender.

Captain Scott was buried in the Christian cemetery on Fort Canning Hill. He was seventy-five years old.

8

1862

In early December of 1861, the Taiping armies of General Li Xiucheng had advanced eastward once again. They captured Ningpo on December 2 and Hangzhou on December 29, and by mid-January 1862 they were massed before Shanghai. Once again General Li offered to spare his foreign brethren in the city if they maintained their neutrality, but this time his offer was couched in the form of a threatening ultimatum, which was delivered to the European ambassadors by Joseph Lambert, an English seaman who had been captured by the Taiping but released for this purpose. Lambert reported that General Li had warned him that if the British or French tried to resist them when they attacked Shanghai, they would cut off the heads of any foreigners who got in their way, and stop all the tea and silk trade; but if the British and French did not interfere with them, all foreigners might go all over the country and trade.

The Loyal King's ultimatum only served to strengthen the Europeans' already fixed resolve to resist any Taiping attack upon Shanghai. The British commander, Brigadier General Staveley, deployed his four thousand regular British troops to man the defences, while eight British warships anchored offshore, ready to bombard the city if it fell to the Taiping forces. Heavy gun emplacements were built to house thirty-pounder swivel guns, which covered all the land and river approaches to the city.

* * *

Augustus F. Lindley, Commander of the Loyal and Faithful Auxiliary Legion of the Taiping army, reported to General Li Xiucheng at his headquarters, which was a large marquee tent festooned with yellow silk banners and the golden lion standard of the Loyal King.

'Are your men ready, and prepared to fight the foreigners if necessary?' the Loyal King asked him.

'They are, Loyal King,' Lindley replied. 'We will do what is necessary to capture Shanghai, even if it means taking the fight to my own countrymen – if they have become so corrupt as to betray their professed neutrality once again.'

'That is good,' General Li replied. 'I know I can count on you, as I can count on all my captains,' as he waved his arm expansively over the heads of his assembled officers.

'But tell me, Commander of the Loyal and Faithful Auxiliary Legion, what progress does your dear wife make?' he said, with a questioning smile.

Augustus F. Lindley had married a Portuguese girl named Marie, who had taken the Taiping cause to heart, and had begun to practice with one of the new Enfield rifles that her husband had managed to relieve from the Qing forces. She had proven herself to be a natural markswoman, and was improving quite dramatically with increased practice. She had recently demonstrated her cool efficiency as a sniper by killing three senior Qing officers, who had momentarily exposed themselves to her deadly fire.

'My dear Marie makes good progress, General Li,' Lindley responded, holding up three fingers to indicate the death of three demon-devils. Then he asked the Loyal King when they would advance upon Shanghai, and the general replied that they would begin their attack in three days' time, because he wanted to give his foreign brethren a few more days to consider their position, in the hope that they might yet avoid a fight with them. Lindley knew that such a hope was vain, and that the delay would only give the enemy more time to prepare. But he made no protest, since it was clear that General Li was fixed in his mind. He would give them a few days grace as Christian brethren, but would crush them without pity if they dared to align themselves with the demon-devils. Lindley knew the city was well fortified and garrisoned, by regular troops as well as foreign mercenaries, but he also knew that the Taiping forces heavily outnumbered them. He also knew that they had brought their own artillery and Western rifles, which had been smuggled to them once the Yangtze had been reopened to trade.

'These three days will give my Marie more time to practice,' he replied, as he prepared to return to his legion. 'I await your command, Loyal King.'

As he stepped out into the January night, Lindley felt something wet land on the back of his hand, and then on the tip of his nose. He turned his eyes up to the grey heavens, and saw the first of the winter snow beginning to fall.

***

Brigadier General Staveley put Captain Charles Gordon of the Royal Engineers in charge of the Shanghai defences. Gordon had been with Lord Elgin and Hope Grant in the 1860 campaign that had ended the Second Opium War, and found it ironic that he, who had been present at the capture of Peking and burning of the Yuan Ming Yuan, was now helping to defend the city for the Manchu. Before he set off to inspect the defences, Staveley asked Gordon to keep an eye on the American mercenary Frederick Townsend Ward and his new Chinese army, now known by their uniforms as the 'Imitation Foreign Devils'.

'We may have need of his Chinese brigade, if the Taiping do attack us,' he acknowledged, 'but I don't want Ward starting the fight on his own account. We must at least maintain the pretence of neutrality.'

Gordon assured Staveley that he would do so. As he stepped out of the British consulate, he felt the first snowflakes brush against his check, and looked up into the thick grey clouds above.

***

The snow fell in sticky white flakes, without respite, for fifty-eight hours, until it lay thirty inches thick over the fields and rooftops, and the wind swirled the heavy wet mass into deep drifts before the walls of Shanghai. When it finally ended, the temperature plunged below freezing, and a cruel frost set in. The Taiping armies were stopped in their tracks on the day that General Li had intended to mount his attack on the city.

'We cannot move,' was all that the Loyal King could say to his loyal captains.

Worse still, the Taiping forces had planned a lightning campaign, and had not brought winter clothing or sufficient food supplies. When they tried to obtain grain and vegetables from the local population, they found that they were no longer welcomed as liberators, but were set upon and harried by local militias organized by the minor gentry. When General Li did eventually try to advance his troops, they were cut down mercilessly, as they plodded forward like oxen in heavy mud through the deep snowdrifts, their bright blood splashing red over the frozen killing field. The Christian missionary leaders in Shanghai proclaimed that the snow blizzard was an Act of Providence, sent to protect God's children from the blasphemous and murderous Taiping.

When the defenders realized that the Taiping forces had lost their critical momentum, they began to send out sorties against them, recapturing some of the small towns and villages around Shanghai, where many of the Taiping leaders had made their camps. In these small battles, Ward's new army of one thousand trained Chinese, supported by regular Qing forces, came into its own. Ward drove the Taiping from Wu-Sung and Guangfulin, the strange uniforms and disciplined fusillades of his well-trained army creating surprise and consternation among the enemy, who were unprepared for this new type of Qing fighting unit. Invigorated by his success, Ward became more ambitious, and in joint operations with regular Qing battalions drove the enemy from Yinchipeng, Chenshan, Tianmashan and other areas around Songjiang, killing and capturing thousands of rebels. His greatest success came in late February, when General Li, furious at the impudence of the American upstart, flung a force of over twenty thousand men against Ward's two thousand defending Songjiang. General Li's men were slaughtered when they ran into concealed artillery that flanked the city, and were driven back with heavy losses.

Li Hongzhang and his merchant backers were well pleased with their investment in Ward's new army. So was Yehonala, now Dowager Empress, when she heard of his successes against the Taiping. In March she decreed that henceforth Ward's army would be officially known as the 'Ever Victorious Army', and she raised him to the title of mandarin of the forth rank, with a peacock feather.

General Li did not remain to watch his soldiers defeated by the combined forces of the Ever Victorious Army and the regular Qing battalions, whose confidence now grew as Li Hongzhang and Ward quickly learned how to best deploy their combined forces in joint attacks against the Taiping. When he received news in June that Zeng Guofan's brother Zeng Guoquan had led a sizeable Qing force down from Anqing and was now threatening the southern gate of Nanking, General Li was forced to withdraw the bulk of his army west again, to try to dislodge the Qing from their new fortifications threatening the Taiping capital.

9

Adi bin Sadat was the son of Sadat bin Badang and his wife Nahu. He was brought up in the kampong where his family had always lived, and was an intelligent young man who took in everything around him. He had not inherited his father Sadat's gift for reciting the Koran, although he loved to hear him incant the sacred verses, but he had a special talent for drawing. He would draw animals and scenes of nature and everyday life, which he would embellish with calligraphic script, earning him the praise of his elders.

He helped his father cultivate their rice holdings and worked with him on their fishing boat. They lived a comfortable and peaceful life, but Adi had a restless spirit. He considered himself blessed, but knew he was capable of greater things, even though he knew it was a sin to presume this. His father had told him he was a descendant of Badang, the great warrior who had saved one of the ancient kings of Singapura. Although he tried hard to accept his lot with humility, Adi wished that he had lived in a time when he could have proven his manhood as a warrior.

He knew there was little chance of that these days, because there were no wars for Malays in Singapore to fight. He had learned how the once great Malay empire had declined over the centuries, and how its remnants had been displaced in Singapore. Sultan Ali was impoverished and powerless, and Temenggong Abu Bakar, like his father Temenggong Daing Ibrahim who had died earlier in the year, was a businessman whose fortunes were tied to Johor rather than Singapore. He sometimes heard other Malays talk about rising against the British authorities, and even talk of assassinating the governor, but he knew nothing would come of it. There were too few Malays, and fewer still willing to go that far. And they were not only dominated by the British, with their soldiers and policemen, but also hugely outnumbered by the Chinese, with their wealth and secret societies, for whom fishermen and farmers and boatbuilders and syces were no match. In any case, he bore no grudge against the British, for they had done him no harm and had left him alone to live out his simple life. He was ambitious, although his ambition had no definite content. But he could dream.

10

In March, Lord Canning retired from his position as viceroy of India, a position he had held since the government of India had been transferred to the British crown in August 1858. His wife had died four months earlier, and his own health was broken after six years as head of the Indian government, including the tumultuous years of the mutiny. He hoped that rest and the bracing weather of the home country might revive his health and spirits, but he died within two months of returning to London, at the age of fifty.

Lord Canning was succeeded in the position of viceroy of India by Lord Elgin, as reward for his services in the late China War. The following year Lord Elgin followed his predecessor and Oxford contemporary to the grave. He died at his home in Dharamsala[ci] on November 23, aged fifty-two, and was buried at the nearby Church of St John in the Wilderness.

***

Later in the year the Town Hall was completed, at the foot of the High Street, next to the Courthouse. Designed by John Bennett, the municipal engineer, it was an elaborate two-storied building with rusticated columns and loggias on the first floor, Italianate windows, and elaborate decorative gables surmounting the four prominent corner pavilions. On the ground floor, the hall was fitted out with

ci City in Kangra district of India, formerly part of the British province of Punjab.

a small stage for concerts and theatrical performances, and quickly became the home of the local *Corps Dramatique*. On the second floor there was a small gallery that could be used as a concert hall or a ballroom. The side rooms served as the offices of the municipal commissioners, who also managed the building. In September the Singapore library was transferred from the Raffles Institution to the Town Hall, where it was housed in two downstairs rooms.

The first steamers of the French Messageries Impériales mail line began service towards the end of the year, as a consequence of the French occupation of the port of Saigon three years earlier. The Singapore agents for the line were the Belgium firm of Hinnekindt, Freres and L. Cateaux.

***

Frederick Townsend Ward's Ever Victorious Army renewed their attacks against the Taiping positions west and south of Shanghai. They continued to demonstrate their effectiveness against even seasoned Taiping troops, earning them the respect of the Europeans, the Qing and the Taiping themselves. By September, Ward's army had grown to about five thousand men, equipped with mobile artillery units and river steamers.

On September 21, Ward ordered his forces to attack the small town of Cixi, close to the southern port city of Ningpo, which was held by Augustus Lindley, with his severely depleted Loyal and Faithful Auxiliary Legion. Lindley gave orders for a disciplined retreat, and called to his wife to leave her station on the wall above the main gate.

'Just one last shot,' she cried out to her husband, without turning her head. She meant to make it count. Aim low, she said to herself, to make sure.

That morning Frederick Townsend Ward did not lead his men

into battle with his walking stick, as was his usual custom, but remained in the rear. As he raised his telescope to his eye to view the progress of the Ever Victorious Army, the bullet took him in the abdomen. He survived long enough to learn that Cixi had been taken, but he died the following morning after a night of insufferable agony. Lindley and his wife Marie escaped west with the remnants of the Loyal and Faithful Auxiliary Legion.

11

Tan Kim Ching, the eldest son of Tan Tock Seng, had successfully expanded his rice business from his godown on Boat Quay and now owned rice mills in Siam and Cochin-China.[cii] He was one of the richest merchants in Singapore, whose domain now extended to mining interests in Pattani[ciii] and the import of silk from China, and president of the Hokkien Huay Kuan,[civ] which was located in the Thian Hock Keng temple in Telok Ayer Street. He was also recognized as the representative of the Chinese community in Singapore – the Capitan China – by the Straits government, and developed a close friendship and business relationship with W. H. Read.

Tan Kim Ching had also developed a special relationship with King Rama IV of Siam, who in addition to granting him special trading concessions, appointed him as the first Siamese consul in Singapore. At the beginning of the year, King Rama asked a favour of him: he wanted someone to provide his thirty-nine wives and concubines and eighty-two children with a modern Western secular education, without trying to indoctrinate them in the Christian religion, which earlier American missionary teachers had attempted to do. Tan Kim Ching asked his business colleagues for advice, and William Adamson of the Borneo Company recommended a young widow, Anna Leonowens. She was struggling to support

---

cii Present-day southern Vietnam.
ciii Province in southern Siam.
civ Association devoted to the promotion of education, social welfare, and Chinese language and culture, founded in 1840.

her young son and daughter by teaching the children of British officers in Singapore; since there were not many of them, it was not a particularly lucrative profession. After interviewing her himself, Tan Kim Ching recommended her to King Rama IV. Later in the year, after sending her daughter to school in England, Anna travelled to Bangkok with her son to take up her position as teacher and language secretary to the court of the Siamese king. [9]

***

John Simpson lived long enough to welcome his great-grandson, Robert John Simpson, into the family, when Angie was delivered of a healthy boy in June. But at the end of the year, almost to the day, he followed his old friend Captain Scott to the grave, and was buried close by him in the Christian cemetery on Fort Canning Hill. Ronnie liked to think that when the nighttime shadows fell, they would rise from their graves and join in ghostly games of chess and carousing. A superstitious thought, he knew, which probably came from reading too much of Burns' poetry, but a comforting one nonetheless.

***

After the death of Frederick Townsend Ward, leadership of the Ever Victorious Army devolved to his second in command, Henry Burgevine. He did not last long, because he would not coordinate his operations with Li Hongzhang's regular Qing troops and because Li Hongzhang did not trust him, Burgevine having formerly served with the Taiping. Li Hongzhang discussed the matter with Brigadier General Staveley, who commanded the British forces in Shanghai, and on his advice appointed Captain Charles Gordon as the new commander of the Ever Victorious Army.

12

Just as her hard feelings toward Auntie Ki had softened over time, so too Ah Keng began to love the old man in her own peculiar way; not as young lovers do, but somewhere between the feelings of a daughter for a father and a servant for a kind master. For despite his selfish interest, it was clear that Bee See loved her for the joy she had given him. One night, after they had made love with a passion that surprised her, Bee Swee asked her what she wished for most of all in the world, and said that he would grant her wish if it was within his power.

She did not stop to think, but immediately replied:

'I wish for my freedom more than anything else in this world, my dear Bee Swee, and would love you forever if you would grant it to me.'

The old man was aghast, and turned a deathly white as the blood drained from his face. His mouth opened and closed but no words came out.

'Oh my love,' she whispered to him, 'do not distress yourself. You asked me and I gave you my honest answer.'

'So you did, my child,' Bee Swee replied in a whisper after he had regained his composure, 'and I respect your honesty. But you know I cannot grant you this, for you would leave me as surely as the sun rises and falls in the sky, and I would wither and die without your sweet love.'

Ah Keng was hurt by his broken promise, for they both knew it was in his power to free her, whatever Mui Chi might say. She felt like pouting, as proud concubines are wont to do, but suppressed her urge to do so. For she knew he was right. If he gave her her freedom, she would leave him and his hateful household.

Then something happened that changed Bee Swee's mind, for it changed everything. Ah Keng became pregnant. Bee Swee was overjoyed. He was convinced that the child would be another son – the son he had always hoped for, the son who would be able to maintain his businesses and name after he died, the son who would honour the memory of his father and his ancestors.

He told Ah Keng that he would make her his wife, and would grant his new wife her freedom once the male child was born. Ah Keng agreed to this, but only after she had brought in a Taoist priest and made him swear an oath on it. This was unheard of, and the rest of the family protested vigorously when they heard of it. They complained that it brought great shame to their family that the master of the house had to swear an oath to a bought concubine, but Bee Swee ignored their protests and made his oath before the priest. Then after their horoscopes were compared and found favourable, the wedding was arranged and took place four months later, with Auntie Ki serving as Ah Keng's *dai kam jie*[cv] throughout the ceremony. The family and their guests carried their false smiles and obsequious bowing throughout the excruciating long ceremony, hoping silently that the old man would eat or drink himself to death before the marriage was completed. Yet Bee See was like a man reborn, for he was a man with a new purpose in life.

Before she left, Auntie Ki had her usual words of advice and warning.

'You must be very careful, my child, for yourself and for your baby. They will want you both dead, and the sooner the better.'

Then Ah Keng told Auntie Ki about Bee Swee's promise to grant her her freedom once the child was born. The old lady gave

---

cv Chaperone.

a low whistle.

'Then you must come back to me as soon as he does – I will keep you safe from them.'

'I cannot,' Ah Keng replied, 'at least not while he lives. If he keeps his part of the bargain, as I know in my heart he will, I could not leave him – and I could not leave our son.'

'As you wish, my child' Auntie Ki responded, 'but keep your ears open and make sure you have eyes in the back of your head.'

And hope the child is a son, she thought to herself.

13

Early in the year General Li launched a new campaign in Anhui province, on the northern bank of the Yangtze, in an attempt to create a diversion and draw the forces of Zeng Guofan and Zeng Guoquan away from Nanking. The campaign proved to be another disaster. The Loyal King's army was bogged down by incessant rain and mud, and his ravaging troops could find no grain supplies – the battling armies had traversed the province so often that there were no supplies to be had, and no new crops had been planted. Starving, they dragged themselves towards the deeply entrenched Qing forces, who refused to be lured out into open combat. Having no resources for an extended siege, and having failed to draw the Qing troops away from Nanking, General Li abandoned the campaign in May, when he received a summons from Hong Xiuquan to return to the city.

As General Li and his army attempted to re-cross the Yangtze and return to the capital, they were ambushed by the well-fed and disciplined forces of Zeng Guofan, now reinforced and equipped with new Western rifles and artillery, and backed by a squadron of armed steamers. The Yangtze was in full spate, and the soldiers of the Taiping army were decimated by crippling fire from the Qing as they forced their way across the river, many being swept away by the roaring waters after being cut down by the enemy fire. Augustus Lindley, commanding a defensive force that had reached the other side and was trying to cover the retreating army, watched helplessly as his wife Marie was shot in the back and swept downriver. Only a fraction of the once proud army made it across the river, after three days of carnage within sight of the walls of the Heavenly City.

When General Li re-entered the capital with his dispirited survivors, he expected to be rebuked by Hong Xiuquan for his failure. Yet the Heavenly King had no words for him, for the Heavenly Father no longer had words for the Heavenly King.

***

Shi Dakai, the Wing King, had campaigned ceaselessly in the west, sweeping back and forth for thousands of miles across fifteen different provinces, trying to establish a secure Taiping base from which to protect and supply the Heavenly Kingdom. Yet for the last three years he had been merely fighting for his survival, since his army had been cut off from contact with the Heavenly City by the northwestern advance of Zeng Guofan and his Xiang army group. By June, Shi Dakai knew there was no use continuing the fight. His once proud and loyal army was exhausted and depleted by battle casualties, disease and desertion. Now he and his personal guard found themselves isolated from the main body of his army after they had crossed the river Dadu in Sichuan province under heavy Qing fire.

Shi Dakai negotiated with the local Qing commander, who agreed to spare the lives of his personal guard – the two thousand veterans who had followed him since the beginning of the rebellion – if the Wing King surrendered to him the following day. That evening Shi Dakai watched heartbroken as his five wives committed suicide, and his infant children were drowned in the river, to prevent them from suffering the cruelties of Qing revenge. The following morning Shi Dakai walked calmly into the Qing camp. He was brought before Luo Bingzhang, the governor of Sichuan province, while his veterans were held under guard.

After six weeks of brutal interrogation, Shi Dakai was declared a traitor and sentenced to death by lingchi. After his body was dismembered, his two thousand veterans were slaughtered by the vengeful Qing troops.

14

Ronnie came back from tiffin with Tan Kim Ching and Tom Scott from Guthrie and Co, and went straight to his son's office.

'I want ye tae cancel anything ye have planned for this evening,' Ronnie told him. 'We're going to a meeting at Tan Kim Ching's house, wi a bunch o' other merchants.'

'I was going to take Angie to dinner and the theatre,' Duncan replied, 'and she'll be very disappointed to miss the play. But if it's important I can cancel, and we can catch the play next week. What's this all about?'

And so his father told him.

***

They gathered at Tan Kim Ching's home, Siam House, at the junction of North Bridge Road and Coleman Street, at seven in the evening. Kim Ching had ordered a cold buffet set out for his guests, but got straightway down to business.

'We have invited you gentlemen to join us tonight,' Tan Kim Ching said, 'in the hope that we might interest you in the formation of a joint stock company. We hope to raise capital for the construction of a series of new wharfs at the closest point of New Harbour, with receiving godowns and coal bunkers, including a graving dock[cvi] for ship repairs, which will be connected to the town by railway or tramway.'

---

cvi Dry dock for repairing and maintaining ships' hulls.

'But won't that cost a small fortune to build,' J. Guthie Davidson of Johnston and Co interrupted, 'especially since you are going to have to reclaim considerable quantities of land in order to run out an enclosed embankment.'

'That is certainly true,' Tom Scott replied, 'which is why we plan to form a joint stock company to finance the extensive work that will be necessary to construct the new wharfs. And we will have to purchase the land at New Harbour, which is currently owned by Guthrie and Co and Maclaine, Fraser and Co, representing Mr Gilbert Angus Bain, now retired to Edinburgh – although both have advised us that they are willing to sell at a reasonable price. We believe, however, that such an investment will eventually produce a very profitable return, and we invited you here this evening to ask you if you would like to join us in such an enterprise.'

'But how do you know it will be profitable?' asked Gustave Cramer of Rautenberg, Schmidt and Co. 'We already have the P & O Company's coal store and depot, and the private wharfs of Jardine Matheson, John Purvis and Co, and the Borneo Company, not to mention the Patent Slip and Dock Company with their own dry dock. Do we really need a whole new series of wharfs and godowns? I doubt there'll be enough business to go around to warrant the expense.'

'Well, that is of course what we are counting on,' replied Tan Kim Ching. 'We expect that the steamer traffic to the port will increase dramatically with the expansion of the trade and passenger routes, and we hope to take full advantage of it.'

'You're takin a bit o' a risk, tho', aren't ye?' said Ronnie Simpson. 'If they bypass Singapore, or there's a serious slump in trade, we'll be in deep …' – he paused a moment and considered his language – '… trouble. Very deep trouble.'

'That is a risk I am prepared to take,' Tan Kim Ching replied. 'I have already purchased two steamers of my own, the *Siam* and

Singapore, for my trade with Siam and China, and don't want to keep paying other companies for the use of their facilities. And I am prepared to pledge a significant amount of my own money to the company – fifty thousand dollars to begin with, and more if it proves necessary.'

Ronnie gave a low whistle, but the others remained silent and thoughtful, except for Tom Scott, who was about to pledge his own capital on behalf of Guthrie and Co. But Duncan beat him to it.

'Simpson and Co will pledge a further twenty thousand dollars,' he said. His father shot him a quizzical look, but did not protest. Ronnie's view was that if Tan Kim Ching thought it a good investment, then it was good enough for him. The son of Tan Tock Seng was a richer man than any of them and had clearly inherited his father's legendary business acumen.

Other merchants soon followed with additional pledges, including Tom Scott, Syed Abdullah, F. Davidson, Pochajee Pestonjee, Wei Koh, J. Cameron, Ong Kew Ho and C. H. Harrison, who all thought the same way as Ronnie. By the end of the evening one hundred and twenty-five thousand dollars had been pledged for the formation of the new company, which they agreed would be called the Tanjong Pagar Dock Company.

As they left Siam house, Ronnie said to Duncan:

'I'm wi you on oor pledge, but how come ye were so sure yoursel?'

'Well,' Duncan replied, 'it may be a bit of a risk in the short term, but in the long term the tonnage is bound to increase, especially after that Frenchman builds his canal to Suez.' Duncan was referring to Ferdinand de Lesseps, who since 1859 had been constructing a canal linking the Mediterranean to the Red Sea – when completed it would dramatically reduce the passage time from Europe to India and Asia.

'Aye, weel, that's if he ever finishes it afore his money runs oot,'

Ronnie replied. He knew that the British government was doing everything in its power to halt and impede the progress of the canal, which was financed almost exclusively by French shareholders.

'Well then, we'll all sink or swim together,' Duncan replied, before bidding his father goodnight.

* * *

As they drove the Taiping from their positions west of Shanghai, Charles Gordon and Li Hongzhang were appalled by what they saw. The countryside had been laid waste by the armies that had fought their way back and forth across it, in their attempt to gain control of the Yangtze. Once there had been luxuriant crops and populous and prosperous towns. Now there were weed-strewn fields and deserted, burnt out buildings, with dead bodies left to rot at the sides of the road, while a few staring, skull-faced orphans peered out from hovels made from broken walls. There were no animals to be seen, no livestock, no chickens, dogs or cats – even the birds seemed to have abandoned the empty wasteland. Gordon wondered how many civilians as well as soldiers had perished in the war that had raged for the past twelve years. It was surely millions, a number that his mind found difficult to grasp, but which in his heart he knew to be true.

* * *

On September 1 a prospectus for the Tanjong Pagar Dock Company Limited was issued, with a notification in the *Straits Times* advising that the company had one hundred and twenty-five thousand dollars in capital, in twelve hundred and fifty shares of one hundred dollars each, with power to increase. The paper also carried an announcement of the appointment of the board of directors, which included Tan Kim Ching, Tom Scott and Ronnie Simpson. Shortly afterwards, the company was registered as a Joint Stock Company in the Straits Settlements, with MacTaggart, Tidman and Co appointed as their agents in London. Under the direction of Mr G. Lyons, who had a shipyard at Tanjong Rhu, work was begun on the construction of an enclosed sea wall and road, along which the shipping wharfs were to be located.

15

In October and November the Qing troops tightened their stranglehold on the Heavenly City. They seized hundreds of tons of stockpiled grain supplies and dug a ten-mile moat around the southern perimeter of Nanking. Then they launched their first direct attacks on the walls of the city, after exploding gunpowder in tunnels they had dug into their base. General Li Xiucheng, who had returned to direct the defence of the city, repelled them without much difficulty. Yet after having made a detailed inspection of the defences, the Loyal King requested an audience with Hong Xiuquan, and told him bluntly that the city could not be held against the demon-devils. Their supply routes had been cut and there were not enough soldiers to defend the city. There were too many old people and children and no grain in the city to feed them. Although there were still Taiping armies fighting in the south, there was no hope of relief, since General Zeng Guofan had the city hemmed in with moats and strong forts. He begged the Heavenly King to abandon the city and seek safety in the north, large parts of which were still controlled by the Nien rebels.

***

The Heavenly King looked down upon his Loyal King in silence for a few moments, and then spoke in a voice that seemed to Li Xiucheng if it was coming from some distant place far from the high stone walls of Nanking.

'I received the sacred command of God, the sacred command of the Heavenly Brother Jesus, to come down into the world to become the only true sovereign of the myriad countries under Heaven. Why should I fear anything?'

The Loyal King assured the Heavenly King of his abiding loyalty, but after his audience was over, he set off to find Hong Rengan. He did not get on well with the Shield King, but at least he could talk to him about real armies and real supplies.

* * *

W. H. Read found that there was strong support in London among the business community and former residents of Singapore, such as John Crawfurd and James Guthrie, for the transfer of the Straits Settlements from the Indian government to the Colonial Office. Yet without some demonstration of the financial independence of the Straits Settlements, the British government was reluctant to grant them the status of a Crown colony. They did not accept the optimistic economic projections of the Singapore Chamber of Commerce, which were at odds with those of the officials of the Straits Settlements and the Indian government.

In the end they succeeded despite themselves. The Singapore Chamber of Commerce and their friends in London had failed to block the extension of the Indian Stamp Act earlier in the year, which assured the future solvency of the Straits Settlements. In consequence the British government became more responsive to W. H. Read's vigorous campaign to get them to reconsider their position on the transfer. At the end of the year they appointed Sir Hercules Robinson, the governor of Hong Kong, to report on the feasibility and advisability of establishing the Straits Settlements as a Crown colony.

16

Adi bin Sadat was on the roof of his family's home replacing some palm fronds. When he completed the job, he edged himself backwards to the top of the ladder he had used to climb up on the roof. His right foot felt for the top rung, but missed it, instead slipping down between the top two rungs. Too late he realized his mistake, and his leg continued down into empty space as he began to slide off the roof. He tried desperately to find a hold on the ladder with his other foot, but he lost his balance and fell backwards, bringing himself and the ladder clashing to the ground. Adi screamed in agony as his twisted right leg broke under him. He screamed in agony again as his father and a neighbour extracted his leg from the ladder and laid him out on the verandah of the house. The pain was intense and he passed in and out of consciousness. When he looked up he could see a bone protruding from his leg. A sudden fear engulfed him – the fear that he would never walk properly again.

'Someone fetch help!' his father Sadat called out.

***

But there was no need to fetch help. Musa bin Osman pulled on the reins, and the carriage stopped in front of the house. Habib Noh stepped down from the carriage and made his way to the verandah. He needed no introduction, for they all knew who he was.

'Please help us, holiness – my son fell from the ladder and has broken his leg,' Sadat begged him.

'I know,' replied Habib Noh in a soft voice, 'I have come to heal him.'

Habib Noh asked those gathered around to step back, then sat cross-legged beside Adi and began to pray. Adi looked up the majdhub. He was shirtless, with his long white beard hanging low over his naked chest. A white mist seemed to descend upon them, until those standing around could see neither boy nor majdhub, but only hear the soft words of the prayer. They knelt in supplication and joined in the prayer.

For a long time nothing happened, but then the mist cleared and Habib Noh said to Adi:

'Rise up young man."

Adi was confused and afraid. But slowly he pulled his legs towards him, and then gently eased himself onto his feet. All the while he expected to feel the pain shooting through his leg, but there was no pain, and when he looked down to where the bone had once protruded he could see no sign of it. He walked slowly in a circle, unbelieving at first, but then full of joy when he realized that the majdhub had healed his leg completely. He fell down on his knees and prostrated himself before the holy man, thanking him for the blessing he had bestowed upon him.

Habib Noh raised him up and smiled in return, showing a set of gleaming white teeth. His eyes were a milky blue, like the heavens when dusk falls.

'Adi bin Sadat, I am glad to be of help, but it is God you must thank. I will visit you again one day, for I have a mind to have some words with you.'

Then he turned to leave, but before he did so Sadat ran into the house and returned with some silver coins, which he pressed upon the majdhub.

'This is all we have, holy one, but please take it with our grateful thanks for the miracle you have wrought.'

Habib Noh looked at him sceptically, and was about to remind Sadat also that it was God who he should thank. But instead he said:

'I thank you for your offering, but have no need of it. I will, however, take it and distribute it to the poor and the destitute.'

With that, he took the silver coins and returned to the carriage. As it pulled away, Adi and his family and neighbours stood in wonder on the verandah until the carriage passed out of sight.

News of the miracle quickly spread throughout the kampong and to the Eastern town.

17

She anchored in the Singapore roads on December 21, at five in the evening, having taken on a Malay pilot for the final leg of her approach – a long, low black ship with raking masts and a stumpy funnel, which slipped in unnoticed in the mist and heavy rain. She was the CSS *Alabama*, the Confederate raider, commanded by Captain Raphael Semmes.[10] The *Alabama* had been secretly built by John Laird and Co at their shipyards in Birkenhead, England, and launched on July 1862. After sailing to Terceira island in the Azores, she was commissioned as a commerce raider, on the authority of Jefferson Davis, the president of the Confederate States of America. Since August 1862 she had captured over sixty Union merchantmen and had destroyed one Union warship, the USS *Hatteras*, off the coast of Texas near Galveston. Captain Semmes had taken the American civil war to the Atlantic, Indian and Pacific oceans, and his aim was to capture and destroy as many of the enemy's ships as he could. He had already inflicted millions of dollars worth of damage to federal shipping, whose owners found it increasingly difficult to negotiate cargoes with merchants who were reluctant to have their goods destroyed by the Confederate raider. Ten days earlier the *Alabama* had captured and burned the Yankee clipper *Contest*, from Yokohama in Japan, bound for New York with a cargo of cotton and tea.

Captain Semmes sent an officer to report their presence to Governor Cavenagh and request permission to take on coal and supplies. Master's Mate George Fullam went ashore that evening to arrange coaling through Cumming, Beaver and Co, the Confederate agents in Singapore. Fullam found that the only coaling facility available was at the P & O Docks on the northern shore of New Harbour, so he arranged to have the *Alabama* coaled there the following morning. Captain Semmes went ashore and stayed overnight with Mr Beaver, who helped him arrange for a notice to be posted in the *Straits Times* advising that the *Alabama* would spend the following day coaling, but would take on visitors on the morning of December 23. After Semmes had left the ship, the US Vice Consul in Singapore, Francis D. Cobb, who had learned of the arrival of the *Alabama* from one of the American captains stranded in the port, took a boat out to the *Alabama*, but was refused permission to board. Cobb was told he could visit on the morning of the 23rd with the others.

The following morning a small crowd of merchants and their wives gathered in Raffles Place to await the delivery of the European mail. The rumour they had heard about the arrival of the *Alabama* was confirmed by the presence of a number of grey and butternut uniformed officers of the Confederate navy outside the offices of the Master Attendant. She had been expected. The *Straits Times* had reported the sinking of the *Contest* and the *Winged Racer* some days earlier, and the USS *Wyoming* had put into Singapore at the end of November, in search of the elusive raider.

Many of the merchants and shopkeepers went down to Johnston's Pier to view the *Alabama*, lying low in the water some miles out in the roads. There were mixed feelings about her presence. Many of the European merchants were sympathetic to the Southern cause, but like the captains of the eighteen Union ships that languished in the port searching for cargoes, others were concerned about the impact on their trade with America, and some had already lost money as a result of the *Alabama*'s trail of destruction.

The *Alabama* weighed anchor around ten, then sailed westward toward New Harbour to take on a supply of coal. She moved through the water at great speed, but seemed to glide across the surface, causing scarcely a ripple. The sky was grey and overcast, and the long black ship looked like some spectral apparition, as it moved in and out of the thin mist that still hung over the ships in the roads.

While she waited for the European mail, Margaret Brown learned from Mrs Purvis that the *Alabama* would be open to visitors the following morning. That night she suggested to her husband that they should take the opportunity to view the *Alabama*, and to her surprise Richard agreed – he said he wanted to see the fireworks fly when Vice Consul Cobb went on board.

The next morning the road to New Harbour was crowded with carriages, wagons and bullock carts as crowds of people came out to view the *Alabama*. They were of all races and from all walks of life. Merchants, shopkeepers, coolies, captains, soldiers and lighterman had all came to view the famous – or infamous – ship. For the women of the European community, it was a major social event. Margaret and Richard Brown travelled by carriage in the early morning, but Richard warned her she would have to find her own way back with some of her friends, since he could not spend all morning gawking at a boat.

The *Alabama* was a thousand-ton war cruiser, very long and narrow; she was just over two hundred feet in length and some thirty feet across. She was powered by sail, and by two three-hundred-horsepower engines that drove a twin-bladed brass screw, which could be retracted when the engines were not in operation. She had a black wooden hull, with three tall pine masts, which were well raked, with each carrying a topmast. She was rigged with Swedish iron wire, and carried square sails on her fore and main masts; her short and stumpy black telescoping funnel was directly ahead of the mainmast. She carried six smoothbore thirty-two-pounder broadside guns on carriages, with two larger and more powerful pivot guns fore and aft of the main mast, a rifled hundred-pounder on the foredeck and a smoothbore sixty pounder on the quarterdeck. She had a complement of one hundred and forty-five officers and men, of whom many were paid British sailors. She sat low in the water, like a dark crocodile lying in wait for its prey.

When they arrived, even Richard was moved by the sight of the long black ship close against the wharf, her guns like cold dark eyes probing the assembled crowd. Yet one thing puzzled him, as he walked over to greet John Purvis, who had arrived in his own carriage.

'Good morning, Purvis,' he said. 'Explain this to me. Why so many Chinese? When we had the China War a few years back, there were plenty of British men of war and steam gunboats to be seen, but the Chinese never paid them any attention. Yet they've have come out in droves to see this American brig, including old men and young boys.'

'Good morning to you, Mr Brown,' Purvis replied. 'I'm not entirely sure, but I think it's the ship itself. Nothing to do with the fact that it's American, although plenty of captains in town would of course protest that adjective. The Chinese call it the 'Kappal Hantu',[cvii] the Ghost Ship. If you'd seen it moving through the mist yesterday morning, you'd understand what they mean. Gave me the shivers just watching it skim over the water like a silver ghost. They've come to see it up close, but you won't find many going on board – I'm sure they consider that very unlucky.'

'Stuff and nonsense,' Richard replied, 'and just typical of the superstitious Chinese.'

'I won't stay long,' he said, turning to Margaret, 'I'll just take a quick look around the ship and get back to the office.'

'As you wish,' she replied, 'but I want to stay awhile. I'll get a

_____
cvii Malay term for 'ghost ship.'

ride back with one of the others. It's not as if I have anything else to do.'

Richard ignored her jibe and they went on board the *Alabama*, where Captain Semmes greeted them. He stood tall and straight in his grey naval uniform, almost six foot in height, with dark piercing eyes and thick brown wavy hair. He had a magnificent handlebar moustache, curled and waxed, with a small goatee beard. He looked exactly what he was, a Southern gentleman and captain of a Confederate warship. He greeted them cordially, in his cultured accent, and directed them to Second Lieutenant James Conrad, who would give them a tour of the ship. Lieutenant Conrad looked equally dashing in his grey naval uniform, but Margaret could tell right away he was no gentleman. He was a tall as Semmes, but clean-shaven, except for a thin moustache, with jet-black hair and soft grey eyes. He behaved like a gentleman, and greeted them politely, but as he reached over to take Margaret's hand and guide her round some provisions on deck that were awaiting storage, he gave her such a look that she felt he was undressing her with his eyes – all the while smiling graciously as if he was an usher directing her to a pew in church. She felt that she should protest his impudence, but said nothing, for all her attention was fixed upon hiding the excitement that coursed like electricity through her body. She had not felt this way for a long time – for a very long time – and had even wondered if such feelings were lost to her.

Just before they began the tour of the ship, they were disturbed by a commotion on board, as US Vice Consul Cobb stormed up the gangplank with his secretaries and demanded to see Captain Semmes, who came forward to meet them.

'I won't waste time telling you what I think of you and your business, Captain Semmes – I just hope the *Wyoming* sends you and your crew to the bottom before the year is out. But I've been told you have a Negro on board, taken from the USS *Tonawanda*. I demand to see him, and that you release him into my custody! He is a free man and you must respect his freedom.'

'Oh, you must mean young Davie,' Semmes replied with a smile, ignoring Cobb's insult. He instructed Master's Mate Fullam to ask Surgeon Galt to bring Davie up on deck.

'Davie is of course free to choose for himself,' Semmes continued, 'and he goes ashore whenever he wants, with or without Surgeon Galt. But he has chosen to stay aboard the *Alabama*.'

David White was a young Negro slave, seventeen years old, who was formerly the property of a businessman from Maryland aboard the USS *Tonawanda*. According to US navy law, captured slaves were contraband and subject to confiscation, so Semmes had confiscated him and brought him on board the *Alabama*. Apprehensive at first, Davie had soon settled down and become a favourite of the Liverpool crewmen. He served at first as a waiter in the wardroom mess, and then as steward to Surgeon Francis Galt, for whom he had formed the greatest affection.

When Davie came on deck, Vice Consul Cobb told him that by virtue of President Lincoln's Proclamation of Emancipation, he was a free man, and thus free to leave the ship with him that day. Davie replied that he knowed that all right, but he was happy where he was, and had no desire to leave. Cobb then grew angry and began to harangue the boy, reminding him of the dreadful condition of slavery and urging him to throw off his shackles. Davie remained unmoved, although he looked increasingly embarrassed, and eventually he turned his back on Cobb and made his way back down to the wardroom with Surgeon Galt.

Before Cobb could protest, Captain Semmes said bluntly:

'I'll thank you to leave my ship this instant, Mr Cobb, or I shall have you removed.'

Cobb turned on his heel and stormed back down the gangplank, with his secretaries in pursuit.

After asking some boring questions about tonnage, beam and engine capacity, Richard returned to his office, while Margaret attached herself to Mr and Mrs Purvis, who seemed interested to learn of the *Alabama*'s adventures, which Lieutenant Conrad narrated with much enthusiasm and animation. He described their encounter with the USS *Hatteras* outside the southern port of Galveston, and showed them the damage they had sustained from her broadside on their starboard side, before they had sunk her. He described their unsuccessful pursuit by the USS V*anderbilt* in the Atlantic, and by the USS *Wyoming* and USS *Jamestown* in the South China Sea. When he was asked what happened to the crews of the enemy craft, Conrad answered that Captain Semmes was famous for his chivalry in that matter. He always did his best to rescue the officers and crew of the ships he sunk, and took them on board if they surrendered – they were disembarked at the nearest port, or put aboard neutral shipping en route to Europe or the Americas.

As he spoke, in his languid Charleston drawl, Margaret began to understand the Chinese fascination with the ship. With its long low deck and high black spars, it really did look like a ghost ship – just the sort of ship that might have taken the Ancient Mariner on his nightmare journey. She imagined the souls of the drowned enemy sailors following the black ship, invisible in the cloudy night and bright daylight, but crying out with the moan of the wind and the howl of the gales as they swept around her. She gave a little involuntary shiver, even though the oppressive humidity of the day was rising as the grey clouds thickened in the sky.

They went below to view the engine room. She was amazed by how immaculately clean it was kept. The *Alabama* had four boilers, which drove two horizontal piston engines. According to Lieutenant Conrad, she could make ten knots under sail alone, and up to thirteen with steam. Having coaled the previous day, they were testing the engines, and the giant brass cylinders rose and fell with great hisses of steam. Margaret stood before them mesmerized, as they danced through the air like two gigantic cobras. There was scarcely any air in the engine room, and she began to feel a little faint. She rolled her neck to clear her head, and gave a sudden gasp as Lieutenant Conrad lent forward and grasped her arms. His hands was strong but gentle as he held her arms tight. His breath smelt of cloves and cigars.

'Are you all right, Ma'am,' he said, his face close to hers, his soft grey eyes locking her own. 'You look like you're going to faint.'

'I'm fine, thank you very much,' she replied. 'It's just a bit hot and stuffy down here, and I was trying to clear my head. Please don't be concerned.'

He bowed to her and released her arms, and she wished he had not. He led them back on deck and escorted them from the ship. Lieutenant Conrad took Margaret by the hand as she stepped onto the gangplank, and briefly brushed his lips across her skin – she could feel the heat of his breath caress her fingers.

'Until we meet again, Mrs Brown,' he said. He bowed, and turned his attention to Tan Hong Chuan, one of the few Chinese who had dared to come on board.

As she rode back to town with the Purvises in their carriage, Margaret could still feel his hands upon her arms; they remained as a ghostly presence, although more like a simmering fire than a deathly shade. She imagined him holding her in his arms again, his lips pressed against hers. Her breasts rose and fell, and she was shocked to discover that she was wet beneath her skirts.

'Are you all right, Mrs Brown,' said Mr Purvis. 'You look quite flushed.'

'I'm fine,' she replied quickly, 'it's just this oppressive heat and humidity.'

Purvis and his wife began to complain about the weather, a favourite pastime among the Europeans, as Margaret laid her head against the back of the carriage and looked up into the sky. The heavy clouds blanketed the heavens a deep grey, as if to mark the presence of the Confederate ghost ship.

18

In the early afternoon Captain Semmes visited the town. Thomas Scott of Guthrie and Co had offered to show him around, and had forwarded an invitation to the captain and his officers to dine with Whampoa at his mansion in Serangoon that evening, which Semmes had gratefully accepted. After enjoying a quick tiffin at Guthrie's godown, they walked around Chinatown and along Boat Quay. Semmes was much taken by the multitude of lighters in the river, by the rich variety of the merchandise in the godowns, and the bustle and activity among the natives. He remarked to Guthrie upon the diversity of the races, the variety of their dress, and the smell of industry and commerce in the air.

'Well, let me take you to the centre of it,' said Tom Scott, 'and we can shelter from the rain.'

It had begun to drizzle, and the skies threatened a downpour. They ducked into Whampoa's offices at the head of Boat Quay.

Captain Semmes was amazed. One of the richest Chinese merchants in Singapore, and thus one of the richest men in Singapore, sat in a dingy, ill-lit office, idly working the balls on an abacus. Whampoa got up to greet them, and welcomed Captain Semmes in his excellent English.

'Why don't you give him a multiplication,' Scott suggested, taking a pencil and piece of paper from his pocket, and handing it to Captain Semmes. 'A large one, three or four figures, and see who gets it first.'

Whampoa grinned, and fingered the balls on the abacus like a musician tuning his instrument.

'All right then,' said Semmes, gamely, 'how about two hundred and forty-three multiplied by seven thousand, five hundred and eighty-one.'

Semmes starting doing the long multiplication with his pen and paper, while Whampoa's fingers danced across the abacus. Semmes had scarcely completed the first line when Whampoa exclaimed, 'One million, eight hundred and forty-two thousand, one hundred and eighty-three!'

Semmes said nothing, but completed his pen and paper multiplication, and then confirmed the figure.

'By God, you're right, sir. So that's why you're a rich merchant and I'm a poor navy captain!'

They all laughed, and then Whampoa told Captain Semmes that he looked forward to his company at dinner.

'I also, Mr Whampoa,' Semmes replied, 'I've heard wonderful reports of your hospitality, sir. They say you do a very fine table.'

Scott and Semmes left shortly afterwards. The rain had held off, so they visited a shop that prepared opium. They crossed over the new iron bridge that had been installed the previous year to replace the old wooden Thomson's Bridge between North and South Bridge Road, and which had been named Elgin Bridge, after the late Viceroy of India. As they approached St Andrew Church, the rain came down again suddenly, and they sheltered awhile in the porte-cocheré at the entrance. As they stood and smoked together, Captain Semmes looked wistfully inside the church.

'If you don't mind, Tom,' he said, 'I think I'll go in and say a little prayer. I'm Roman Catholic, but I see this church is Episcopalian despite the name. Which is near enough. It's been a long time and I don't know when I'll get another chance.'

Or if I ever will, he thought to himself. The *Wyoming* and *Jamestown* were close at hand, he knew, and the *Vanderbilt* and a dozen others were in the Atlantic waiting for him to return.

'Of course not,' Scott replied, and Semmes went into the church, where he stood alone in the shadows and made his peace with his God. When he returned, the rain had stopped, and thin strips of sunlight pierced through the breaking clouds. Steam rose from the plants and palms around the church, as if the island itself were a living, breathing thing.

'An interesting place, this Singapore,' Captain Semmes said as they walked back to town.

'But I'll tell you what strikes me most,' he continued. 'I've been walking around all afternoon, and have only seen a single woman – a very doubtful specimen of the lowest type, and almost certainly a whore. I saw a few ladies down at the *Alabama* this morning, but where do you keep the rest of them?'

'You've spied our Achilles heel,' laughed Scott. 'You'll see more out at night, especially upon the Esplanade, when the band is playing or the boats are racing, but we really have a desperate shortage of women, except among the Malays. The Chinese have it particularly bad, except for the Peranakans, who've been here for centuries and married Malay women and their descendants. There wasn't an honest woman from mainland China here until about ten years ago. The ratio among the Chinese remains pretty dreadful, so it's no wonder they fight among themselves so often, or succumb to liquor and opium. There'll be women at Whampoa's tonight, although none of them single, I'm afraid. A single woman is like a princess in Singapore, and has the pick of the crop.'

'I'm not looking for a female companion,' Semmes replied, with a laugh, 'I have a wife and children back in Mobile. Although I must say I do look forward to their company, after so many months at sea. They remind you of the blessings of civilization, and the wisdom of the creator.'

'Well said,' Scott exclaimed, 'I'm going to try that one on my missus!'

When Margaret got home that afternoon, she went straight to her bedroom. She pulled off her clothes, which she felt were suffocating her, and lay in her undergarments on the bed. Her heart was beating fast, and her thoughts were racing through her head. For the last nine years she had lived a life of resigned sufferance of a situation that she had to admit was of her own making, although she felt like a prisoner trapped in a cage. Now for a brief moment she had dreamed of another possibility, even though she had no illusions about the character of Lieutenant James Conrad. His was a life of passion and danger, but it was a real life, not the dreary pretence of her own life – which she could scarcely call a life, and which she could no longer bear.

She had fought her way back from the melancholy that had enveloped her when her son Thomas had been sent to military school, and had steeled herself to live on until she saw him again – for she knew there was no escape from Singapore. But this day had demonstrated to her that her inner strength was a complete illusion, and how hopeless her life was. She lived only for her son, whom she could not see, and might never see if Richard continued to exercise his cruel power over her. It was no longer enough – she had sensed again the passion of life, only to realize that it was lost to her.

She no longer wished to go on living. She rose from her bed, and went to check if Richard still kept his loaded Colt navy revolver in the bureau. It was still there, and she ran her fingers over the cool steel of the barrel as she drew it out of the drawer. If she did it now she would be at peace, and her slow torture would be at an end.

But then she put the gun down and closed the bureau again. It was not peace she wanted, but life! She would find a way, whatever the cost and whatever the danger. She rose and dressed and busied herself with the preparations for Christmas, the following day being

Christmas Eve. Although there was not much to plan for, since the merchants in Singapore treated Christmas Day as any other day – at work by ten, tiffin at noon, home at four for drinks and dinner.

Early in the afternoon she received a note from Richard telling her that they had been invited to dine with Captain Semmes and his officers at Whampoa's mansion in Serangoon that evening. She knew Richard would hate it, but she also knew he would not dare turn down an invitation from one of the most influential Chinese merchants in town. And James Conrad would be there. Please God let him be there, she thought without shame.

19

Whampoa had taken care not to invite any Union captains or the US Consul to dinner, but had included some British and French naval officers as well as some of the leading European merchants and their wives, including Richard and Margaret, yet the conversation had naturally turned to the civil war and its effects. Captain Delacroix asked Captain Semmes if he had heard whether the port of Charleston had succumbed to the Federal siege, and Semmes replied that as far as he knew it had not. Semmes had heard that General Robert E. Lee had achieved great victories in the face of overwhelming odds, although he bemoaned the loss of General 'Stonewall' Jackson at the Battle of Chancellorsville, which Lee had likened to the loss of his right arm. This had probably cost him his recent defeat at the battle of Gettysburg, Semmes regretted.

Captain Johnson of HMS *Steadfast* raised the question that was foremost on the minds of the Yankee merchant captains whose ships were stranded in Singapore.

'I mean no offence, Captain Semmes,' he said quietly, 'but how do you answer those of your countrymen who say you are little more than a pirate, preying on defenceless merchantmen rather than taking the fight to the Union warships.'

Many of the captains and merchants present looked at each other in discomfort, and some raised their eyebrows, because the question was offensive. Yet Semmes remained as inscrutable as Whampoa, and replied in his measured Southern drawl.

'Well, Captain Johnson, if I'm a pirate then so were most of

England's captains in your war with Napoleon. Your British navy saw fit to board and seize any French merchantmen and worse, any neutral ship that was trading with the French. We fought and sunk the *Hatteras*, which was a Union warship, and no doubt someday soon we will have to fight the *Wyoming*, or the *Jamestown* or some other ship, but we are fighting an economic war as well as a military one, and against the odds in both cases. We have precious few fighting ships, while the Union navy has blockaded nearly all our ports, and brought our cotton exports to a fraction of what they were, to the great hardship of your mill-owners and workers in the north of England. And while we have risked our own lives to pick up the survivors of the *Hatteras* and all the merchantmen that we have burned, and seen them disembarked in safe ports or neutral ships, the Union army fires shells from five miles out into Charleston, with little care as to whether they land on the shore batteries or the homes of the families that live beyond.'

'Aye, the mills are suffering for sure,' said Tom Scott, 'although I have to confess the war has been a boon to the merchants here who deal in Chinese and Indian cotton, not to mention the huge demand for tin that the war has created. New mines are opening up on the Malayan peninsula almost every week.'

'Why is that?' asked Margaret, and got a scowl from Richard for interrupting the men's talk.

'Because of all the tin canned food that feeds both our armies ... and our navies,' said Captain Semmes, with a grin.

'Well, I perhaps should not say this,' Scott continued, 'and I know the captains of the twenty odd Union ships locked up in Singapore would curse me for it, but I think there is a fair amount of sympathy here for your cause, and not only the natural one for a weaker side getting the better of the stronger. What Britain fears most is a United States of America, since it poses the greatest threat to her industrial might and overseas trade. She would be happy if the South were to prevail, although of course she regrets the heavy price you are paying in your fight for independence from the North.'

'Both sides are paying a heavy price,' Semmes replied. 'This war is the first really modern war, pitting gigantic cannon and ironclad ships against each other, and soldiers armed with repeating rifles and rapid-fire gunnery. But it is also the sheer bloody work of man against man, of sword against sword and bayonet against bayonet.'

'What do you estimate the casualties of the war so far, Captain Semmes,' asked Scott.

'There were twenty thousand casualties in a single day at the battle of Sharpsburg, or Antietam as the Yankees called it,' Semmes replied. 'This may very well turn out to be the deadliest war of the century. I regret to admit that we will probably end up with close to half a million dead on both sides.'

A hush fell over the company as they contemplated that awful figure, but then Whampoa broke the silence.

'These are terrible losses, and that your war is a great tragedy I do not deny,' he said in his careful English. 'Yet I am afraid to say that they pale in comparison to the losses in the great war against the Taiping rebels that continues to rage in my own country. For over ten years the armies have crossed and re-crossed the plains and rivers and mountains, and the dead are estimated in millions – perhaps as many as ten to fifteen million – with perhaps more innocents dead from pillage, starvation and disease than from military action. And I know not when it will end.'

Once again, a hush fell over the company, which only Whampoa himself could dispel.

'However, let us not dwell on these sad matters' he continued, 'but let us hear the news from Britain and France, and enjoy this fine food.'

His servants came forward at his command with more dishes, and poured more Champagne.

After the meal was over, Whampoa offered to show them round his house and gardens, although he said they were also free to stay at the table with their brandy and cigars and his tame orang utan, who, like Raffles' many years before, was also partial to his brandy and cigars. Richard stayed with the ship's captains, who were not much interested in houses and gardens, while the *Alabama*'s officers and some of the merchants and their wives went on the tour. Whampoa's home was a simple three-storey white house, but elaborately furnished with Chinese and European furniture, statuary and paintings. He led them through the rockeries and bamboo woods of his gardens to show them what he considered to be his prize possession, a spectacular giant lily known as Victoria Regina, which was a gift from the King of Siam. The giant lily floated in a circular pond at the centre of his gardens, and seemed to follow the silvery shadow of the full moon as it crossed the still black waters. It was one of the most beautiful vistas that Margaret had ever seen, and she lingered by the pond when the others left, unable to draw her eyes away from the flower and the image of the moon on the black waters.

Then she felt someone touch her lightly on the shoulder, and she knew it was him. She turned around slowly, choosing her words carefully, but she had no chance to speak, for Lieutenant Conrad slipped his arms behind her and kissed her directly on the mouth – not savagely, but softly, as if he had known her all these years. She made no attempt to protest, for she knew that this was what she had wanted all along, and knew that he had wanted it too. She returned the kiss, and their hands began to explore each other's bodies as their kisses grew ever more passionate. He placed his hands upon her breasts, and she felt her nipples rising under her corset. She knew where this would lead but she did not care, and did not protest when he lifted her up and sat her down upon a marble pedestal, then raised her skirts and pulled down her drawers. She was as mad with desire for him as she could feel he was for her, and she covered his face with kisses as he pulled down his britches and entered her. She stifled her scream, though it was a scream of pure pleasure, and he pleasured her as none had done before. When their passion was spent they looked at each other in silence, amazed at their lovemaking but not by their mutual passion – for they had both known it from the moment they had met.

Eventually he broke the silence, as she rearranged her clothing and her hair.

'I hate to leave, my love, but we had best get back, or we'll both be in trouble – and I might need to fight a confounded duel if your husband were to get upset. I suggest that I go ahead and you follow on, and we both pretend that we got lost on the way back – easy enough to do in this Chinese puzzle garden, I'm sure. I'd like to say that I hope we can meet again, but we both know I can't. We sail at first light in the morning.'

'Take me with you!' she exclaimed, clutching his arm. 'Take me back with you on the *Alabama*.'

'I can't do that,' he said quietly, with a cool smile. 'Semmes would never allow it.'

'You could do it if you wanted to,' she replied. 'You could hide me on board, and when we were out to sea it would be too late to do anything. If you loved me you would not hesitate.'

Yet even as she said it she knew that love had not entered into it. She was just one of James Conrad's many conquests in the many seaports he had visited, where wives were bored to madness in their living death while their husbands drank and whored and made their money. He would love her and leave her in his usual way – she was perfectly sure of that.

He said nothing in response, but instead stood looking at her with a puzzled expression on his face as he played with his moustache. James Conrad had known many women in his many ports of call, and he considered it good sport to seduce the wives of merchants, officers and governors often practically under their noses. The moment they consummated their passion, he immediately lost interest in them, and could scarcely give them the time of day. But this woman was different. She had aroused and pleasured him like no other, and he wanted more, he wanted more right now, even though he was cool-headed enough to know it was too dangerous. It would be too dangerous to take her on board the ship as well, but he was no stranger to danger, and he thought it more than worth the risk. Semmes would be furious, but there was little he could do about it once they were at sea. The worst he could do was put her ashore at some other port, and perhaps him with her. There were worse things, he thought to himself – he had some money saved, and no fear of reprisals after the war was over – for he knew the South had already lost, even though Semmes would never admit it.

So he told her he would do it, and they made their plans.

20

When Lieutenant Conrad returned he told them he had got lost, but had enjoyed his exploration of the gardens in the moonlight. When they asked him if he had met with Mrs Brown on the way back, he told them he had not, and expressed some mild concern. Yet nobody seemed to suspect anything when Margaret returned a few minutes later, although Semmes gave Conrad a quizzical look, and Richard scowled at her – but only because she had embarrassed him by getting lost. The dinner party broke up shortly after, when a messenger came from the *Alabama* to inform Semmes that a fight had broken out in Colonel Emerson's bar and billiard hall, between the Yankee merchant sailors who were stranded in Singapore on account of the *Alabama* and the junior officers and seamen from the *Alabama*. The Yankee sailors had called Jefferson Davis' mother a whore and the president of the Confederate States a bastard, and the men from the *Alabama* had answered these insults with their fists and Colonel Emerson's furniture. Semmes and his officers arrived with the police in time to prevent any fatal injuries, and Semmes paid Colonel Emerson for the damage caused to his property. Colonel Emerson said the mates were just having a bit of a lark, but thanked him for his trouble nonetheless.

Richard sat in silence in their carriage as they returned to their home on River Valley Road, then told the driver to take him back into town as he let Margaret out of the carriage.

'Don't wait up for me,' he called out to her in jest.

She went upstairs and began to prepare. She stripped off her evening gown, and put all her jewels and all the cash she could gather into a small travelling bag, along with a change of clothes. She put in the picture taken with Thomas long ago at Dutronquoy's London Hotel. She dressed herself in her riding gear, and then slipped quietly out of the house and into the stables. She saddled her horse and walked him out into the moonlight, only mounting when she was some distance from the house. Then she rode towards New Harbour and the *Alabama*. She knew it was not safe for a woman to be out by herself in the middle of the night, but she had no care for her safety, and not just because she had Richard's loaded pistol. She was free, and alive, and the devil could take anyone who dared to interfere with her.

She knew that she had little to fear from Richard. He would not be back until the early morning, and would probably be too drunk when he returned to notice she was gone. As she rode through the night, she thought of her son alone in London. She wondered how he would spend Christmas Eve at the Academy and wondered if he would think of her, if only for a short while.

***

When Captain Semmes returned to the *Alabama* that evening, he wrote in his ship's log:

> *Weather variable, with occasional showers of rain. Raining heavily in the afternoon. Visited the city, and was astonished at its amount of population and business. There are from 80,000 to 100,000 Chinese on Singapore Island, nearly all of them in the city; from 12,000 to 15,000 Malays, and about 1,500 Europeans. Singapore being a free port, it is a great entrepôt of trade. Great quantities of Eastern produce reach it from all quarters, whence it is shipped to*

Europe. The business is almost exclusively in the hands of the Chinese, who are also the artisans and labourers of the place. The streets are thronged with foot passengers and vehicles, among which are prominent the ox, or rather buffalo cart, and the hacks for hire, of which latter there are 900 licensed. The canal is filled with country boats, of excellent model, and the warehouses are crammed with goods. Money seems to be abundant and things dear.

The moving multitude in the streets comprises every variety of the human race, every shade of colour, and every variety of dress, among which are prominent the gay tartans and fancy jackets of the Mohammedan, Hindu, etc. Almost all the artisans and labourers were naked, except for a cloth or a pair of short trousers tucked about the waist. The finest dressed part of the population was decidedly the jet blacks, with their white flowing mantles and spotless turbans. The upper class of Chinese merchants are exceedingly polite, and seem intelligent ... Their shaved heads and long queues, sometimes nearly touching the ground, are curious features of their personal appearance. The workshops all front upon the streets, and these busy, half-naked creatures may be seen working away as industriously as so many beavers all day long, seeming never to tire of their ceaseless toil.

A few miles beyond the town the whole island is a jungle, in which abounds the ferocious Bengal tiger. It is said that one man and a half per day is the average destruction of human life by these animals. Visited opium-preparation shop. It pays an enormous license. All this beauty fails to reconcile the European ladies to the country, I was told. The eternal sameness of summer and heat and moisture weigh upon and oppress them, and their husbands being away all day on business, they wilt and pine for their European *homes. The life seems agreeable enough to the men.*

As Semmes climbed into his bunk and fell asleep, Margaret tethered her horse behind the P & O wharf, and went to meet Lieutenant Conrad in the *Alabama*'s skiff.

***

Margaret and James Conrad crept down to the wardroom and into his cabin, which was scarcely large enough for them to stand in. But it mattered little, as they tore at each other's clothes like old lovers, and clambered into his bunk. They drove each other to heights of passion that neither of them had known or ever imagined. She, who had never before known the real passion of physical love, and he, who thought he had experienced all the nuances of love that the ladies of Charleston and the ports of the world could offer, were amazed that they had found their soul mates is this Eastern port. They made love over and over as the ship lay at anchor, she screaming silently in pleasure as the hours spun by. And then he was up and dressing at six bells, winking to her as she stretched out like a cat upon his bunk.

'My duty, my love. We're shipping out of here within the hour. Keep quiet and lock the door behind me, and don't open it unless you hear me whistling "Dixie".' He whistled the tune softly under his breath. 'I'll come back with a bite for breakfast as soon as I get the chance.'

Then he kissed her quickly and slipped out of the cabin, closing the door quietly behind him. She slid down from the bunk and locked the door, then peered out through the tiny porthole. There was no unusual activity on the P & O wharf, only a few natives moving here and there, and no sign of Richard or the constabulary. She hoped that the note she had left him, saying she had gone on an early morning ride – to clear her headache in the fresh morning breeze – had deceived him if he had read it. She need not have worried. Richard had been with his drinking companions to the bar rooms and brothels of Malay Street, and had tumbled into his bed drunk as a dog just before dawn. He would not wake for hours, and none of the servants would dare to wake him.

But Margaret did not know this, and she bit her lip anxiously while she waited for the *Alabama* to get under way. After what seemed to her an eternity, she heard the cables running up as the anchors were lifted, and felt the ship suddenly shudder as the engines were fired up, and the great pistons began to pound beneath her. Then they were moving, and she watched the skyline of Singapore grow smaller and smaller as they steamed out of New Harbour. Well, she thought to herself, there is no going back now.

She had no regrets. She felt freer than she had felt since her father died and, much more, she felt a real woman at last. She had no illusions about James Conrad, who she feared would tire of her, but she did not care. She had escaped, and she would make her own life for herself, whatever fate had in store for her.

Captain Semmes followed the Chinese war steamer *Kwan-Tung* out of the harbour at eight thirty in the morning. The day had begun fair, but they suddenly found themselves in heavy rain and mist, as they steamed northwest into the Straits of Malacca. Shortly after they entered the Straits, Captain Semmes summoned Lieutenant Conrad to the bridge.

'Lieutenant Armstrong has just given me the roster of officers and seamen. Two men jumped ship in Singapore, and we took on two more, so we should all be present and accounted for. But then who did you bring on board last night, Lieutenant Conrad? Mr Fulham reports that you came on board with a second party.'

'Just the Irish boy Michael O'Brian, Captain Semmes,' Lieutenant Conrad replied. 'I'm afraid the young gentleman was rather the worse for wear through drink, so I did what any Southern gentlemen would do and saw him back safely on board.'

'Don't lie to me, Conrad,' Semmes snapped, 'and don't talk to me about Southern gentlemen. O'Brian was one of those who jumped ship. So, who did you bring on board last night? I demand an answer, sir.'

'You've caught me red-handed, I must confess,' Lieutenant Conrad replied, with a thin smile. 'But I regret that I cannot oblige you, captain, for I am honour bound to keep the matter a secret.'

'Your honour be damned, sir!' Semmes exploded. 'You will have no secrets on my ship! Master's Mate Evans, take the helm. Lieutenant Howell, call out a squad of your marines, and follow me. Semmes marched back across the deck and down into the wardroom, where he made to open the door of Lieutenant Conrad's cabin, only to find it locked.

'Who have you got in there,' Semmes said, turning to face Lieutenant Conrad. 'Not one of those Chinese whores, I hope. Open up in there!' he commanded, rapping on the cabin door with his bare knuckles.

'Open up in there or we'll break down the door,' he roared, as Lieutenant Howell arrived with his marines.

Lieutenant Conrad coughed politely, as if he was interrupting a conversation at a society gathering.

'I beg your pardon, captain,' he replied, 'but she's English and she's no whore.' Although, he thought to himself with relish, the way she had behaved last night would have astonished the madams of many of the world's finest brothels.

'She is Mrs Brown, who you may remember meeting at Whampoa's last night. She has left her husband, and I have promised to take her back to Charleston to start a new life. Margaret, please open the door before Captain Semmes has me clapped in irons,' he called out to her.

There was a sound of movement in the cabin, and a few minutes later a decidedly dishevelled Margaret opened the door and stood defiantly before Captain Semmes, who was for a moment flabbergasted at the sight of her.

Semmes quickly recovered his composure and said to her, 'My pardon, Mrs Brown, but I cannot have a woman on board my ship. We're going to turn around and bring you back to your family as soon as we can, and I apologize for any inconvenience we may cause.'

'Is that wise, Captain Semmes?' Lieutenant Conrad responded. 'We know the *Wyoming* is out there looking for us, and she could trap us if we go back. In any case, what's wrong with taking a woman on board? We took the niggra, so what have you got against Mrs Brown?'

'If the *Wyoming* finds us, we will come out and fight her in the open sea,' Semmes snapped in reply, 'and as for Davie, I ...'

His voice froze as he watched Margaret pull out a heavy Navy colt revolver, cock the hammer and place it against her right temple.

'I have no family, Captain Semmes, and I am not property to be returned. My husband sent my son back to England when he was six, and will not let me return to see him. He keeps me bound to him in Singapore while he spends his nights drinking and whoring on Malay Street. I'll not go to back to him, and if you are intent on taking me back, I will blow my brains out right here before your eyes. I mean it!' she exclaimed, her voice rising and her eyes growing wild. 'I'd rather be dead for sure than return to a life in which I am as good as dead!'

Captain Semmes looked at her carefully, and then spoke to her in a calm and soothing voice.

'Please put the gun down, Mrs Brown. You have made your point and I do not doubt you.' Captain Semmes recalled the words he had written the previous evening, and suddenly felt sorry for her.

I'll not be a hypocrite, he thought, even to myself.

'You may stay on board, Mrs Brown, but I would not entertain any high hopes of us returning to Charleston. There are many Yankee ships out there who mean to send us to the bottom of the ocean, and you have placed yourself in great danger. However, I will respect your wishes, although I beg you to allow us to let you off in some friendly port, or aboard a ship returning to England. I would be willing to furnish you with sufficient funds to secure your safe passage.'

Margaret slowly lowered the colt and uncocked the hammer. Semmes heaved a sigh of relief.

'I'm most grateful for your offer, Captain Semmes,' she replied in a firm voice, 'but I have made up my mind to stay with James, come hell or high water.'

'As you wish madam, tho' hell and high water it may very well be,' Semmes replied. 'But I must take my leave and attend to my ship. Good morning to you, Mrs Brown.' Semmes bowed, and turning on his heel, marched off back on deck, motioning Lieutenant Howell and his marines to follow him.

'Nicely done, my love,' James said to her with a wide grin after Semmes had left. 'Now that's what I call spirit!'

Then he leaned forward and whispered in her ear.

'I hope it never comes to it, my love, but if you ever want to blow your brains out again, put the revolver in your mouth. Pointing it at your temple is very dramatic, I'll grant you, but not likely to get the job done. The recoil would mean you'd only blast a fragment from your frontal lobes, and you'd likely survive, but with your mental faculties very severely impaired. I wouldn't wish it on my worst enemy.'

'You're such a charmer,' she laughed, replacing the revolver in her bag. She moved towards him, beginning to unbutton the shirt she had hastily put on.

But he stilled her. 'Later, my love,' he said, blowing her a kiss as he stepped back out of the cabin. 'I'm on duty, remember, and we have Yankee merchantmen to find.'

She sank back on the bunk, and peered out of the porthole at the breaking clouds as the *Alabama* sped northward. She was amazed at herself, but she had no fear of what might happen if the *Wyoming* caught up with them. This was adventure, this was passion – this was life!

21

James returned soon after with a mug of coffee and some buttered eggs and toast, which she devoured ravenously. Half an hour later, Mr Parkinson, the wardroom steward, came down and informed Margaret that whenever she was ready, she could come up on deck and take the air, now that the crew had been informed of her presence aboard the *Alabama*. He told her she should feel at home, since many of the crew were from Liverpool, and some of the officers were English. She made up her face as best she could, then went up on deck dressed in her riding gear, minus her hat and crop, with her hair tied back with a black ribbon.

'Good morning, Mrs Brown, I'm very pleased to have you aboard,' said a tall man with a black beard and a Welsh accent. 'I'm Dr Herbart Llewellyn, the acting surgeon. You've come up in time to see the action. We're about to put one across the bows of that trader.'

He led Margaret across to the starboard deck and handed her his telescope, so that she could view the merchantman that the *Alabama* was bearing down upon at full speed. Llewellyn indicated that she should put her hands over her ears, but the starboard pivot gun boomed out before she could respond, and her ears echoed with the sound.

Captain Semmes ordered the engines slowed and a boat lowered. Lieutenant Armstrong and a party of sailors and marines were sent across to inspect the *Martaban*, which had turned around in response to the *Alabama*'s warning shot.

'But she's flying an English flag,' said Margaret in surprise.

'Surely Captain Semmes does not intend to destroy an English ship?'

'That may be,' Llewellyn replied, 'although from the looks of her she's more likely out of Boston than Liverpool, I'd say. But Armstrong will check her papers.'

They watched as the *Alabama*'s boat made her way across to the *Martaban*, and Armstrong and his party boarded the ship.

When Armstrong came on board the *Martaban*, he demanded to see the ship's papers. Captain Pike told him that the vessel was originally registered as the *Texan Star* in Boston, but that she had been sold to Mr Currie, an Englishman in Moulmein,[cviii] and was carrying a cargo of rice for sale in Singapore. He produced the Ship's Register and Bill of Sale, which Armstrong inspected.

'You will have to accompany me back to the *Alabama*, Captain Pike,' said Lieutenant Armstrong, 'so that Captain Semmes can examine these papers.'

'I refuse to do so, sir,' replied Captain Pike. 'This is a British vessel and protected by the British flag.'

'As you wish, sir,' replied Lieutenant Armstrong. 'But I am taking charge of this vessel until I have consulted with Captain Semmes.' He ordered the marines to take up positions on the deck of the *Martaban*, and sent the boat back to the *Alabama*. It soon returned with Captain Semmes and a party of seamen in another boat. When Semmes came on board, he went straight to Captain Pike's cabin and asked for his papers. He then sat down on a chair and looked over the Ship's Register and Bill of Sale.

'Do you have a certificate showing this transfer was legal, Captain Pike? I'll not be humbugged by sham papers.'

'The papers are legal,' Captain Pike replied, 'you have seen them for yourself.'

Semmes got up from his chair and stood before Captain Pike.

'Listen to me very carefully,' he said, 'do you state that this was

---

cviii Port City in Moulmein (Burma).

a bone fide sale?'

Captain Pike said nothing for a few moments, and then replied, 'I do not state this.'

Captain Semmes continued, 'Do you not know that this was intended merely as a cover to prevent capture.'

Again Captain Pike was slow in replying, but eventually admitted, 'Yes, I do know it. I cannot pretend to you otherwise.'

'Then I shall burn your ship,' said Captain Semmes.

Captain Pike tried to protest, but Semmes ignored him and turned to Lieutenant Armstrong.

'Haul down that flag and burn this ship, sir,' he commanded.

Armstrong had the flag taken down, and directed the crew from the *Alabama* to drop anchor and clew up the sails. Captain Pike was informed he could take two small trunks with him, and that his officers could take one bag each. When these were assembled, they were ordered to row in their own ship's boats to the *Alabama*, where they were held on deck under armed guard. Lieutenant Armstrong and his men gathered up some bolts of canvas, two chronometers, a deep-sea line and lead, two hams and all the poultry on board, which they sent back to the *Alabama*. Then they smashed the skylights, and flung lengths of tow steeped in tar into the ports between the decks. As they left the *Martaban*, or the *Texan Star* as Armstrong now referred to it, they fired the tar-soaked tow – by the time they made it back to the *Alabama* smoke was billowing from both ends of the doomed ship. As Captain Pike and his crew watched helplessly, the *Martaban* burst into flames, blazing like a warning beacon to other Union merchant ships in the vicinity.

Lieutenant Conrad relieved Captain Pike of the keys to his trunks, and then searched them. He removed the Ship's Register Registry and Bill of Sale, and four hundred Federal dollars that he found hidden among his clothes. Once again Captain Pike protested, but once again his protests were ignored. One of the seamen from the *Martaban* then cried out to Lieutenant Armstrong:

'Did ye get the cat? Surely ye did no leave the cat on board!'

'I'm afraid we saw no cat, and nobody mentioned the cat to us,' Armstrong replied.

'Bad luck will surely follow ye for burning a poor cat alive,' the seaman cried out, before Benjamin Mecaskey, the *Alabama*'s bosun, told him to hold his tongue or he would take his own cat to him.

'We meant no harm to the cat,' Captain Semmes declared, in a voice loud enough for everyone to hear, including the Liverpool seamen, who were a superstitious bunch. 'But that particular superstition is as worthless as the one about having niggras or women on board,' he continued, nodding to Davie, who returned a broad grin, and Margaret, who gave a little bow. The crewmen of the Alabama roared in laughter, and gave the captain a loud hurrah, although some of them retained their secret doubts.

Lieutenant Conrad walked over to where Margaret was standing with Dr Llewellyn, watching the *Martaban* burning in the distance, and said cheerfully:

'A good day's work, don't you think?'

'I cannot believe you just burned a British ship,' she replied. 'Do you want to bring down the wrath of the British navy upon you?'

'Oh, I don't think we need worry about that,' Conrad replied. 'Semmes is sure his papers are a fraud, and the flag means nothing. We regularly fly British colours to disguise our approach to the Yankees, and they do the same. In any case, I doubt they have anything this side of Point de Galle able to catch the *Alabama* or match her guns. And I'm sure Semmes will send off a letter explaining his action to the British authorities, as soon as we get to port or come across a real British brig.'

'What will happen to these men?' Margaret asked, indicating the crew of the *Martaban*, who were being led down to be kept as prisoners in the forward hold.

'Semmes said he would drop them off at Malacca, unless we meet up with trouble before then. But I'll be off duty later, so why don't we have a little private dinner in my cabin. Not enough room to swing a cat, living or dead, but Mr Parkinson can rouse us up something – perhaps one of those chickens we took on yesterday – and I've got a few bottles of fine reds left in my locker.'

'I'd be delighted,' she said, meeting his eyes and smiling in anticipation of the night ahead.

But the day's work was not over. In the late afternoon the *Alabama* came across the *Sonora* and the *Highlander*, anchored ten miles off Malacca. Both ships were boarded and burned, their crews put into their ship's boats and set on course for Malacca. Captain Semmes put in briefly to Malacca that evening, where he released Captain Pike and his officers and crew, after they had signed a statement stating that they would not serve against the Confederate states, unless and until they were officially exchanged for Confederate prisoners. He also delivered a hastily written letter to the British authorities explaining his actions with respect to the *Texan Star*, which had been falsely represented as the *Martaban* under a British flag.

In the early evening, as they steamed out of Malacca, Captain Semmes assembled all hands on deck and thanked them for their day's endeavours. To Margaret's delight, he said that he thought Mrs Brown had turned out to be a very good mascot indeed, to which the men gave a hearty cheer. Then, with the sun setting in golden streamers over her bows as Christmas Eve drew to a close, the *Alabama* steamed west on a course that Semmes had set for Cape Town and the Atlantic.

As James and Margaret went down to his cabin for dinner, James apologized that Parkinson had nothing for desert.

'Oh, I can think of something,' she said gaily, giving him an openly lascivious smile in the darkness of the wardroom.

22

As the *Alabama* steamed west and into the new year, Margaret felt that she was on a glorious holiday and honeymoon combined. Everyone on board was friendly and courteous to her, and Surgeon Galt found he had a new rival for young Davie's affections. During the day she took the air on deck and read from Semmes' considerable library, and during the night she flung herself into her lover's arms and afterwards slept as deep and as peacefully as a newborn babe. She told James of her ruined family and her disastrous marriage, and he told her about Charleston, about the mansions on the Battery and the fine townhouses on the cobbled streets. He had a sister and an aging father back home, he said, but had received no news of them for about two years. Although Major General Gillmore's siege had not yet managed to break the city, James knew that it was only a matter of time before it was starved into surrender, or caught in the path of Brigadier General Sherman's army of destruction, which was marching from Atlanta to the sea.

As they passed south of Ceylon, they hailed an English ship, the *Shrilanka*. Captain Semmes passed off his ship as the USS *Dakota* in search of the *Alabama*, in order to discover if there were Union ships in the Bay of Bengal. Semmes was greatly amused when the captain of the *Shrilanka* told him that he should abandon his pursuit, since the *Alabama* was much bigger than the *Dakota* and iron plated. He was also relieved to hear that the *Alabama* had last been reported at St Simon's Bay, off the coast of Mozambique. They pressed on through the Bay of Bengal, and burned the Union merchant ship

Emma on January 14. When they passed across the equator on January 30, Semmes was confident enough that no Union warships were in the area to take a week out to make some repairs to the *Alabama,* and rest the crew at the Comora islands, where they took on fresh meat, fruit and vegetables. James and Margaret swam in the surf and stretched out on the silver sands. At night they dined on spicy dishes as the stars danced against the blue black sky.

They set off again southwest in early February, and on March 11 they anchored off Cape Town, where Captain Semmes was outraged to learn that the British authorities had seized the Confederate cruiser CSS *Tuscaloosa.* While in Cape Town they received newspapers reporting the progress of the war, but they made depressing reading. The Union armies were strengthening their stranglehold on the South, and all but two of her ports were securely blockaded. Semmes knew he ought to dock the *Alabama* in Cape Town, because her hull and engines were badly in need of repair, but he feared that the authorities might seize the *Alabama* as well when they heard about his destruction of the *Martaban.* They took on new shells and powder, which Second Assistant Engineer William Brooks complained were of very poor quality, and departed Cape Town on March 25.

***

'Good news, gentleman,' W.H. Read announced to his guests at his home on Orchard Road. 'The Governor of Hong Kong had recommended the transfer of the Straits Settlements to the Colonial Office. We shouldn't count our chickens, but I feel that victory is within our grasp!'

'Hear, hear!' replied his guests, who included long-time supporters of the transfer, such as Robert Carr Woods, Abraham Logan and Ronnie Simpson.

23

It was a difficult first labour, but just before the lunar New Year Ah Keng gave birth to a healthy baby boy. Bee Swee was overjoyed, and was as good as his word. Although Mui Chi tried to pretend that the deed of sale was lost, she dutifully handed it over to her father-in-law when Bee Swee threatened to disown her and turn her out on the street. When Ah Keng received the cancelled bill of sale with Ho Bee Swee's chop upon it, she burst into tears, and loved the old man almost as much as she loved her new son, who lay curled up at her breast.

* * *

As a dutiful wife, Ah Keng observed the traditional one-month confinement period, during which she took special care of herself and her baby by eating heaty foods^{cix} and taking tonics for her blood. At the end of the month, Ho Bee Swee held a celebration, during which he distributed an odd number of red hard-boiled eggs to his friends and relations, who responded by giving hong bao red lucky packets for the child. After the celebration was over, Ah Keng carried her baby, whom they had called Ham Choon, into the courtyard at the centre of the house, which was laid out with bamboo and other ornamental trees. As she stepped out into the **sunlight, intending to make her way to the shade of the small pavilion in the centre of the**

---

cix Foods believed to improve circulation and avoid chills, such as read meat and chillies.

courtyard, she suddenly turned to one side, when she saw a large butterfly with brilliant blue wings alight on a nearby fern.

'Look my precious,' she whispered to Ham Choon, 'look at the beautiful butterfly.'

The words had scarcely left her mouth when she felt the wind on her cheek, and saw the huge flower pot smash onto the stones beside her, spraying her with earth and pottery shards, one of which caused a small cut on her left ankle. Sheltering her child, she looked back upwards to the balcony. She could see no one, but she heard the hasty footsteps of someone fleeing from the scene. And she knew that if she had not suddenly turned towards the butterfly, the heavy earthen pot would have landed on her and her baby.

She went immediately to tell her husband what had happened. Bee Swee summoned his family before him, and demanded to know who was responsible. He cursed them all, condemned his other sons as useless, and warned them that if any harm came to Ah Keng or his new son, he would disown them and turn them out on the street.

Mui Chi pleaded their innocence, and told her father-in-law that she had already punished and dismissed the servant girl who had accidentally knocked over the heavy plant pot. But Bee Swee told Mui Chi that he did not believe her, and that from this moment forth he was putting his new wife Ah Keng in charge of the household. They would all take their orders from her, and severe punishment would come to anyone who disobeyed or threatened her.

They left the old man's presence, their heads hung in shame, but their hearts blazing in anger and hatred. While Ah Keng attended to her baby in the nursing room, Mui Chi came to her and prostrated herself on the floor at her feet. She begged Ah Keng's forgiveness for her past behaviour, and promised that she would obey her new mistress in her every word and deed. She also begged Ah Keng's permission to visit her father-in-law, so that she could prostrate herself before him and demonstrate her genuine contrition. Ah Keng could not easily forgive Mui Chi for her past cruelties, but she was embarrassed by her fawning entreaties, so she granted Mui Chi permission to visit Ho Bee Swee. The baby was fussing, and she did not reflect much upon Mui Chi's apparent change of heart.

***

When Mui Chi entered, Bee Swee was lying upon his bed, resting after his day's exertions.

'Why have you come?' he demanded, as he turned towards her, his face revealing his displeasure at being disturbed.

'First wife Ah Keng has given her gracious permission for me to visit, to ask your forgiveness for my past behaviour. I have been an unworthy daughter-in-law,' she said, as she sat down on the edge of the bed and reached out to take his hand.

'So you have,' Bee Swee retorted, as he pulled his hand away, 'you and my useless first son.'

Then Bee Swee saw the cruel intent in her eyes, and made to rise and cry out. But Mui Chi had already seized the pillow and pressed it hard down over his nose and mouth, and held it firmly over his face as he struggled desperately for breath and life. Ho Bee Swee fought with all the vigour of his rejuvenated essence, but it was not enough to overcome the youthful energy and strength of Mui Chi, and his will to live was but a thin reed swept away in the torrent of raging hatred and malice that Mui Chi bore towards him.

***

When Ah Keng returned with Ham Choon to the bedroom, so that Bee Swee could kiss him goodnight, she saw Mui Chi sitting on the edge of his bed. She no longer looked contrite and a thin smile passed over her face. Taken by surprise, Ah Keng turned her attention to Bee Swee, and to her horror saw no expression on his pale face – save for the vacant stare of the dead.

'I am afraid that my father-in-law has passed over into the spirit kingdom, and that you no longer have a husband,' Mui Chi said in a cool tone.

'What happened?' Ah Keng asked, but the moment she did she realized what had happened. Mui Chi had suffocated him – she could see the discarded pillow by his head.

'Who knows? He was an old man. Perhaps he was worn out with overexertion,' Mui Chi replied, with a sneer she did not attempt to disguise. 'For all we know, you might be a fox-spirit or ghost who has drained his essence with your sex.'

'Don't be foolish,' Ah Keng responded, 'and don't take that tone with me, Mui Chi! I am still his first wife and still in charge of the household. Go send for the undertaker and the Taoist priest, while I attend to my dead husband.'

Mui Chi rose, but she did not leave the room to do Ah Keng's bidding. She went and stood in the doorway, from where she addressed her longtime adversary, while Ah Keng bent over her dead husband and gently closed his staring eyes with her fingers.

'No one in our family remembers any such thing, I assure you,' Mui Chi said, her thin smile returning to her face, 'which means that I remain in charge of the household, and that I am the one who gives the commands. And my first command is that you give your child over to me, that I may ...'

'I know exactly what you mean to do!' Ah Keng exclaimed, her face turning red in anger as she rose from the bed with Ham Choon in her arms. 'You will never have my child!' She made to leave the bedroom, but Mui Chi remained in the doorway, blocking her exit.

'You will not leave here alive,' Mui Chi hissed, 'you or your baby!' Then she stepped forward and tried to pull Ham Choon from

Ah Keng's grasp. Ah Keng clasped the child to her body with her left arm, and fought back with her right, like a woman possessed, tearing at Mui Chi with her nails and kicking at her with her slippered feet. The two women spun round and round as they fought for the baby, until they collided with a bedside table. Mui Chi fell crashing to the floor, upsetting the table and the oil lamp upon it, which burst into flames as it smashed against the bedroom wall.

Ah Keng managed to keep her balance, still clutching a bawling Ham Choom in her left arm, as the flames raced up the silken screens and wall hangings around the bed. As Mui Chi struggled to get up, hampered by her bound feet, Ah Keng kicked her hard in the stomach, and then knocked her back down to the floor with a fierce blow from her clenched right fist. Then she turned and ran out of the bedroom, leaving her dead husband and sister-in-law. She raced down the stairs, clasping her infant son to her breast, then ran out of the main door of the house and into the welcoming darkness of the moonless night. As she ran, she heard Mui Chi call out for help, and then loud cries of alarm as the servants discovered the fire. Ah Keng had left without a thought for her money or her jewels, but she had snatched up some of the red hong bao packets from the table in the entrance hall as she passed it by. She made her way back towards town in the darkness, a darkness only relieved by the light from the flames that soared skyward from her former home.

24

When Ah Keng arrived at Auntie Ki's house two hours later, the old lady took a long time to respond, and at first demanded to know who was disturbing her rest at this time of night. But when she heard Ah Keng's voice, she opened the door immediately, and fussed over her and the baby.

'What happened to you?' she exclaimed. 'And why have you come on foot, and in the middle of the night? Everything seemed so happy and harmonious when I came this afternoon for Ham Choon's celebration – and all those lucky packets!'

When Ah Keng told Auntie Ki her story, the old lady nodded her head with understanding.

'Did I not warn you that something like this would happen? You should have taken my advice and left when I told you. But at least you are safe, you and your baby son.'

'But how will we survive?' Ah Keng sobbed in reply, as the real nature of her new and reduced situation sunk in. I have no money, except for these,' she said, handing Auntie Ki the hong bao packets she had grabbed during her flight from the house. How will I pay for my father's medicine, and how will I be able to support my baby?'

'Do not worry, 'Auntie Ki replied, with a smile, 'we will surely find a way.'

A sudden thought flashed through Ah Keng's mind and filled her with horror. Did Auntie Ki mean to sell her once again? Well, she would do it if needs be, she resolved to herself. She would become a concubine again, if that was the only way she could support her baby and her father. She had not lost her looks, and Auntie Ki could find her another suitor.

Once again, the old lady seemed to have read her mind.

'Do not worry, Ah Keng,' she replied. 'I do not own you anymore, and you have been like a daughter to me. We will find some other way.'

Ah Keng breathed a huge sigh of relief and gratitude when she heard these words.

'As Ho Bee Swee made you his first wife, he must have provided for you and the child in his will. But we cannot count on that, since we can be sure the family will fight to have the terms of his will changed, by bringing all sorts of false charges against you – perhaps even false charges of murder. Even if you were to win in the end, the court case could tie up his estate for years and years, and at the moment only Mui Chi has control of his cash.

'But I will make a solemn contract with you, Ah Keng, if you will agree to it. I will do my best to help support you and your baby, and look after your father, if you will agree to say prayers for my spirit when I die, and tend to my grave. It is all I ever wanted. I was a mui tsai myself many years ago, and sold as a wife to a shopkeeper. He died soon after, leaving me without children and only a small amount of money after the funeral expenses were paid. I determined to make enough money to ensure that I would be able to pay some sister to pray at my altar after my death, and decided that the best way to make money was to go into the mui tsai business myself. I even trained one of my younger girls as a long-haired nun, who was supposed to remain celibate and worship my ancestral tablets. But the pig of a pork-seller who lives next door managed to persuade her to part with her virginity, so I was forced to sell her to him. I got a good price, for the man was besotted with her, but it made me realize that there are some things that money cannot buy. I ask only one thing of you, Ah Keng, that if you agree to do this for me, you will remain faithful to my trust. If you do not think you can do that, then please tell me now, I beg of you.'

'I promise you Auntie Ki,' said Ah Keng, taking the old lady's hands, 'that I will honour your memory when you die, since you have been like a second mother to me. I promise you this without condition, although I would be grateful for your support, at least until I can get back on my feet. But what will we do for money when the red packets run out?'

'I have some money saved, 'said Auntie Ki, 'if we need to use it. But we should save that if we can, and find some other source of income. I suggest that we start taking in laundry. Starting tomorrow.'

* * *

But there was no need for them to take in laundry. The next day they learned that the whole family had perished in the fire, so desperate were they to preserve their precious jewels and belongings. The servants had managed to escape with the children, refusing orders to continue fighting the fire when it became obvious that it was beyond their control. The children's parents had been killed when the roof had collapsed upon them, while they were rifling the cupboards and chests in Ho Bee Swee's bedroom. Their greed had been the death of them.

The following day Ah Keng received a visit from Mr Sng Chon Yee, Ho Bee Swee's manager. Mr Sng offered his condolences over the death of her husband, and said he had come to explain to her the terms of the old man's will. He told her it was a complicated instrument, and that it would take some time to sort things out, but that she would be well cared for. Mr Sng advised Ah Keng that Ho Bee Swee had anticipated that in the event of his death the family would contest his will, so he had been instructed to set up a separate trust in her name, for the future well-being of his wife and son. Ho Bee Swee had also anticipated that his family would threaten the lives of Ah

Keng and her son – as Auntie Ki had also warned that they would – so he had left instructions that in the event of their premature death the whole estate would be willed to the Fuk Tak Chi Temple[cx] on Telok Ayer Street. As things turned out, Mr Sng continued, none of these careful instructions had proved necessary. Since Ho Bee Swee's four other sons and their wives had all died in the fire, the whole of his estate would devolve on Ah Keng and her infant son.

Ah Keng could not believe her ears when she heard this news. She knew what it meant – she was free at last, and free of worry about how she would be able to look after her child, her father and herself.

'Well, you know what this means, Auntie Ki!' she exclaimed, with a squeal of delight.

'What does it mean, my precious,' Auntie Ki replied cautiously, wondering how Ah Keng would treat her now that she had attained complete independence.

'It means we don't have to take in laundry! It means we can get the best medical attention for my father! It means we can buy a bigger house, and have our own servants.'

Auntie Ki breathed a sigh of relief when Ah Keng said 'we'. She had wondered if Ah Keng would abandon her now that she had come into her own, and might no longer feel bound by the terms of their earlier contract.

While they were thus considering the implications of Ah Keng's good fortune, Mr Sng interrupted them with a polite cough.

'Excuse me, ladies,' he said. 'There is one matter that we need to discuss rather urgently, and on which I must have your decision. There are seven grandchildren, three boys and four girls, who need to be placed somewhere, and some sort of consideration ought to be extended to the servants, who saved their lives. I can easily find

cx Oldest temple in Singapore, dedicated to Tua Pek Kong, the god of prosperity, founded by Hakka and Cantonese immigrants in 1824.

434

homes for the boys, but I am not sure what to do about the girls.'

Ah Keng, who only a few moments before had discovered her financial independence, quickly asserted her new authority.

'Do not be concerned, Mr Sng, I will take responsibility for all of the grandchildren. I will likely retain most of the servants, although I will need to interview them personally before committing to any long-term engagement – some of them had close ties to Mui Chi, and may still harbour some resentment. I want you to immediately secure us a temporary home of sufficient size to accommodate us all, while I decide whether or not I want to rebuild on the old site.'

'That is no problem,' Mr Sng replied, 'since one of Mr Ho's own rental properties at Tanglin recently fell vacant. You can easily stay there until the financial matters are sorted out. I will instruct the servants to bring the children to the house and prepare it for you. I will see to it at once.'

And with that he wished them good day, and left them to their thoughts and their dramatically changed situation.

'I hope our contract still holds, Auntie Ki,' Ah Keng said. 'I hope you will still look after my father in return for my promise to honour your ancestral tablets.'

'Of course,' Auntie Ki replied. 'Nothing would give me greater pleasure. Your father and I have become good friends these past few months, and I hope we may continue for many years with our pipes and our games of xiangqi.[cxi] He is quite a good player you know.'

'There is one last condition, Auntie Ki,' Ah Keng said. 'You must free your remaining mui tsai. I will pay you a good price for their bills of sale.'

Auntie Ki agreed to do so, but the girls objected. They wanted Auntie Ki to find them good husbands in Singapore, which she easily did, since there was still a severe shortage of eligible women in the settlement.

---

cxi Chinese chess.

25

The last two remaining Taiping strongholds outside of Nanking, Hangzhou and Changzhou, fell to Li Hongzhang in March and April. Hundreds of thousands of defiant Taiping rebels were slaughtered in the fierce hand-to-hand street fighting. Judging that the rebellion was nearing its end, Li Hongzhang decided that it was time to disband the Ever Victorious Army, which had grown so large and effective that he had come to fear it. Captain Gordon, who was sick to his stomach with the bloodletting of the past year, readily agreed, especially when Li offered him generous demobilization bonuses for his officers, and compensation to the wounded. [11]

***

In April Hong Rengan lead a force out of Nanking to the countryside around Lake Tai, two hundred miles to the west, in the hope of securing desperately needed supplies. But he failed to secure any in the ravaged land, and when he made his way back to Nanking in May, he found the city ringed fast with massed Qing troops. The Shield King was forced to return west and make his base at Huzhou, south of Lake Tai.

***

The Qing armies now commanded every strategic hill around Nanking, and had surrounded the city with a double line of breastworks, with forts erected at half-mile intervals. None but women and children were allowed to leave the city, and none were allowed to enter. General Li watched helpless as the Qing bombarded the walls and gates of the Heavenly City with their new European rifled cannon, and drove deep tunnels towards the city walls. The Loyal King rode out with his veterans in an attempt to recapture some of the hills and secure new grain supplies, and ordered counter-tunnels dug to flood those of the Qing. Yet his tired and hungry veterans were beaten back, and the Qing opened new and deeper tunnels to replace those that were destroyed. Now it was only a matter of time before the city fell to Zeng Guofan, who wrote to Yehonala in April promising that he would capture the rebellious city in the next few months.

Yehonala's reply was blunt and to the point.

'I thank my loyal general for his promise. Accept no surrender. Kill them all, every last Taiping!'

26

There was no food to be had in the Heavenly City. The soldiers and citizens were starving and dying. Once again General Li requested an audience with the Heavenly King, and begged him to decree what could be done to relieve the distress of his loyal followers. Hong Xiuquan's answer left the Loyal King aghast.

'Everyone in the city should eat manna. This will keep them alive.'

The Loyal King knew to what the Heavenly King referred. The Book of Exodus, which like all God-followers he had read, described how God had saved the faithful in the wilderness by spreading manna among them. Yet the manna had fallen from the sky, and the only thing falling into the Heavenly City was the shot and shell of the European artillery that the Qing had purchased from their new allies.

Then to Li Xiucheng's amazement Hong Xiuquan came down from his throne and walked out into the open courtyard of his palace, where he got down on his hands and knees and began gathering the weeds that had grown up between the flagstones. He squeezed them into a ball, which he declared he was going to eat. He issued a decree commanding his followers to follow his example, so they would all have something to eat. Then he went back into the palace and began to eat the weeds for his evening meal. At that moment General Li knew that all was lost, and began to make his own secret preparations.

Hong Xiuquan grew sick in April, although whether it was

from malnutrition or from eating weeds his doctors could not say. He revived for a few weeks in May, but then his health grew steadily worse. Hong Xiuquan had only recently turned fifty, but knew he had not long to live, and that his dream of destroying the demon-devils and establishing a Taiping Kingdom of Peace on Earth was lost forever.

On May 30, Hong Xiuquan issued a final decree to his followers. The time had come, he declared, for him to visit Heaven, where he would ask his Heavenly Father and Heavenly Brother to send a celestial army to defend the Heavenly City.

Then he swallowed the poison that he had ordered prepared for him.

The poison was supposed to be fast acting, but unfortunately was not, and the Heavenly King lingered on in excruciating agony until he died early on the morning of June 1, as the rising sun sent streamers of golden light across his golden palace. Hong Xiuquan had decreed years before that the Taiping dead were not to be buried in coffins, but in shallow graves in the bare earth, since they would soon all rise up to Heaven. In accord with his decree, the Heavenly King was wrapped in a yellow shroud of silk and buried by his women in the gardens of his palace.

Five days later, Tiangui Fu, the Young Monarch, ascended the throne of the Heavenly King, and the ministers and generals paid homage to him. Yet he ruled in name only, with General Li making all the final decisions and dispositions. The news of Hong Xiuquan's death did not damage the morale of the Taiping troops remaining in the Heavenly City, who still believed that the Heavenly King had been sent by God to deliver them, and would send his celestial armies to save them. But General Li did not.

27

Adi bin Sadat knelt toward Mecca and said his prayers, then rolled up his prayer mat. He sat cross-legged on the floor of his small bedroom and began to complete the Arabic inscription he had been forming, using a dried bamboo pen and black ink. It was a popular verse from the Koran:

'And he found you lost and guided you.'

He was engrossed in his work, and was startled by the voice.

'You have a fine gift, Adi bin Sadat.'

Adi looked up and was surprised to see Habib Noh sitting in front of him, his milky blue eyes fixed upon him. He had not heard the holy man enter his bedroom or announce himself.

'You have a yearning to live the life of your ancestor, do you not, Adi bin Sadat.'

'I do, master,' he replied, 'and know it is unworthy of me.'

'There is no sin in celebrating your ancestors, even though they were not of the faith. But your path will not be their path, and that you know already.'

'I do,' Adi replied, his head bowed.

'Do not be despondent,' Habib Noh said, rising from the floor, 'but take my hand and come with me.'

He reached out his hand and Adi rose from the floor and took it.

As he did so a thick white fog descended upon them and blocked out the everyday sounds of the kampong – birds singing, cattle lowing and mothers calling out to their children.

They stood for many moments in the white silence until the fog finally cleared and Adi found himself standing on the walls of a fortress, as the sounds of battle roared from the plain below.

'Be not afraid,' said Habib Noh, who stood beside him, 'no one can see you or touch you.'

Adi saw the rajah, mounted on a magnificent war elephant, leading his warriors and driving the enemy back towards their ships near the mouth of the river. Then he watched in horror as the enemy soldiers dragged the rajah down from his gilded saddle, and one raised his huge battle axe for the killing blow. Yet before he could bring the weapon down a giant of a man flung a great stone that killed the soldier instantly, and then helped the rajah drive the enemy forces into the sea.

Before Adi could ask, Habib Noh said:

'He was your ancestor Badang, who attained the strength of ten men.'

Before Adi could reply, the thick white fog and silence descended again.

Then they were climbing a hill, and came upon a keramat.[cxii] Habib Noh stopped and whispered a prayer, and Adi bowed his head. He knew where they were, they were on Bukit Larangan – Forbidden Hill – before the keramat of Iskandar Shah. They carried on up the hill until Habib Noh stopped a short distance from a clearing, raising his arm to indicate that Adi should do the same. They were standing behind a tall Malay, who was watching a sad procession of men, women and children passing through the clearing and into a dark cave cut into the rock. Adi watched in amazement, when at the last moment a giant of a man seemed to hail the Malay with his raised sword, before disappearing into the cave, which closed behind him.

'Was that not Badang, the great warrior,' Adi asked, in a hushed

---

cxii Tomb.

voice.

'It was, and the man you see before you lived on the island the year that the British came. His name was Badang bin Aman. He too was a healer and a visionary.'

'What he dreamed was the passing of the ghosts of old Singapura … the passing of Malay sovereignty over the island.'

Adi was about to ask if this would be ever be returned, but before the silent fog descended again, he already knew the answer.

* * *

Then the fog lifted one last time, and he was sitting in his bedroom facing Habib Noh again.

'They are the past, but you are the future. And your future lies not in force of arms, but in this,' as he pointed towards the verse from the Koran that Adi had scripted.

Then all a sudden, Habib Noh was gone.

28

The *Alabama* continued north up the coast of Africa. She chased the USS *Rockingham* through the night of April 22, and sank her with a broadside the following morning. She battled on, burning Union merchant ships and releasing neutrals, but the voyage took a heavy toll on the cruiser. The copper sheeting that Semmes had hoped to secure in Cape Town was now peeling from her hull, drastically reducing her speed. On June 11, she limped into Cherbourg harbour on the coast of Normandy, where Captain Semmes requested permission from the French authorities to dock the *Alabama* and conduct the extensive repairs she required. When he met with the Master Attendant, Monsieur Rabillet, Semmes likened the *Alabama* to a weary foxhound.

'We're limping back after a long chase, footsore, and longing for quiet and repose,' he said.

After they put off their prisoners the following day, James came down to tell Margaret the good news.

'The captain aims to give us two months' shore leave. So, let's pack our things and find ourselves some good rooms before the Georgia boys get the best of them.'

They rented the top floor of a pension with a fine view of the harbour, and the next day they lunched at a waterfront café, where they feasted on new lamb and potatoes and green beans, washed down with a fine Bordeaux. A few puffy white clouds drifted across the clear blue sky, and a gentle sea breeze fluttered the shade above their heads. They finished their meal with a bowl of strawberries, large and juicy at the height of the season. They felt the way that young lovers do, and looked forward to the days and nights ahead of them.

But as they walked along the promenade a few days later, they saw young Davie come running towards them, waving his arm to attract their attention.

'Cap'n Semmes wishes yor 'tention in his cabin, Lieutenant Conrad,' he declared, his eyes wide. 'Immediately,' he finished, pointing to where the *Alabama* was berthed, and then ran off in pursuit of the other officers.

'What's wrong?' Margaret said, as she looked at him anxiously. 'Do you think there is trouble?'

'I suspect there is,' Conrad replied. 'I don't see Semmes holding a soiree with the *Alabama* in such a state of disrepair. Go back to the hotel – I'll return as soon as I find out what this is about.'

When James returned, the news was grim, although he made light of it. Semmes had discovered that the US consul in Cherbourg had contacted the warship USS *Kearsarge,* which had made its way to Cherbourg from the Netherlands, where it had been hunting the *Alabama* and other Confederate vessels. The *Kearsarge* was cruising at the breakwater, just outside the three-mile limit. They were in no state to make a run for it, he said, for the copper plating that was peeling from their hull would slow them down too much. But Semmes would never surrender his ship. He had sent a message to Mr Bonfils, the Confederate commercial agent in Cherbourg, to be forwarded to the US consul and the captain of the *Kearsarge,* John Ancrum Winslow, stating that he intended to fight as soon as he could make the necessary arrangements. If they could wait until the *Alabama* was coaled, he would leave the harbour and fight the *Kearsarge* in the open sea on Sunday, June 19. Semmes had received a reply through Mr Bonfils that it had always been Captain Winslow's intention to fight him, but that he could wait a few days more.

'But that's only three days away!' Margaret exclaimed. 'And the *Alabama* is in no condition to fight.'

'I know my love, but Semmes reckons we have a fair chance of beating them, if we can put one through the *Kearsarge* with our Blakely before we get in range of their guns. He means to get in close quickly and board her, since we cannot outgun or outrun her. The *Wyoming* and the *Jamestown* may not be far off, so we had best fight the *Kearsarge* before they arrive. If we can capture it, we can transfer our flag.'

***

James had to return to the *Alabama* during the day, while they prepared the ship for battle and practiced their fighting drills, but he returned to Margaret's arms in the evening. In the wardroom and steerage, the officers joked and fooled around despite the grim business ahead, and most of their jokes related to the state of their nerves. They chaffed poor Davie about his courage, but he grinned broadly, and told them he knew they would bring him through it all right. They prepared their shot, shell and canister, they cleaned and loaded their rifles and pistols, and they sharpened their swords, cutlasses and boarding hooks.

The night before the battle, Semmes allowed his men shore leave, but ordered them back on board before midnight.

***

James and Margaret said little during their meal, and both drank sparingly. They sat most of the time holding hands and looking into each other's eyes. When they returned to their room, he said to her, in his usual laconic manner:

'I don't doubt we'll win the day tomorrow, and we've been through worse scrapes, but just in case I want you to keep this.'

He placed a large black tin box on the table, and opened it with a key from his waistcoat pocket. In it were English gold sovereigns and banknotes, Spanish silver dollars, and wads of Federal and Confederate banknotes. He told her there was enough in the box to keep her comfortable for a good many years, if anything happened to him – and if she did not live to excess, he joked. He told her not to bother with the Confederate money at present; it was worthless as currency now, but she might be able to make some money later by selling it as souvenirs of the war. He told her to pack her bags after he left and to go down to the docks at seven in the morning, where the Englishman John Lancaster had agreed to take her aboard his yacht the *Deerhound*. Lancaster would take the *Deerhound* out to watch the battle, which would give her a better view. More important, he said, although Captain Semmes did not know this, Lancaster had agreed to pick up Confederate survivors if the *Alabama* was sunk by the *Kearsarge*, and take them all on safely to England. If the *Alabama* prevailed, Lancaster would send her back on board. John Lancaster was a wealthy mining engineer and coal magnate, and the *Deerhound* had been built in the same Laird shipyard as the *Alabama* – he was also a Confederate sympathizer.

They went to bed early, before the sun had set, and made love and talked, and made love and talked, until it was time for him to leave. She thought he looked very handsome in his grey and butternut uniform, with its brass buttons, and told him so. He grinned and gave her a last kiss, then smoothed his thin moustache.

'Champagne tonight, I think,' he said, then turned and left the room.

29

Captain Semmes was confident of victory, but took the precaution of lodging the logbooks of the *Alabama*, her bullion and papers, and his own collection of captured hydrometers with the Confederate agent in Cherbourg, Mr Bonfils.

When Semmes first heard of the approach of the *Kearsarge*, he had summoned First Lieutenant John McIntosh Kell, the executive officer of the *Alabama*, to his cabin to discuss their prospects in a fight with the Union ship. He had told Kell that he thought he could whip the *Kearsarge*, since the ships were evenly matched; both were wooden vessels with screws, and carried about the same number of guns. Kell had expressed concern about the quality of their powder and ammunition, which had deteriorated further through long exposure to dampness on the high seas, and condensation from the freshwater condenser. He also noted that although they had eight guns to the *Kearsarge*'s seven, the Yankee ship had two heavy Dahlgren guns that were more powerful than anything the Alabama had on board. Yet it could not be helped, he said; they would just have to get in close before the *Kearsarge* had them at a disadvantage.

In any case, as they both knew well, they had no choice but to fight. And it would give them a chance to answer those critics who called them pirates, preying on defenceless merchantmen. Several newspapers had already taken up their cause, and were claiming that the *Alabama* would soon show the world what she was made of. In the billiard halls and barrooms of Cherbourg, large sums of money were being staked on both ships.

The die was cast. News of the impending naval duel had been telegraphed throughout Europe, and parties were travelling down by train from Paris, renting every available hotel room with an ocean view and hiring private boats to watch the battle from out at sea. Photographers had come to capture the battle on wet plates, and the painter Édouard Monet would later capture it on canvas (based upon newspaper reports).[cxiii] Semmes had no doubt that other Union ships would have been alerted, so this was his only chance to break out of Cherbourg – although he had no clear idea what he would do if he sank or captured the *Kearsarge*. He would think about that tomorrow, he said to himself, as he prepared for an early night. His last thought before he went to bed was that tomorrow was Sunday, and that Sunday had always proved to be his lucky day in the past. The *Alabama* had been commissioned on a Sunday; she had sunk the *Hatteras* on a Sunday; and now he hoped Sunday would bring him success against the *Kearsarge*.

***

Sunday June 19 broke fair, with a clear blue sky and only a few scattered clouds. By early morning, a great crowd of people had gathered along the waterfront, on the hill overlooking the harbour, on the roofs of houses and along the naval fortifications, in preparation for the battle. There was a festive mood in the air, as if they were about to view a regatta or firework display.

Captain Semmes came out to inspect his ship at nine o'clock. He found her in good order. The decks had been scrubbed and

_____

cxiii *The Battle of the Kearsarge and the Alabama*, Oil on Canvas, now hangs in the Philadelphia Museum of Art.

holystoned;[cxiv] the brass work was polished and shining. The sails and rigging had been repaired, and Lieutenant Kell had had the men freshen the paint. Sand had been spread out on deck to staunch the flow of blood and prevent men slipping, and buckets of water had been filled to put out fires. The officers and crew were resplendent in their dress uniforms, neatly brushed with their buttons shining, as if preparing for a review – but the gunners, who were stripped to the waist, reminded them that they were not. Below decks, the surgeons laid out their knives and saws and bandages.

A local chaplain came on board and conducted a short service, after which Captain Semmes ordered the engines fired up, and sent a signal to the *Couronne*, a French ironclad that was to lead them out into the English Channel. The *Alabama* got underway just after nine thirty, and followed the *Couronne* out past Fort Du Homet and point De Querqueville, at the mouth of the harbour. The *Deerhound*, flying the flag of the Royal Mersey Yacht Club, followed close behind, her band playing Dixie, to loud cheers from the men of the *Alabama* and many of the crowd on the dockside. Margaret, who had come on board at seven, strained to see if she could spot him on deck. She saw an officer who looked like him, but she was not sure, for they were still some distance away.

cxiv A soft and brittle sandstone used to scour the deck of a ship.

30

As they moved out past the three-mile limit, the *Couronne* turned around and headed back to Cherbourg. The *Deerhound* stood off, but followed the *Alabama* out to watch the engagement at close quarters. The sky was clear and the sea quiet as they moved out towards the English Channel, with only a light westerly breeze. Captain Semmes had moved all his guns to the starboard battery, which gave the *Alabama* an awkward list, but his aim was to attack with his starboard battery and get in the first shots, then come in close to board the *Kearsarge* before she could bring her Dahlgren guns to bear. If they could board her, Semmes had no doubt that his men would quickly overcome the Yankees.

Captain Winslow was conducting morning service when his lookout spotted the *Alabama*.

'Here she comes!' he cried out from the crow's nest.

Winslow clamped his bible shut and ordered his men to their stations. The *Kearsarge* turned around and steamed out to sea, with the *Alabama* in pursuit.

'See, them yeller Yankees are running away without a fight!' cried one of the sailors on board the *Alabama*.

Lieutenant Kell quickly silenced him. 'They're doing nothing of the kind, Shields,' he snapped. 'They're simply taking the fight safely out of French territorial waters. They'll turn around as soon as they're ready, mark my words!'

At about seven miles out the *Kearsarge* turned around and steamed back towards the *Alabama*. When the two ships were about a mile apart, the *Alabama* suddenly sheered, and fired a broadside from her starboard battery. Most of her shells burst overhead and did little damage, except for minor tears in the *Kearsarge*'s rigging. Semmes then tried to bring his ship in closer so that he could board, but the *Kearsarge* was more streamlined and could move faster – the *Alabama* was still slowed by the copper sheeting peeling from her hull – and quickly evaded the *Alabama*. While Captain Winslow tried to put his ship between the *Alabama* and the shore to make sure she could not escape back into Cherbourg, Captain Semmes kept sheering the *Alabama* and pouring starboard broadsides into the *Kearsarge*, forcing the ships into a circular track, as each tried to gain the advantage and rake the exposed stern of the other.

Semmes knew that once he was locked into that dangerous circle the *Alabama* was in grave danger, for as the two ships swerved towards each other and exchanged broadsides the *Kearsarge*'s heavy Dahlgren cannon would soon take their toll. The *Alabama* managed to send a shell from her Blakely gun into the bulwark of the *Kearsarge*, below the main rigging, killing two sailors and a gunner; another pierced her steam funnel and exploded inside, but caused only minor damage. Semmes and Kell were shocked that their shot and shell failed to penetrate the hull of the *Kearsarge*, even when she was struck directly; unknown to them, the *Kearsarge* had been fitted with armour plating, with linked iron chains fixed across her port and starboard sides, and camouflaged beneath wooden planking. The *Alabama* only succeeded in blasting away the wooden shell, but her fire never penetrated the chair armour.

Then Semmes heard Kell cry out and the sailors cheering, and turned to see that a shell from their Blakely gun had struck the sternpost of the *Kearsarge*, just above the rudder! With the steering disabled, she would be a sitting duck, and Semmes could bring the *Alabama* in close and board her. But he and the crew let out a collective gasp of horror when they realized that the shell had not exploded, and the *Kearsarge*'s Dahlgrens ripped into the *Alabama*'s bulwarks, smashing the wood and showering deadly splinters across the deck, one of which struck Semmes on his right hand. Quartermaster Hobbs bound his wound quickly, while Semmes surveyed the carnage before him: the deck of the *Alabama* was awash with blood and body parts.

***

From the deck of the *Deerhound*, Margaret strained to see what was going on, and tried to get some sense of how the battle was going. At first, she thought the *Kearsarge* was badly damaged, because she was belching out thick black smoke and the *Alabama* was almost smokeless, until Mr Lancaster pointed out that it was just the difference in the coal they were using. But he confessed that the smoke from the *Kearsarge* made it deucedly difficult to see what was going on. He lent Margaret his binoculars, but all she could see were shadowy figures moving back and forth across the decks, as the two ships poured an incessant fire into each other.

***

The first broadside from the *Kearsarge* had brought down the *Alabama*'s ensign from the spanker-gaffe, but did little damage, and the flag was quickly remounted on the mizzenmast. But the *Kearsarge*'s Dahlgren cannon soon began to take their toll. Lieutenant 'Fighting Joe' Wilson, in charge of the *Alabama* aft pivot gun, died in the first wave of eleven-inch shells from the Dahlgrens. Two other gunners who took over from him soon suffered the same fate. Captain Semmes directed the steering and shelling from the forward deck, barking his instructions to Lieutenant Kell while he held the *Kearsarge* in his telescope, only pausing to change hands when his right hand was wounded. A shell exploded over the forward deck, shredding the bodies of the unfortunate sailors beneath it, and spewed their severed limbs and entrails across the deck, which ran red and slippery with their blood.

'See to the decks!' Kell called out to Mr Fullam, the Master's Mate, who led a party of hands who shovelled the grisly remains of their comrades over the side of the ship, and spread new buckets of sand across the deck. Seeing the destruction wrought by the Dahlgrens, Semmes called out a thousand-dollar reward to anyone who could put them out of action.

'I'll take you up on that,' cried Lieutenant Conrad, his once pristine grey uniform stained dark red from the blood of the men who had been blown to pieces around him. He made his way down the starboard side of the ship toward the aft pivot gun, which had just lost its fourth crew. He was about halfway down when a large chuck of shrapnel blew away the back of his head. He took a few stumbling steps forward, a puzzled look on his face as his brains poured out behind him, then tumbled overboard into the churning wake of the *Alabama*.

The *Kearsarge* now targeted her Dahlgrens on the *Alabama*'s water line. One shell crippled her rudder, making the ship near impossible to control; another pierced the engine room and the main coal-bunker, sending up a dense cloud of choking coal dust, and opening up a gaping hole on her water line, into which the seawater poured. Chief Engineer Miles Freeman came up on deck to report to Captain Semmes that the seawater had extinguished the fires in the engine room, and that the engines were rapidly losing pressure.

Semmes knew that his only chance of survival was to make a run for it back to Cherbourg, although it broke his heart to admit defeat. He ordered the fore and aft sails set, but Captain Winslow immediately recognized what he was trying to do. He quickly drove past the *Alabama* to cut off her line of escape, raking her with another deadly broadside as he did so, which opened up more gaping holes on her waterline. The *Alabama* was now beginning to sink, and already settling in the stern. Semmes sent Lieutenant Kell below decks to evaluate the damage; when he returned he advised Captain Semmes that the *Alabama* would go down in about ten minutes.

Semmes had no choice but to order the colours to be struck, but felt he had to justify himself to Lieutenant Kell.

'After all,' he said, 'this is the nineteenth century. It will not do to sacrifice every man on board.'

Unfortunately, two of the gun crews fired off their last shots just after the colours were struck, which brought on another furious broadside from the *Kearsarge*. Kell ordered that a white flag be raised, and when it was hoisted, the *Kearsarge* ceased firing. The battle was over, and the *Kearsarge* had finally defeated the legendary Confederate raider.

Lieutenant Kell ordered the able seamen to grab what they could cling to and jump overboard. Master's Mate Fullam directed the wounded to one of the *Alabama*'s surviving boats, and took them across to the *Kearsarge*, where he offered Captain Winslow the surrender of the *Alabama*. Fullam asked Winslow if he could return to bring back more wounded, and Winslow said that of course he must.

When Fulham returned to the *Alabama* with the empty boat, Lieutenant Kell and Surgeon Llewellyn helped load the remaining wounded aboard. When they were nearly done, Semmes told Llewellyn to get into the boat, but he said he preferred to stay with Captain Semmes and Lieutenant Kell.

'And I have to find Davie,' he explained to them.

One of the surviving crewmembers helped Semmes off with his coat, while another, covered in grime and coal dust, helped him pull off his boots. As he stripped to his underwear, he was pleased to see that Llewellyn had managed to rescue Davie from below decks. The boy was trembling violently, but he was alive. Semmes drew back his left arm, and flung his sword far out into the sea. Then he dived overboard, followed by Lieutenant Kell. Soon after they were joined by Llewellyn and Davie, who jumped into the water together holding hands.

Captain Semmes turned in the water to take a last look at the *Alabama*. Her stern had already gone under, and her bow was rising dramatically into the air. For a moment she lingered nearly erect in the water, her slim black hull straight backed as if in a final salute, before plunging down into the depths.

* * *

The Deerhound came up from behind the *Kearsarge*, heading for the surviving Confederates in the water. As she passed by, John Lancaster called out to ask if anyone on board needed help.

'No,' Captain Winslow cried back, 'but for God's sake do what you can to save them!'

The *Deerhound* lowered her two boats, and began to collect the Confederates in the water. When Lieutenant Kell was pulled on board one of the boats, he was relieved to see that Semmes had also been rescued; he was lying flat in the boat, white faced and exhausted but alive. When Kell saw a launch pulling out towards them from the *Kearsarge*, he told Semmes to keep quiet and lie low, and covered him with some sailcloth. Then he donned a *Deerhound* cap that he borrowed from a sailor and took up one of the oars. When the *Kearsarge* launch pulled alongside, the officer on board demanded to know if Captain Semmes had been rescued. In a calm voice, Kell replied that he very much regretted that the poor man had drowned. The launch pulled away to report this news back to

Captain Winslow, while the surviving Confederates, some forty-one men in all, were taken aboard the *Deerhound*.

Margaret desperately searched the faces of the battle worn and weary survivors as they came on board, and her heart sank as the realization dawned that he was not among them. She recognized Captain Semmes, who was wrapped in a blanket and talking to Captain Jones, the chief officer of the *Deerhound*.

'Captain Semmes!' she cried out as she made her way towards him. 'Do you have news of Lieutenant Conrad? Did he survive the battle?'

Semmes looked at her gravely, and she could tell by his expression that James was dead.

'Lieutenant Conrad was a gallant officer who behaved with great courage and steadfastness, but I am sorry to inform you that he was killed by enemy fire while performing his duty for his country. I am very sorry, Mrs Brown – I truly wish he could have shown you Charleston.'

She did not cry, and she thanked Semmes for his thought. She did not cry later that day, or any of the days or nights that followed. She missed him terribly, but she knew she would survive. She had lost him, but she had not lost what he had given her – her strength and her freedom.

***

Captain Semmes and Lieutenant Kell pressed Captain Jones and Mr Lancaster to make full speed for England. To this they immediately consented, and the *Deerhound* swept north and steamed past the *Kearsarge* on her way to Southampton, to the great umbrage of Captain Winslow and his officers, who had expected the remaining Confederates to be handed over to them as prisoners of war. Some of Winslow's officers urged him to pursue and fire upon the

Deerhound, but he would not, for she was a neutral ship with women and children on board. Winslow had no intention of causing an international incident and bringing the British into the war on the side of the Confederacy at this late state of the conflict. Gideon Welles, the Secretary of the Navy, would have his stripes if he did such a thing.

On board the *Deerhound*, Semmes was glad to see that Surgeon Galt had survived, and asked him if there was any news of Assistant Surgeon Llewellyn.

'I did not see him killed, so I suppose he must have been put aboard with Mr Fullam and the wounded,' Galt replied.

'He was not,' Semmes replied, 'we saw him and he decided to stay on board. He had to look for young Davie, who I'm glad to say he found.'

Semmes saw the look of horror on Galt's face.

'What's wrong man?' he cried. 'You look like you've seen a ghost!'

'Llewellyn could not swim – he told me so himself,' Galt replied. 'And neither could Davie.'

* * *

The ghost ship now lay at the bottom of the English Channel. But the *Alabama* had achieved much during her twenty-two months and seventy-five thousand miles of cruising. She had burned, sank or bonded sixty-five Union vessels, causing over five million dollars of direct losses, and many millions more by stranding Union ships in foreign ports around the world, on the mere rumour that the *Alabama* was cruising in the area. The 'wolf of the deep', as she had come to be known, had now gone to the deep, but news of her victories had brought hope to a beleaguered South, when she had commanded the seas from Savannah to Singapore.[12]

31

The year had been very bad for business in Singapore. Two of the oldest and most respected European firms had suspended payments, with liabilities of over a million dollars. Their default had a dramatic ripple effect, undermining the market in manufactured goods, and causing many Chinese businesses to collapse in their turn. The Chinese businesses were heavily indebted to the European firms, who, in fierce competition between themselves, had been pressured to offer more and more extended lines of credit to their Chinese counterparts, and hold their promissory notes long after they became due. While this arrangement normally served to oil the wheels of trade and commerce, in the wake of the failure of such old and established firms, the whole system threatened to come apart. In June the Chamber of Commerce declared that the terms of credit for buyers of imports should be reduced from three months to two, and contemplated the imposition of a policy of cash sales – although in the end this was considered to be impracticable. Yet it was very much a case of shutting the door after the horse had bolted. Many European firms were now in desperate financial straits because their Chinese debtors had defaulted on their loans, having failed to find a market for their merchandise.

***

The Tanjong Pagar Dock Company was also in trouble. A monsoon storm that had roared into New Harbour had almost completely washed away the embankment, adjoining road and seawall that had been laboriously built out from the shore at Tanjong Pagar, as the foundation for the new wharfs for the company. The whole construction project would now have to begin again almost from scratch, with all the money that had been ploughed into the original work wasted. It was also becoming increasingly clear that they had all grossly underestimated the cost of the project. They would have to raise considerably more capital, or the Tanjong Pagar Dock Company would soon join the ranks of the bankrupted European firms.

***

It had taken almost a year, but now Ah Keng and her son, Ham Choon, her father Wang Zuoxin and Auntie Ki were able to move into the new house that Ah Keng had arranged to have built especially for them at Tanglin, although not on the grounds of Ho Bee Swee's old house, which the Buddhist monk who had conducted the funeral services had declared to be unlucky. She had another house built on the original grounds, which she rented out along with her other properties, under the careful management of Mr Sng. After the appropriate rites and ceremonies had been conducted, they moved in with their servants and Ah Keng's stepchildren. Like a dutiful wife, Ah Keng made offerings at her late husband's altar, in gratitude for the freedom he had given her, and for the son she had borne to him.

And after a respectable period of waiting, Wang Zuoxin and Auntie Ki were married in a ceremony for which Ah Keng spared no expense, despite the tut-tuttings of Mr Sng. She was delighted that she who had once thought she had lost all her family, now had a new family of her own.

32

They arrived in Southampton on Sunday evening. Margaret spent
the night in Kelway's Hotel, and took the morning train to London,
where she took a room in the Kings Arms in Woolwich, close to the
Royal Military Academy. She sent her son, Thomas, a note saying
that she would be seated at one of the outside tables of Mr Collin's
tearooms at three o'clock on Wednesday afternoon, the weather
being fine. She would be delighted if he could join her for afternoon
tea, if it was convenient for him; if not, could he please suggest
another time and place. She had wondered about saying 'grateful'
or 'honoured' instead of 'delighted', but stayed with the honest
truth. She said nothing about what had passed in Singapore or on
her voyage with the *Alabama,* and did not try to explain herself –
although she knew that Richard would have written to him and
done his best to poison her reputation. She would explain herself if
he came, if he still wanted to see her.

Thomas did desperately want to see her, but he did not come
to tea at Mr Collin's establishment and he did not reply to her note.
He stood in the window of the bookstore on the corner, watching
her, pretending to be looking through a pile of remaindered books.
His father had written to him, saying she had been a faithless wife,
who had taken a score of lovers, many of the lowest kind, and that
she had run away to sea with a Confederate officer – the vilest
scoundrel it had been his ill-fortune to come across. His father had
warned him that the pair might end up in London, and that she
might try to meet with him. He had absolutely forbidden it, and

said that if Thomas were seen with her he would withdraw him from the academy and cut off his allowance – he would be out on the streets to fend for himself. He knew his father meant it. He had told Thomas that he had hired a man to watch over him – spy on him, if truth be told – and report his comings and goings. So, he dared not risk meeting her, but had to see her.

Although she was some distance away, and the window glass was misted, he could see that she was still as beautiful as he remembered. He stood watching her in silence for the full hour she waited for him, snapping at the shop assistant when the man asked if he could be of service. His heart almost broke when she finally got up to leave, for he could see her sadness even in the distance. He waited until she was out of sight, then left the bookshop and returned to his barracks. After mess that evening, he took from his locker a small box made of camphor wood, which his mother had given him as a parting gift. He lay down on his bed and closed his eyes as he inhaled its fragrance. All the smells and sounds and sights of Singapore came back to him, a vivid dream of traveller's palms and frangipani and sunshine shimmering on sparkling white stone.

***

Margaret paid her bill and asked the porter to order her a hansom cab. As she picked up her bag, the manager stepped out from behind his desk.

'Beg pardon, madam, but we just had a delivery for you.' He handed her a small package – there was no note and no return address.

When the hansom arrived, she climbed in and gave the driver directions to a boarding house that Captain Jones had recommended. He said his wife always used it when she was in London. It was reasonably priced, but very clean, and the woman in charge was a fine cook as well as a good source of information about the city. She did not know what she was going to do, but the money she had banked would last her for a long time, if she did not spend it foolishly. She thought she might visit America after the war was over – to start a new life there as they had intended to do.

She absentmindedly pulled the wrapping from the small package, and gasped when she saw what was inside. The camphor box – the one she had given him so many years before. She put it to her lips and kissed it, breathing in the memories it held.

He had been there. He had not been able to meet with her, and she thought she understood why. Richard had somehow prevented him. But it was enough to know he had been there, at least for the moment. One day, she hoped, he would come to her, when he was as free of his father as she was now free of her husband.

***

In April, the Singapore Gas Company, a branch of the London Gas Company, had laid out gas pipes through the main streets of the town, and on May 24, the Queen's birthday, the gas lamps were lit for the first time. They provided a great source of puzzlement and amusement to many of the natives and not a few Europeans, who were surprised by the fact that the pipes on which the gas fires were supported were not themselves hot to the touch. Whampoa was also greatly impressed by the new marvel, and immediately arranged to have gas lighting installed at his home on Serangoon Road, happily agreeing to pay the cost of having the gas line laid from the town to his house.

For many years, the Courthouse located in John Argyle Maxwell's house had been plagued by the noise from Stephen Hallpike's boatyard and blacksmith's shop, which was located adjacent to it on the east side of the river. To avoid the constant interruption of their work, the municipal commissioners decided to build a new Courthouse at the eastern mouth of the river.[cxv] The foundation stone for the new Courthouse, which was designed by Major McNair, was laid on July 4.

---

cxv Where it became the centre wing of the Empress Place Building (which now houses the Asian Civilizations Museum).

33

On July 19, Zeng Guofan gave orders for his troops to fire a series of deep tunnels that had been dug under a section of the eastern wall of Nanking and filled with explosives. The huge blast that followed cut a hundred-and-eighty-foot-wide breach in the wall, hurling great stones into the air, which came crashing down on defenders and attackers alike. The waiting Qing soldiers threw themselves into the open breach as massive reinforcements drew up behind them. For nearly an hour the desperate Taiping defenders managed to keep them in check, but then the Qing broke through and began their slaughter, killing, dismembering, raping, looting and burning.

The Young Monarch and his two younger brothers fled from the Heavenly Palace to the Palace of the Loyal King. General Li had two of his men bring them horses, then made everyone take off their clothes and dress themselves in Qing uniforms that he had stripped from his dead enemies and saved for this purpose. They made their way through the chaos in the city to an abandoned temple on high ground near the western wall, which gave them a clear view of the destruction taking place before them. As night began to fall, Lai Han-ying, the captain of General Li's personal guard, spotted a breach in the wall near the Eastern Gate, and they rode pell-mell for it. They all made it through except for Tiangui Fu's two younger brothers and two guardsmen, who were trapped and cut down by Qing cavalry who recognized them by their long hair, which had fallen out of their helmets in their mad dash across the city.

As the Qing massacred the twenty thousand souls remaining in the city, General Li and his guardsmen rode south with the Young Monarch. They had not gone far when General Li's mount stumbled and fell, trapping the Loyal King's legs beneath him. The others stopped to help, but General Li ordered them to ride on.

'Take the Young Monarch to safety, Lai Han-ying, my trusted captain! He is the only hope for our people!'

Lai Han-ying grasped Tiangui Fu's bridle, and they rode off into the night.

* * *

The victorious Qing soldiers discovered the decaying body of Hong Xiuquan in the palace gardens. Zeng Guofan gave orders that his head be struck off, and paraded on the end of a lance by a company of Bannermen throughout the provinces, to demonstrate to every subject of the young Emperor Tung Chih that the Taiping King was truly dead. Hong Xiuquan's body was thrown upon a bonfire built in the palace courtyard, along with the bodies of his many wives and concubines, some dead and some living.

* * *

General Li managed to extricate himself from under his horse, and fighting back the pain in his legs, made his way to a ruined temple, where he passed out from exhaustion. When he woke the next morning, he discovered that he had been robbed in the night – all his weapons, valuables, and most of his clothes had been taken. Another band of robbers confronted him as he scrambled to his feet to escape from the temple, and demanded a ransom from him. When he could not pay them, they handed him over to a passing Qing patrol.

General Li was taken before Zeng Guofan, who interrogated

the Loyal King. Li Xiucheng pleaded with Zeng Guofan to show mercy to the surviving Taiping veterans in the city, and send them back to their villages where they could practice their trades. Such an action would surely reflect well upon him, Li Xiucheng declared, and would help persuade the remaining Taiping forces to surrender.

Zeng Guofan told General Li that he could not spare them, for he was commanded by the Dowager Empress to destroy every last Taiping rebel. He did not tell him that he was also under explicit orders from the Dowager Empress to bring the Loyal King back to Peking in an iron cage, so he could be put on public display before his execution. Yet Zeng Guofan could not bring himself to so humiliate the man who had proven to be such a noble adversary. He asked General Li to compose his own account of the Taiping rebellion.[13] When the Loyal King had completed his account, he was beheaded.

34

For the next few weeks Adi wondered at the journey he had taken with Habib Noh, and wondered what the majdhub had meant when he had said that his future lay in the verse from the Koran that he had written.

Then one day Habib Noh suddenly appeared before him as before, only this time he held a book in his hands, which he handed to Adi. The frontispiece, which was beautifully illustrated, displayed the title, *Cermin Mata Bagi Segala Orang Yang Menuntut Pengetahuan.*[cxvi] He turned the pages, each of which was as beautifully illustrated as the frontispiece. It looked like it had been handwritten, but he could see that it was not – he had never seen anything like it before.

'It is called lithography,' Habib Noh told him. 'The Jawi[cxvii] text is printed from metal to resemble a handwritten text, so it can be recreated many times over without laborious copying by hand.'

'Not that there is anything wrong with copying by hand,' the majdhub continued, 'but if you are going to advance the poetry and literature of the Malay you must learn this technique. And that is your destiny.'

'But how will I achieve this, holiness?' Adi replied.

'You will go to the Reverend Keasberry's[14] school in River Valley Road. You will live as a boarder and work as an apprentice at his press, where you will learn lithography and book binding, so

---

cxvi *An Eye Glass for All Who Seek Knowledge*
cxvii Alphabet for writing Malay language based upon Arabic script.

you can publish the literature of your people. I have arranged this through Temenggong Abu Bakar, who was a student at the school and who has recommended you to Reverend Keasberry. However, you should bring along some samples of your work in case the Reverend has any doubts.'

'He is of course an unbeliever and will try to convert you to Christianity. You must resist, but you must also learn the methods by which he is able to proselytize so effectively, and use them to in the service of your faith.'

'I will do as you command, your holiness, but ...'

'But what about your father?' Habib Noh interrupted him. 'I know, I know, how will he manage his rice fields and fishing without you? Do not worry, I have arranged for the Temenggong to send one of his men to work with your father, who has agreed to our arrangement. He is grateful that you will be able to use the talents that God has given you.'

'How can I thank you, holiness?' Adi began, but knew how the majdhub would respond.

'Do not thank me. Serve God,' he said.

'Goodbye, Adi bin Sadat. We will not meet again.'

And then he was gone.

And so, Adi bin Sadat went to work for the Reverend Keasberry, who was happy to take him on when he saw the work that Adi had brought.

35

Lai Han-ying and his guardsmen managed to bring the Young Monarch to the safety of Huzhou, south of Lake Tai, where Hong Rengan, the Shield King, still held the city with a sizeable Taiping force. They were joined shortly after by Augustus Lindley and the six surviving men from his Loyal and Faithful Auxiliary Legion.

They had scarcely arrived when the city was surrounded by Qing troops commanded by Li Hongzhang and soldiers of the Ever Triumphant Army, a mixed force of Chinese and Filipino mercenaries, commanded by French officers, which had been modelled on the disbanded Ever Victorious Army. When in August it became plain that Huzhou would soon suffer the fate of Nanking, the Shield King led a small force that broke out of the southern gate of the city. Hong Rengan and Lai Han-ying continued south with the Young Monarch, while Augustus Lindley turned northeast and made for Shanghai, which he reached without challenge. He took a room at the new Clarendon Hotel where, after a long bath and a short meal, he continued work on his memoir of the Taiping rebellion, which he had begun some months before. [15]

Hong Rengan had no clear plan, but found himself leading the Young Monarch back in the direction of Thistle Mountain, where the great rebellion had begun. They never reached it. One night in November, four hundred miles southwest in Guangchang, a Qing patrol raided their camp. Hong Rengan was captured and interrogated, but Lai Han-ying and the remaining force managed to ride off with the Young Monarch. A few days later they ran into a

Qing ambush on a bridge. Lai Han-ying put up a brave fight, and in the confusion Tiangui Fu managed to escape – he fled through the hills, hiding by day and stumbling through forests and across rivers by night. The Qing soldiers cut off the long hair of the Taiping soldiers they had ambushed on the bridge, as souvenirs of the great rebellion, and left their bodies for the carrion dogs and birds, believing they were all dead. But Lai Han-ying was not dead. When night fell he managed to crawl to safety, and after weeks of travelling and avoiding Qing patrols, he managed to reach his home village of Cuiheng[16] in Guangdong province, where he lived in quiet obscurity.

A Qing patrol captured Tiangui Fu on October 25. He confessed to his Manchu interrogators that he was the son of Hong Xiuquan, the Heavenly King, but claimed that he had taken no part in the rebellion. Tiangui Fu was beheaded on November 18, a week before his fifteenth birthday. Five days later, Hong Rengan, the Shield King, the cousin of Hong Xiuquan and friend of Dr James Legge, was beheaded in the Jiangxi capital of Nanchang. All the kings were now dead, and the Taiping rebellion was over.

36

In January, Mr Casteleyns took over the Hotel de l'Esperance on the corner of High Street and the Esplanade, and transferred his Hotel de l'Europe from Beach Road to the new site. Also in January, the old brick bridge linking Hill Street and New Bridge Road, which had been built by George Coleman and named Coleman Bridge, was replaced by a new wooden bridge, of inferior quality, which was also named Coleman Bridge.

***

Sarah Simpson looked at her husband Ronnie. He was beaming like the Cheshire Cat from *Alice's Adventures in Wonderland*, peering through his spectacles at the invitation card.

'I always knew that my friendship with the Temenggong wid pay off,' he said with a grin. 'Noo his son Abu Bakar is inviting us on a cruise around the island in his new steamer the *Johor*, including a picnic in the grounds of his new Istana in Johor Bahru. Next Monday, Easter Monday in fact. Says the Governor and his wife will be there, wi' a' the leading residents of Singapore, which I suppose must include us!'

'Sounds like fun,' Sarah replied, 'Abu Baker is famous for putting on a good spread. And it will be good to get some fresh sea air.'

***

The *Johor* was a seventy-five-ton iron-screw schooner-rigged paddle wheel steamer, which had been built in West Hartlepool in England. Since her arrival in in Singapore, she had been overhauled at the Patent Slip and Dock Company, at the westerly reaches of New Harbour, close to Telok Blangah. On the morning of Saturday, April 15, she was anchored about one hundred feet offshore, between Pulau Hantu[cxviii] and the far end of Pulau Blakang Mati. The Temenggong's younger brother Inche Wan Abdul Rahman was on board, supervising the loading of the silverware and making arrangements for the picnic on the Monday morning. He had asked Abdul Talip, the captain of the *Johor*, to start up the engines at noon and steam out of the harbour and into the Singapore roads at two o'clock, where they would lie at anchor off the Dalhousie Pier, ready to take on the Temenggong and his picnic guests on the Monday morning.

Inche Wan Abdul Rahman had invited Hussein Bin Abdullah and Inchi Ibrahim, the two eldest sons of the late Munshi Abdullah, to join him on board that morning. The three men were old friends, having attended the Reverend Keasberry's Malay school in Telok Blangah together with Temenggong Abu Bakar, and were looking forward to a run out to sea in the new steamer. Hussein Bin Abdullah arrived on board the *Johor* shortly before noon, and was greeted warmly by Inche Wan Abdul Rahman. Hussein told him his brother was delayed because he had to close up the Telok Blangah school before he left, but would surely make it on board before they set off at two.

Also on board the steamer that morning were Captain Wishart and Mr Hugh Bain, the superintendent and engineer of the Patent Slip and Dock Company, who were supervising the construction of

cxviii Ghost Island.

deck seating for the guests by a gang of Malay carpenters. At noon, just after Captain Wishart and Mr Bain had returned to shore, Inche Wan Abdul Rahman instructed Captain Talip to start the engines. Captain Talip pulled the starting lever, but nothing happened. The engines would not start. Captain Talip waited a moment then tried once again, but once again nothing happened. After a third failed attempt, he consulted the *Johor*'s European engineer, John Miller, who suggested that they call back Mr Hugh Bain, the engineer from the Patent Slip and Dock Company. Inche Wan Abdul Rahman hailed Captain Cleghorn, the master of the Dock Company's tug steamer the *Henrietta*, who was passing close by. Captain Cleghorn came on board, and sent the tug back to fetch Mr Bain.

Captain Cleghorn went down with Mr Miller and Captain Talip to check on the engines, while Inche Wan Abdul Rahman went to explain the delay to Hussein, and to his own younger brother Haroo. A few minutes later Mr Bain arrived back on board with Henry Sandhurst, a boilermaker from the Dock Company, and they went to join Captains Cleghorn and Talip, and John Miller, in the engine room.

* * *

Inchi Ibrahim was running late and trying his best to make up for it. After he had closed up the school, he ran to his house to change his clothes. Then he walked briskly towards the wharfs where he planned to take a sampan out to the *Johor*. He knew he would have no trouble getting one – there were always plenty plying their trade between the Borneo Company, Jardine Matheson and P & O wharfs. On his way he spotted some Malay boys playing marbles in a five-foot way, and noticed that one of the boys, whom he recognized as one of his students, Abdul Rahman bin Andak, was crying. Inchi Ibrahim bent down and asked Abdul what was the matter. The boy told him that his young sister, whom he loved dearly, was very sick, and he was afraid that she might die. Inchi Ibrahim spoke gently to the boy, and did his best to comfort him. He told Abdul that he hoped she lived so that she could grow up in the world with him, but that if she died she would be taken straight to Heaven, like all young children who are specially chosen by God.

* * *

Inchi Ibrahim bade farewell to Abdul Rahman bin Andak, and stepped out from the five-foot way onto the street. As he turned to walk towards the wharfs, he was stopped in his tracks by the sound of a massive explosion coming from New Harbour, and the sight of a black funnel and rigging blasted high into the sky. His heart tore in his breast, and he knew right away. His brother was dead. He began to run towards the wharfs, as fast as his feet could carry him.

* * *

Inche Wan Abdul Rahman had heard a curious hissing sound, then turned to locate the source. As he did so, an enormous explosion had roared out from the engine room, blasting the mainmast to pieces and hurling the funnel into the air – which then came crashing down destroying the port paddles. The bridge and after-cabin were smashed to pieces, the silver cutlery and tableware swept overboard like ocean spray. Inche Wan Abdul Rahman was struck on the head by a piece of splintered wood from the mainmast, which knocked him unconscious for a few moments. When he came to, he was momentarily blinded – he stumbled across the deck and fell into the water, but managed to swim away from the burning ship. Others were not so lucky. Captain Cleghorn, Captain Talip, Hugh Bain, John Miller and Henry Sandhurst were killed instantly, because they were standing close by the boiler when it exploded, as was John Young, the European gunner on the *Johor*. Hussein bin Abdullah, the late Munshi Abdullah's eldest son, was struck down dead by a shard of iron that blew out from the exploded boiler, and lay in a pool of blood with the bodies of the Malay sailors who were killed on deck, twenty-five souls in all.

***

Captain Wishart was the first to reach the stricken ship in the *Henrietta*, where he took on board Inche Wan Abdul Rahman and a wounded Malay sailor. He was closely followed by a small armada of sampans and lighters, who picked up the remaining survivors in the water. Eventually all the bodies were found and accounted for, except for Captain Cleghorn, whose body was not found until the following morning, and the bodies of Inchi Mohamed Yahya bin Abdullah, the Temenggong's treasurer, and Mat, Captain Talip's servant, which were never recovered.

The European dead were buried in the new European Cemetery on Bukit Timah Road on Easter Sunday and Easter Monday, and occupied the first graves in the cemetery, except for a Dutch seaman who had been buried there on the Saturday afternoon, when the *Johor* had exploded.

***

'Do they know why it exploded?' Sarah asked Ronnie when he broke the news about the tragedy of the *Johor*.

'Weel, the cause was simple enough. The boiler was heated red-hot while it was empty, and when the cold water hit it naturally exploded. At first, they blamed the Malay bosun and his inexperienced crew, but Dunman thinks the fault lay with Miller, the *Johor*'s engineer, who was responsible for the boiler. Turns out the man was far tae fond of the bottle, and he gave them no end of trouble on the way out from England. A real tragedy though – old Munshi Abdullah's eldest son died in the blast, and his younger brother only escaped because he was delayed on his way to the ship.'

***

Temenggong Abu Bakar was horrified by what had happened to the *Johor*, and wanted nothing more to do with the cursed vessel. He donated her to the Patent Slip and Dock Company, who patched her up and used her as a tug in the harbour.

37

1866

In March, the Tanjong Pagar Dock Company held an extraordinary general meeting, chaired by Mr C. H. Harrison, one of the directors. Mr John Greenshields, of Guthrie and Co, advised the directors that the original cost of the construction had been greatly underestimated, and that if the project were to continue, the capital would have to be raised from three hundred thousand dollars to six hundred thousand dollars. Mr Samuel Gilfillan and Dr Robert Little proposed a motion that the capital sum be raised to six hundred thousand dollars. The motion was carried unanimously, including the vote of Ronnie Simpson, who turned to his son with a wry grin, and said:

'In fur a penny, in fur a pound!'

Ronnie was one of the directors of the company, although they had yet to be paid, and the company had yet to pay its first dividend.

***

The majdhub Habib Noh died on Friday, July 17,[cxix] aged 78, at the home of Temenggong Abu Bakar in Telok Blangah. Adi bin Sadat joined the thousands of mourners from Singapore and the surrounding islands who came to pay their last respects to the beloved holy man. After the funeral ceremonies at the Temenggong mosque, the mourners prepared to follow the coffin to the Bidadari

---

cxix 14 Rabiul Awa 1283 in the Muslim calendar.

Muslim cemetery. But when the bearers tried to lift the coffin onto the funeral carriage, they found they could not move it – it was stuck fast to the ground. The bearers called out for strong men to help them lift the coffin, but when they tried to lift the coffin together, they could not lift it an inch from the ground. The mourners were dismayed and stood in hushed silence and fear, wondering what this could portend. Then Inche Wan Abdul Rahman, a brother of Temenggong Abu Bakar, came forward and told them he remembered that Habib Noh had told him he wished to be buried in the small cemetery at the top of Mount Palmer, where he used to spend many hours meditating and praying. When the bearers heard this, they managed to lift the coffin onto the carriage without any difficulty, and Habib Noh was brought to his burial place on Mount Palmer. A shrine – the Keramat Habib Noh–was later built over his tomb.[cxx]

***

On August 8, the British parliament passed 'An Act to Provide for the Government of the Straits Settlements', which declared that the 'Islands and Territories known as the Straits Settlements, namely Prince of Wales' Island, the Island of Singapore, and the town and port of Malacca and their Dependencies should cease to form a part of India, and should be placed under the Government of the Queen as part of the Colonial Possessions of the Crown.' On December 28, by order of council, April 1 1867 was designated as the date upon which the act would take effect, when the government of the Straits Settlements would be transferred from the Indian government to the Crown.

---

cxx The tomb was refurbished in 1890 by Syed Mohamad bin Ahmad Alsagoff.

In September the previous year, Mr W. J. Du Port had come out from Europe to supervise the construction of the work on the retaining wall and embankment for the Tanjong Pagar Dock Company. By August, the seawall had been extended to over two thousand feet, and the wharfs completed for a distance of seven hundred and fifty feet, enough to accommodate four ships. In addition, four coal sheds, capable of holding ten thousand tons of coal, had been erected, the first storehouse completed and opened for business, and a substantial iron godown was under construction.

38

On March 15, Governor Cavenagh stumped down Johnston's Pier to board HMS *Pluto* for Penang. He acknowledged the guard of honour provided by the Singapore Volunteer Corps, and replied graciously to the address that had been presented to him by W.H. Read on behalf of the Singapore Chamber of Commerce, as he had responded graciously to the toasts in his honour offered at the public dinner that had been held for him three days previously. Yet Governor Cavenagh was not a happy man. He had seen the Straits Settlements through their difficult financial years, and had resolved the perennial problem of financial deficits by ensuring the extension of the Indian Stamp Act, which in his mind had rendered the colonial transfer quite unnecessary. Despite his financial constraints, Cavenagh had presided over the extension of the law courts, the police force and the prison system, and had managed to maintain peaceful if not cordial relations with the merchants of different races, the government officials and the press. He had also presided over an extensive program of public works. Although the Indian government had agreed to suspend the transportation of new convicts after the Indian Mutiny, Singapore still maintained a sizeable convict population, which Major McNair had deployed in the construction of new roads and public buildings, including the new Town Hall and Courthouse. Yet for all his good work he had been dismissed with scarcely a by your leave. The Colonial office had still not officially informed him that Major-General Harry St

George Ord, the former governor of Bermuda, was replacing him. It galled him no end that he had first heard about Ord's appointment through a chance remark that W.H. Read had made at a meeting with the municipal commissioners in January.

The following day, Harry St George Ord, who was to be the new governor of the Straits Settlements when she became a Crown colony on April 1, arrived in Singapore aboard the P & O mail steamer.

**

On the morning of April 1, W. H. Read led other prominent merchants and dignitaries to the inauguration of the new government, which took place at noon in the Town Hall. A large crowd was gathered outside, and the proceedings were communicated to them through government interpreters. Shortly after noon, Major-General Harry St George Ord entered the building, and strode upstairs to the dais prepared for him on the second floor, to the accompaniment of a seventeen-gun salute from Fort Canning, and the presentation of an honour guard by the 8th Madras Infantry and the Singapore Volunteer Corps. Major-General Harry St George Ord was a short, dumpy man with grey hair and drooping grey moustaches. He was dressed in the uniform of the Royal Engineers, with a bright red stripe down each leg, but he had none of the martial demeanour of Colonel Cavanaugh, even with his wooden leg. He paid no attention to the merchants and dignitaries or the honour guard, but took his seat upon the dais without removing his hat, and waited stone-faced for the proceedings to begin.

The Orders in Council establishing the Straits Settlements as a Crown colony were then read out, to loud cheers from the assembled audience. Then Sir Benson Maxwell, the Recorder, administered the oath of office to the governor, and to the newly appointed founding members of the new legislative council, W. H. Read, Mr F. S Brown of Penang, Thomas Scott of Guthrie and Co, and Dr Robert Little. A few days later Whampoa was sworn in as the first Chinese member of the council.

***

The first meeting between the new governor of the Crown colony and the legislative council of the Straits Settlements did not go smoothly. Unlike the genial and practical Colonel Cavenagh, Governor Harry St George Ord, who insisted upon being addressed as 'Your Excellency', was cold and aloof, and considered himself the representative of her majesty the Queen, with a mandate to act as a 'new broom' in the Straits Settlements.

W. H. Read and other members of the legislative council pressed the new governor with advice on how to bring about the administrative reforms that had for so many years been denied by the Indian government. Yet they quickly discovered that the new governor felt no need for their advice, and made his own decisions with or without their support – and more often than not without it. They were particularly incensed that his first priority as governor was to order the construction of a new government steamer for his exclusive use, and the construction of a new government house on land fronting Orchard Road that had once comprised part of the nutmeg estates of W. H. Read and Mr C. R. Princeps.

39

1868

On May 11, John Crawfurd, the second resident of Singapore, who had negotiated the Treaty of Friendship and Alliance with Temenggong Abdul Rahman and Sultan Hussein in 1824, died at his home in South Kensington, London, at the age of eighty-five. Earlier in the year he had been elected as the first president of the Straits Settlements Association, which had been formed to promote the interests the new Crown colony in the home country.

***

The previous year Temenggong Abu Bakar had visited Europe and England, where he had been received by Queen Victoria and befriended the Prince of Wales, later King Edward VII. One thing he learned on his trip was that his title of Temenggong was unfamiliar to European royalty, which determined him to change his title to one more befitting of his regal station. In June, with the approval of Governor Ord, he assumed the title of Sri Maharaja of Johor.

***

The Tanjong Pagar Company continued to expand. By the end of the year the wharfs had been extended to fourteen hundred and fifty feet, an additional coal shed had increased the storage capacity to seventeen thousand tons, and new goods sheds and machine shops had been added. Over a hundred steamers and over fifty sailing ships had berthed during the year, and repairs made to about a quarter of them. The company was beginning to earn income, but still not enough to pay the directors or a dividend to the stockholders.

40

1869

In January, Alfred Russel Wallace published *The Malay Archipelago*, a lengthy account of his travels in the region, which included detailed descriptions of the flora and fauna of the various island groups, and their peoples, languages and social organization. In the book Wallace maintained that the varied animals and plants of the Malay Archipelago were geographically distributed between two distinct regions, separated by a deep-water channel running between Bali and Lombok, which later came to be known as the 'Wallace line.' In chapter two of *The Malay Archipelago*, Wallace described the time he had spent at St Joseph's Church in Bukit Timah with Father Anatole Maudit, whom he described as 'truly a father to his flock'.

* * *

On Friday, February 6, a jubilee ball was held in the Town Hall to celebrate the fiftieth anniversary of the founding of Singapore. The second-floor hall was decked out with red drapery and tassels, and lined with the flags of the principal nations, arranged alphabetically. At the upper end of the hall, on a seven-foot pedestal, stood a bust of Sir Stamford Raffles, backed by the flag of the Singapore Volunteer Corps. The tribute to the founder was surrounded by the stacked Enfield rifles of the Singapore Volunteer Corps, and was flanked by two twelve-pound howitzers, hung with red and white ensigns, and by colourful Malay and Chinese trophies and flags.

Governor Harry St George Ord was in attendance, as were His Highness Abu Bakar, Sri Maharajah of Johor, Chief Justice Sir Peter Benson and Lady Maxwell, most of the members of the legislative council, the officers of the Artillery Regiment and Her Majesty's 73rd Regiment, foreign consuls and ambassadors, and many local merchants and dignitaries. While the band of the 73rd played, the dancing began at nine and continued until midnight, at which time the company adjourned to the theatre on the first floor for supper, which was provided by Messrs Früchtnicht and Leerholf.

W. H. Read, the chairman of the jubilee ball committee, rose and proposed a toast to Her Most Gracious Majesty the Queen, to which the company enthusiastically responded, and the band played 'God Save the Queen'. Then Read gave a short celebratory speech:

When Sir Stamford Raffles had directed the first tottering steps of his bantling[cxxi] on the road he intended it to follow, he returned to England, leaving as his successor Mr Crawfurd, a true friend, whose loss we had lately to lament, and of whom it may be truly said Singapore was engraved on his heart, as, for nearly half a century, he never ceased to promote the best interests of the Settlement. To him succeeded, as governors, Indian civilians whom experience and long residence had entitled to advancement, and military men, whose distinguished conduct in the service of their country, justified their selection. One and all have readily adopted the policy traced out by our illustrious founder, and, in consequence, have achieved the success which must be the highest reward that ambition can covet.

I beg to propose a toast to the Governor, Sir Harry St George Ord,[cxxii] and his dear wife Lady Ord.

---

cxxi Very young child.
cxxii Harry St George Ord was knighted upon his appointment as governor of the Straits Settlements.

Governor Ord thanked Mr Read and the company for the honour paid to himself and to Lady Ord, for whose absence he apologized, and recounted a brief history of the founding of the settlement, with all due credit to Sir Stamford Raffles. And with none to Colonel Farquhar, thought Ronnie Simpson to himself, with not a little bitterness.

Governor Ord concluded by looking forward to the continued commercial success of Singapore, and asked the company to join him in a toast to 'the prosperity of the settlement'. After the toast was drunk, the dancing was resumed upstairs, and went on until the early hours of the morning.

***

Was it really fifty years ago? Ronnie thought to himself. When he had stepped out of the longboat with Raffles and Farquhar on the bank of the Singapore river? He was now eighty-two years old, and all of his contemporaries were dead and gone. Raffles, Farquhar, Temenggong Abdul Rahman, Sultan Hussein, Captain Pearl, Badang the fisherman, Lieutenant Ralfe, Francis Bernard, Captain Methven, John Morgan, William Flint, Mr Oates, Joseph Johnstone, Alexander Guthrie, Tan Che Seng, Syed Omar Aljunied, Naraina Pillai ... their faces seemed to float before his eyes in a trail of memories, ending with the deaths of Captain Scott, his own father, and last year, John Crawfurd, the second resident of Singapore. He was now perhaps the only living survivor of those early years. What a change they had wrought, and what greater changes were surely to come, after he joined his father and Captain Scott in the Christian cemetery on Forbidden Hill.

***

Saturday, February 7, the day on which Raffles had signed the treaty with Temenggong Abdul Rahman and Sultan Hussein fifty years before, was designated jubilee day, and a public holiday. Sports were held on the Esplanade, although they were poorly attended, unlike the Chinese theatre, which drew huge crowds.

**

Government House was completed in April, and the sparkling new building was quickly recognized as an architectural gem that rivalled George Drumgoole Coleman's best work, and provided the young Crown colony with a colonial building to be proud of. Set high upon a magnificently landscaped hill, the new government house looked like an English palace or Italian palazzo, but was constructed in the symmetrical and cross-shaped form of the traditional Malay istana.[cxxiii] The elaborate facades, porticoes and ornate cornices stood in white splendour, reflected the shimmering sunlight like the walls of some magic castle, while the high-ceilinged rooms and long marble-floored arcades made the inside light and airy. Like Coleman's earlier works, Government House was constructed to allow for maximum ventilation, and the high shuttered windows opened out onto beautiful vistas of the town and the ocean beyond.

The new Court House was completed later in the year, once again by convict labourers and to Captain McNair's design. The neo-Palladian building, with its high wooden louvered doors and pitched clay tile roof, made an impressive mark at the mouth of the river. Inside, the high-ceilinged rooms were exquisitely decorated with Doric columns and plaster moulding and cornices.

---

cxxiii The building now serves as the present-day Istana, the official residence and office of the president of Singapore.

41

The previous year a new bridge had been erected at the mouth of the river, linking Raffles Place with the new Court House. The steel structure had been shipped out from Glasgow, and the bridge was the last major work completed with the use of convict labour. Governor Ord had wanted to call the new bridge 'Edinburgh Bridge', in honour of the recent visit to the colony by Prince Alfred, the Duke of Edinburgh. However, the new legislative council managed to prevail over the governor on this matter, and persuaded him to name it Cavenagh Bridge, after the last Indian governor. It was an impressive structure, and a great convenience to those who wished to travel across the mouth of the river, although it put out of business many of the boatmen who had previously ferried passengers for a cent per ride. It was also a source of great inconvenience to the tonkangs[cxxiv] that ferried goods from ships in the roads or New Harbour to the godowns on Boat Quay. Cavenagh Bridge sat so low over the river that they could not travel under it at high tide, but had to wait for low tide to pass through. Although the bridge had been constructed to commemorate the fiftieth anniversary of the founding of Singapore, it was opened without ceremony on the day that Colonel Collyer declared it ready to receive road traffic.

* * *

In October Governor and Lady Ord opened the Tanjong Pagar

---

cxxiv Boats used to carry goods along rivers and shorelines.

Dock Company's new graving dock, which was called the Victoria Dock. Four hundred feet in length and sixty-five feet wide, the dock was built of granite, and closed by a teak caisson[cxxv]; its two chain pumps could drain the dock in six hours. Governor and Lady Ord joined Thomas Scott, the chairman of the company, aboard the government steamer the *Peiho*, and followed by the government's other steamer, the *Rainbow*, they steamed through New Harbour and berthed at the new dock. The day had been declared a public holiday, and the huge crowd that had gathered cheered when the governor declared the Victoria Dock officially open.

***

In November, ten years after it had been begun, the Suez Canal was finally completed. The French Princess Eugenie, on board the *Aigle*, led a small fleet of sixty-eight vessels from the Mediterranean to the Red Sea, and the Suez Canal was declared officially open. Within a very short space of time, ships from Britain and Europe travelling to China abandoned the traditional route by the Cape of Good Hope and the Straits of Sunda and travelled via the canal through the Indian Ocean and the Straits of Malacca. The time taken to make the journey to Singapore was more than halved – a steamship could now make the journey from Britain to Singapore in just over forty days.

As a result, Singapore's trade increased dramatically, and the new Crown colony, the Tanjong Pagar Dock Company, and Simpson and Co entered the new decade on a wave of spectacular commercial success, the likes of which Sir Stamford Raffles and

---

cxxv A large watertight chamber, open at the bottom, from which the water is kept out by air pressure and in which construction work may be carried out under water.

Colonel William Farquhar could never have dreamed of.

***

Ronnie and Sarah Simpson were about to embark on a trip to Europe, and their family had organized a party for them the night before they left. Mrs Jessie MacFarlane had recently come out from Glasgow with her husband Mr Andrew MacFarlane, who had taken up a position with George Armstrong and Co. She asked Sarah if she and her husband were going home to escape the climate. She had heard that the tropical heat was enervating to Europeans, and often led to neurasthenia.[cxxvi]

'Oh, that's stuff and nonsense, Mrs MacFarlane,' Sarah replied. 'I love the weather here, and find the sunshine and sea air quite invigorating. But I wanted to see my homeland one more time before I die, and Ronnie felt the same.'

'So do you still feel that way, Mrs Simpson?' Andrew MacFarlane inquired. 'Do you still feel like England's home?'

'No, not really,' Sarah replied, 'although I have fond memories. I've made my home here, and have never regretted it.'

'Does that mean you now feel like a citizen of Singapore, since the Settlements have become a Crown colony?'

'No,' Sarah replied. 'I feel part of me is bound to this beautiful place, while part of me is bound to my homeland, the place of my birth and my upbringing. I don't identify myself with one place or the other, but treasure them both. I think that once you've lived in more than one place as long as I have you're bound to feel that way. You might find that an alarming thought, that one no longer has a home, or a people, to identify with. But I find it liberating. I can slough off old prejudices like a snake sheds a skin, and seek out

---

cxxvi An early diagnostic term describing chronic fatigue and weakness.

the best of both worlds, and all the worlds I come to know. Once you see the world with open eyes, you feel as much at home in Inverness, London, Paris, Calcutta, Singapore or Shanghai. And I'm sure I'd feel the same way if we packed up and went off to Borneo, or America!'

Mr and Mrs MacFarlane looked at her with puzzled frowns, and wondered if perhaps she had been too long in the sun after all.

But Ronnie said, 'I ken exactly whit ye mean.'

'America ...' he continued. 'Now there's a thocht!'

Notes

1 James Legge (1815-1897) was a Scottish missionary and sinologist, who worked for the London Missionary Society in Malacca and later in Hong Kong. During his time in Hong Kong he began his monumental work of translating the Chinese classics into English, published as *The Chinese Classics: with a Translation, Critical and Exegetical Notes, Prolegomena, and Copious Indexes*, (5 vols.) (London: Trubner, 1861–1872). In 1876 he took up the first Chair of Chinese Language and Literature at the University of Oxford.

2 James Brooke remained the Rajah of Sarawak until his death on June 11, 1868, age sixty-five, after suffering the last of three strokes. He was buried in the cemetery at St Leonard's Church, Sheepstor in Devon. He was never the same man again after the Singapore inquiry. Tired and dispirited, worn out by smallpox and malaria, and – as he saw it – betrayal and treachery, he spent most of his later years fruitlessly trying to negotiate with the governments of Britain, France and Holland to transfer Sarawak to them in exchange for compensation for the money he had invested in the state. He initially delegated the day to day running of Sarawak to his nephew John Brooke Johnson Brooke (1823-1868), also known as Brooke Brooke, and nominated him as his successor to the title of Rajah of Sarawak in 1851. However, two years later James had a falling out with Brooke Brooke and relieved him of all authority in Sarawak, naming his younger nephew Charles Johnston Brooke (1829-1917) as his successor. Charles Johnston Brooke became the second White Rajah of Sarawak after James' death in 1868. His son, Charles Vyner Brook (1874-1963), became the third and last White Rajah of Sarawak in 1918, ceding Sarawak to the British government as a Crown colony in 1946.

3 Thomas Church died three years later in London, on 19 August 1860.

4 It was not until 1887 that the waterworks were finally completed, thirteen years after Tan Kim Seng had died in Malacca. To recognize Tan Kim Seng's contribution, the municipal commissioners erected a three-

tiered ornate iron fountain in his honour in Fullerton Square. The Tan Kim Seng fountain was moved to Esplanade Park at Connaught Drive in 1925 and renovated in 1994. In 2010 it was gazetted as a national monument.

5 James Bruce, the eighth earl of Elgin and twelfth earl of Kincardine, was born on July 20 1811, the son of Thomas Bruce and Mary Nisbet, the seventh earl and countess of Elgin. His father was famous – or infamous, according to his critics – for having saved – or stolen – the friezes from the Acropolis in Athens, which came to be known as the 'Elgin Marbles', and which he had eventually been forced to sell to the British Museum at great financial loss. Educated at Eton and Christ Church, Oxford, where he took a first in Classics, James Bruce had had a distinguished diplomatic career as governor of Jamaica and then as governor-general of Canada, during which time he managed to prevent the British province from being annexed by the United States, and successfully negotiated the Reciprocity Treaty with the United States in 1854.

6 Frederick Townsend Ward (1831 –1862) was born in Salem, Massachusetts. He worked first as a sailor and then as a 'filibuster', raising private armies for wealthy sponsors, and learned his trade as a soldier while serving as a lieutenant with the French Army in the Crimean war.

7 Given the huge profits that were made by American traders shipping ice to the American South, India and Asia, including Hong Kong, Whampoa and Gilbert Angus set up a warehouse next to Coleman Bridge on Boat Quay in 1854, with magnificent wrought-iron balustrades. Unfortunately, they overestimated the demand and the Ice House lost money from the beginning, closing in 1856.

8 Yehonala continued to effectively rule China – via palace intrigues and alliances, and through the short reign of her son Tung Chih (1861-1875) – as Empress Dowager for the next forty-seven years.

9 Anna Harriette Leonowens (1831 –1915) served the King of Siam for six years, as teacher and later as secretary to the king. She wrote a book based upon her experiences, published in 1870 as *English Governess at the Siamese Court*, later adapted as the musical *The King and I* (1951) by Rodgers and Hammerstein.

10 Captain Raphael Semmes (1809-1877) was born in Charles County, Maryland, and joined the US Navy as a midshipman at the age of fifteen. He served with distinction as captain of the USS *Somers* in the Mexican American War of 1846, and rose to the rank of commander. He resigned

his commission in January 1861 to take up an appointment in the Confederate Navy. He demonstrated his prowess as a commercial raider while serving as commander of the CSS *Sumter*, before taking up his commission as captain of the *Alabama* in August 1862.

11 Charles George Gordon (1833 –1885) was a British army officer who served in the Crimean war but made his military reputation as commander of the Ever Victorious Army. Impressed by his service, Yehonala awarded him the Imperial Yellow Jacket, the very highest military distinction, which earned him the nickname 'Chinese' Gordon. On his return to England in 1864 Gordon was promoted to lieutenant-colonel (later major-general) and appointed Companion of the Order of the Bath. However, he is best remembered as having been killed in action defending the city of Khartoum against the forces of the Mahdi [Muhammad Ahmad (1844-1885), the self-proclaimed Islamic redeemer] in 1885.

12 Captain Semmes was brought to England aboard the *Deerhound*, and eventually made his way back to Richmond, Virginia, where he commanded the James River Squadron. After the fall of Richmond, Semmes formed his sailors into an infantry unit called the 'Naval Brigade', which surrendered with General Joseph E. Johnston's army on April 26, 1865. He was later arrested for treason, but the charges were eventually dropped. In subsequent years he worked as a lawyer, a professor of moral philosophy and English literature, and editor of the *Memphis Bulletin*. He published his account of the voyages of the CSS *Alabama* as *Memoirs of Service Afloat During The War Between the States* (Baltimore: Kelly, Piet & Co.) in 1869. He died on August 30, 1877 of complications from food poisoning after eating contaminated shrimp.

13 Later published as *Loyal Prince Li Xiucheng In his Own Words*. Reprinted as *Taiping Rebel: The Deposition of Li Xiucheng* (Cambridge: Cambridge University Press, 1976).

14 Benjamin Peach Keasberry (1811-1875) and his wife Charlotte came to Singapore in 1839 as independent missionaries, under the auspices of the American Board of Foreign Mission. They made friends with John and Alexander Stronach of the London Missionary Society, which they joined later in the year. Keasberry learned Malay from Munshi Abdullah (1796-1854), and started a small school for Malays at Kampong Glam, where he taught the boys printing, English, and arithmetic, and on Sundays he preached in Malay to his small congregation of Christian converts – both Malay and Peranakan Chinese – from an attap hut on North Bridge Road. He also taught the Malay classes at the Singapore Institution. When the American Board moved its operations to China

that year, they deeded Reverend Keasberry the plot of land on River Valley Road on which the London Missionary Society Mission chapel stood and allocated him an allowance of fifty pounds a year. They also arranged for the type from the Penang Mission and the press from the Malacca Mission to be shipped to Singapore, so that Keasberry could set up a new press. Keasberry converted one section of the old chapel into a commercial printing and binding shop and used part of the profits to set up a school for Malay boys in another section. The boys were taught English and Malay, but also learned the printing trade, including lithography, type setting and book binding, with the older boys working as paid employees of the press. Munshi Abdullah and his son helped with the teaching and with translations of Malay and Arabic texts.

15 *Published as Ti-Ping Tien-Khow; The History of the Ti-ping Revolution* (London: Day and Son, 1866)

16 This was the village in which Sun Yet-Sen (1866-1925), the revolutionary leader of the Kuomintang and provisional first president of the Republic of China was born, and where he was inspired by the stories of the Taiping rebellion recounted to him as a child by the aged veteran Lai Han-ying.